Hot in the City

by

John Money

A Pete & Dud Novel

Text copyright © 2019 John Money
All Rights Reserved

Published by Regency Rainbow Publishing
Cover by Maria Spada Design at www.mariaspada.com

Acknowledgements

This is another of my novels with a foot in the dim distant past. Not something originally penned at a campsite in Scotland, but a lot of the notes that rest behind this tale were scribbled (almost illegibly) in an altogether different country back near the turn of the century (and millennium) when I lived in Luxembourg. That might explain some of the 'tourist board' references to the small country but wasn't an influence on the story itself other than for the occasional location piece.

Peter Cooke, the main protagonist, is a work of pure fiction – unlike him I have never been a widower nor – as far as I'm aware' a father to a teenage daughter. But that is not to say that I've not had first-hand experience of caring for such a stranger creature – my thanks, therefore, go to Niamh who was inspirational in the creation of Suze Cooke. Nothing like her, I hasten to add, but she certainly got me to entertain the idea of such a character.

My most sincere and full thanks, and my gratitude must once again go to the one person I have found who surpasses all others, and who cares for me as we share our love. **Sara Avila** has changed my life for the better in every way – despite MS affecting us both – and it is thanks to her that I continue to tell my fictional tales. Dear readers, once more turn your backs now if excess emotion disturbs you – because I just need to say to Sara, I love you and always will.

Inspirations and history aside, I must also thank everyone who has provided me with lovely feedback over the years, and I always have to acknowledge your collective part in this story and all of my tale.

Regency Rainbow have, as ever, been a great incentive to me, and their collaboration with cover designer Maria Spada has helped so much in the creation of this book.

Website addresses are listed at the end of this book.

Part 1

1

When I was a teenager, one of my favourite pieces of graffiti was the one that went *'Insanity is hereditary – you get it from your children'*. Now that I'm a father, I've begun to realise that it's true. Suzanne's a great kid though, and I've got to admit that I'm really proud of her; she's smart, witty and beautiful – a ringer for her dear-departed mother. However, she's just coming up for sixteen and need I say more? Julie, her mother and my wife, died a little over four years ago, and it's not been the easiest of times for either Suze or me, although in some ways we're a lot closer than we were before it happened.

It was Suze who inadvertently got me involved in all this; just one casual comment over breakfast. I should have known better, of course, so I can't really blame her for what happened afterwards – and for all I know, is still happening.

I'm Pete, by the way; Peter Cooke and, yes, I have heard all the comments before, since, unfortunately, I also somewhat resemble my late namesake; six foot one, but dark-haired and a chain smoker. I do not, however, drink heavily (well, that heavily), although the events of the past few months have given me a more than adequate excuse to start.

The one casual comment, the catalyst of catalysts, was actually directed at one of Suze's friends, the rather alarmingly over-endowed Samantha who had been staying over with us for the weekend.

"So, what exactly does your Dad do?" Sam asked my dear, sweet, only offspring.

"When he can be bothered to do anything, he's a computer hacker," she charmingly replied.

"I am not!" I protested, "I run a computer security company; PC Security in fact. Sam, don't listen to a word Suze tells you."

"I never do," Sam simpered.

I made a mental note to have a word about Sam's behaviour with Suze; her friend was beginning to seriously worry me.

"Charming," Suze giggled, "But it amounts to the same thing anyway. You spend most of your time trying to break into people's computer systems. Even *you* refer to it as hacking."

"These people *pay* me to try to break into their systems," I explained doggedly, "They employ me to find out how secure their systems are. Calling me a hacker might be technically accurate on one level, but it's highly misleading. I hope you don't tell everyone that's what I do for a living."

Suze gave me one of her most radiant smiles, "Of course not. I tell them that you're locked up in prison after being caught smuggling heroin into the country in the boot of your clapped-out old Mini."

"Suze!"

"Just kidding, Pa," she grinned at me.

"You'd better be," I admonished, smiling despite myself. Her grin does that to me.

"That's actually pretty interesting," Sam chipped in, "Only my Dad uses computers a lot where he works. He was banging on about some sort of security breakdown on Friday night just before I left to come here."

"At least one daughter around here actually listens to their father," I said. Suze poked her tongue out at me.

"Maybe I could have a word with him on your behalf?" Sam offered, "There might be some work in it for you."

"That'd be very kind of you. I'm, er, not exactly that busy at the moment." I ignored Suze's *'You can say that again'* and continued, "What sort of company does your father work for, Sam?"

She shrugged, an alarming gesture in the rather too small robe she was wearing, "Something in the City, I think. The company does a lot of business with the European Commission. I'll get him to explain all about it if he's interested in using you."

"Thanks," I nodded.

And that was it. One casual remark from Suze, my protestations and Sam's offer. Less than a week later I was already out of my depth and sinking further.

2

Sam's father called me early the following morning, the Monday, and we arranged to meet at his office at eleven. Suze appeared in the kitchen just as I was hanging up.

"Was that for me?" she yawned.

"Not every phone call is for you. And, as it happens, that was Sam's father. He wants to discuss his problem with me."

"Sam or the computer thing?" she grinned.

"Not nice, fruit of my loins," I chided, smiling, "But that reminds me, does she have to wear such revealing things while she's staying here? I could almost see her, er, nipples in that robe yesterday."

"You should see her at that club she goes to," Suze shrugged, "She's not known as Sam the Mams for nothing. Anyway, you shouldn't be looking."

"With breasts that size it's hard to look at anything else. Come to that, it's hard to *see* anything else. Just don't let me catch you wandering around like that."

"I won't," she promised faithfully.

"Good girl."

"I won't let you catch me, that is."

She dodged my attempted swat and ran, giggling, from the kitchen. Is it any wonder, I ask you, that my hair's beginning to go grey?

After I had changed into one of my better suits, I asked Suze if she wanted me to drop her off at school.

"I am *not* going to be seen in that clapped-out old banger," she told me.

"It's not a clapped-out old banger, it's a classic car," I explained, for what seemed like the thousandth time.

"It's a forty-eight-year-old rusty Mini. Christ, it's even older than you!"

"Forty-eight is not old for a classic car! Now, do you want a lift or not?"

Suze gave me her trademark grin, "As long as you promise to drop me off a few hundred metres from the school. And if you promise to pretend to be a kidnapper or something, should anyone happen to see me in the old banger."

In the event, I got my own back by driving her right up to the school gates.

I left the precious Mini at the station and boarded the first London-bound cattle truck, cursing loudly about the lack of a smoking carriages these days. Just one hour later, we'd managed to cover the fourteen miles into the Capital, and I gratefully lit up on the Charing Cross concourse. After double-checking the address Sam's father had given me, and finishing a second Marlboro, I wandered out into the early Summer sunshine and climbed into the first taxi on the rank.

"Gresham Street, please."

"Another bleedin' City job," the driver sighed back.

There are times when I find it hard to believe that New York cabbies are supposed to be the least charming in the world.

Instead of directing the cabbie to the exact location of Sam's father's office, I had him drop me outside the Guildhall. I've always been fascinated by the history of the City and given that I was twenty minutes early for my appointment I decided to have a quiet stroll; see what new changes were being made to the area. In recent years many of the older buildings had been torn down to be replaced by modern edifices. Sometimes, as with Leith House this was a positive improvement but all too often this was not the case; Mappin and Webb's former site being a perfect example. After my quiet stroll, I was glad to see that no other sacrilegious acts were in the process of being perpetrated and I arrived at the office in high spirits.

I had rather expected the building to be a bank of some sort from the brief discussion I'd had earlier and so I was a bit surprised to find that the location was a nondescript office block. Inside, the décor was

4

ultra-modern, all smoked glass and chrome, a thick, dark carpet covering the floor of the reception area. I crossed to the large desk and presented myself to the security guard.

"Peter Cooke to see James Forsythe. I have an eleven o'clock appointment."

The guard checked a large book and then handed me a pass bearing the word 'Visitor', "Mister Forsythe's office is on the third floor," he told me, "Please make sure you hand back the pass when you leave."

I crossed to the elevator and was whisked silently upwards. A young woman was waiting for me as the doors slid open.

"Good Morning," she said with a broad smile, "You must be Mister Cooke?"

I nodded, "To see James Forsythe."

"If you'd like to follow me?"

"Lead on." *Like* to follow her? I would have crossed rivers of molten lava to follow her. She was almost as tall as me, her figure lithe and slender inside her clearly expensive business suit. Her hair was a mass of blonde waves trailing down to her waist and her legs were long and shapely. Just recently, Suze had been pestering me to start dating again – as much, I think, for the nights in alone that she would get, rather than my happiness – and although I'd been reluctant, this vision of feminine beauty I was now following could make me change my mind in an instant. The walk through the plush building was all too brief as far as I was concerned – although to be fair, if we'd had to cross the Sahara to get to Forsythe's office, I would still have thought it far too short a journey.

She knocked on his door and opened it without waiting for a reply, ushering me inside. James Forsythe was standing by a large window, gazing down into the street below, seemingly lost in thought. A big man, in every sense of the word, he could have been aged anywhere between thirty and fifty. As far as build went, Sam certainly took after her father. He looked around when the young woman coughed politely.

"Ah, sorry about that!" he boomed, "Wool-gathering, I'm afraid. You must be Peter Cooke?" He offered me a large hand.

"The very same," I smiled, trying not to wince as his grip seemed to grind the bones in my right hand into powder.

"Take a seat, dear boy," he gestured to a large leather chair beside his desk, "Tea, coffee?"

"Coffee, please."

"Jennifer, my angel, would you see to that?"

"Certainly, James." The young woman smiled briefly in my direction and quietly left the office, closing the door behind her.

"Absolute stunner, isn't she?" James laughed.

"Quite."

"My daughter tells me you're a widower," the big man went on, settling himself into his own chair, "Maybe you'd like me to put in a word for you? Jenny's rather shy around men."

She hadn't appeared at all shy to me, but there again, I wasn't in possession of the same level of self-confidence that James Forsythe clearly had, "I, er, I'll think about it."

He gave a loud chuckle and pushed an ashtray and an ornate box across his desk, "Cigarette?"

"Please," I nodded opening the box, "It always seems rather strange these days to be able to smoke in an office."

"Know what you mean, dear boy, but I guess that's one of the perks when you work for the government. Tell everyone else not to do something and then carry on doing it yourself, what?"

"The government?" I asked, surprised, "I was led to believe that this was some sort of bank, Mister Forsythe"

"Please. Call me James, dear boy," he gave another chuckle, "And in some ways you could say that we are a bank." He went on to explain about the company, "When I say that we work for the government, I mean we're employed by them. Basically, we carry out certain, shall we say, *financial transactions* on their behalf. Mainly with the European Commission and a few other European financial institutions."

"I wasn't aware that the government used outside agencies for such things," I shrugged, lighting the cigarette.

"Most people aren't. Let's just say that there are certain types of transaction that the powers that be prefer to keep entirely separate from the normal, everyday ones. I really can't say too much about the exact nature of these deals, although I will give you a more detailed overview if you decide to accept our commission."

I nodded thoughtfully, "What exactly is the nature of your problem?"

Before he could reply, the door opened and Jennifer reappeared, bearing a large tray. She set it on the desk between James and I and then proceeded to pour two cups of coffee, "Milk or cream?" she asked me with a smile.

"Er, neither, thanks."

She set the cups before us and, with another smile, departed once more.

"Sure I can't put in that word?" James chuckled as I watched her departing form.

"Er, maybe. I'll give it some thought." I was frantically hoping that he couldn't see the blush that I felt burning on my cheeks.

"Now, where were we?" he went on, "Oh, yes. The nature of our problem. It's actually a little embarrassing, really, dear boy. In essence, it seems someone is either hacking into our systems and generating false transactions which disappear into unnamed accounts all over Europe, or maybe there's actually someone inside the organisation carrying out the dirty deeds."

"I take it that's the reason that you're looking for someone from outside to investigate this?"

"Quite so, dear boy. It was rather fortuitous when my little Sam mentioned what you do for a living."

I decided not to question the term 'little Sam'. "It does rather sound like it's the sort of thing that I do. How long do you think it's been going on?"

"Ah!" James gave a rueful smile, "That's actually a little difficult to determine. You see, dear boy, as I said before, the genuine transactions that we carry out are not exactly standard; it's a trifle difficult to separate the real ones from the others. Our best guess is that it's been going on for about three to six months."

"What sort of size of transaction are we talking about here?" This was beginning to genuinely interest me, "And roughly how many do you think have occurred?"

"On average, I would have to estimate about one million a time. As to the number, maybe one per week."

I nearly choked on the mouthful of coffee I had just taken, "How much?"

"As I say, it's a best guess, dear boy, but our audit team reckon we're short by about fifteen to thirty million."

"What on earth do the government have to say about it?" I asked incredulously.

"Oh, it's just a drop in the ocean to them," James replied airily, "But of course, they would rather it was stopped."

"I can imagine." I tried hard not to sound too sarcastic, "What would you pay me, and what are the terms of your contracts?"

"Oh, you can name your own figure, dear boy. After all, it's you that's the expert in this field."

"I, er, that is... How do you even *know* I'm an expert?"

James gave another booming chuckle, "We work for the government. I had you checked out this morning."

"Checked..." I shook my head.

"Don't worry, dear boy. You have a very good reputation. If you'd like the assignment, just sort out the terms with Jennifer."

"I would like it."

"Marvellous," James rose and grasped my still-smarting hand, "When can you start?"

"Thursday?"

"Perfect! Get Jenny to introduce you to Barry Grant; he's our head of computer operations. Come back when you're through and I'll take you to lunch, if you're free?"

"Sounds marvellous," I smiled, still finding it difficult to believe how easy it had all gone.

He led me back through to the reception area where Jennifer was waiting, leaving me to sort out the terms with the extraordinarily attractive young woman. The terms turned out to be extraordinarily attractive as well. Afterwards, she introduced me to Barry Grant who, under the circumstances, was surprisingly friendly, and within half an hour I was set up with all the equipment I would need when I was working on-site.

Lunch was a sumptuous affair and it was three o'clock before I finally bade James Forsythe farewell outside his club and hailed a passing taxi. Suze was already at home by the time I arrived.

"Hi, Pa," she greeted me, evidently having forgiven me for the lift to school that morning.

"Hi, yourself."

"How'd it go?"

"Absolutely brilliantly; I start on Thursday. Remember to thank Samantha for me, would you?"

"Great," she beamed, "And you can thank her yourself; she's coming over tomorrow. How much lovely loot are they going to pay you?"

"One hundred and seventy-five pounds an hour," I replied airily.

Her eyebrows shot up, "How much?"

I repeated the amount.

"Wow! We'll be able to afford a really good holiday this year! Perhaps you can even get yourself a proper car."

"Slow down, princess. Anyway, I thought you weren't going to come with me on holiday ever again?"

"Since you'll be that well off, I'll make an exception," she grinned, "Besides, if you go on your own, you'll only make me stay with aunt Paula."

"I thought you liked it there?" I grinned back at her, "I seem to recall you having a crush on their next-door neighbour's son. What's his name?"

"I do not have a crush on Eric!" She blushed charmingly, "Anyway, he's already got a girlfriend."

"Oh, you poor lovelorn thing."

"What about you being lovelorn?" she changed the subject quickly.

"I am not lovelorn! And as it happens, I'll be working with an extremely attractive young woman by the name of Jennifer."

"Oh?"

9

I described her in detail.

"Wow!" Suze breathed when I'd finished, "Perhaps you could ask her to come on holiday with us? It'd be like a real family again—"

She suddenly trailed off, "Sorry," she muttered.

I crossed and put an arm around her shoulders, "It's okay, princess. Maybe you're right about me dating again. I know it's been difficult for you without a mother around. Especially at your tender age."

She turned and hugged me, "I'm okay. Or at least, I am now. But I do worry about you; being on your own, I mean."

"I'm not. After all, I do have you, don't I?" These little sessions of mutual support had been growing less frequent over the time since Julie's death, but every now and again they sprung up in the middle of a seemingly unrelated conversation. That night I'm not sure who needed the comfort more.

3

I spent the next two days doing some research into James Forsythe's mysterious company – and trying to avoid Samantha, whose simpering was reaching new heights following her successful introduction of me to her father. Not unsurprisingly, I found out very little more than what Forsythe had already told me. While not exactly a quango in the true sense of the word, ETA Services' sole income was from government departments – officially for 'banking services and functions'. It had been established in mid-2016 and its activities had grown steadily during the three years it had been in existence. Exactly what those activities were, however, seemed shrouded in mystery.

When I arrived at the offices on the Thursday morning, a different security guard at the downstairs reception gave me a new, semi-permanent 'Consultant' pass, and a lecture on the importance of handing in visitors' passes when I handed back the one I had been issued with on the Monday. Upstairs I was delighted to be greeted by Jennifer, her former business suit replaced on this day by a blood pressure-threatening short skirt and silk blouse combination.

"Nice to see you again, Peter," she smiled at me.

"Likewise. Please call me Pete."

"Pete it is, then. You must call me Jenny."

Resisting the urge to inform her that I would call her anything she liked – and at any time she liked – I nodded happily.

"Let me show you where all the important things are," she offered, gesturing for me to follow her, "We'll start with the coffee making facilities and the washrooms."

I happily trotted along behind her, mindful that I probably looked like an eager puppy, albeit a rather large one, and then back to the reception area.

"Well, that just about covers our little domain," she said, "Where would you like to start this morning?"

"I'd really like to see James first. There's a few more details about the organisation that I need to know before I can really get started on the work."

"He assumed that you would," she offered me another of her radiant smiles, "But I'm afraid you'll have to make do with me; James is away for a couple of days visiting some business contacts in Brussels. If that's okay with you, let's retreat to my office and we'll discuss matters there."

"That's, er, perfectly okay," I nodded, bemused. I had thought that Jenny was a high-powered secretary or personal assistant to Forsythe, but I was quickly disabused of that notion when we reached her office. The sign on the door read "Jennifer Winter, Executive Director"; the same job title that Forsythe had. Inside, the office was, if anything, even more sumptuous than Forsythe's and I had just settled into the giant leather chair that Jenny had indicated, staring around somewhat dumbstruck, when I was brought back to the present moment by her laugh.

"Don't worry, Pete," she smiled, "I guess I don't really look the part, do I?"

Earlier confusion was now joined by embarrassment, "I, er, that is…" I took a deep breath and sighed deeply, "Sorry, but no, you don't. I guess

I was a little confused on Monday, what with you bringing us coffee and everything."

She laughed again, the sound raising the hairs on the nape of my neck, "We don't stand on ceremony here. It's probably something to do with the nature of our business, and, believe me, after working in investment banks, it takes some getting used to."

Jenny settled herself on the edge of her desk and I feigned a cough to try to cover the fact that my eyes had been magnetically drawn to her gorgeous long thighs, "Excuse me," I muttered.

If she had noticed my errant gaze, she didn't comment. Still smiling she began, "James informed me of how much he told you on Monday about the nature of our business, and I would hazard a guess that you've been doing a little research of your own since then?"

I smiled and nodded, "Not very revealing though." Given the proximity of her legs, I wished I'd chosen another phrase.

"We are – we have to be – highly secretive," she went on, "Although the activities that we carry out on behalf of the government are commonplace in the European Union as a whole, they are not, shall we say, the norm in this country. The transactions that we carry out are strictly off-budget and do not appear in any audit of either the Treasury or the government as a whole."

"Greasing palms?" I asked, trying not to look too annoyed.

Jenny sighed and nodded, "There are all too many phrases for it, but essentially, that is correct. In order to protect the interests of many important and diverse British institutions and companies, it is common practice to... ensure that certain individuals within the EU are content with their lot, as it were."

"Having told me this, aren't you concerned that I might wander out and phone the nearest journalist?"

"If you've done your research thoroughly enough, you'll have found no mention of us in any press cuttings agency. True?"

I nodded, "Presumably everything is covered by some D-notice ruling?"

"Absolutely. To be frank with you, I'm not altogether happy with what goes on. But that's just a personal view; we must face facts and recognise that we are involved with the EU regardless of membership status, and for the protection of our own industries we must play by their rules. I can see your distaste with such things, but I hope this won't compromise your assignment with us. You really are the ideal man for the job, and I'm so looking forward to working with you."

Her last words might well have been a deliberate ploy to keep me there, but in truth, I wasn't too bothered about the company's place in the scheme of things anyway. The idealism of my left-leaning youth had been replaced with a much more pragmatic view. And then, of course, there was one hundred and seventy-five pounds an hour to consider. "You needn't worry on that score," I told her, "The only thing that could compromise my position here is not knowing the exact nature of your operations. Are you in a position to let me into all the details of your activities?"

Jenny slid easily off the edge of the desk, "I'm delighted you've taken that viewpoint," she smiled, "As far as answering any further questions you may have, I'd be happy to. That is, after you've signed this." She reached across her desk and handed me a document.

"There's no need," I said when I saw what it was, "I've already signed it."

"Oh, of course." She took back the paper, "You had a contract with the Ministry of Defence. Back in '14, wasn't it?"

"I'm not the only one who's been doing their homework."

Happily – for me – she settled back on the edge of the desk, "Well then, what do you need to know?"

Half an hour later I was considerably better informed, and considerably more amazed. The activities of ETA Services were manifold and quite diverse, but all revolved around transferring millions upon millions of pounds into bank accounts across Europe and beyond; there were some people out there getting very rich indeed. "Okay, that just about covers the business side of things. One last question and I'll stop impersonating the Spanish Inquisition; what are your priorities for me? In other words, do you want me to first concentrate on stopping the activities of our mysterious hacker, or would you rather I spend my time trying to identify him – or her, of course?"

"Definitely the former. The embarrassment factor alone mitigates in that direction."

"In that case," I said, "I'll need a profile of all employees – both past and present – and details of their access rights to the systems and so on. In addition, I'll need a full technical and functional specification of the computerised systems, together with information concerning the software authors."

"I'll get my secretary…" she paused and laughed, "Sorry. I'll get my secretary to get you the profiles – I take it you'll need mine as well?"

"I'm afraid so."

"Very well. As far as the computer documentation goes, Barry can provide you with that. But, tell me, why do you need information concerning the software authors?"

"Quite often," I said, "the original authors leave a sort of 'back door' into systems. This is mainly for emergency situations where front-end access becomes impossible, but occasionally a disreputable person will use this for various nefarious purposes. I'll need to check out the company, or companies, that supplied the systems."

"Sounds sensible. It also sounds a rather daunting task. Do you have any idea when your preliminary work will be completed?"

I shrugged, "Maybe a week?"

"Fast worker. Is there any other way I can offer you assistance?"

The juxtaposition of the two sentences sent a shiver up my spine, "I, er, think that's all for now." During the three quarters of an hour or so that I had been closeted in Jenny's office I had become less concerned with her beauty and thoroughly engrossed in my profession. Now, however, Suze's last comment to me that very morning came racing back into my mind. *'Pa? Don't pussyfoot around. Just ask the woman out, okay?'* As 'the woman' rose once more from her desk, I very nearly followed my daughter's advice. It was probably only the seventeen years since I'd last asked a woman out that stopped me. Instead, I rose, and awkwardly offered Jenny my hand.

She glanced down, surprised, and then grasped it lightly, "I'll come and find you at lunchtime," she smiled, "There's a wonderful little wine bar just a few doors down. If you would like to, that is?"

Swallowing hard, I nodded, "I'd be, er, delighted."

Although the lunch wasn't quite what I had expected – Barry Grant and Jenny's secretary, Alice, joined us – I was still on cloud nine by the time the end of the day arrived. Even the dreadfully boring chore of poring over staff profiles had not seemed too onerous. Barry had left some time before, patting me on the shoulder on his way out, and, absorbed in my reading, it was only a polite cough that alerted me to the fact that the office was almost totally silent. I looked around, first surprised to see that the place was empty, and then again when I saw Jenny standing behind me, smiling broadly.

"We may want to make fast progress on this matter," she said, "But that doesn't mean that we want you working round the clock. It's already half-past six, Pete."

"It's easy to get wrapped up in this stuff," I said, nodding at the heap of files on the desk, "But I guess that's pretty much it for today; things start to blur after a while."

"Good." She hesitated for a moment and then continued, "If you've time, perhaps we could help each other unwind for an hour back at the wine bar?"

I started and swallowed hard, "That'd be great," I managed, probably looking like some hyperactive nodding dog on the back shelf of a car. Trying very hard to keep my feet in contact with the plush carpet, I floated after her towards the lifts.

I couldn't – and still can't – believe how nervous I felt during the first part of that hour. Gone was Jenny's business-like approach and no mention was made of ETA Services, computer fraud or the European Union. Instead we talked about ourselves. Or rather, Jenny talked about herself, and bullied information out of me with a series of questions. By the time we left, I felt fifteen years younger, and was desperately trying to work out how such a beautiful woman, with such a wonderful personality, could be single and unattached at the age of thirty.

We walked down to Cheapside in search of cabs and turned to say our farewells.

"I was right," she smiled, "I am going to enjoy working with you."

"Likewise." My heartrate was approaching that of a hummingbird.

15

It nearly stopped altogether when she leant forward and brushed my lips oh-so briefly with her own. Although it was hard to be sure in the crimson-hued sunset, I was almost certain that she blushed before she turned and held up an arm. Stunned and transfixed, I could only stare as a cab made a screeching U-turn and stopped at the kerbside, Jenny quickly climbing into the rear.

"See you tomorrow," she called as the cab pulled away.

It had already reached St. Paul's before I could manage to mutter a rather belated, "Yes, and thanks."

Suze was yawning on the sofa when I finally reached home.

"Hi, Pa," she called when she heard the door open.

"Hi, yourself. Sorry I'm late."

"What kept you?" She came through to the hallway, "You said you'd be home by seven."

"You'll make someone a perfect wife one day," I smiled, pecking her cheek, "Or an archetypal one, at any rate."

"Charming," she giggled, "But if I was your wife, I'd have already been on the phone to a lawyer. Since when do you wear *Obsession* and hang out in wine bars?"

I gave her a smug grin, "If you must know, Sherlock, I took your advice."

"You actually asked out this Jenny woman?" she stared at me incredulously.

"Pretty much." I didn't want to spoil my nascent Lothario image with the actual truth.

"And?"

"And nothing! She's a very nice person."

"When are you going out with her again?"

"It's not like that," I said, "We've only spent an hour together in a wine bar."

"I can see I'm going to have to give you a few pointers."

"I am not taking pointers from my own daughter. Besides, you're the wrong sex to be giving pointers to me."

"Not these days, Pa. These days, the girls often do most of the running."

"No!" I insisted, "I'm sure I can manage. Now, isn't it time for your bed?"

"Save that one up for Jenny," she giggled, dodging around me before I could react.

4

The following day, I spent almost as much time plucking up the courage to ask Jenny whether she'd like another after-work drink as I did studying the staff profiles. She'd been tied up with some government officials for most of the day and the longer I went without a chance to ask her, the more nervous I became. When Barry Grant patted me on the shoulder and said that he was off early on the grounds that he was visiting relations that weekend, I nearly jumped out of my skin.

Just before five, I heard Jenny's door open and watched surreptitiously as she showed her visitors out of the office. Summoning every last ounce of my courage, I was waiting for her when the lift doors opened.

"Jenny!" I said, a little too loudly for comfort, "I mean, Jenny. I was, er, wondering... that is, would you like a, er, wine or two after work?"

"I'd love to," she nodded. My heart seemed to soar, "Oh, hang on though," she grimaced. My heart plummeted like a stone. "Tell you what? I've got to leave early tonight, but if we go now, I'll have time for a couple, okay?" she smiled. I was beginning to feel queasy.

"Suits me," I nodded, back in puppy-dog mode, "I don't think I could stand another profile today. I'll just grab my jacket and case."

We met up in the downstairs reception area and strolled out into the early evening throng, "Have you got around to reading mine yet?" she asked, "My profile, that is."

Turning to face her, I was presented with her physical profile, and it took an extraordinary effort not to comment on its perfection, "Actually, no, I haven't." Her file was safely tucked in my briefcase for later perusal.

"It won't be very interesting," she said, holding open the door of the wine bar, "I've led a very dull life, really."

This segued into a series of stories and anecdotes about her past, and once again the time seemed to fly by. So much so that when she glanced at her watch sometime later, she let out a small curse.

"Bugger! It's already seven," she gave a laugh, "Oh, well. I prefer your company to my mother's any day of the week. I'd better just give her a quick call though, she's a terrible worrier."

"I'm sorry," I said, "I wasn't keeping an eye on the time."

"It's not your fault. As I said, you're wonderful company. I'm not usually so relaxed around men; you're very considerate and gentle."

"I'm a softy, in other words."

"No!" she protested with a laugh, "A little... lacking in experience, maybe."

"That is an understatement. You'd better make that call."

Jenny clapped a hand to her mouth, "You see? You'd made me forget about my own dear mother already."

When she returned she was smiling broadly.

"I take it she wasn't too upset with you?"

"Not at all. When I told her that I was having a pleasant drink with a very nice man, she was delighted. I've time for another, if you're having one?"

"I'd love to."

One turned into two and it was after nine before we finally left. Once more we walked down to Cheapside, and once more we stopped at the kerbside.

Perhaps it was the wine, or perhaps I was finally relaxing in Jenny's company, "I really enjoyed that. I hope we can do it again soon?"

She nodded, a lop-sided smile in her face, "Count on it."

One thing was very different between that night and the preceding one. When Jenny reached forward to offer me a kiss, I made sure she couldn't pull away as quickly as the night before. Perhaps she wouldn't have done anyway. Whatever. It was wonderful.

By the time I arrived home, vowing to take a taxi to the station every morning, Suze was already in bed. On the coffee table in the sitting room was a short note from her:

'Dear dirty stop-out,

Hope you had a wonderful time with your new ladyfriend, and I hope for your sake she   isn't too much of a lady! I want all the juicy details in the morning!

Love you, Pa,

Your wonderful, amazing, gorgeous daughter, XXXXXXX'

I was in far too good a mood to wake her up in revenge. Besides, I was worried that if I did, I really *would* start telling her all the juicy details.

5

I probably read Jenny's profile a dozen or more times that weekend, and even indulged my precious daughter's obsessive curiosity by describing Jenny to her in minute detail. The profile itself didn't reveal much more about her background than I'd already heard from Jenny's own lips during our few hours together in the wine bar; she was well-educated at a private school in Kent, went to Cambridge where she earned a first in International Banking, took a further year in post-graduate studies, and then started her career with a top investment bank. She had been head-hunted by James Forsythe himself for the position at ETA. From what I could gather, reading between the lines, her family had been average middle-class, middle-England, and moderately wealthy. Judging by Jenny's six-figure salary at ETA, she was not short of a few bob in her own right.

The small photograph of her, which belied the commonly held belief that no-one could look good in a passport-size photograph, somehow became accidentally detached during the weekend, lodging itself inside my wallet.

On Sunday evening, my darling daughter attempted to give me another of her pep talks.

"The only two things I ask," she grinned, "Is that when you stay the night at her place in town, firstly you call and let me know – so I can organise an impromptu orgy here – and secondly, you make sure you have enough protection with you."

"Suze!" It was bad enough coming to terms with the fact that my sweet little girl was rapidly approaching adulthood without her lecturing me on the responsibilities that brings. Especially sexual responsibilities. "For a start, I barely know the woman and whatever happens between us will stay exactly that way: between *us*, Jenny and I, that is. For another thing, I don't even like you *joking* about orgies and stuff like that."

"Joking?" she giggled, "Oh, Pa," she went on when I didn't return her grin, "Don't fret about me. I'm going to save myself for a really nice guy; I've got no intentions of jumping into bed with half the blokes I meet; that's Sam's department. You're not going to be one of those over-protective daddies who gives every guy I go out with the third degree, are you?"

"Probably," I sighed.

She came around the table and sat on my knee, "Really, Pa. Don't worry, okay? I'll still be your little girl for a good while yet. Remember, up to now, I haven't even had a steady boyfriend."

I gave her a hug, "I know, princess. It just takes a little getting used to. You growing up, I mean." I glanced down at her body, now full of the graceful curves of womanhood. So reminiscent of her mother.

She stood up, "Talking of growing up, any chance of an advance on my pocket money? Only I've just graduated to the next bra-size."

I groaned and reached into my wallet, "I suppose that's one thing I've got to be grateful for," I said, handing her twenty pounds, "Unlike your friend Sam, at least you actually *wear* one."

The following morning, I called for a taxi to take me to the station in hopeful anticipation of being over the limit by the time I arrived home – then spent the journey into the City wondering how Jenny would react when she saw me. I needn't have spent the time fretting; it turned out that she was away on some sort of business trip until the Thursday morning. Initial disappointment was greatly tempered by an e-mail she had sent me, apologising for having forgotten to mention the trip, and saying that she was looking forward to seeing me on her return.

Without the distraction of her presence in the office, the completion of the staff profile checks went much quicker and I was already poring through the system documentation by the Tuesday afternoon. On the Wednesday, I arranged to meet with the management of BISCO, the company that had supplied ETA with their software, and I returned to the office a very happy bunny – there were, and only ever had been, two people working for BISCO and they were good enough to show me how I could easily get into the system through the back-door that they had left; hardly the offer of guilty men.

This news at least narrowed down the possible range of culprits, and on the Thursday morning I began the first of the procedures designed to trap an aberrant user within ETA itself. After first clearing all security rights to the systems, I had expected a barrage of moans and complaints when each user was told to input new passwords – and into a format containing both numbers and letters, at that – and was not at all disappointed. I listened eagerly to the grumblings, noting the names of those who grumbled loudest; if anyone had been using dual identities to illegally access the system, this would now be no longer possible.

This was an extremely long shot since I had studied the raw data of the illegal transactions within the systems, hoping that the perpetrator had missed some vital audit check which might have revealed his identity. I had been, not surprisingly, disappointed; the villain – or villains – were clearly good at what they did, and simply changing the security settings and passwords was unlikely to trip him, her or them up.

Forsythe, who had returned from Brussels the previous afternoon, came bustling up to my desk shortly before lunch.

"I say, dear boy, Barry tells me you've changed everyone's password thingies."

"More accurately, James, they have to change their own; set everything up from scratch."

He gave a booming chuckle, "Don't suppose you could spare me five minutes to help me with mine, could you? Only I'm hopeless with the damn things."

"Of course," I said, grateful for a distraction from waiting for Jenny to appear. I followed him through to his office and gave him a brief description of what I had found out so far, and what the password ploy was meant to achieve. He cut me off quickly.

"As I said, dear boy, I don't have the faintest clue about all this IT nonsense. Jenny's yer girl for that sort of thing, she's been taking a keen interest in this problem ever since it came up," he gave another chuckle, "A little bird tells me you and she were seen canoodling in *Spritzers* the other evening. Good man, I say."

"Hardly canoodling! She was, er, just supplying me with some background information."

"How awfully disappointing for you."

I left his office fifteen minutes later to find that Jenny had returned in my absence and had closeted herself in her office to deal with a number of important calls. I rather hoped that, like Forsythe, she would have trouble with her passwords, but she had still not emerged from her office by five o'clock, and Captain Paranoia was trying – fairly successfully – to convince me that the beautiful young executive was deliberately avoiding me.

By five to six, I was one of only four people left in the outer office and was just, reluctantly, pulling on my jacket when her door finally opened. Her head appeared in the doorway, luscious blonde hair flowing loose and free around her perfect features.

"Oh, Pete!" she called, "Not going are you?"

I looked down at my watch and shrugged, "It's getting on for six."

"I know," she grimaced, "Sorry, but I've been absolutely up to my neck in stuff since I got back. I was wondering – if you're free that is – whether you could hang on for a couple of minutes; let me know what progress has been made?"

"Of course," I nodded, trying to hide my disappointment. She only wanted to talk business, it seemed. I walked across to her office and closed the door behind me.

"Actually," she gave a shy laugh, "The progress report can wait to the morning."

To my amazement – joyous amazement – she stepped up to me and after the slightest hesitation, kissed me fully and firmly on the mouth. After a few seconds, she broke the contact and stepped back, blushing slightly. "Sorry–" she began.

"Don't be," I interrupted, breathlessly. The fact that it was she who had instigated this moment gave me the courage I so desperately needed, "I've, er, missed you."

"I'm glad. And the feeling's mutual."

I can't really describe what I felt right at that moment; astonishment, joy, elation, relief. A mixture of all of those and more. I gave a nervous laugh, "I feel like some dopey adolescent." Although I regretted those words the second they were out of my mouth, Jenny's reaction instantly repaired the damage to my pride.

"I know," she gave a girlish giggle, "Silly, isn't it?"

The tension in the air, an almost audible electrical crackling, dissipated at once, "So much for thinking I'd grown up."

She stepped back up to me and we kissed again, "Sorry about dragging you in here on a pretext," she said when we finally parted, "But we have a strict office rule: no relationships between members of staff, and that includes executives."

"Don't apologise," I smiled (probably idiotically), "But am I strictly an employee?"

"I guess not, but there again, I wouldn't want anyone to think that you're treating me any different to anyone else in this investigation of yours."

"As far as the investigation goes, I won't."

"Good," she smiled, "But I think maybe we'd better find somewhere a little more discreet for after-work socialising–" she stopped suddenly and looked quickly up at me, blushing as she did so, "That is, if you'd like to socialise out of work?"

"Nothing would give me greater pleasure, er, are you free tonight?"

She was, and we spent another wonderful two hours together in a quiet Italian restaurant, the evening ending all too soon. All the way home, I tried to imagine what I'd done to deserve such luck.

There was a growing magnetism between us, which manifested itself the following morning when I spent nearly two hours closeted in Jenny's office, describing the progress of the investigation. Or, at least, one hour describing that, and almost all of the other lapsing into contented silences, stealing the occasional kiss, experiencing a frisson of pure excitement at every touch.

We both left the building early that evening, separately, to maintain appearances, and met up in a quiet wine-bar close by the Barbican. We were still there when it closed at ten, the last customers to leave. Our stroll back towards St. Paul"s was slow and I felt a distinct reluctance to part from this wondrous woman; it was, after all, Friday, which meant I wouldn't see her again for two whole days and three whole nights. When we reached the main thoroughfare, we stopped and Jenny turned towards me, already moving into my eager embrace.

"I wish I could invite you home with me," she whispered, "But, well, living with my mother…"

My heart seemed to be thundering in my chest, "Likewise," I smiled, breathing heavily, "But, Suze…"

"Do you think your daughter would approve of me?" She had a shy smile on her beautiful face.

"She'd adore you. She takes after me in many ways–" I stopped, suddenly aware of what I had just said, "Perhaps I can organise things so that you can come down one weekend?" I suggested to cover my embarrassment.

"That would be wonderful."

It took another fifteen minutes for us to finally go our separate – and in my case, at least, rather frustrated – ways. I only just managed to catch the last train back home.

I was surprised to find Suze still up when I quietly let myself into the house. She was sat on the sofa, seemingly half-asleep, the television burbling quietly in the corner.

"Hi, princess," I said softly.

24

She turned a bleary eye in my direction, "Hi, Pa." Her grin looked lop-sided.

"It's a bit late for you to be up, isn't it?"

"Been out. Not been in long."

"Anywhere nice?" I was surprised. Suze seldom went out of an evening, and certainly not without telling me first. If I'd got home at a reasonable hour, her absence would have been highly alarming.

"Sam came 'round and she persuaded me to go to a club," she said slowly.

Her voice seemed slurred and I crossed to where she was sitting, "Have you been drinking?"

"Jus' the one." She gave an exaggerated nod.

"Suze!" I began to protest, but stopped when she burst into tears.

"I'm sorry, Pa!" she wailed as I took her into my arms, "They said it was fruit juice; I didn't know any different until I began to feel a bit strange. Please, believe me?"

"It's okay, honey," I sighed, stroking her hair, "I do believe you. But perhaps you'll believe me now when I say that Sam's not a good influence?" Trust me, sometimes you have to be hard at such times; just occasionally the message will stick.

"It wasn't just her," she sniffed, "But I guess she was the one who persuaded me to go out in the first place."

I was about to reply; something to the effect that she should stand on her own two feet or some such nonsense, when I realised something else was amiss, "What on earth are you wearing?" I pulled back to get a better look. She was wearing a low-cut, short-skirted party dress – not part of her own wardrobe – and, more pertinently, no bra.

She pulled the front of the skimpy garment higher up her half-exposed breasts, "It's... one of Sam's old ones. She reckoned everyone would be wearing that sort of thing. I... didn't want to feel like the odd one out, but none of the guys... did anything, anyway." Her voice tailed off to a whisper, her eyes fixed firmly on the carpet in front of her, "I'm sorry, Pa."

I truly didn't know how to react. On the one hand, I could remember myself as a teenager feeling like an idiot for not being dressed in the correct fashion, but on the other hand... Suze was still not sixteen; she was my darling little daughter. Seeing her dressed like that; so much like her mother and perhaps even more attractive, I couldn't help but imagine what the young guys thought when they saw her. And someone – I was determined to find out later who it was – had duped her into drinking alcohol; something she'd never touched before. Not knowing what to say while I tried to be rational and calm about the situation, I pulled her once more into a tight hug. I could feel tears of my own prickling at the corners of my eyes, as Suze's dampened the front of my shirt.

She pulled back after a minute or so to dry her eyes, and nervously glanced up at me, trying to gauge my reaction. Her mouth dropped open, "Oh, Pa! I really didn't mean to upset you! I promise, it won't happen again, really I do!"

I shook my head, "It's okay. I guess it's just that sometimes I don't want my little princess to grow up. Just promise me you've learned an important lesson from tonight, okay?"

"Oh, I have," she nodded, suddenly appearing a lot more sober.

"Okay. Let's make that the end of it," I gave a snort, "I wonder what Forsythe makes of his... errant daughter?"

"Thanks, Pa," Suze uttered a huge sigh of relief, "You're great. And as far as Sam's father goes, he's seldom home. Sam reckons he's having an affair with some City type."

"Sam probably would think that." The storm seemed to have passed, "Just promise me you'll use that wonderful brain of yours in future; don't depend on someone else for your ideas?"

Suze smiled at last, "I promise. I never want to feel this stupid ever again."

"Naïve, maybe, but not stupid."

She gave me a rueful grin.

"Tell you what?" I said, "Go and get changed into something a little more... appropriate, and I'll put some coffee on. I could sure use one, and I wouldn't mind betting you could as well." She nodded and stood, unsteadily, then made her way to the door, "Suze?" I called softly. She turned to face me, "You know something, princess? You're growing up to be a truly beautiful woman."

Her smile became radiant, "Thanks, Pa."

It's not a common occurrence during fatherhood, but sometimes, you just know when you've made the right decision over something.

6

Over the weekend, I broached the subject of a possible visit from Jenny with a still rather shamefaced Suze. I had expected her to be pleased with idea, but her enthusiasm when I mentioned it bordered on the hysterical.

"Of *course* I wouldn't mind! I've been just *dying* to see her after all you've told me. Now, you won't chicken out or anything, will you? And don't worry about the sleeping arrangements. I'm not one of these dumb kids who thinks their parents' sex lives stop at the moment they, themselves, are conceived—"

"Suze!" I interrupted, alarmed once more with the way my sweet, innocent, little daughter seemed to manage to raise the subject of sex – or, rather, my sex life – at every turn, "All I wanted to know was whether you'd mind."

"Don't be an old silly," she giggled, "But you really must consider the bedroom arrangements, I mean—"

"Enough! One more word about bedrooms, sex or anything like that, and I'm phoning your aunt Paula and getting her to put you up for the entire weekend."

"You wouldn't dare!"

"Try me."

"Okay, then," she sighed, "No more advice... but—"

"Is Paula's number on the speed dial?"

"Alright, alright, I give!"

I patted her on the head, "There's a good little girl."

"Little woman," she puffed out her chest, raised her chin, and then spoiled the effect by bursting into giggles.

I had another 'progress' meeting with Jenny on the Monday morning and was delighted when she confirmed that she would be free the following weekend – or, at least, up to Sunday morning – and would love to come and stay with Suze and me. Jenny would have to leave then because of an important meeting in Luxembourg scheduled for early on the Monday. I made a point of mentioning Suze because, despite her enthusiasm and eagerness, I was worried over what she would make of 'sharing' her father for a couple of days; it hadn't happened since Julie died.

The week passed slowly, constant monitoring of computer system usage bringing a new meaning to the word 'tedium' but punctuated by three evenings in the company of Jenny. There had been no further instances of rogue transactions, and by the Friday everyone was beginning to hope that I had at least found a way of stopping the nefarious dealings, even if I was making little progress on identifying the perpetrator.

Jenny had suggested that we drive down to my house in her car since she would need it on the Sunday, and I happily agreed. Although I have a personal pride in my classic Mini, I've yet to find anyone else who seems to share my adoration of the little beauty. Jenny left the office at five, and I followed ten minutes later, quickly walking to the Guildhall entrance where she had arranged to pick me up. One thing that hadn't been mentioned during the planning of our clandestine rendezvous was the make of car that she would be driving, and I studiously ignored the car that pulled up shortly after I had arrived there.

A loud honk drew my attention to the vehicle and my jaw sagged as I saw Jenny's blonde hair through the slightly tinted windscreen. I dashed to the kerb and climbed into the luxurious interior.

"An Aston Martin DB7," I breathed in awe as Jenny pulled away.

"Lovely, isn't she? I just adore her."

"I can quite see why." I decided not to mention what sort of 'Classic' car I actually owned.

The closer we got to my house, the more nervous I became. I could vaguely remember taking girlfriends home to meet my parents for the first time, and the feeling I was experiencing as Jenny's Aston drew closer was, if anything, even more nerve-racking. When she finally turned into the street that I indicated to her, I took a few deep breaths, composing myself for what I was beginning to expect to be an agonising ordeal. I was half expecting to see Suze standing by the side of our driveway, but, marvellous little thing that she is, there was no sign of her.

I took Jenny's suitcase from her and unlocked the front door of the house while she set the Aston's alarm. "Suze! We're home."

"Hi, Pa!" she called from somewhere near the back of the house.

"Come on in," I smiled as Jenny joined me on the front step. She followed me into the living room, and I set her bag next to the sofa. She grasped my hand as I rose, and I realised for the first time, that I wasn't the only one that was feeling nervous. I gave her a reassuring, if tight, smile, and turned towards the doorway to the kitchen when I heard Suze approaching.

My lovely daughter stepped confidently into the room, already smiling, drying her hands on a tea-towel. When she first caught sight of Jenny, Suze's jaw dropped before the smile returned, even brighter than before. "Pa told me you were beautiful," she said softly, "But he wasn't doing you justice. You must be Jenny?"

Jenny laughed delightedly, "Yes, and you must be Suzanne?" She turned to me, "I adore your daughter already."

"That's Suze," my daughter told her, "Take a seat, you two, and I'll fix you drinks. Lucky man," she giggled at me.

To my continuing astonishment, my kitchen-shy princess had spent the time since she'd returned from school preparing a lovely meal for Jenny and me, and astounded me further by insisting that we eat it on our own, taking herself off to do some revising for the last couple of GCSEs that she was currently sitting.

Afterwards, she joined us for an hour, struggling gamely not to ask too many questions of our guest – and knowing Suze, struggling even more gamely not to mention the S-word. At ten o'clock, feigning yawns, she declared herself exhausted and retired for the night, leaving Jenny and I alone.

"I think she likes you," I said to her.

"She's adorable," Jenny smiled, "I really have to congratulate you on bringing up such a wonderful daughter."

"Thanks," I said, compliments of Suze's behaviour being the only sort that I am truly comfortable with.

Later, I showed Jenny to the guest bedroom, taking her case inside and setting it on the bed. I turned to find her standing directly behind me. Since Suze's greeting, Jenny and I had been perfectly relaxed, as comfortable in each other's company as if we'd know each other for a few years rather than a few weeks. Now, a tension sprang up.

"I'd, er, better let you get some sleep then?" I swallowed as quietly as I could.

"I guess so," Jenny seemed to sigh.

"Well, then..."

"Yes, well then..."

I'm fairly certain we were wearing matching blushes. To cover the embarrassment of the situation, I kissed Jenny deeply, holding her tight for a moment. I tried not to remember my daughter's advice on sleeping arrangements. *Perhaps*, I told myself, *I should listen to her in future.*

"You know?" Jenny said quietly when we broke the embrace, "I'm very tempted to ask you to stay with me tonight?"

"And I'd be very tempted to do so." I blushed harder.

"Maybe it's a little too soon, though?"

"Yeah, maybe."

"And there's your daughter to consider."

"My who? Oh, er, of course." I don't often not think about Suze, but really, under the circumstances, could you blame me?

I left quickly before the situation got out of – or, perhaps, into – hand.

Saturday was idyllic, the weather hot and sunny, the skies clear of even the tiniest hint of cloud. Jenny and I went for a long walk across the fields surrounding the village, Suze, determined not to play gooseberry, staying behind at the house. She left us alone that evening, as well, visiting Sam, and pointedly saying that she would return no sooner than nine (and equally as pointedly, no later than ten).

Jenny and I spent a long time that evening cuddling on the sofa; the world's oldest teenagers, and we eventually retired after midnight. Once more I escorted her into the guest room and embraced her. We were no less nervous than we had been the previous night and the tension was even higher. I could clearly feel the firm contours of her lithe body through the delicate blouse she was wearing; could tell that she was neither wearing anything underneath, or in need of its support.

That night we took things a bit further – but only a little – and I retreated, uncomfortably, to my own room still able to feel the impression of firm nipples in the palms of my hands. I was fairly certain that we'd never be able to sleep in separate rooms under the same roof after that night.

As Jenny prepared to leave the next morning, Suze said her goodbyes and then left us alone once more. Our own goodbyes were far more passionate and took far longer. Before she finally left, Jenny promised that she'd call me from Luxembourg, and that when she returned on the following Friday, she wanted to take me out somewhere special. I waved her beautiful car, carrying its even more beautiful contents, a rather frustrated goodbye, and returned to face the Inquisition which I just *knew* was coming.

Bless her to Heaven and back, my darling daughter restricted herself to just one question and one comment: "Did you?" And "Moron!".

7

I hadn't really been looking forward to the following working week – excepting the Friday, of course – and my mood took a distinct turn for the worse when I arrived at the office on Monday morning. Forsythe and Barry Grant were standing in the upstairs reception area when I stepped out of the lift, and as soon as they saw me, they beckoned me over.

"What's up?" I asked them.

Forsythe answered, "Another rogue transaction, dear boy. Barry, here, tells me that just under two million US Dollars were automatically transferred into a Swiss bank account – numbered, of course – at eight thirty this morning."

Barry took up the story as I let out a despondent groan, "I had only just arrived and was about to start checking the audit logs and back-ups when I noticed activity on one of the modems in the comms room. Before I could get at the administration terminal the line went dead. When I checked the data, there was the new transaction, unfortunately with a status of 'complete', and, as with the other ones, no audit information whatsoever."

I nodded thoughtfully, "In a way, this is good news. At least we now know our perpetrator is getting into the system from outside. It still doesn't rule out one of the staff members, but that's a less likely scenario now. It also means that our mystery hacker has a thorough knowledge of accessing the database directly – otherwise they would have left an audit trail after the modifications we made last week."

"The data also matches the pattern of the other rogue deals," Barry added, "So we should be able to determine exactly how many previous transactions are not genuine."

"Quite. I'll let you deal with that." I crossed my fingers, "Any trace?" Just the previous Thursday I had set up trace devices on all incoming lines.

Barry handed me a piece of paper, "Modem three – the one that deals with our supposedly secure land line – was active for two minutes and nine seconds. No time, unfortunately for a full trace but at least we've had one small piece of luck. It was telephonically instigated rather than directly through another computer. I would have thought the latter was both easier and harder to trace."

"Yes, most nefarious types can mask IP addresses, but this could still be a remotely triggered call. Perhaps it's too much to hope that's not the case but at least it's something." I scanned the sheet he had handed me, "0203," I smiled, "Not nearly long enough for a full trace, but at least we know that the final call, triggered or not, was from the Greater London area. That narrows it down to… What? Seven million people and about the same number of landlines?"

Barry gave a wry smile, "Excluding kids and the elderly, probably closer to five."

"It's not much use then, dear boy?" Forsythe chipped in.

"On the contrary," I assured him, "For a start, to carry out a full transaction and audit scrub in just over two minutes shows an in-depth knowledge of the data structures that you use. It would therefore seem likely that he's a former employee."

"That should narrow it down," he nodded, "We don't have a massive turnover of staff here."

"Not necessarily. He could have spent hours inside the system, before we had the traces set up, learning the data structures and how deals are transacted. In other words, he could be a computer fraud specialist and not a former worker. Additionally, this doesn't actually rule out current employees. Yourself and Barry were both here, but most of the others don't start until nine-thirty; since our hacker probably lives in Greater London, there'd be plenty of time for him to get into work after carrying this out. And," I added, "It also doesn't rule out the possibility that someone inside ETA has simply given all the necessary information to a third party and had them break into the system. Or in other words, we can't even definitely eliminate you and Barry."

Barry nodded thoughtfully, "You said *probably* lives in Greater London; doesn't the 0203 mean that he must?"

I shook my head, "Hacking has reached amazing levels over the last couple of years; it's perfectly possible to have calls routed through a dozen different exchanges – that's what I meant about 'triggered calls'. The trace will only give us the last number used in that chain. Given the facts that our hacker has been so careful and that he is fast and efficient, we really can't guarantee his location."

"Or in other words," Forsythe sighed, "This little piece of luck, as Barry called it, really doesn't help us in any way?"

"As far as identifying our perpetrator, not really," I agreed, "But at least we know for sure that the transactions are being generated outside of the office itself."

"Is there *any* way we can prevent this?" Forsythe pressed me.

"We could disable all of the incoming lines, but as you well know, some transactions *have* to be generated off-site," Jenny had explained to me that when senior representatives of ETA were meeting officials from various government departments, it was often necessary to generate transactions immediately, even from abroad, "And there's also all of the outside information sources that you use; Reuters feeds, BACS, funds transfer systems, and so on. Disabling the lines is not really an option at this point."

"Couldn't we tighten up access to the data area itself?" Barry asked.

"If we tighten it up any further, we're going to strangle it. Our perpetrator clearly knows all of the access tricks in the book; we've already got four levels of security in place."

"What about the outgoing lines? Couldn't we put some sort of delay on the transaction processing in that area?" Barry went on.

"Same problem as disabling the incoming," I shook my head, "As I said, some transactions have to be carried out immediately."

"Couldn't we get BISTO, or whatever they're called, to add something to the system?" Forsythe asked.

"BISCO, and, no, that's not a practical option," I said, "To make a series of modifications that would have any effect on our hacker would take weeks for a start, and besides, if he's being supplied with inside information, any changes made would simply be passed on to him."

"All a bit of a catch-22, then?"

"Maybe, but at least we've got somewhere to start now. I'm beginning to get one or two ideas about how we can at least stop the transactions taking place, although I'll need a day or four to get the necessary information together."

"Ideas such as what?" Forsythe asked.

"If you don't mind, I'd rather not say for the moment. The less any information of that sort gets into the public domain, so to speak, the more chance there is of being able to put a stop to it all. What I will tell you, is that the first thing I'm going to be doing is to try to reproduce the hacker's methods," I was really beginning to enjoy myself for a change, "I'm going to go back home where all of my kit is and attempt to break into the system. I'll need someone at this end to monitor my efforts and see what happens."

"It'd better be me," Barry said, "I think it would be better if we don't let this little bit of information go any further than us three."

"I agree for now," I said, "Before I go, Barry, I'll let you have the details of what you need to be checking for. After my initial attempts, I'll need to get someone else in at this end who knows almost as much as I do about the hacking processes themselves, and my partner is just the man for the job. Does that sound okay with you, James?"

"Dear boy," he chuckled, "I've only understood one word in a dozen so far; whatever you need to do, please just do it. The sooner we get this matter resolved the better as far as I'm concerned." He left Barry and I discussing details of my planned system invasion and returned to his office.

What I hadn't said through all of the discussion was that my prime suspect was Barry Grant himself, and in truth I didn't need him to monitor my first efforts but wanted him to feel that he wasn't under suspicion. When I had told him what I wanted him to do, he left me in search of a much needed coffee and I called my long-time partner, David Moore – known as 'Dud' through his association with me, for reasons that are patently obvious.

"Pete!" he exclaimed, after I'd given him a brief explanation of my predicament, "You're not actually doing something for a change are you?"

"Why on earth do I put up with you?"

"Because you know I'm the best," he replied smugly, "So, what do you need me to do?"

"Meet me at my place about one and I'll fill you in."

"Telephone lines have ears, I take it?"

All the telephone conversations at ETA were recorded – even from private mobiles – as they are at most financial institutions, "Quite so, Dud. Can you make it?"

"It will be a pleasure," he laughed, "Sounds intriguing."

"That's an understatement," I told him before hanging up.

Just as I replaced the handset, the telephone rang.

"Peter Cooke," I announced.

"Pete, so glad to have caught you!"

"Hi, Jenny. Already arrived in the Grand Duchy?"

She grunted, "Hardly. I've been at Heathrow since six-thirty; the bloody plane was cancelled at the last minute and I've got another half hour to wait before the next one. Why does it always happen on a Monday morning? *And* when I've got an important meeting?"

"Poor thing," I smiled at the receiver, checking also that no-one could overhear me, "But it's great to hear from you. I really enjoyed the weekend."

"So did I," her voice softened, "I can't wait until Friday."

"Me neither."

"Pete... Is there any chance that you might be able to stay in town that night?"

Feeling deliciously adolescent, I felt a surge of butterflies in my stomach, "I should think that would be okay," I managed.

"Great! Well, until then, I'll call you every day, like I promised."

"That'll be wonderful... Oh, hang on; there might be a small problem with that."

"Oh?"

"We've had another break-in here," I went on to explain briefly what had happened and what my plans were.

"Sounds as if you're on the case," she said when I'd finished, "I'll call you at home then."

"Better use my mobile number. All of my landlines will be used for the hacking processes." After I gave her my number, I hung up, a very happy bunny indeed. The promise of a lovely woman come Friday, work that was fascinating and growing more interesting by the day, and a chance to work with Dud. All in all, not bad for a Monday.

I arrived back home just before midday and was surprised to find Suze curled on the sofa, still in her dressing-gown, earphones squawking in each ear.

"Hi, princess," I called loudly, hoping not to make her jump out of her skin.

She started and turned to face me, one hand on her racing heart, "Hi, Pa. What are you doing home?"

"I could ask the same question. In fact, I will. What are *you* doing home?"

She grinned, "Never listen to a word I say, do you?"

"I try not to," I agreed, reasonably.

After rolling her eyes, she said, "GCSEs, remember? I've only got two left to do and we're allowed to stay at home to study for them. By the end of the week I'll be finished with exams for another year, and, in case you'd forgotten, I'll be sixteen!"

"Oh, right," I nodded. I had forgotten about her last two exams, although not her birthday, which was on the Wednesday, "But that doesn't look much like revision to me." I nodded at the earphones, which were now silent.

She uncurled herself gracefully and crossed to where I was standing. Holding one of the earphones close to my right ear, she pressed the 'Play' button on the Samsung hanging in its cover, clipped to the belt of her robe.

"The three principal forms of land formation are volcanic activity, glaciation–"

"Okay, you're revising."

"My own father doesn't even trust me," she sighed dramatically, the back of her right hand on her forehead.

"Just trying to look after your wellbeing and your future, princess."

"I know," she grinned, "And I suppose I should be grateful. At least you do take an interest in what I get up to, unlike some fathers I could mention."

"Sam's, for instance?"

She nodded, grimacing, "He disappeared again yesterday evening and didn't come home."

"Well, he was at the office bright and early this morning."

"Maybe Sam's right when she says he's got some fancy woman in London."

37

"I couldn't imagine anyone fancying him," I said.

"Pa! It's all very well you being a surrogate mother, but you don't have to sound like one of those gossipy housewives as well."

"I'm learning from you," I grinned, "Now, why don't you go and get yourself dressed; Dud will be here in about an hour."

"Great!" she laughed delightedly. Dud was her favourite among my small circle of friends. "Will he be working here with you?"

"Only for today. Until Thursday, at least, you'll have to put up with me."

"Oh, damn," she sighed.

"I take it you've still got a crush on him then?"

"I do not!" A light blush flowered on her cheeks.

Although Dud Moore was only a year younger than me, he had the boyish good looks and charm of a much younger man. Dud was never short of female company, and I'd yet to meet a woman of any age that didn't take an immediate liking to him. "I'll be able to get a real answer by the way you dress," I teased Suze, "Probably that little party number you wore the other Friday."

Her eyes opened wide in surprise, "Pa! That's not nice. And you promised that episode was finished."

"Sorry, princess, just teasing," I couldn't help but grin, "Have you made up your mind what you want for your birthday yet?" Apology and appeasement – what more could a daughter ask for?

"How about a new father?" She ran, giggling, from the room.

By the time Dud arrived, customarily half an hour late, Suze was dressed in faded jeans and a baggy sweatshirt. This clear indication that she wasn't dressing to please our visitor in any way shape or form; that she most definitely did *not* have any sort of crush on him, was rather spoiled by the way she flew to the door when he knocked. She led him into the living room by his hand and flashed a warning look at me, indicating that I'd better not say anything to embarrass her.

"Hiya, Pete!" he beamed, "And Hiya, Suze!" he gave her a quick peck on the cheek, which, along with its counterpart, immediately turned the brightest shade of crimson.

"Hi, yourself," I smiled.

Suze scurried from the room in order to make coffee, and presumably calm herself down a bit. Her crush on my friend had started just the previous year when he had told her that she was 'the most beautiful fifteen-year old he had ever set eyes upon', and ever since she had been giggling nervously whenever he was present.

"So, what's the story?" he asked me when we were settled with our coffees, Suze sitting in one of the armchairs, trying hard to make it look as if she were engrossed in a geography textbook.

My detailed account of the problems at ETA and my plans to solve them, fascinating as they obviously were, had Suze finally concentrating on her revision.

When I'd finished, I asked Dud what he thought.

"Sounds like you're the man with the plan. I'll be there sharp at nine Wednesday morning; shouldn't take us more than a day or so to crack it."

"My thoughts exactly. But that's pretty much it for today, anyway. Fancy a beer or two down at *The Duke?*" I studiously ignored Suze's imploring look.

"What a pleasant thought," Dud agreed.

"Er, Pa?"

"Just popping out for an hour or so, princess."

"But–"

"I'll be back by four, at the latest."

"But–"

"Probably bring back a takeaway, if that's okay with you?"

"Pa!"

"Of course, if you were dressed a bit smarter, I'd offer to take you with–" Suze was halfway up the stairs before I'd finished.

8

Tuesday proved to be another exercise in tedium, the ETA systems' defences woefully inadequate for an experienced hacker, and I told

Barry Grant at two o'clock that there was nothing more I could do until Dud Moore went to the offices the next day. Probably as relieved as I was to be freed of the boring duties, he rang off gratefully. I was just preparing for a trip to the local shops when Jenny rang.

"Hi, Pete," she greeted me, "How's it going?"

"Hi, yourself," I sighed, suddenly content with my lot, "Not bad. I've got some idea of how we might be able to combat our hacker."

We went on to discuss progress briefly, and each other at length. I was still talking to Jenny when Suze returned from school. My darling daughter rolled her eyes theatrically, made a few gagging gestures, and then disappeared to her room to change. By the time she had come back down, I had rung off.

"I didn't need to ask who that was," she grinned.

"How did your last two exams go?" I was determined for the moment to change the subject.

She shrugged, a gesture identical to one that her mother had often made, "Great, I think. Guess I'll find out for certain in a couple of months. But best of all, I've only got three days of school left before the hols. Any idea where we're going yet?"

"I haven't even got a clue *when.* It's pretty much down to how I get on at ETA."

"Talking of ETA," she began, disingenuously, "Any idea whether Jenny will come with us?"

"No," I said, giving her a mock-stern look. I took a deep breath, "But while we're on that subject, I was wondering whether you'd mind very much if I, er, stayed out on Friday night?"

"Yes!" Suze punched the air delightedly, "I mean, no, of course I don't mind. Where are you two going?"

"I haven't the faintest idea. But there are some conditions attached."

"Aren't there always?"

"I'll let you stay here alone as long as there's no going out to clubs and getting drunk—"

"Pa! I promised. Remember?"

"If I didn't think I could take your word for it, I'd hardly let you stay here alone so soon after the last little episode, would I?" I grinned, "I'm just laying down some ground rules. Second condition, although I know you'll be sixteen by then, I don't want any boys coming around, okay?"

"Don't worry," she smiled, "But would it be okay of I invited Sam and Donna over? Have a sort of small party?"

"As long as you make sure Sam behaves herself – and as long as you promise to clear up any mess you make. Who's Donna, by the way?"

"She joined the school a couple of months ago," Suze said, "She's really nice; one of those girls that all the others envy. Great looking, really intelligent, witty."

"A bit like you then?"

"I wish," she groaned.

"Well that's how I describe you to people."

She tilted her head to one side, the tiniest of blushes flowering on her cheeks, "Really?"

"Really."

"You'll adore Donna, then. I'll see if she can stay over on Saturday night, as well. Give you a chance to meet her."

"There's no need," I said her, "Other than for Sam, I trust your judgement implicitly. But if you really want me to meet her, I'd be happy to."

"Any other conditions?"

"None. Now, are you sure about your birthday present?"

Suze nodded happily, "It sounds fantastic. But isn't it a bit expensive?"

I'd suggested that she might like a state-of-the-art computer, together with a digital camera and a few other peripherals, since Suze was becoming interested in graphic design, "It's a special birthday, for a special daughter. And we're not exactly hard-up, you know?"

"Well, if you're sure, then it'd be wonderful." She crossed the room and gave me a big hug, "Love you, Pa."

"Even when I'm not buying you expensive gifts and letting you stay home alone?"

"Even then. Or is that, especially then?"

41

The following morning, I made sure that when Suze woke, her new toy was all set up and ready to run in the small study next to my office, and it was all I could do to persuade her to get showered and dressed for her antepenultimate day at school. It also took me the best part of five minutes to dry her kisses from my face. At times like that fatherhood is the most wonderful of institutions.

Suze had barely been gone ten minutes when Dud called, and the world of work reasserted its unwanted presence. Dud and I have always worked well together, and we were soon totally engrossed in what we were doing; me at one end tirelessly hacking into the systems, he at the other, setting up ever-more elaborate defences. We took a short break for refreshments around two in the afternoon – and so that I could empty my overflowing ashtray – and then settled back to the task in hand. By five we were both surprised to find that I could no longer access any of the systems.

"You sure you're trying down there?" Dud asked me as yet another attempt failed.

"My hardest. Any ideas?"

He listed a dozen, all of which I'd already tried. We never discussed what the other person was actually doing since that would produce a bias in one or the other of us and may even lead to serious oversights.

"Well, it's looking good, then," he said, "There's only one other way in that we can't close down, and as far as I can see, they don't have the facility."

In recent years, much has been made of satellite and microwave technology, but few people realise that they are already widely used in the computer industry to allow computers to communicate without the need for wireless links and landlines.

"Barry assures me they don't have," I said, "But since you're there, why not have a quick look round? Call me back in ten, I'm busting for a pee."

"Will do, Pete."

When he called back, he confirmed that there didn't appear to be any other feeds into the systems. Satisfied that we'd done all we could, we chatted about other matters for a few minutes before hanging up.

Shortly afterwards, Suze came bursting through the front door.

"Hi, princess."

"Hi, Pa," she gave me a quick hug, "Sorry I'm a bit late, but I stopped off for a coffee on the way home with Donna."

"That's okay," I shrugged, "What do you fancy eating tonight? It is your birthday, after all."

"Takeaway? Only, I'd really love to start getting to know the computer."

"Fine by me," I agreed readily. It wasn't just Suze that was kitchen-shy, "Indian okay?"

"Perfect. By the way, can me and the girls order out on Friday night?"

"Given the mess I just know there'll be in the rest of the house, at least that way the kitchen should be relatively habitable by the time I get back."

"Not fair!" she protested with a giggle, "Oh! And another 'by the way'; Donna said she'd love to stay over Saturday as well – if that's still okay with you?"

"Of course it is. Fickle little thing, aren't you?"

"Fickle?"

"A few weeks ago it was Sam this, Sam that. Now all you seem to talk about is this Donna."

"Well, she's nice," she said, defensively, "I hope you like her, as well."

"If she really is like you, I'm bound to. It's just going to be the three of you on Friday, then?"

"Definitely. Just me, Donna and Sam. No boys, and no going out to a club."

"Good girl," I patted her head.

I spent the Thursday checking on the defences that Dud had installed and then had a brief meeting with Barry Grant and James Forsythe to give them an overview of what we had done (not wishing to give sufficient detail in case Grant really was the perpetrator).

"Sounds impressive anyway, dear boy," Forsythe chuckled when I had finished, "So what do we need to do now?"

"Pretty much nothing for the time being," I said, "Just monitor the data with the utmost care. I'll need some time to work on a contingency plan in case our villain manages to break the defences, and I'll do my best to see if I can trace the culprit, although without him slipping up, there's not much I can do. I'm desperately hoping that my work here is coming to an end."

"What sort of time-scale do you reckon for the contingency plan – and, please, don't try to explain what it is, dear boy?" Forsythe asked.

"A day with BISCO, probably three more here. One week, tops."

"Would you be prepared to be kept on a retainer for a few more weeks after that?" Forsythe asked, happier now that he was talking figures.

"Certainly."

"I rather think that we should maybe keep you available at all times," Forsythe nodded, "Never can be too careful, as we've just found out."

"You wouldn't be the first company to do so." The lovely thing about retainer fees is that if you've done your job right in the first place, you're earning, as Dire Straits once put it, money for nothing.

"Splendid, dear boy. I'll get Jenny to sort it out with you when she comes back from wherever it is."

"Luxembourg," I said, hastily adding, "Or I think that's where she said."

"It is," Barry Grant confirmed, "Is there anything that you'll need me to do, other than analysing the data?"

"Hopefully not," I said, smiling to myself. He'd seemed rather sullen all day.

9

Friday finally arrived and I treated myself to a late start at ETA, taking a leisurely breakfast and carefully packing a small overnight bag, trying hard to ignore Suze's ribald comments. After she had promised me for the tenth time that she, Donna and Sam were going to have a quiet girls' night in, she finally left for her last day at school for that year. The weather matched my mood – sunny and hot – and I strolled into the office just after ten.

Barry Grant was standing by his desk, reams of paper sprawled across its usually tidy surface. "Any news?" I asked.

He turned and gave me a hard, tight smile, "Oh, yes. Our hacker has been back at work."

My heart sank for a moment until he let out a loud laugh, "Four attempted break-ins, zero successes!"

"Yes!" I dropped my bag and attaché case, and punched the air, "Any traces successful?"

"Progress there as well," the systems manager nodded happily, "A fifth telephone number, 2. Any idea where that is, I haven't had time to check?"

"West of London. But it's still a vast area. Never mind, though. If he becomes desperate enough, he'll soon slip up. This is great news."

"What is, dear boy?" Forsythe emerged from the lift.

"Our hacker's been at work again, but the defences managed to stop him," Grant replied, grinning from ear to ear. I was beginning to think that my suspicions about him might have been wide of the mark.

"What marvellous news," Forsythe boomed, "This calls for a celebration! Well done, Pete, dear boy. Alice!"

Jenny's secretary, who had returned one day earlier than Jenny herself, poked her head around the doorway of the small office kitchen, "Yes, James?"

"Champagne, dear girl! Fetch a glass for yourself," he added, magnanimously.

Later that morning, I called the two guys at BISCO, the software authors, and arranged to meet them the following Tuesday, and then spent a leisurely hour in the local wine bar, continuing the celebrations with Barry Grant (*and* trying to divert my mind from what lay in store later that evening). When I got back to the office, Jenny had still not arrived, and I was beginning to worry.

The second my phone began to ring half an hour later, I snatched it up from the desk where it lay, "Peter Cooke."

"Pete! It's Jenny, I'm calling from the airport car park."

"That's great!" I heaved a huge sigh of relief, "When do you think you'll get back here?"

"I'm not going to," she said, my heart sinking, "I'm going straight on to the hotel. Could you meet me there?"

"The hotel?" I hadn't really had the slightest idea as to what her plans for the evening might be, but a hotel most certainly didn't feature. I'd rather assumed that if we were going to stay anywhere, it would be at her place.

"I thought it would be rather romantic," she said, nervously, "You don't mind, do you?"

"Not at all," I beamed, seriously doubting that she would have booked two rooms.

"It's the *Rathbone*, do you know it?"

"Off Charlotte Street?"

"That's the one." A nervous giggle escaped her, "Room 201. We're checked in under the name Underwood."

I desperately resisted the urge to shout "Yes!", and took a deep breath, "A fan of *Lord of the Rings*, I take it?" I asked, trying to change the subject.

"Very clever. But I had to use a pseudonym because James and one of the other directors sometimes go there. I hope you don't mind?"

"Of course not. What time do you think you'll arrive, only I've pretty much finished here for the day?"

"Knowing the M4, probably an hour at least. But you can turn up at any time; the room's pre-paid and all fully booked."

"I can't possibly let you—"

"Too late," she gave another girlish giggle, "I'll let you pay next time, if it makes you feel better?"

Next time, I grinned to myself, "Well, okay. I'll see you up in the room about four, then?"

"Can't wait."

"Likewise."

After I hung up, I left the office as nonchalantly as I could – not an easy task when you're outpacing an Olympic sprinter – and once outside, decided to head for St. Paul's tube station. If I took a cab, I'd arrive at the hotel in about ten minutes, and I wasn't sure that I could stand to wait for three-quarters of an hour or so. The Underground method turned out to be a reasonably good idea, the journey of less than a mile to Tottenham Court Road taking thirty minutes. The hotel was only a five-minute walk from the station, and I arrived a little breathlessly.

The receptionist, a pretty, dark-haired girl with a name tag bearing the legend 'Philomena', surprised me by saying that 'Mrs. Underwood' had arrived a few minutes earlier and was waiting upstairs for me. I took the electronic key-card from her and walked as casually as I could manage over to the lifts. I took a few deep breaths as the lift doors opened on the second floor and then stepped out, crossing the wide corridor to room 201 in three strides. As I stood there for a moment, trying to compose myself, the door opened a crack and one of Jenny's beautiful blue eyes appeared. When she saw me, she threw the door open and literally dragged me into the sumptuous room.

How can I describe that first night of passion? I could say that I performed like a love-god, a stallion, a modern-day Casanova. I could say that we spent the entire night locked in each other's arms, each of the ten or more times we made love better than the last; that we received complaints from other guests when our passions climaxed in thunderous shouts of pure ecstasy.

Or I could be honest.

We did make love more than once. Twice that number of times, in fact. The first time, which started just seconds after I'd been dragged into the room, was as clumsy and unsatisfactory as any such act had been for me this side of adolescence. We were simply far too nervous. We decided that a meal was called for – time to calm our ragged nerves – and ate in the third-floor restaurant; steak for me, lobster for Jenny. Afterwards we retired to the bar and sipped chilled Chablis until the sexual tension between us dictated a retreat to the room. Once inside, we undressed each other slowly, relishing the delay before we climbed more certainly into the king-size bed. The second time was altogether more satisfying, and I have to admit that Jenny's beautiful, lithe and supple body was the most amazing thing I'd ever seen, let alone been able to explore in such intimate fashion. Why the bloody receptionist chose that time to telephone and see if we needed an alarm call in the morning is beyond me.

Actually, it wasn't as disruptive as it might sound, and the humour of the situation finally dissolved the remaining tensions between us, allowing us to fully enjoy each other, and our togetherness. Sometime after midnight, we both fell asleep, locked in each other's arms.

I woke after nine to find Jenny sitting on the edge of the bed, sipping coffee.

"Morning," I yawned happily.

She turned to face me, a warm smile on her face, not a stitch of clothing on her gorgeous body, "Morning, Pete. Sleep well?"

"Wonderfully."

She set the coffee cup back in its saucer and pulled back the duvet before sliding her lissom form back into the bed. I pulled her tightly against me and kissed her deeply, relishing the sensation of naked flesh on naked flesh; something, I realised, I'd missed more than almost anything else over the previous four years. When we broke the embrace, Jenny propped herself on one elbow and studied my face.

"You're a remarkable man, Pete Cooke."

"And you're a beautiful lady, Jenny Winter."

She gave a soft laugh, "Actually, I meant you're remarkable because I feel so comfortable with you. I don't... usually get this intimate with men, this quickly."

"I'm not exactly experienced in that way either," I smiled, "With women, I mean."

She let out a sigh that verged on the plaintive, "I wish we could stay here all weekend."

"Me too," I agreed readily. I had a lot of catching up to do.

"But I'm afraid I've got to be leaving soon."

The sense of disappointment was almost crushing, "You must?" I asked, trying to mask my emotions.

"I really don't want to but…"

"If you must, then you must," I said, "But I hope this won't be the last time that we… that we're together."

"It better not be!" she laughed, leaning forward to kiss me once more.

I wondered whether this might be the precursor to another bout of love making, a sort of 'goodbye for now and remember me' type of thing. I was quickly disabused of that notion when she pulled back and sat up.

"So soon?" I asked, emboldened by the night of intimacy.

"Sorry, but yes. I hope you're not too disappointed?"

"As long as there's a next time, why should I be?"

"Let's make it soon," Jenny said, "Maybe… if you don't mind, that is, I could come down to your place?"

"Next weekend would be marvellous."

"I'll put it in red in my diary."

With that, she rose and stretched languidly, and it took all of my strength not to leap out of bed and drag her down onto the plush carpet. The woman, I promise you, would have raised more than just smiles in a monastery.

We showered – separately, unfortunately – and then dressed, before grabbing a quick breakfast in the ground-floor restaurant. Reluctantly, we checked out and strolled into the cool morning air, our free hands locked tightly together. I walked Jenny to the underground car park where her precious Aston Martin had been garaged for the night, and, after a final kiss, watched dreamily as she drove away.

Although I was a bit disappointed that our clandestine rendezvous had ended so abruptly, the elation that I felt at the memory of the previous night made it hard for me to concentrate on anything around me. I was fortunate that the bus had good brakes.

I reached my house at almost exactly midday, and for the first time in more than twenty-four hours, turned my thoughts towards my little princess. More exactly, I began to wonder what sort of havoc she and her friends had wreaked in our home. I let myself in and peered into the living room.

I had imagined that it would resemble a bomb site, but if anything, it was tidier than usual. The same applied to the kitchen and the small study where Suze's precious new toy was located. "Impressive," I muttered to myself, trailing back into the living room. On the coffee table, I spotted a note that had escaped my previous attentions.

"Dear, darling, Pa – or should that be Casanova?

Have gone go-karting with Donna and we'll be back around six. Will eat on way back so don't bother to make us anything (as if you would!). Hope you and the gorgeous Jenny have sore backs this morning (I didn't really mean 'backs' but I'm sure you'd get mad if I wrote anything else).

Love you to bits,

The light of your life, the fruit of your loins,

Your wonderful, amazing, gorgeous daughter, XXXXXXX"

Sometimes, you don't know whether to laugh or cry.

The two girls eventually arrived home at seven, both breathless, having ran the last mile – whatever happens to all that energy you had as a teenager? Donna proved to be every bit as beautiful, witty and intelligent as Suze had described, and I was immediately taken with her. The only real difference between the pair of them was Donna's sense of complete self-confidence, a highly tuned awareness of herself, her looks and her talents. I hoped that some of it would rub off on Suze; Donna was clearly a much better influence than the dangerous Sam.

Unusually, I was content to be in the company of Suze and one of her friends, and I was surprised to find myself almost disappointed when Donna left after a late Sunday breakfast.

"So, what do you think of her?" Suze asked eagerly after she had seen Donna off.

"A vast improvement on Sam," I smiled.

"Anyone could see that! I meant what did you really think of Donna herself?"

"She's everything you said she was. A thoroughly charming young woman."

50

To my surprise, Suze let out a huge sigh of, what sounded like, relief, "Great!"

"Is my opinion that important to you?"

Suze suddenly seemed three or four years younger than she actually was; more like the gawky thirteen year-old that was forever blushing and stumbling over her words, "Well, she's a really g-g-good friend," she stammered slightly, "And I really would prefer it if you liked her. I can't really explain why."

I shrugged and determined not to press her on the issue; my experience of teenage girls suggested that I'd never understand them, anyway. Instead, I changed the subject, "I think I might be finished at ETA in a week or so if nothing else happens there. Perhaps we could start planning that holiday you keep harping on about?"

"I do not harp!" she protested, returning to her real age, "But will Jenny be coming with you?"

Unbelievably, this was the first mention she had made of my beautiful new lover since she had arrived home the previous evening. I imagined that she was sparing me the embarrassment in front of her friend, "I haven't asked her yet."

"Not even last night when you were... you know? I mean, you did, didn't you?"

"Suze!" It was my turn to protest, "I'm pretty sure that you won't like it if I start prying into your love-life whenever you get around to having one, will you?"

"Ah! But I might remain celibate for the rest of my life. If I don't share your secrets, then I'd never have any experience of a sex-life at all."

Teenagers should come complete with a manual. I mean, what on earth does one say in those circumstances? "If you must know, we spent a very pleasant night together, okay? And that's all I'm prepared to say on the matter."

"Good for you," she giggled, "So, will you ask her to come with you. On holiday, I mean."

"Suze!" I gave her a mock-scowl, "As far as the holiday goes, I'll wait and see. She'll be coming down next weekend, by the way. Is that okay with you?"

"Of course! Need any pointers?"

I rather spoilt my stance of indignation by laughing, "Enough! Are you sure you don't mind her... being here?"

"Don't be silly. Besides, I was going to ask you if it would be okay if I spent Friday and Saturday night at Donna's. She invited me over in return for staying here."

The idea had immediate appeal. Not only would that mean that Jenny and I would be undisturbed at my place, if Donna was anything like the good influence that she appeared to be, the more time my little princess spent with her the better as far as I was concerned, "Are you sure you're not just saying that so that Jenny and I don't have a precocious kid under our feet"

"I am not precocious! Spirited, maybe."

"Okay, then. You can stay at Donna's"

"What, no conditions?"

"Only the usual ones," I smiled. The next weekend having been organised, I turned the subject back to the proposed holiday, "Any idea where you'd like to spend a couple of weeks lazing by some pool?"

Teenagers, I've found, have a never-ending ability to surprise, "Actually, Pa," she replied, thoughtfully, "I'm not that sure I really want to go with you."

"Oh? This time last week you were already packing your suitcase."

She shrugged – that mother-like gesture that could almost reduce me to tears, "I guess I'd like to spend a little more time here, that's all. What with my new computer and new friends and everything..."

"You honestly believe that I'd leave you here alone for a fortnight?"

"Pa, please? I mean, look how well behaved we were Friday when you weren't here."

I stared hard at her, "One night is a hell of a lot different from a fortnight. And besides, all I know about Friday night is that you cleaned up well after yourselves; I've no idea what you actually got up to."

"So you don't really trust me after all?" she moaned petulantly, once more the thirteen year-old.

"I do. But a fortnight is a hell of a long time. What exactly are you planning to get up to while I'm away? Have you got a boyfriend, for instance?"

"Pa!" She was now verging on angry, "I have not got a boyfriend and even if I had, I wouldn't betray your trust like that. I'm really not into boys, and all I'd hoped I could do was have my own space for a while; get to grips with that graphic design software you brought home the other day. Maybe invite Donna over for an evening or two."

It had always distressed me to see Suze upset or angry, and now she was close to tears, "Okay, ease up, princess. I didn't mean to imply that I don't trust you, because I do. But what if I *do* go away without you and there's some sort of disaster here? I'd never forgive myself if anything happened to you and I wasn't around to prevent it in the first place."

"Pa, I'm sixteen! You're not going to be able to protect me from every little everyday hazard for the rest of my life. In two years, I'll be off to university – hopefully. What will you do then? Room with me?"

God, I hate these spats. Especially when there's an element of truth in what Suze is protesting about. "Princess," I sighed, pulling her into my arms, "I know I'm a little... over-protective at times," I ignored her groan at the word 'little' and continued, "And I guess some of that is because of your mother; I feel the need to protect you for both of us." The mention of her mother caused her to relax a little in my grip, "It's hard to let go, Suze."

"I know," she sighed, her anger dissipating, "But maybe a fortnight apart will help the process. It's not just you being over-protective, you know? *I've* got find out what it's like not to be dependent on you for everything; stand on my own two feet for a change."

I eased her away from me so that I could stare into her lovely blue eyes, "Everything you've just said makes perfect sense. But until you have kids of your own, you'll never know how hard it is to watch them grow up and start to grow away."

"I *won't* be growing away, Pa," her voice held a plaintive edge, "You'll always be the one person I'll love the most. Always. Please, Pa? I really do need a little time on my own."

It was my turn to be close to tears. The rollercoaster ride of parenthood; what joy! "Oh, Suze," I shook my head, "Why can't I ever deny you?"

Her eyes opened wider, "You mean, you'll let me? Stay here, I mean?"

"Do you promise to behave properly?"

"Of course, Pa," the sincerity in her eyes dissolved the last of my reservations, "If you like, I won't invite *anyone* over while you're away; not even Donna."

"That's not necessary. I suppose if we're going to do this, we'd better do it properly," I sighed inwardly. Letting Suze go was harder than letting go of a window-ledge when you're dangling over a hundred-foot precipice by your fingertips, "I *should* say that you should consider the house yours while I'm gone – no rules, no conditions. But that's asking a bit too much of me, just yet. If you promise just the one thing, then I'll agree."

"Anything at all." The look of sincerity was even deeper.

I took a deep breath, "Just promise me you won't let any boys... stay over?"

Her serious expression disappeared in an instant, and she hugged me tightly, "Oh, Pa! That's an easy promise to make, and even easier to keep. Like I said, I'm really not into boys; or at least, not yet, anyway. You'll really let me stay here alone?"

I returned her hug – as much for my comfort as anything else, "I'm not sure I really know what I'm doing, here, but, yes, you can stay here alone."

The stream of thank yous lasted a full three minutes.

10

I broached the subject of a holiday with Jenny first thing on the Monday morning while we were closeted in her office to discuss what had happened at ETA the previous week (it hadn't been mentioned once on Friday night).

"It's a lovely idea," she smiled, "But I guess I couldn't take a whole two weeks. Perhaps five or six days, though?"

As far as I was concerned, five or six days might be enough to do some permanent damage to my back – and it was far better than no days at all, "Why not? I'll have to stay for a fortnight, though; I've sort of promised Suze."

"That's settled then," Jenny kissed the tip of my nose, "Where were you thinking of going?"

"Anywhere hot," I returned her kiss, my hands brushing the front of her silky blouse, "Any ideas?"

"You choose." She groaned at my touches, "I love to laze in the sun."

The thought of that lithe, lissom body covered in suntan oil was almost too much to bear, and my caresses became firmer. Among other things. "I'll go around to that travel agency on Cheapside at lunchtime, then," I managed. I swear that if Alice hadn't phoned through with a message for Jenny, I would have ended up with carpet burns on my knees and elbows. I hate to think where Jenny's would have been.

By the end of the afternoon, I was the proud – and eager – possessor of two tickets to Nice airport, dated twelve days later, and a reservation for two weeks at a hotel on the coast near St. Raphael. I also possessed an air of elation that I hadn't experienced in more years than I cared to remember.

If Jenny had been delighted with my choice of destination, Suze was even more enthusiastic; she probably harboured secret fears that I'd hole up at the nearest hotel to home.

"Really romantic," she sighed, "That Jenny's a lucky lady. Come to that, so am I. No second thoughts about leaving me behind?"

"Several hundred thoughts. But don't worry, I'm not going to change my mind. As long as you're a good girl for the next two weeks until I leave," I added, "And you can start by pouring your wonderful father a beer."

Given the speed with which it was poured, I was amazed that the head was only a couple of centimetres thick.

The rest of the week turned into a long, boring grind. Putting together my contingency plan was as much a process of information-gathering as anything else, and this was my least favourite sort of work. To exacerbate matters, Jenny had returned to Luxembourg on the Tuesday and wouldn't arrive back until Friday evening, the plan being for her to drive straight down to my house when she did so. At home, Suze's boundless gratitude began to grind as well. I was fortunate that Donna spent a couple of evenings there, providing sufficient distraction for Suze for her to leave me in peace.

On the positive side, there had been no more attempted system break-ins, and by the time I left on the Friday afternoon, with only two more working days scheduled for the following week, I was optimistic that between us, Dud and I had put paid to our mystery hacker's nefarious activities.

I arrived home to find Suze packing a bag for her stay at Donna's.

"Hi, princess," I greeted her when I located her in her bedroom.

"Hi, wonderful father of mine," she beamed, "Looking forward to your couple of nights of passion with the lovely Jenny?"

"Yes, and I sincerely trust you're *not* looking forward to a couple of nights of passion with any guys?"

"Pa! How many more times? Guys don't figure in my life at the moment!"

"Just being a concerned, caring father," I grinned.

"Concerned, caring mother-hen, more like."

"Cluck," I nodded.

She went on to tell me, excitedly, about all she and Donna had planned for the next two days, and, though I hate to admit it, most of it went in one ear and out the other; Jenny's imminent arrival dominated my thoughts. It was almost a relief when Suze finally left, so that I could sit and fret alone.

When Jenny still hadn't arrived by eight, I was beginning to fear the worst. By nine, I was wearing a thin strip in the carpet with my constant pacing, and at half past, I had two cigarettes alight at the same time. The sound, ten minutes later, of the throaty Aston Martin engine was one of the most wonderful noises I'd ever heard in my life. By the time Jenny had parked the sports car and taken a suitcase from the back seat, my front door was open, and I was trying desperately not to hop from foot to foot like some hormone-crazed adolescent.

It took less than three minutes to convey Jenny's one piece of luggage into my bedroom, and less than thirty seconds to convey her clothes to the four corners of the room. We didn't leave the room, other than to use the bathroom, until ten the following morning.

"I've said it before, and I'll say it again," Jenny smiled at me from over the rim of a coffee mug, "You're a remarkable man, Pete Cooke."

"And you're a wonderful lover."

"Think what I might be like with some more practice," she gave me a lascivious grin and stood slowly, letting her robe slip to the kitchen floor.

As I've said before, she really had the most amazing body, full of long, graceful curves, every part of her, perfectly proportioned. As she stood there, unashamedly naked in the middle of my kitchen, I found myself with absolutely no choice; drawn as efficiently as any moth to any flame. Each time we had made love had been better yet than the time before, and that morning, nestled among a hastily strewn pile of towels, was no exception. As I entered her, and as she gave an almost animalistic grunt of pure pleasure, I had no thoughts for anyone, or anything, else; just that one moment, that one overpowering desire.

By the time she left on the Sunday morning, I felt sated, exhausted, and not a little sore. If, as she had told me, sun, sand and sea made her even hornier, I was beginning to dread what sort of state I'd be in by the time she left me in St. Raphael. 'Perhaps,' I thought, 'I'd better consider giving up smoking.'

Suze arrived home just after Jenny had left, took one look at me, and burst into a fit of giggles.

"Okay," I sighed, "What's the joke?"

"You know that expression?" she managed, still giggling, "The one about looking like the cat that got the cream? Well, I know what it really means, now."

"Is it that obvious?" I asked, alarmed.

"If you had a little notice hanging round your neck saying 'I had lots of great sex last night' it couldn't be more obvious!"

"Enough!" I protested. I glanced down at her, "You're not wearing a bra!"

"Pa! For a start you shouldn't be looking, *and* I don't really need one anyway."

"You do with a blouse like that. You can, er, pretty much see through it."

"Don't worry, I was wearing a jacket on my way back," she sighed, "I'm no exhibitionist."

"I hope you didn't go out anywhere dressed like that?"

Suze looked genuinely shocked, "Of course not! The clip on the one I was wearing last night broke and I didn't have a change with me. Donna's mother drove me over here to pick one up – Donna's are too small for me – but there was only one light on; your bedroom light. I decided I'd better not come inside in case I disturbed you."

"Silly thing," I said, both relieved and grateful, "This is your home as well as mine. Jenny's presence doesn't change anything."

Suze shrugged and gave her disarming grin, "I guess I didn't want to put you off your stroke. After all, you haven't had much practice recently."

"Suze!" I decided to change the subject quickly, "Well, go and put one on now, or at least change into a less revealing blouse or T-shirt, or whatever. If you're quick, I'll take you down the *Duke* for some lunch."

"You'd let me go down there with you without a bra on?"

"It's not as if anyone can tell – with a different top on, at any rate. It's your body; all I ask is that you don't go around looking like you do right now."

Suze, bless her, modestly held an arm across her chest, her cheeks reddening slightly, "I..." she began, dropping her gaze to the carpet.

"What?"

Her eyes still engrossed in the Axminster, she muttered, "I wish I could... bring myself to talk to you about some things."

This was most unlike my normally open, candid daughter, "Suze, princess, you can talk to me about *anything*. Remember what I used to tell you after... after your mother died? From then on, I was going to be both mother and father to you. There's no subject that you can't discuss with me."

She glanced up at me for a second and then back down to the carpet. She took one deep breath and then said quickly, "It's just what you said about it being my body and that you didn't mind if I didn't wear a bra. Well, when that one broke last night, and I couldn't – or at least, didn't – come in to get one from here, Donna sort of laughed a bit. Said she almost never wears one now, and really likes the feeling of freedom. And, well, I guess I found out she was right; it really does feel nice."

"And your point?" I asked softly, bemused.

She finally raised her eyes to mine, "You know Sam?" she broke off to roll her eyes, "Dumb question. It's just that some of the guys – and some of the girls, come to that – refer to her as a 'slut' and stuff like that. And *she* never wears a bra, as you very well know. I was wondering whether the two things are related, like, if you don't wear one, does that make you a slut, I guess. I'm just so confused."

"Of course it doesn't, princess," I sighed, pulling her into a hug, "Maybe if you go around wearing see-through tops, it'd give people that impression, but it's really more the way people act that give others these thoughts. You've said yourself that Sam's always keen to let the guys get a good view of her, and you've said that she sleeps around a bit. In most people's view that does make her a bit of a slut, as you put it. You never act like that, I'm sure. If you like to feel a bit of freedom

59

under your T-shirts or your blouse, then fine, go without a bra. Unless you get into a clinch, or go jogging maybe, no-one's even going to notice." I was on firm ground here, for once; Julie had gone through exactly the same dilemma when I'd started dating her. Of course, there might have been a tad of bias in my advice back then, but it really *is* one of those things I believe in, "It's not just what you wear that makes you a particular type of person, Suze, it's much more how you act, okay? Surely you know that from what you see in other people?"

She finally relaxed against me, giving me a small hug, "You're right. It's just that after spending so long around Sam, Donna's opinions seem a bit strange. I mean, that's what got me so confused, I guess. Sam never wears a bra because she wants guys chasing after her, but Donna doesn't because she just likes the feeling."

"And what would be your reason?" I grinned down at her upturned face.

"You know very well!" she managed a giggle.

"Well, there you go then." It was almost funny to see the normally grown-up thinking, near-adult, Suze, so confused and her almost child-like innocence. I guess I also felt reassured that she wasn't growing up and away from me so quickly, after all.

"Thanks, Pa. And are you really sure you don't mind if I don't, well, wear one to the pub?"

"Just promise me you won't jog round the bar, okay?"

Suze swatted my arm. It was worth it, just to prove that I still had *some* value as a parent. In the event, she came back downstairs after changing in a jet black, loose and baggy sweatshirt. In that she really *could* have gone jogging and no-one would have been any the wiser as to her underwear situation.

11

The last couple of days at ETA felt more like a chore than a worthwhile way of earning a few hundred pounds, but the first of them, at least, was brightened by Jenny's radiant presence before she left on the Tuesday, bound for Geneva. After she had departed, I went through to James Forsythe's office for what he called a de-briefing session.

"So, dear boy, your last day with us, then?"

"I'm afraid so, James," I nodded, trying not to appear too delighted at the prospect.

"All sorted out on the retainer front?"

"Jenny arranged everything yesterday. I'll poke my nose round the door every couple of weeks or so, just to make sure the defences are holding up, but should anything happen in the meantime, she and Barry have my mobile number and Dud's if I'm away anywhere."

"Splendid! No chance of any progress on identifying our interloper, I suppose?"

I shook my head, "Whoever he is, I'm fairly certain he's caught on to the fact that we're after him; that's probably the main reason why we've not had any further attempts at break-ins."

"Oh, well, at least we're secure. Now, dear boy, how about I take you round to my club for a spot of lunch, what?"

Over a particularly delicious Lobster Thermidor, I gave him a brief outline of my contingency plan – but judging by the gradual glazing of his eyes as I spoke, it held little interest for him. He muttered something about being computer illiterate and changed the subject. I can't say I was too disappointed.

At five, I took everyone to *Spritzers* for a last drink, and the wine, combined with the earlier intake at Forsythe's club, left me feeling decidedly under the weather by the time I reached home. Suze was clearly unimpressed.

"What am I going to do with you?" she sighed, settling me on the sofa and handing me a steaming coffee mug.

"Sorry." I tried to keep a straight face. I have a tendency to giggle when I've had a few too many.

Suze gave me a mock-scowl, rolled her eyes and then sat beside me, "Still, I suppose I can use this to my advantage. You know Donna and me went karting a while back?"

I nodded a little too vigorously and said something like "Vroom".

Trying hard not to giggle herself, Suze went on, "Well, there's a course starting at the club Saturday week, and I'd really love to go on it. It's just for three days, but it's intensive and me and Donna would have to stay at the hotel nearby."

"That's Donna and I."

"You're not going to be staying with Donna," she giggled, "I will be. But, what do you say? Can I go on it?"

"Don't see why not."

"The course isn't too expensive, and if Donna and *I* share a room at the hotel, that'd save a bit, as well."

"Ah!" My nodding dog impression was coming along nicely, "You want some more money?"

"Would you mind?" she asked, oh-so-sweetly, "I'd really love to go with her."

"Of course I don't mind, my darling daughter." Despite a fit of hiccups, which for some reason I found incredibly funny, we managed to work out how much extra cash Suze would need, and I counted out the correct amount from my bulging wallet to the accompaniment of her endless stream of 'thank yous'.

The following morning, I rose late and carefully carried my hangover down to the kitchen where I found coffee and Paracetamol waiting for me. What more could a father ask of a daughter?

As Saturday approached at a far too leisurely pace for my liking, I busied myself around the house, intent on cleaning it from top to bottom before I left it in the care of my offspring. It took me a while to realise that it was already pretty much spotless, and I marvelled at the fact that I hadn't even realised how much of the burden of domestic chores Suze had taken on herself. I was both impressed *and* embarrassed.

"Princess?" I asked her on the Thursday evening, "Why didn't you tell me you were doing all that housework?"

She shrugged – *that* gesture again, "You've been pretty busy over the last few weeks – for a change – so I reckoned it was only fair. Besides, it's a bit alarming when you go the fridge and discover the bacon grazing on the lettuce."

I winced, "You really don't have to do all of it by yourself. *Or* be quite so sarcastic!"

"You're volunteering to help?" She raised an eyebrow, "And it's 'descriptive', not 'sarcastic'."

"Actually, I was thinking more of getting someone in to do a few things. Maybe a day a week or some such. Along with extra English lessons."

"Why doesn't that surprise me?"

"Perhaps you could try to organise something while I'm away?"

"Me?" This suggestion clearly *did* surprise her.

"Why not? Like I always say, it's as much your place as it is mine. And besides, you know what I'm like around women."

"Who says it has to be a woman?" she gave me that mock-scowl, "You're not turning into some sort of sexist pig now that you've got yourself a ladyfriend, are you?"

"I just assumed—"

She interrupted me with a very melodramatic sigh, "Men!"

I stuck my tongue out at her and failed miserably to keep a straight face, "It was a perfectly natural assumption to make. And anyway, since when have you been one of those burn-your-bra feminists?"

"I have not burnt my bra!"

"I bet you're not wearing one," I commented, smugly.

"Low blow, father of mine. You never see supermodels wearing bras, and you'd hardly call *them* feminists. *And* I noticed that Jenny doesn't wear one, either. I can't exactly see her in a pair of unisex dungarees and a number two haircut."

"Leave Jenny out of this," I grinned, "And let's get back to the point. Would you mind organising it?"

"I guess not. And, actually, I'd probably prefer a woman to do it anyway. I really couldn't stand the thought of some guy rummaging through my knickers."

"Good girl," I patted her head, "My thoughts exactly. Now, how about a beer?"

"You know I don't drink," she replied, disingenuously.

"Tell you what? If my darling, dutiful daughter pours her wonderful daddy one, I'll let her have a sip, okay?"

She gave another melodramatic sigh and crossed to the fridge, "Not only does my own father treat me like some sort of modern-day Cinderella, *now* he's encouraging me start boozing!"

"I'd hardly equate one sip with boozing!"

She poured the beer into my favourite tankard and took a tentative sip, "Oh, yuck! How on earth could anyone drink this stuff?"

I took the beer from her and drank a mouthful, "Thanks, princess. And it's very reassuring to hear you say that," I smiled.

"Well, for the time being at least, that's another thing you don't have to worry about over me. Boys and booze are definitely off my agenda for now."

"You mean they don't go with the radical-feminist, girl-power image?"

"I am neither of those! I am my own person; a free spirit, not constrained by any media-hyped vision of what should be, nor by the peer-pressure that affects so many at my age."

"Nor by a bra."

Her swatting accuracy and power were definitely improving.

When Saturday finally managed to put in what seemed like a belated appearance, I was awake at six, and packed and ready to leave by eight. A rather pointless exercise since the Nice-bound plane wasn't due to take off until four. By midday, I could sense that Suze was getting anxious for me to leave.

"For the eighth time," she groaned, "I promise! No guys, no boozing, keep the indoor fireworks to a minimum, no ordering a swimming pool to be built in the garden while you're away, no turning the kitchen into a printing press for forged tenners, no–"

"Okay, I get the picture! I'm just, well, worried a little, that's all."

She crossed and hugged me tightly, "Don't be. There's really no need. I'm a big girl now and I've made my promises. Just enjoy yourself in France and concentrate on having a good time. Which I'm sure will be pretty easy with the lovely Jenny there. And remember, when she leaves, you've still got another eight or nine days in which to have a holiday fling or two."

"I'm not that sort of guy!" I protested, trying hard not to let it show that the thought *had* crossed my mind. "Now, you will be okay here, won't you?"

"I'll be fine! In fact, I'm going to spend the first couple of days just relishing the peace and quiet. Just imagine! Two whole weeks without having to start every other sentence with "I promise"!"

Her giggles were, as ever, infectious, and I hugged her tightly, "Sorry princess, but I guess I just can't help fretting."

"And *I* guess, it's good to know you care," she said, more seriously.

"I do. More than anything else in the world."

"Likewise." She reached up and kissed my cheek, "Now, are you sure you've got everything you need? Suntan oil, books to read, clean underwear, one gross of condoms?"

"Suze!" I made a mental note to pick up some of the latter at the airport.

A loud honk from outside indicated the arrival of the taxi I'd booked to take me to Heathrow – I wasn't going to trust my precious Mini to any airport car park – and Suze didn't even bother to try to disguise her sigh of relief. Within two minutes I had been bundled out of the front door and into the back of the taxi.

12

Pessimist that I occasionally am, I was convinced that some last minute hitch would prevent Jenny from getting to the airport, and so I was even more delighted than I would normally have been to find her already there, waiting for me by the Bodyshop kiosk, as arranged.

I took that to be a good omen, and, if you believe in such things, that is exactly what it turned out to be. Our flight left on time and arrived a few minutes early. The coach from Nice to St. Raphael was air-conditioned and spotlessly clean. The hotel turned out to be a dream, the weather joyously hot. And best of all, there was Jenny.

Wherever we relaxed, heads turned. Whether we were laying by the pool, her lithe, half-naked form glistening in the sun, or dining in one of the marvellous seafront restaurants, her smartly-tailored sundresses emphasising her wonderful figure. She had been right, too, when she had told me that the sun and sea did lovely things to her sex-drive. The word 'insatiable' springs to mind.

The first Friday was Jenny's last day, and we stayed in our room until after eleven.

"I guess I really must get going," she whispered as I caressed her gently after a third bout of love making.

"Shame," I sighed.

"Promise me you'll call as soon as you're back?"

"Try stopping me."

"Don't worry, I'm not about to try to stop you. From doing anything," she added.

After she left, I wandered down to the poolside bar in search of much needed refreshment, a Stephen King paperback in one hand and a pack of Marlboro in the other. As I sat, sipping an ice-cold beer, I was surprised to find myself feeling slightly relieved. I'd not really given much thought to the relationship I was having with Jenny, content to let things drift along at their own pace and in their own time; more content still to simply relish every act of sex. But for whatever reason, it suddenly seemed a little strange.

In the dim, distant past, I'd always been the faithful type, and throughout the thirteen years I'd been married to my lovely Julie, I'd never even been tempted to be unfaithful. But now... Somehow, my relationship with Jenny didn't seem as concrete as those I'd had before; less a true relationship than a sharing of mutual feelings – mostly revolving around sex. When the pretty little dark-haired Maria asked me for a light a few minutes later, I found myself studying her discreetly in a way that I hadn't studied any woman for more years than I cared to remember. When she accepted my offer of a drink, I felt the same thrill as I had when I'd been a teenager 'out on the pull', as we used to say.

The thrill was even greater as she agreed to my suggestion that she might like to come back to my room when I asked her later that evening.

I felt no guilt and no regret as I slowly undressed her and none afterwards, as we lay sweating and panting in that glow of post-coital bliss. She had to leave the next day, she told me as we lay there, still entwined, and she asked me whether I would mind if she stayed the night. I ask: would *you* have kicked her out the door?

Perhaps I was catching up on the long, lonely years since Julie had died. Alternatively, perhaps this was just some mid-life, early male-menopause sort of thing. I didn't know then, and I don't to this day. Nor, come to that, did I, or do I, care. Whatever the reasons behind it, I spent the final week of my glorious holiday in a sort of testosterone-induced haze, surprised at my ability when it came to attracting the women. Maria was followed by Anastasia (and, no, I don't believe that was her real name, either); Anastasia by Yvonne, and Yvonne, finally, by Elaine.

All of them were completely different from each other; in looks, age and even behaviour. The would-be thirty-something Russian princess had auburn hair and the body of a regular work-out freak. She was superficial and, perhaps with some justification, vain. Yvonne claimed to be twenty-six but was probably closer to thirty-six, as was her bust measurement, her hair dyed blonde, her manner laddish.

Elaine, however, was my favourite. She, too, claimed to be twenty-six, but I would have put her no older than twenty. She was a natural blonde, that honey-tinted shade that always reminds me of Goldie Hawn, and it was her body, not her manner, that I thought of as 'laddish'; small, pert breasts, narrow – almost boyish – hips. What I liked most about her, though, was her air of innocence and modesty, somehow very much in keeping with her appearance. When I first undressed her, she was shy, coyly covering her nakedness with her delicate hands. When I told her how beautiful she was, she didn't seem to believe me – although I think the heights of passion I reached with her might have caused her to reconsider this. I had wondered whether she might be upset when I told her that I had to leave the following day, but she surprised me by simply holding me tight and thanking me for 'the most thrilling experience'. I was surprised further to find out it was *me* that was a little upset at the thought of leaving *her*.

Still, I guess that's what holiday romances are all about and as I stepped onto the coach, ready to be taken back to the airport at Nice, all in all, I didn't feel much in the way of regrets.

All of those lovely ladies had succeeded in taking my mind off the one truly lovely lady I had in my life, and my thoughts turned towards Suze and, I have to admit, the chaos that I was convinced I would find when I arrived home. The taxi journey from Heathrow seemed to last for hours, my mounting tension having some sort of Doppler effect on time, no doubt, and when we finally pulled up outside the house (which to my surprise was still standing) I was out of the car in a flash.

The catalogue of fears that I had created during the journey dissipated as the front door opened, and Suze waved happily to me, clearly fit and well. She dashed down the drive and threw herself into my arms, smothering my face and neck with kisses.

"Missed you, Pa!"

"Missed you, too, princess," I almost didn't lie.

I paid off the amused-looking driver and took my suitcase into the house, trying not to make it too obvious to Suze that I was giving the place a once-over *en route*. Precious thing that she is, she groaned, rolled her eyes and took my hand.

"Come on, doubting Thomas, let's have a tour of inspection. Then you can tell me all about your holiday."

She led me from room to room – even into her own sanctum sanctorum – and I had all my fears quickly laid to rest; the house was immaculate. Back in the living room, she set me on the sofa and poured me a beer.

"Okay," she said, handing my tankard to me, "Let's hear all the gory details! And you can start by telling me how many lucky young ladies succumbed to your charms."

"It was wonderful," I smiled at her eager expression, "And so were all the ladies." I hadn't intended to mention anything about my conquests, but whether it was tiredness after the long journey home, or a reaction to Suze's obvious good behaviour in my absence, I can't really say. I told her – very briefly – about the successes I'd had.

"I don't know whether to be proud of you or appalled," she shook her head in wonder when I'd finished, "What about Jenny?"

"We're more… friends, I suppose. Not really an item as such."

"I wonder if *she* thinks that? Oh, well," she added with a theatrical sigh, "I suppose it *was* my suggestion in the first place."

"Enough about me," I said, determined to change the subject, "How was it here?"

"Wonderful. The karting course was out of this world and I'm going to save up and go on the advanced one in a few weeks. I've done tons of stuff with the camera and the computer, as well, and me and Donna had the greatest of times–" she broke off abruptly.

"What's up?"

Suze gave me a funny look, the expression impossible to read, "Nothing's up," she said after a pause, "Really. We just had a… great time."

"Something's up."

She shook her head vehemently, "No, honest. I…" she trailed off again, and then put on her broadest grin, changing the subject quickly, "And we've got a new cleaning lady. Her name's Terri, and just to please you, I picked her because she's about thirty and really pretty."

"As long as she can clean." I decided not to press Suze on her earlier hesitation. In my humble experience, it's better to let kids find their own time and place to tell you things that are troubling them; the more pressure you exert at the wrong time, the tighter they clam up.

"She really is pretty," Suze went on, clearly on happier ground, "She's Donna's mum's younger sister."

"Her aunt, in other words," I smiled.

My princess rolled her eyes, "Obviously. I was just pointing out that she's a close blood relation of Donna's, so that you'd know just how pretty she is."

"Oh, I see. And is she married, or whatever?"

"Why? Interested?" she fired back.

"No, but I know you. I'm sure you just advertised for a young, single woman and requested photographs."

I received a smug smile, "I didn't have to advertise. Terri overheard me when I was telling Donna about it, and she volunteered."

"What day will she be round?" I shrugged, at once believing my precious princess and also wondering how much engineering went into the 'overhearing' bit.

"Mondays. Nine in the morning to two in the afternoon."

"Nine! That's the middle of the night."

"Oh, I get it. Now that you've done a few weeks work, you're going to be lazing in bed all day."

"Not true," I protested unconvincingly. If I couldn't convince myself, how was I supposed to convince a rightfully suspicious daughter? "I'm on a retainer at ETA and I'll need to pop in from time to time."

"Oh, that reminds me," she went on, "Dud called and said he'd like to see you on Tuesday, if you're free. And he also said that he hoped you weren't going to turn back the clock and become a shag-happy teenager again. Do you want me to phone and tell him it's too late, or will you do it?"

"Suze! And must you use such language?"

"I'm just quoting Dud verbatim," she giggled, "And besides, how would you like me to have translated that?"

"I get your point. Did he say what it was about?"

Suze shook her golden tresses, "No. It was just a quick call."

"You didn't manage to keep him on the line for half an hour like normal, then?"

"Maybe I'm getting over that crush," she shrugged, blushing.

"The one you never had?"

"That's the one."

She went on to describe the 'awesome' karting course, a really funny movie she'd seen at the local cinema, a great new graphic design book she'd bought, and a wonderful meal that she had cooked with her own bare hands. There was something, though, that she wasn't mentioning.

I retired early, and rose late the next morning, the Sunday, thoroughly rested and pretty much relaxed. Suze was poring through the

Review supplement in *The Times* on her tablet and whistling a Taylor Swift number.

"Glad to hear you've finished with that Little Mix phase you went through," I said, pouring myself a coffee.

"I only liked one of them!"

"Which one? Jade? Perrie?"

"I meant one of their songs!" she almost snapped.

I glanced across, surprised to see a slight blush on her cheeks. While I had her off-balance, I tried to *subtly* raise the issue of what she wasn't telling me about her time there alone, "So what aren't you telling me about the last couple of weeks?"

Off-balance or not, I had clearly picked the wrong time to ask. To my intense astonishment, my normally even-tempered, level-headed little princess, picked up the tablet and stood up, "Nothing! There's nothing wrong, okay?". She turned on her heel and flounced from the room.

"Well, I thought that went pretty well," I sighed aloud to myself.

When I suggested later that morning that she might like to accompany me to the *Duke* for some Sunday lunch, she unusually refused, saying that Donna had invited her over. "At least she doesn't give me the third degree all the time," she added as she left in a huff and on her bicycle.

After a few much needed beers and a generous helping of roast beef and yorkshire pud, I returned home and called Jenny. A voice-mail message informed me that she was out of the country until the following Friday, and I can't say that I was too disappointed. I next called Dud.

"So, how'd it go?" he asked, "Get plenty?"

"You're as bad as my daughter," I groaned, "But, as it happens, yes thanks."

"Good man. It's about time you were back in the real world."

"Talking of my daughter, Suze said you wanted me to call you; something about meeting up on Tuesday, or some such?"

"Too true. If nothing else, you can tell me all about Nice."

"St. Raphael, actually, but why do you really want to see me?"

Dud grunted, a trademark sound that I immediately recognised as an indication of a potential problem, "I've got the distinct impression that there's some activity at ETA," he explained, "It's a bit of a coincidence, actually. Something I spotted when I was working nearby last Monday."

"Which was?" If Dud had one infuriating habit, it was that he never came straight to the point. Unless sex was involved.

"Did we, or did we not, check for external feeds?" he asked.

"We did."

"And did we, or did we not, check the roof for dishes and microwave transmitters?"

"We did not, because you can't see the roof from street level and there's reputedly no easy access from the office."

"But you can see it from Tower 42," Dud said, finally coming to the point, "And there's a bundle of dishes and stuff up there."

"It's not necessarily anything to do with ETA, though. There's another half-dozen companies in the building."

"True," Dud said smugly, "But that Barry Grant guy was standing up there with a couple of technicians."

"You could see who it was from half-way up Tower 42?"

"With my binoculars, yes," he laughed, "Actually, I was scanning the rooftops for sunbathers."

This I could well believe. During the summer, many of the rooftops were used by sun-worshippers, and many of the young ladies, confident that the distance of taller buildings renders themselves next to invisible, quite often sunbathe topless – if they wear anything at all. Dud had graphically, and kindly, proved this to me a couple of years previously, "Well, well," I said thoughtfully, "Presumably you want to meet up in town and maybe pay ETA a quick visit?"

"They don't call you the Sherlock Holmes of computer fraud for nothing."

We arranged to meet at Charing Cross early on the Tuesday morning, agreeing that we wouldn't give anyone at ETA advance notice of our visit, and I hung up a few minutes later, perturbed.

Suze arrived home at seven, just as I was leaving for the pub, her mood better, but by no means back to her normal, serene self. I was tempted to ask her what was wrong once more, but, probably wisely, thought better of it. I got back much later than I had intended, and my precious princess was already in bed, her room in darkness.

Donna's aunt, Terri, turned out to be every bit as attractive as her niece; moreso, in fact, since she was that much older. Her hair was the same dark-auburn and her figure lithe and supple. Not that I took much notice, of course. She further endeared herself to me by insisting on making me coffee, and by complimenting me on my 'wonderful' daughter.

"Nice, isn't she?" the wonderful one asked me when Terri had left.

"Quite pleasant," I said, airily.

"You should ask her out for a drink or something."

"Hang on. Just a couple of days ago, you were intimating that I should be considering Jenny's feelings."

Suze shrugged, "Well, it's pretty clear to me you're not that interested in her outside of the bedroom, so I thought—"

"Suze!" I interrupted, "I know you're growing up and that your father's life impinges on yours, but that's taking things a little too far. Come to that, you seem to find it okay to talk about my relationships and problems, but you won't even tell me what's bothering you about the last couple of weeks."

Once again, I was in for a surprise. This time her outburst was closer to tearful than angry, but it was nonetheless totally out of character, "Pa! Will you just drop it, okay? There are some things in my life which are *mine*; private things! If I'm confused or upset, it's my business and it's got nothing to do with you!" I was left standing, slack-jawed, in the kitchen, as she dashed from the room. The sound of her bedroom door slamming could probably have been heard in Edinburgh.

This time her strange mood seemed to last longer, and it was almost a relief to leave the house early the next morning.

13

Dud was waiting for me when I arrived at Charing Cross, and he ordered a coffee for me while I lit up a much-needed Marlboro.

"So, Sherlock," he grinned, "The plot thickens, as they say."

"We don't know anything for sure," I replied through a cloud of blue smoke, "But I had a quick look-see at e-mail activity originating from ETA, and it's all been rather frantic since last Friday."

"Pete!" he admonished, laughing, "Are you telling me you've been illegally accessing their confidential communications?"

"Since I'm on a retainer as a security expert, there's nothing illegal about it." The question of legality is moot at the best of times, but I really did feel justified in a cursory examination of what was happening at the site, "And anyway, I didn't actually open the files; I was just monitoring activity."

"So, you won't be offering me odds on whether or not they've had another break-in?"

"No chance. Although I'd rather have thought they would have been in touch with me if something had occurred."

"Well, I guess there's only one way to find out for sure," Dud said, draining his coffee, "Shall we?" he nodded towards the exit.

"Good idea, Watson."

"And on the way," he added, "You can fill me in on what you got up to down in St. Tropez."

"St. Raphael," I sighed. For someone that spent most of his working life paying close attention to the tiniest of details, Dud had an amazing propensity for forgetting the most basic pieces of information.

"It at least explains why you don't have much of a tan," Dud was saying as the taxi pulled up outside the ETA offices.

"I never tan much, anyway, but which would you rather be doing? Laying in the sun—"

"Or just laying," Dud interrupted with a laugh.

I paid the taxi driver and led Dud up to the third floor. Neither of us were unduly surprised to find James Forsythe in animated conversation with Barry Grant.

"The very man!" he boomed as we stepped from the lift. Grant said something under his breath which I couldn't catch.

"James," I greeted him, "I thought we'd just pop in since I've been away for a while. Any developments?"

"I should say so, dear boy. It seems our mystery man has been back at work. Barry? You'd better fill Peter in with the gory details."

I exchanged a quick look with Dud and then turned my attention to the systems manager, "What happened?"

Grant sighed, "Friday morning, approximately eight-fifteen, twelve million US Dollars disappeared into a numbered account in Geneva."

"Seems our hacker is making up for lost time," I said, "Any trace? Any clues as to the method of access?"

Grant gave Forsythe a jet-black look, "None of the telephone, wireless or land lines were compromised," he said with great emphasis, "And so I have to assume that access was achieved by our wonderful new microwave link." The word 'wonderful' was imbued with pure venom.

"A new microwave link?" I raised an eyebrow, ignoring Dud's muttered comment.

"James?" Grant said, almost pleasantly, "Perhaps you can explain?"

Forsythe nodded, "As you know, dear boy, our instructions are received directly from central government. It was someone there that ordered us to have the wave link thingy installed."

"But it's almost impossible to protect microwave links," I said slowly, "Surely whoever dealt with the government department in question raised this issue; I explained it all to everyone when I was last here. Come to that, who *was* involved with the decision?"

Forsythe shrugged, "As usual, Paul and Jenny."

"Paul?"

"Surely Jenny or I mentioned Paul to you?" Forsythe looked surprised.

"As far as I recall, I didn't even see a staff profile of anyone named Paul. Who is he?"

"Paul Stephenson, the third executive director. He was originally something high up in the Civil Service. It was him who helped set up ETA in the first place."

"Well, this is all news to me," I sighed, "Dud? I'll leave you to do what you can with the microwave. Perhaps Barry can show you where everything is?" I waited until Barry had led Dud into the computer room and then continued, "James, I'm going to need this Paul Stephenson's profile. I'm not going to say anything too much at the moment, but if anyone has the MMO to carry out the illegal transfers, it's him."

"MMO, dear boy?"

"Means, motive and opportunity. I can't believe no-one mentioned this guy to me before."

"I really can't quite believe it myself," Forsythe shrugged his massive shoulders, "Obviously he seldom comes here; being our principal liaison with the government, he tends to work directly in Westminster, but I'm amazed that neither Jenny or I had told you about him. I can see what you mean about the motive and opportunity business, though."

"Let's not jump to conclusions. But I really must have a look at his staff profile."

"Come with me," Forsythe nodded, "I'll see what I can find."

I followed the executive into a small office near the rear of the building and stood beside him as he opened a locked filing cabinet. In the top drawer were three large files, each bearing the name of ETA's executive directors. I had already seen Forsythe's own, and the photograph from Jenny's still nestled in my wallet. Forsythe withdrew the third file and handed it to me.

"Thanks," I nodded, opening it. I looked down and sighed, "Hardly very illuminating, is it?"

Forsythe looked over my shoulder at the sheaf of blank pages which was all Stephenson's file contained, "That's bloody weird," he said, taking back the file, "I know he's a rather, shall we say, *shadowy* figure – has to be in this line of work – but this is very strange. Perhaps I should say, it's all rather suspicious."

"My thoughts exactly. I think I'll need to have a word with him."

"I'll go and see what he's up to this week," Forsythe said, "I only got back this morning and I'm not up to speed with things as yet."

I followed Forsythe through to his office and lit a Marlboro while he made a telephone call. The introduction of this new element to the puzzle was intriguing, the main question being why neither Jenny nor Forsythe had so much as mentioned Stephenson's name. Although I had led Forsythe to believe that my suspicions already centred on the former civil servant, in truth I was beginning to have my doubts in entirely different directions. I listened carefully to the one half of the conversation I could hear and nodded when Forsythe hung up, "He's away until Friday, then?"

"Quite so, dear boy." Forsythe looked perplexed, "Apparently he's accompanying Jenny on her trip to Brussels. They left on Friday morning according to Stella. And before you ask, Stella is his personal secretary, but has no connection with ETA."

"Is that normal? I mean, him and Jenny travelling together?"

"Not at all," Forsythe's frown deepened, "As a rule, Paul stays in town here, while Jenny or I do the globetrotting bit."

"Any chance of getting in touch with either of them?"

Forsythe's usual air of bonhomie seemed to have evaporated, "Don't worry, dear boy, that's exactly what I intend doing." He reached for the phone.

It was ten minutes before he hung up, his face thunderous, "What the bloody hell's going on here?"

From what I'd heard, there had been no sign of either Jenny or Stephenson in Brussels, and whoever Forsythe had spoken to there clearly wasn't expecting either of them, "Are you absolutely certain they were due in Brussels?" I asked.

Forsythe glanced up at me and sighed, allowing his anger to dissipate slowly, "Both their secretaries were adamant that it was Brussels they were going to. I'm going to have a quick check on airline tickets and that sort of thing; see if I can shed any light on the matter. However, before I do, I think that I'd better let you have some background information, dear boy."

"What sort of background information?"

"Personal, dear boy, personal," Forsythe sighed once more.

I listened in stunned silence as I was told – in graphic detail – how Jenny and Stephenson had been carrying on an affair for the past year; how Stephenson's wife knew nothing of it, and how Forsythe himself had helped cover their tracks. "It's the sort of thing I'm rather good at," he told me, a little shamefaced, "I, er, have been known to have the occasional dalliance myself."

I judiciously refrained from commenting that, given his own daughter's suspicions, he really wasn't that good at covering tracks, "So you think that maybe they've cooked up some scheme between themselves and now they've done a runner?"

"Seems rather plausible, dear boy, doesn't it?"

It rather did. "Well, the first thing we're going to do is disable that microwave connection," I said, determined to keep my mind on business matters and away from Jenny, "That way, if it *is* them, they'll have lost the power to carry out any more transactions. Do you think there'll be a problem with anyone in the government?"

"I know one or two of the bods up there. I'll have a quiet word over lunch. What else can we do, though?"

"You know I was talking about a contingency plan in case anything continued to happen?" I smiled.

"Indeed, dear boy. Although I seem to recall a dearth of detail."

"Quite. Look, I know you're not, er, technically minded, but I need you to tell me if you think my plan is feasible."

"Fire away," he chuckled, "But, please do try to keep it simple."

I was taking a chance on bringing Forsythe into my confidence on this matter, but I really didn't have much of a choice, "Well, the systems you currently use receive transaction orders from either an outside source – say, a mobile telephone connection – or from direct input at a keyboard in these offices. Follow me so far?" He nodded firmly and I continued, "The transactions themselves are then sent over telephone lines directly to the banks concerned. My plan is to disable that ability."

"So we won't be able to send *any* transactions?" he asked, two bushy eyebrows raised questioningly.

"Not by telephonic or electronic means."

"Then how on earth, dear boy, can we carry out our business?"

"James?" I smiled, "How long have you been in the banking business?"

"Twenty years—" he began, before a slow smile spread over his face, "Oh, dear. How silly of me."

"Not really," I sympathised, "That's one of the main troubles with high-tech systems; people become dependant on them – start to believe that there's no other way of conducting business. However, that doesn't mean that the good old manual methods aren't still available."

"So I take it that you mean we should carry out manual transfers of funds, then?"

"Absolutely. I've checked out the logistics, and it should be possible to carry out manual transfers anywhere within mainland Europe in less than eight hours. I know that I've been told that there's a need for immediacy in transfers, but if anyone in the government is really interested in stopping these illegal transactions, then I can't conceive of another way of proceeding."

"Another word or two over lunch should sort that out. Exactly what sort of thing did you have in mind?"

"Bankers' drafts. The guys at BISCO told me that the facility is already present in your systems, so I'm suggesting that we disable the outgoing transfer facility, that you generate a bankers' draft for each transaction and then have a secure courier company deliver it in person to the foreign bank in question."

"Sounds feasible," he said thoughtfully, "And, I take it you can recommend such a company?"

I handed him a business card, "I've used this mob in similar circumstances, and they're extraordinarily efficient and completely trustworthy."

Forsythe chuckled softly, "Takes me back a bit. The good old bankers' draft. All these couriers flying around the City carrying what are effectively million-pound notes."

I nodded. Bankers' drafts bear no name, just a sum of money – they are as good as hard currency, and, just as with cash, whoever bears the draft has sole possession of it. "Remember the time when some idiot dropped two of them in Gresham Street?"

Forsythe let out a booming laugh, "Ninety-one, I think. Some poor sap found them and gave them back to the bank, didn't he?"

"Sap is the right word." The guy had effectively just found eight million pounds which he could have deposited anywhere in his own name. Instead, when he returned the two drafts, he was rewarded by the bank with a whole bottle of champagne. Lovely institutions, banks, aren't they?

"Well," Forsythe announced, business-like and full of determination, "To sum up, you need me to find out from my contacts in Westminster whether they mind the microwave thingy being disabled, and whether they'd object if the transfers aren't made instantaneously. Is that right?"

"Absolutely."

"And if both answers go your way, how soon can we carry out whatever's necessary to change transfer methods?"

"We can disable the link in about two seconds – just unplug the damn thing, in fact. And as far as disabling the electronic transfer and switch to drafts goes, that'd take maybe fifteen minutes."

Forsythe looked astonished, "That all, dear boy?"

"That's all," I agreed. Thanks to the two guys at BISCO, I could easily access the internal workings of the transfer system through their hidden back door.

"In that case, I think I'll organise an early lunch with my contacts. I'm sure they'll be willing since it's something of an emergency, what?"

I left him arranging his meeting and went in search of Dud. I found him sipping coffee and chatting quietly to Grant.

"Hi, Sherlock. What's the news?" he greeted me.

"News aplenty. If you don't mind, Barry, I'd like a word with Dud in private?"

"Use the computer room," he said.

Ten minutes later, Dud looked over at me and nodded, "Sounds like your Jenny and this Stephenson guy are our culprits all right."

"Not necessarily. They might just have decided to have a few days away in some hotel somewhere. And she's not *my* Jenny, by the way," I added.

"That's possible, but pretty unlikely. If they've been keeping their affair under such tight wraps up until now, why risk anything by disappearing for a few days like this? My guess is that they're doing a

80

quick tour of all the banks that the money disappeared into and are about to set up home in Switzerland or some place."

"*My* guess would be that the money has already been moved from those banks," I said, "After all, Jenny's had the opportunity on all of her business trips. If they have done a bunk, then I'm pretty sure that's the last we'll see of them."

"I bet you're pretty pissed-off right now," Dud smiled sympathetically.

"Not really. I'm not even sure that I actually believe all that I've been told today. I guess we'll find out a bit more pretty soon."

We left the confines of the computer room and made our way back to the reception area where Forsythe was changing his club tie.

"All arranged, dear boy," he boomed, "And I've run a check on airline ticket purchases. Both of them were issued with tickets to Brussels leaving last Friday, returning Friday this week. Phillipa checked with BA, and according to them, they were both on the nine-twenty flight."

I sighed, "It doesn't really tell us very much; they could be anywhere by now. When will you be back?"

"About one, I should think."

"We'll be here."

In the event, he arrived back early, a somewhat puzzled look on his face.

"Curiouser and curiouser," he told Dud and me, "Seems our boys in the government had never heard of this microwave thingy, and on top of that, neither of them were aware that the transfers had to be made immediately. As far as they were concerned it could take a minute, an hour or a week; just so long as they were completed, and discretion assured."

"Okay, pal," I smiled at Dud, "Let's get the system sorted."

Within twenty minutes, ETA had half-abandoned the electronic age and were, as far as I was concerned, once more proof from illegal activities of the villain – or villains. Unless, of course, Forsythe was somehow involved. Satisfied that we could do no more for the present, we left the building and made our way back to Charing Cross via a couple of pubs.

"Well, Pete," Dud grinned as we waited for our trains, "Looks like that's the last you'll be seeing of the wonderful Jenny."

"I wouldn't be so positive," I shook my head. I was sure I'd missed something in all this, some things just weren't adding up.

14

I explained to Suze that evening what had happened, trying hard to ignore her sullen attitude.

"Typical men!" she snorted contemptuously when I told her about Stephenson, "Never faithful."

"Hang on, princess," I said, carefully, "I never once cheated on your mother."

She looked hard at me for a moment and then shrugged, "Maybe you're just an exception."

I couldn't really reply to that. I'd known far too many husbands and boyfriends that had strayed, "It's not an issue of men or women. After all, a man can hardly have an affair on his own, can he?"

"I bet they would if they could!"

With this creeping tendency towards the more radical feminist attitude, I was beginning to doubt that Suze's new friend was such a good influence after all. "Suze," I went on, sighing, "People are people; all different, all with their own individual weaknesses and strengths. Don't try to generalise so much."

"Generalise?" she gave a gentle snort, "Archetypes don't just appear from thin air. No smoke without fire and all that."

I decided that I wasn't getting anywhere. "I'm off to the *Duke*," I told her, "And before you say it, yes, I'm aware that's a very 'man-thing' to do." I picked up my jacket and struggled into it.

"Pa!" she called as I made for the door.

I turned and faced her, a lop-sided smile on my face, "What's up, princess?"

She was about to say something, I'm sure, but evidently changed her mind, "Nothing."

"Love you, princess."

"You, too, Pa," she said quietly.

Sullen, moody, crabby, irritable. There are many words in the dictionary to describe Suze's temperament over the rest of that week, and none of them had applied to her before my holiday. I was becoming increasingly concerned.

Friday afternoon, I phoned Forsythe to see if there was any sign of the missing executives, and was told that he'd received a brief call from a hotel receptionist with a French accent, saying that she had been asked to tell him that the couples' stay had been extended into the following week. He had been unable to find out exactly when they were planning to 'return', or even which country they were staying in. He promised to call me as soon as he heard anything, and after he had hung up, I called Dud to relay the news.

"You believe him?" he asked me the one question I was finding it difficult to answer whenever I asked it to myself.

"I really don't know."

With nothing but problems and confusions to occupy my mind, I decided that an early trip to the *Duke* was in order and arrived home at nine a little worse for wear. Suze was sitting on the sofa watching an American sit-com and looked up sharply as I bumped my way into the room.

"Drunk again?"

"Just had a bit too much teenager-repellent," I grinned. A strange look came over her beautiful features, and at first I thought she was about to unburden herself. Once again, I was left in the dark.

"I'd like to stay over at Donna's tomorrow night," she said, "Any objections?"

I decided that I wasn't in any fit state to start a discussion on the subject, "I guess not."

"Good," she managed a half-smile, "Want a coffee? Or should that be, need a coffee?"

"That'd be nice," I nodded. If my ears hadn't deceived me, she'd actually been quite civil.

For the rest of the evening, although the atmosphere wasn't exactly relaxed, there was distinctly less tension in the air. I hoped and prayed that the mysterious storm was finally passing.

When I came down to the kitchen the following morning, the air was once more tension-filled. However, it was a different kind of tension, one with a distinctly nervous edge. Suze wasn't quite pacing the room, but every movement she made was sharp, her natural grace seemingly having deserted her.

"Hi, princess," I announced my presence.

Suze seemed to start, her head turning so quickly in my direction that her blonde hair swirled around it, "Oh! Hi, Pa," she managed a quick smile, "Coffee?"

"Please," I nodded, keeping my features neutral, picking up the post, "What's on your agenda for today?"

I noticed her hand was trembling slightly as she set my coffee mug in front of me, "I'm, er, probably doing a bit of shopping."

"Food or fun?" I smiled at her, hoping an old in-joke might help calm her a little.

She didn't even seem to have heard me, "Look, Pa..."

"What's up, princess?"

"I... can't!" she wailed.

She made to dash from the room, but I caught her around the waist, pulling her gently into my embrace, "What can't you do?"

"You'll hate me!" She gave another cry, the depth of despair in her voice almost reducing me to tears like the ones pouring from my daughter's eyes.

"I'll never, ever hate you, princess. Whatever have you done to make me think that?" I tried desperately not to conjure up images of just *what* she might have done; I'd really never seen her so upset with herself.

"Then you won't like me anymore," she said despondently, between gentle sobs.

"I don't *like* you now," I tried to keep my voice light, "I *love* you. More than anyone or anything in this whole wide world. And I always will. Now, please? What's so awful?"

"I... I don't know how to tell you... You're going to think I'm weird; I just know you will."

"I've always thought that," I was finally rewarded with a choked laugh and a half-hearted swat, "How many more times, princess? You can tell me anything. Please? I hate to see you so upset."

"I... don't know how – where – to start."

I could feel her beginning to relax against me, her resistance to me gradually dwindling. My heart was pounding hard, still dreading what she was about, I felt sure, to tell me. "How about you start anywhere you like? We can sort out details later."

Apparently she was unable to look at me, instead, she buried her head on my chest. Ever-so slowly she began to speak.

"Pa... I've told you before that I'm not... into guys, right? Well, it's always seemed a little bit strange to me – most of the other girls in my year have been dating for a while now, or going loopy every time someone mentions Leonardo de Caprio. Some of them have even, you know? Slept with guys? Me, I've never had any interests in those directions; always preferred female company, couldn't even understand what all this guy-thing fuss was all about.

"When you were away, I sort of mentioned the subject to Donna. I've found it easy to talk to her, to trust her, and I guess... I respect her and her opinions. When I told her about the guy-thing, I was only trying to find out what she thought on the subject – mainly because she's so different from Sam that way; never mentioning guys and stuff, never showing any interest. I really, really, really, only brought up the subject because of that. But that's when something really weird happened; something that I'd never expected.

"When I said what I thought, Donna went really quiet and then, after a little bit, she laughed, and for pretty much the first time since I started hanging out with her, she got all embarrassed; couldn't seem to look at me. I asked her what was wrong – what I'd said to upset her... and that's when she told me."

My precious daughter stopped talking for a few moments, evidently bracing herself for what was to follow, and even then I knew what was coming.

"Pa, she said that she felt just like me about guys; that she knew there was something different about her. Different from the way most girls felt. After what seemed like the longest time, she turned and looked at me and I could see just how scared she was, and I think I now know just how she felt right then – you'll never know how hard this is, Pa.

"She just came out with it. *'Suze'*, she whispered to me, *'I'm pretty sure I'm. you know? Gay?'* When she said it, and, well... you don't need to know all the details about what she explained afterwards. When she said it, it was like a light going on in my head. I could recognise everything, every feeling that Donna was going through. Just like that, I realised that maybe that's what had drawn me to her... The fact that we shared the same feelings. And that we shared the same sort of feelings for each other.

"Pa... I guess what I'm trying to say is that I really think I'm gay. In fact, I *know* I am. So, there you go. You wanted to know what was wrong and now you do."

I've no idea how desperately difficult that enormous revelation must have been for my wonderful girl; can't comprehend the level of courage it took for her to tell me. And if any one of you reading this has had any difficulty in understanding why I love and cherish her so much, perhaps now you'll understand.

"Suze, baby? Why on earth did you think that would make me think you're weird, or hate you, or whatever?"

She recoiled from me, her eyes flashing up to mine for the first time since she'd started speaking. Confusion registered on her features. "You... don't think it's weird?"

"How could I?" I smiled, "How many times have I wittered on about every individual being different? How we shouldn't conform to what other people say is normal? It goes just as much for your sexuality as everything else in life. If you're gay, then that's the way you are. Besides, you're young yet. It may even just be a phase you're going through." I held up a hand to silence the protests that she was beginning to make, "And whether it is or not, doesn't matter to me. Only your happiness matters. If that can be achieved between you and another girl, then fine, so be it. It doesn't make you weird, or strange. Just be honest with yourself, be true to your own feelings."

Her face still registered a mixture of surprise, disbelief, and, slowly creeping in, relief, "You really don't mind?"

I pulled her back into my arms, "Of course I don't. Now, have you told Donna this? Is that's what's been bothering you?"

Suze had started crying softly as I hugged her, and now she stopped, sniffed and then finally looked up at me, "No," she gave me a lop-sided smile, "I told Donna what I felt. And... I told her that I realised I felt... that she was something – someone – really special to me. I thought for a minute that I'd really put my foot in it because she just stared at me. And then she let out this huge sigh of relief and... told me she felt that way about me; that she'd been so scared of telling me, of how I'd react if she ever did."

"You don't have to go into details," I assured her, stroking her hair.

"No," she shook her head, "I've come this far, I want to finish. Pa, Donna and I, well... we're an item, I guess you could say." Suze's eyes went back to their study of the carpet.

"I'm really pleased for you. She's a very nice young woman."

Again, her face registered surprise as she looked up at me, "You mean it, don't you?" she breathed. I nodded, "But aren't you shocked? Hurt?"

"A little surprised, maybe, but not hurt, or disappointed, or angry or anything other than happy that you've discovered something about yourself that can only bring you happiness. If you'd stayed confused about the way you felt – sexually, I mean – then you'd never be able to live life to the full; to take true enjoyment in what you did. Now, perhaps you can."

I don't think she'd ever before hugged me as tightly as she did at that moment, "Oh, God! That's such a relief. I didn't think I'd ever be able to tell you about... how I am. But I should have known better, shouldn't I? You're the most wonderful father a daughter could ever have."

"Look at it this way," I smiled down at her, "I've always been worrying about you getting mixed up with the wrong sort of guy. At least I don't have that to worry about anymore."

It took a second or two before she realised that I was trying to joke with her. When she did, her transformation back into my precious princess was complete. For the first time in more than a week, she allowed me to experience the pure, unadulterated pleasure of one of her giggles. "Don't get too carried away," she beamed, "I might just ditch Donna and take up with someone like Sam."

"Don't you dare!" I laughed.

The sense of relief – of release – was almost palpable; a near-physical feeling. We celebrated Suze's 'coming-out' with coffee, hugs and kisses, and, most importantly of all, with laughter.

I can recall – albeit barely – the trauma of discovering that girls are not just there for pigtail-pulling and name-calling; that there's this genetic imperative that means that sex becomes a serious issue. That was hard enough for me. But for Suze, it must have been so much harder – to come to terms not just with the question of sex, but of sexuality. I was truly happy for her, and, maybe more than that, I was relieved for her. In the months – years, even – leading up to her revelation, I'd been concerned what sort of guy she would end up with; and, as any father of any daughter could tell you, I'd grown positive that whoever he was wouldn't be good enough for my precious little princess. In some ways, therefore, I was relieved for myself as much as Suze, and I hadn't been altogether joking when I'd mentioned that fact to Suze earlier. Mostly though, I was so full of admiration for her, and I'm almost positive I could never have made such a revelation to my parents. Maybe it's different for guys, although I'm not so sure it is.

Perhaps her revelation was also made easier for me because of all the things I'd been fearing about her reticence to discuss what she'd got up to in my absence. In any case, I was just so very happy to have the real Suze back.

During that long morning, we discussed many things, but the subject of Donna was always returned to. It was clear to me long before Suze finally mentioned it, that my sweet little girl had fallen in love. I'm just so very glad that the feelings between her and Donna appeared to be mutual.

One of the things discussed was whether she wanted to make public her sexuality, and it was clear from what Suze told me that, although she didn't really object, she would prefer not to at that time. I promised her that I wouldn't say anything to anyone other than Donna – who had apparently already told her own parents – and Terri, who was the only other person Donna had told. I think Suze and I were both happier that the ground rules had been cleared up.

As Suze was becoming more and more relaxed about the situation, I decided to clear up one more thing. Having been the 'surprisee', as it were, it was only fair to turn the tables – and only fair to show my princess that I was perfectly serious in my attitude to her. "I don't want to pry, or for you to go into any details that you probably find embarrassing, but when Donna stays over next, would you prefer to share a room?"

She gave the most impressive impression of a goldfish, "You mean... sleep together?"

"Unless you intend to take it in turns, yes. Look, I'm not really asking whether your relationship is... *that* physical, but if it is, then I don't want you thinking you have to sneak around behind people's backs, or try to engineer situations so that you two can be on your own. I'd much rather you could be comfortable and open. Too much sneaking can really damage a relationship; trust me on that."

"Pa, you're amazing," she shook her blonde tresses, "A couple of hours ago, I was still thinking that I'd never be able to tell you anything about the way I feel, and now, this. I thought Donna's parents were pretty good about things, but you're on an altogether different plane." Suze took a deep breath before continuing, "Well, I guess since you've been so good with me – so honest – I'd better follow suit. If you really wouldn't mind, then, yes, I'd like to be able to share a room with Donna when she comes over."

Somehow, Suze managed to keep her eyes fixed on mine as she told me that, and my admiration for her – and, to some extent for myself, and how I'd handled the situation – rose a notch or two, "Then that's settled then," I smiled.

I took her to the *Duke* that lunchtime for a small celebration, the toast: 'Honesty and self-awareness'. Somehow, my precious little princess seemed to have aged by a few years in just a few hours, and as we walked back home together after lunch, I was struck by how adult she looked and acted. I just wished I could do the same.

On the Sunday evening, Suze returned from her overnight stay at Donna's with the young lady in question tagging along behind her. I could tell the second that they walked into the kitchen where I was – unusually – doing some much-needed washing up, that Donna was extremely nervous, Suze quietly confidant; a complete reversal of their normal attitudes.

"Hi, girls," I greeted them.

"Hi, Pa."

"Hello, Mr Cooke."

"For the millionth time, that's *Pete*, Donna," I smiled, "And, relax. As I told Suze, I'm very happy for you both."

"I told you he was amazing, didn't I?" Suze grinned at her friend. Her girlfriend, I should say.

Donna still seemed tense, but she managed a tight smile, "You certainly did. Thanks, Mr... Pete."

Suze giggled, "He's most definitely the mutt's nuts."

"Suze! Where on earth do you pick up these expressions?"

"Well, you wouldn't want me to call you the dog's–"

"Enough! What on earth's wrong with the cat's whiskers?"

"Too feminine, and after all your recent conquests–"

"I'm going to put you up for adoption if you carry on," I couldn't help but laugh, "Now, I'm off to the *Duke* in a few minutes. Want to join me?"

"Actually, Pa, we were going to watch a video," Suze grinned, "And, if it's okay with you, could Donna stay over tonight?"

I tried not to smile as I saw Donna holding her breath, her left hand curled into a tight fist, "Of course. I've made up the bed in the spare

90

room," I paused long enough for Suze's face to fall before continuing, "There's a lot more room in there and I thought you two would prefer it."

Donna's face registered pure shock, Suze's, on the other hand, darkened into a mock scowl, "Don't think I don't know you said it that way on purpose," she chided, "But I suppose I'd better say thanks."

"Er, yes, thanks, Pete," Donna added quietly.

"*De nada*. But if you two really want to show your gratitude, you could finish these dishes for me." I threw the damp teacloth at them, water spraying over them both.

That simple gesture cleared the remaining tension from the air, and I left for the pub a few minutes later to the sound of their combined giggles as they splashed around in the kitchen.

15

I had forgotten that Mondays had become our cleaning day and was therefore rather surprised to come down to the kitchen that morning to find three women chattering happily.

"Oh, Hi, Terri. Hi, girls." I yawned.

"Hi, Pa."

"Morning, Pete," Donna even managed a broad smile.

"Hello, Peter," Terri greeted me, "I've been hearing very nice things about you."

The two young girls left the kitchen at a near-dash.

"That's me," I nodded, pouring myself a coffee, "Nice to the bone."

"So it seems," Terri said in a rather more earnest tone than I would have imagined, "I'm really glad to hear that you took such a mature attitude to the girls' situation. Many parents would have got all reactionary."

I shrugged, "I don't see why. It's all perfectly natural. I'm just full of admiration for Suze – and Donna, too, I suppose – for plucking up the nerve to actually tell me."

"To some people it's anything but natural," Terri smiled, "But you're right; it was tremendously brave of them both. Donna confided in me first – too scared to tell my sister, I guess – and it was pretty traumatic for her."

"I can well imagine after Saturday." It was easy to see why Donna had chosen to confide in Terri; now that I had seen them together, the similarity between the two was remarkable, and it followed that they probably shared a lot of the same thought processes as well, "I'm really happy for them."

"Me too. And I'd also like to thank you for letting them... share a room. I think it's given them a tremendous boost to their self-confidence."

"That'd be a nice side-effect," I smiled, "But it was really just so they would feel comfortable; I still vividly recall all the sneaking around I used to go through as a teenager in those sort of circumstances."

"Oh, God! Me too," Terri laughed, "I'm sure some parents deliberately loosen a couple of floorboards whenever they knew some boyfriend or girlfriend was going to be staying over."

"I once tried to convince an irate father that I was a sleepwalker," I nodded, grimacing at the memory."

"Ouch! I take it that wasn't believed?"

"No. And I've still got the scars to prove it. Some fathers have no sense of humour."

"I always had more trouble with the mothers," she said, "Very protective of their little boys. Once, I was caught... well, in the act, as it were, and despite our protests, this old cow really wouldn't believe that we were just trying out some new yoga positions."

"How terribly untrusting," I laughed. For some reason, I was distinctly glad to hear that Terri didn't share her niece's sexual orientation.

"Quite. Up until then, I always thought I had a really trustworthy face, as well. Another coffee?"

"Please."

What happened next just proves that no farce ever written can actually do justice to real life. Terri took my mug and stepped around

the chair I was sitting on, making for the coffee machine. Quite simply –
and honestly – she stumbled, taking two quick steps backwards, and
collided with my chair. Unable to control her momentum she fell
backwards into my lap and had I not grabbed her, she would no doubt
have toppled right over me and onto the floor. I held on tightly for just a
few seconds to be sure that she had regained her balance when, of
course, Suze and Donna reappeared.

"Pa!" my precious giggled, "I hope you're going to pay Terri extra for
that!"

"That's my aunt," Donna laughed along, "Just can't resist the guys."

"Enough!" I protested.

"Yes, absolutely," Terri agreed, struggling upright, "It was a simple
accident."

"Would you believe it?" Suze rolled her eyes at Donna, "After all
their going on about openness and honesty, and being aware of your
sexual imperatives, they can't even admit that they fancied a little
hanky-panky and got caught in the act!"

"Double standards there, alright," Donna agreed.

Despite our heated protests, the two girls left the room giggling fit to
bust.

"Sorry about that," Terri sighed after they had gone.

"Don't be," I shook my head. I was wondering how I'd be feeling if
we really had been up to something…

"Er, just off to the shops, Pa," Suze called from the living room,
"Need anything?"

"See if you can pick me up a new daughter," I said levelly, hiding a
smile, "One that isn't so quick to judge perfectly innocent situations."

"Charming!"

That afternoon, after Terri had left, Suze, of course, was waiting to
grill me. "Well?" she asked eagerly before I even had a chance to close
the front door after our new cleaner.

"Yes, thanks. Yourself?"

She rolled her eyes, "You know very well what I mean. What did you
think of her? Our new help, I mean."

"It seems such an odd word, these days, doesn't it? Help."

"Fess up, father."

"She's lovely," I relented, "If Donna's as similar to Terri as you keep telling me, it's easy to see why you fell for her."

"That's great! So, when are you going to ask her out? Do you want me out of the way next Monday, maybe, so that you can have a bit of fun here all by yourselves?"

"Listen up, my little matchmaker," I sighed, "I haven't given the matter a single minute's thought." This was at least true. There's a big difference between one minute and thirty.

"Bet it won't be long," Suze giggled, "You seem to have turned into some sex-crazed monster recently."

"I have not! And come to that, there's only one person in this room that's slept with someone in the last few days." I was interested to see how Suze would react to that comment; to gauge how her self-confidence really was holding up.

To my intense delight, she stuck out her tongue, "Jealousy will get you nowhere."

16

A happy and contented calm seemed to settle over the Cooke household in the next few days and the only storm cloud on the horizon remained the mysterious goings on at ETA. On the Thursday, I received a rather garbled message from Forsythe saying that both Jenny and Paul Stephenson had returned the previous evening, and that they were now officially together, Stephenson having left his wife. Their trip to Brussels had been nothing more than an extended dirty weekend so that the pair of them could plan their future lives together. I called Dud with the news.

"You believe that?" he asked.

"Sounds feasible," I shrugged – a rather pointless gesture during a telephone conversation.

"So, what's the next step?"

I'd been giving this some thought, "For a start, I'm going to get to see this Stephenson guy. There's something altogether too fishy about him for my tastes. Then I'm going to meet up with Jenny and see what she has to say for herself."

"Business-wise?" Dud enquired, disingenuously.

"Of course. As far as personal involvement goes, that's obviously over with." As I was speaking, Suze came into the room.

"I should hope so," she piped up, loud enough for Dud to hear, "Especially now that you've got the lovely Terri in tow."

"Terri?" Dud asked.

I gave the light of my life a very dark look, "She's just our new cleaner, if you must know," I said, "An aunt of one of Suze's friends, and Suze seems to feel she's an ideal candidate for my attentions."

"An aunt of my girlfriend," Suze corrected me with a shy smile.

I gestured to her silently, trying to find out whether she wanted me to tell Dud about her new-found sexuality. In the event I needn't have bothered. To my surprise, she took the receiver off me and proceeded to tell Dud all about it herself.

Later, after the call had ended, I asked her why she'd done it.

"I guess I needed to hear how someone else – someone outside our families – would react. Dud seemed the ideal choice, somehow."

"You really are becoming at ease with it, aren't you?"

She nodded, "Thanks mostly to you. So, when are you going to see that trollop, Jenny?"

"I wouldn't exactly call her that." Actually, I probably would have, "But I'd better get something organised pretty quickly."

I called Forsythe back and asked him to arrange meetings for me with Jenny and Stephenson. He returned the call fifteen minutes later, saying that they'd both agreed to be present at ETA the following Monday. As far as I was concerned that was ideal, since Terri would be cleaning that morning, and I was finding it rather difficult to keep my mind off her. I once more called Dud and asked him whether he'd like to come along.

"Wouldn't miss it for the world," he laughed, "All that stuff that's going on down there has really got me intrigued."

"You're not alone."

"I'll meet you at the usual place, then," he said.

Happy that there was nothing I could do immediately, I decided that a quiet weekend was called for and, since Suze had invited Donna over, we spent two glorious days as a rather esoteric threesome; the widower, and the widower's daughter and her girlfriend. Odd, it might have been; great fun it most certainly was.

Before I left on the Monday morning, the postman – an irascible old sod called Humphrey – brought the Cooke household even more cheer.

"Well, open it then," I urged Suze, who was staring nervously at the official-looking envelope.

"I'm scared to," she admitted.

"So much for your new-found self-confidence," I grinned.

She stuck her tongue out at me, and then tore open the envelope, closing her eyes at the same time. She took a long, shuddery breath and then stared down at the single sheet of paper she had withdrawn. The look on her face told me all I needed to know.

"So, how many passes?" I asked, impatiently.

She let out a small, surprised laugh, "All," she said simply, with one of those from-mother-to-daughter, trademark shrugs.

"All ten?" I tried not to sound too surprised.

She nodded, a smile beginning to spread slowly over her features as the news sunk in, "Eight As and 2 Bs. I thought I'd done pretty well, but..." she trailed off, gave a single, shrill cry of delight and then rushed over to where I was standing, hugging me tightly.

"Clever, clever, princess," I laughed, returning the hug, and kissing the top of her head. It's very hard to describe the feeling of awe that offspring can sometimes invoke, and this was one of those moments; not only was my lovely, fun-loving daughter beautiful and witty, she was clearly also very intelligent. She had taken ten GCSE subjects against the advice of her headmistress, who had thought that it would prove an excessive burden – especially as poor Suze missed almost an entire year of schooling after Julie died – and not only had she passed them all, she'd passed them with exceptionally good grades. It made my measly six and a scraped pass at A-level look rather paltry.

"I can't believe it!" she cried delightedly.

"I can, my little smart-arse. And it's wonderful news."

"I prefer 'cute' to 'smart'," she giggled, her joy overflowing, "But, yeah, it's fantastic. You'll never know how relieved I am."

"Probably not. So, what does it mean for the future?"

"That's easy," she grinned up at me, swinging from side to side in my arms as she used to when she was much, much younger, "Back to school next month, and three A-level courses. *And* I get to choose the subjects I really want to do. Pass them, and it's off to university!"

"You are truly amazing, my little princess. When I get home tonight, we'll have to go out and celebrate. Call Donna and see if she'd like to come along."

"I promised to call her anyway to see how she did." She reached up and gave me a quick peck on the cheek, before almost floating over to the sofa and pulling her phone out of her pocket.

Although I was already running late, I waited to see what the news was, surprised by my interest in how Suze's girlfriend had fared. It turned out to be more glad tidings; nine passes out of nine, and I left the girls chatting happily, for once not caring about the soaring cost of the household phone bills.

Dud was quite understanding when I turned up at Charing Cross almost half an hour late.

"Where the bloody hell have you been?" he grinned, "This Terri woman lose the keys to the handcuffs, did she?"

I ignored his questions to facilitate the lighting of a Marlboro, and then told him about Suze's results.

"That's great," he enthused, "It's good to know she takes after her mother in the brains department as well as the looks, right?"

"True," I agreed, my chest beginning to ache from all the prideful puffing out it had been doing, "Although, to be honest, the results were a bit of a surprise after what that miserable old headmistress of hers told me."

"Suze seems to be full of surprises recently. What on earth did you think when she told you she was gay?"

I laughed and shook my head, "I was less shocked than you might imagine, although I didn't see it coming. I suppose relief was my first true feeling; no more worrying about what sort of guys she'd start bringing home – and what they'd get up to with my little angel."

Dud nodded thoughtfully, "And I guess that means you're not likely to become a grandfather before you're forty."

"There's that added benefit, as well, although I hear adoption and surrogacy are still options. Suze had been going on a about starting a family when she was still young, so that I wouldn't be too old to baby-sit for her."

"That sounds like your Suze: always practical. What's her, er, girlfriend like?"

"Totally charming, and very pretty. This Terri is her aunt."

"So you said," Dud nodded, "Talk about keeping it in the family."

"I am really not interested in Terri for the minute. But they'll both be there tonight when we go out and celebrate. Why don't you join us?"

"Love to but can't," he grinned, "Remember that blonde I went out with last year?"

"Lynn, Linda, something like that?"

"Lydia. Long blonde hair, big green eyes, and really big–"

"I remember," I interrupted, "They weren't green as well, where they?"

"Black and blue by the time we finished some of our sessions. Anyway, she's coming back today from her Japanese jaunt, and wants to pick up where we left off."

"As far as I can recall, wasn't that in the back of a taxi on the way to Heathrow?"

He shook his head, "No. The ladies' room in the departure lounge. This time it'll have to be the arrivals, though."

"What time's she due?"

"Four," he said, "So I'd rather we kept things fairly brief today; I've got a bit of shopping to do before I meet her."

"Presumably in a chemist's shop," I grinned.

"You know me too well, partner."

"Well, don't worry," I assured him, "We should be finished by lunchtime. That is, if we get a move on; it's almost ten already and I said we'd be there at nine-thirty."

"Let's get to it, then. I can't wait to hear what you're gonna say to that trollop, Jenny; it should be the mutt's nuts."

"So that's where she's picking it up from. I didn't think it was from one of her friends."

"Pardon?"

"Nothing," I grinned, "Just a little mystery solved."

Dud shrugged, "Well that's okay then. Now, let's see if we can solve a bigger one."

Thanks to unusually light traffic, we arrived in the City less than ten minutes later and quickly made our way up to ETA's offices where we were met with a rather alarming sight.

James Forsythe was pacing furiously up and down the reception area, firing angry questions at the frightened-looking Alice, Jenny's secretary.

"What the bloody hell do you mean by that?"

Alice was clearly out of her depth and close to tears, "I really don't know where she is Mr. Forsythe," she almost wailed.

"But you're her bloody secretary. It's your job to know! Surely you must have some idea?"

"James!" I called before he could harangue the poor girl any further.

He spun on his heel and looked across to where Dud and I were standing, "Ah! Peter, perhaps you can shed some light on the situation? Heard anything from Jenny?"

"Nothing. Should I take it that she's not turned up?"

"I should bloody well say not," he bellowed, "Nor has Paul. And that isn't even the worst of it. Grant!" he roared, bringing to my mind an image of the local bird population simultaneously taking wing.

The systems manager appeared from the computer room, "You yelled?" he said sourly.

"Wouldn't you?" Forsythe shouted, "Tell Peter, here, what's happened."

"You'd better come through with me," Grant suggested to Dud and I, "It's a bit quieter in the computer room."

I nodded and followed him into the relative peace amid the humming, bleeping machines, "Don't tell me there's been another break-in?" I asked immediately the door had closed behind Dud.

"Not exactly," Grant sighed, "But we do have a problem; a big one."

"Which is?" Dud asked.

"Someone – or more likely, some *ones* – have generated a transfer and the accompanying draft, and then disappeared with it. To me, one thing makes it look as if it's a final, parting shot."

"And that is?" I pressed him.

"The draft is for two hundred million US Dollars," Grant replied, his tone neutral.

"Jesus wept!" Dud whistled.

"How long ago was this?" I asked.

"This morning, about eight, would be my guess. And I reckon that he, she or they, knew that time was short."

"How so?"

"They made one crucial mistake," he sighed, "The draft is country-specific and post-dated."

"Post-dated? That means we might be able to stop them lodging the damn thing. Which country are we talking about? How long have we got?"

My urgency didn't faze Grant at all, "Luxembourg, and four weeks from today. As I said, they must have been in a tremendous hurry, and accidentally typed in the wrong month."

I looked at Dud, "Jenny and Stephenson missing, along with a bankers draft. Seems pretty clear to me."

"As crystal, as far as I'm concerned," he concurred.

"Well, thanks for the info, Barry. I guess we'd better have a word or two with Forsythe."

"Rather you than me," Grant gave me a tight smile.

Dud and I left him in his Forsythe-shelter and went back into the reception area. Forsythe was still pacing the floor, the only evidence that Alice had been there, a small pile of soggy tissues next to her desk.

"James?"

He stopped pacing and turned to face us, "Ah! What do you reckon, then?"

"It looks fairly obvious, doesn't it?"

"Bloody obvious, more like," he nodded, veins pulsing on both temples, "And there's no reply from her flat, either."

"Not even her mother?" I asked, surprised. I was to be further surprised.

"Mother? I doubt whether even Doris Stokes could get in touch with her; she's been dead ten years."

"But I thought..." I trailed off and sighed, "I'm beginning to think that I can't trust a single word that the bloody woman told me." I was also, for the first time, beginning to think that maybe I'd said too much to the 'bloody woman'; she was the only person I'd discussed the contingency plan with before the day it was set in place.

"So what the bloody hell are we going to do about this?" Forsythe asked, almost plaintively, "I can't for a minute imagine that our bods at Westminster are going to turn a blind eye to this little disaster."

Knowing the current administration, I wasn't so sure about that, but I chose not to mention it. "Well, we know where they're headed, and we've got four weeks to recover the damn draft before it's of any value to them. I would suggest that you contact Interpol or Europol and maybe get some detective firm to try to find them. We'll do what we can to help."

"Not either of the 'pols," Forsythe shook his head, "We can't, er, afford any police involvement. Remember, these transactions aren't exactly... totally within certain legal limits, shall we say?"

I sighed deeply, "I never realised that they were quite that bad. Jenny certainly never gave that impression when..." Once more I trailed off, rolling my eyes. "I'm getting the impression that I've been misled from day one."

"Seems so," Dud agreed.

"Look," Forsythe boomed, "I'm prepared to offer you a five percent reward for the return of the bloody draft. I don't care how you do it, or who you employ, just don't involve the authorities, okay?"

Dollar signs – millions of them – flashed briefly in front of my eyes, "If I agree to take you up on that," I said slowly, my mind processing faster than any Intel chip, "I'll need to be paid for my time and any expenses occurred."

"You've got it, dear boy," Forsythe told me, his voice mellowing, "And the reward offer stands."

"Dud? You up for some detective work?"

"I'm your Watson, Sherlock."

We left Forsythe fuming quietly and went into the nearest bar to discuss the situation.

"For a start," I said, "We'd better find out whether they really have flown the coop. After all, they've got four weeks to kick their heels before they can use the draft."

"Stephenson's wife might be able to help, and we'd better have someone keeping an eye on Jenny's flat," he suggested, "Why don't you get in touch with Dean Samson?"

Dean was a former employee of mine back in the days when the firm was still fairly small, and he had left to set up a detective agency, specialising in computer-related crime. "Good idea. Not only is he good, he's cheap. I guess we'd better work on the premise that our two villains have already left the country, though. It might even be worth a trip overseas. Any idea where exactly Luxembourg is?"

"Not a clue, but do you really think they'd go straight there and then wait around for four weeks?"

"Probably not, but it's worth a try," I shrugged, "If nothing else, we could establish a couple of contacts over there to keep an eye out for the pair of them."

"I must admit, I could use a break."

"I'll get in touch with Dean, then. If he can find out whether they've done a runner, then we'll at least know what we're up against and where we might be able to start."

"I'll leave you to get on with that," Dud said, "And I'll pop back to ETA; we'll need photos and addresses and all that happy shit."

"Believe it or not, Stephenson's file is blank. Maybe Forsythe can give you his home number, though. Or rather, his wife's home number."

"They don't call you Sherlock for nothing," he laughed, draining his beer, "I'll be back in ten."

Dean Samson was delighted to hear from me, and even more delighted to accept the offer of some work. By the time Dud returned, Dean was already on his way to meet us.

"Get the info?" I asked.

"Almost," he grinned, handing me a piece of paper, "That's Stephenson's number, but unfortunately, Jenny's photo is missing from her file."

"Ah!" I winced, "Er, actually, I knew that; it'd just slipped my mind." Trying hard not to blush, I took out my wallet and extracted the missing snapshot.

"How sweet," Dud commented.

Dean arrived ten minutes later, causing the early lunchtime customers to turn their heads and stare. I promise you, if you ever see Dean, you'd stare as well. He stands nearly seven feet tall, is totally bald, and, in his own words is 'as black as black cat at the bottom of a mineshaft'.

"Yo, dudes," he grinned, perfect white teeth the starkest of contrasts to his ebony skin.

"Yo, yourself," I grinned back. When Dean smiles, it's hard not to return the gesture.

"So, you've got yourself some runaways?"

"Probable runaways," Dud pointed out.

We explained the situation to Dean, and he left with a promise to have some information for us before the day was done. I didn't doubt for a moment that he would – somehow, his mere presence when someone is asked a question tends to lubricate their tongue.

"Well, I guess that's about all we can do for now," I said to Dud, "You'd better get off to Heathrow and get your love-life active. I'll call you on your mobile when I hear from Dean."

"If you hear any strange noises in the background, no funny remarks, okay?"

"Now, would I?"

All the way back home, the only thing I could think about was the fortune that waited for us should we succeed in our quest. Even if we *didn't* succeed, there was still a very nice income from our efforts.

Suze, Donna and Terri were sat round the kitchen table when I got there, and I was struck by the fact that they all appeared to be the same age. No three weird sisters, these.

"Hi, intelligent ones, and Hi, Terri," I grinned.

"Charming," Terri laughed, "And I'll have you know, I've got a master's degree in zoology. It's probably what makes you seem halfway attractive."

"Touché," I laughed, wondering just how much of a come-on that line was.

"So, how'd it go, Pa?" Suze beamed, clearly still delighted by her exam successes.

"Very strangely."

"Did you get to call her a trollop?"

"No. It seems she's done a runner. Or at least, that's the current thinking. The plot hasn't so much thickened as congealed." I went on to explain what had occurred. "The only problem about Dud and I going over to Luxembourg is that we don't speak the lingo. Come to that, I don't even know what lingo they speak there," I finished.

"Mainly French and German, but they do have their own 'Luxembourgoise'. On top of that, because of the European Commission and the Court of Human Justice being located there most of the population speak pretty good English," Donna told me.

"Grade A geography pass, I take it?"

"European studies, actually," she grinned.

"And as far as the language problem goes," Suze chipped in, "I got A passes in both French and German. It'd be great to come along with you when you go."

"That's 'if' we go." The idea of Suze – and perhaps Donna as well – coming with Dud and I held quite a bit of appeal. For a start, their combined knowledge would be a great asset, and in addition to that, they'd be a lot cheaper than professionals. (That last bit is a joke, by the way). "I guess it might be okay, but when does school start back?"

"Just over three weeks," Suze grinned, "You'd really take us along? I mean, both of us; I wouldn't want to go without Donna." The two young girls exchanged a surprisingly shy and caring look.

"Of course I'd take both of you," I assured her, trying to hide my smile, "Well, that's settled then. If Dean confirms that they've scarpered, we'll organise ourselves a jaunt to Luxembourg. Er, Donna? Just where is the damn place?"

"South of Belgium, between France and Germany," she replied promptly.

"Oh, Pa!" Suze groaned, "You're hopeless with geography. You know one time?" she addressed the other two, "He actually got lost on his way to his own office?"

"That's not strictly true. I'd just forgotten that we'd moved."

"You'd moved three weeks before," Suze giggled.

"It's easy to forget little things like that when you've a fourteen-year-old pest at home," I returned.

"Don't be mean," she giggled.

"Quite right," Terri agreed.

Donna gave a shy laugh, "I'm glad Suze doesn't take after you."

"Enough!" I protested, "It's bad enough with Suze, without the rest of you ganging up on me!"

I was saved by the bell. Or rather, the irritating cheep-cheeping of my mobile. I went through to the relative peace of the living room and answered it.

"Yo, dude!"

"Yo, Dean. What's the score?"

He let out a loud chuckle, "Seems you and Dud guessed good; one Paul Mark Stephenson and one Jennifer Helen Winter boarded the nine-twenty five-BA flight to Luxembourg this morning. Each of them had two pieces of luggage as well as carry-on bags. Looks like this ain't no short stay. Also, I managed to get a couple of photos of Stephenson from his old lady."

"That's great news. And well done, my man."

"I've got a man keeping a casual eye on Winter's place," he went on, "It's not unusual for these guys to fly out and then fly straight back. It's a pretty good way to throw people off the scent."

"Good thinking. Dud and I are planning on going out there to see what we can find out, and I'll keep my mobile on me at all times. Give me a call if there's any developments at this end."

"Will do, my man. Happy hunting."

I rang off and checked my watch. It was ten to five, and I guessed that Dud would have finished greeting Lydia. I was wrong.

"You do pick good times to call," he panted.

"Er, where exactly are you?"

After a couple more grunts he said, "In the back of my car. Now..." another grunt, "Do me a favour and call back in ten minutes? Actually," grunt, grunt, "Make that twenty."

Tempted as I was to make it five minutes, I left him in peace for a whole half hour.

"Thanks, pal," he laughed when he picked up, "So, I take it there's some news?"

I related Dean's conversation.

"When do we leave, then?" he asked.

"How about Wednesday? I'd like to get there as soon as possible, but I need to do a little research first."

"Sounds okay to me. It'll at least give me a whole day to, er, catch up on things with Lydia. I'll need a bit of a break after that to recuperate," In the background I heard her throaty chuckle. "Want me to sort out the tickets and hotels and stuff?"

"Leave it to me," I said, "We've still got to check with Donna's parents to see whether they mind her going. Just as a by the by, what's Lydia's surname, by the way? I was rather hoping it was 'Kettle'."

"What? Oh, right," he laughed, "But I'm afraid not; it's Fleming, as in Ian."

"Shame. But, anyway, I'll give you a call tomorrow with the flight details."

"Catch you then, Pete."

106

Suze and Donna had come into the room while I'd been speaking to Dud, and my little daughter was clearly excited by the news.

"Wednesday, then?" she asked.

"Looks like it," I nodded, "You'd better check that it's okay with your parents, though, Donna."

"I'm right on it," she grinned, "My battery's flat though so may I borrow your phone?"

I handed her the mobile, "As long as they're not holidaying in Australia."

"No, New Zealand."

"That's okay then," I nodded sagely.

"How long will we be there?"

"Four of five days, I guess. Maybe six."

I went through to the kitchen while Donna made the call and was just pouring myself a coffee when the highly excited Suze dashed in, colliding with my back in her eagerness, "They said it was okay! Oops, sorry."

"Have you ever thought about leaving home?"

"No, but I have got you booked into an old folks' place."

17

I spent the following morning arranging our expedition and carrying out research into the destination country. This, despite a slight hangover from the previous night's celebrations. I had rather hoped that such a small place – only nine hundred and ninety-nine square miles, in all – would have a shortage of banks. Instead, it seemed to have more than London and New York combined; banking was clearly an essential part of their economy, a fact that Donna was happy to confirm. The only plus side to come out of the investigations was that almost all of the banks were situated in and around the country's capital city, which, rather confusingly, is also called Luxembourg. At least we could base ourselves there, rather than trailing around somewhere different every day.

During the afternoon, I checked in with Dean Samson – no developments to report – and with Simon Jefferson, a former client who was something of an expert in offshore banking and investment. He was able to provide me with some interesting facts, not least of which was that the land-locked little country was considered offshore for investment and banking purposes.

"Sounds bloody strange," I commented.

"Not really," he laughed, "Remember, Luxembourg was one of the three founder members of what was then the Common Market, along with Belgium and The Netherlands. When the bigger boys joined, there were all sorts of trade-offs and, to be frank, rather shady deals done."

"One last question," I said, "What's the currency there? I'm assuming the Euro, but I'd better get along to the bank anyway."

"It is, but most places over there will accept anything, even Sterling. Currency conversion is even more common now that the Euro's upon us."

"Sounds good, and thanks again, Simon."

"No problem and have fun over there. Not only are there about a million banks, there's probably the same number of bars and clubs. At weekends, the place simply doesn't sleep."

"I'm looking forward to it already."

When I got back from the bank armed with hundreds of Euros the two young women were chatting across the kitchen table.

"So, when do we leave, Pa?"

"The twelve fifteen flight tomorrow afternoon, Heathrow, terminal two; check-in is two hours beforehand. You'd better get packing; I know how long it normally takes you."

"Already done," she grinned, pointing to a case in the corner of the room.

"Good grief!" I feigned shock, "A new world record. Perhaps it's because you don't have to worry about which bras to pack these days."

"Pa!" she blushed charmingly.

I noticed that Donna was blushing as well, "Are you all packed?" I asked her.

"It's in the hallway," she nodded.

"Er, Pa?" Suze's tone of voice indicated that she was about to ask something that might embarrass her.

"What does my little princess need to know?"

"I was just wondering... That is, how many rooms did you book at the hotel?"

"Are you wearing blusher?" I grinned.

"Stop teasing!"

"I was only going to point out that I think you've used a little too much, that's all."

"I really am going to put myself up for adoption," she groaned, "The rooms?"

"Three. And before you ask, Dud and I are not sharing." I grinned as she and Donna exchanged another of their shy looks.

When the taxi arrived at half-past ten the following day, Suze and Donna were inside it almost before it came to a halt. I followed at a more leisurely pace – necessarily so, since I had been left to carry out all the bags. During the journey to the airport, the young pair acted more like excited schoolkids than the young adults they were, although this might not have been that noticeable to the driver, since I wasn't, in truth, much better.

I've always enjoyed travelling, especially when it's to a place I've never visited before, and there had been all too few opportunities in recent years, my duties as a single parent meaning that I had been limited in the jobs I could take on. Now that Suze had reached an age when she was capable of caring for herself, I promised myself that I'd not pass up such opportunities in the future.

One thing, though, that I really didn't enjoy about travelling was flying. Not the actual flight itself, but the bloody airports at either end of the journey. Heathrow, in particular, was one that I detested the most. Despite the best intentions of the planners and designers that seemed to be constantly remodelling the terminals, the places were always crowded, confusing and progress through the check-in procedures to the departure lounge itself seemed to take forever. That morning, though, was an exception, despite having to collect our tickets from the Air-France desk, and all three of us were soon quickly browsing through the shops on the far side of the security gate. Dud, looking tired, joined us soon after, and we retired to one of the cafeterias for some sustenance. Airline food also rates as one of my pet hates about the whole flying business.

To my surprise, the flight departed on time and we were soon winging our way back across the City, the aircraft seeming to follow the Thames. I turned back to point out a couple of landmarks to Suze and Donna, who were sitting behind Dud and I, to find my daughter hugging Donna whose eyes were tightly closed.

"What's up?" I asked softly.

"Donna's scared of flying," Suze shrugged, "She didn't want to tell anyone in case we decided not to take her."

"Oh, Donna!" I said softly, "Why didn't you say? I would have booked us on the Shuttle or driven over."

She managed to open one eye a fraction, "S-s-sorry, I thought m-m-maybe this time I'd b-b-be okay."

"Well, look," I soothed, "The flight's only fifty minutes or so, and when we get there, I'll find the railway station and you and Suze can travel back by train. How does that sound?"

"But you've already b-b-booked the flights," she almost wailed.

"It's not a problem. And besides, all of the expenses are being paid for by ETA, okay?"

"Well, if you're s-s-sure?"

"I am. Now, cuddle up to Suze and maybe try to get a bit of sleep, okay?"

Donna did as I suggested, and I turned my attention back to Dud, who, unlike my daughter's girlfriend, was thoroughly enjoying the flight, his nose pressed against the window beside him.

"Apparently Donna's scared of flying?" I explained quietly, "I told her I'd book them on the train for the return journey."

Dud gave me a bright smile, "You're a kind man, Pete."

"That's me," I grinned. A genuine compliment from Dud was rare indeed.

Fortunately for Donna, a tailwind reduced the journey time by ten minutes, and the landing in Luxembourg was as gentle as could be.

When the plane finally taxied to a standstill, I reckoned that everyone on board must have heard Donna's sigh of relief.

Showing my expertise in such matters, I was quickly out of my seat and had retrieved our hand luggage (mine consisting of a large plastic bag containing four hundred Marlboro) and was facing forward ready to disembark, ever the expert in such matters. A kind gentleman in front of me indicated that we were to exit from the rear of the plane, through a door I didn't realise even existed. The Boeing 737 was some fifty metres away from the terminal building, and we, rather charmingly I thought, descended steps onto the tarmac itself before walking across to the small two-storey structure.

Inside, we passed quickly through passport control and then made our way up a tiny escalator to the baggage reclaim area. If all airports are like that one, I might not object to them quite so much. The reclaim area there is no more than fifteen metres on a side, and there are just two carousels, one of which was already in motion. Less than two minutes later, we had recovered our bags and passed through customs. Actually, I use the word 'customs' very loosely, since it consisted of a wooden trestle table, manned by one bored-looking official who didn't so much as glance up from his newspaper as we passed him.

The arrivals hall is a long, high-ceilinged room, which also serves as the check-in area, and booking hall, and contains a single, small shop. Using Suze, her arm firmly around the still-quivering Donna's shoulders, as a translator, I managed to purchase a map of the City centre. To be exact, the *town* centre since that's how it's referred to locally. There was a brief problem because I didn't have a banknote smaller than one hundred Euros (which was not much less than one hundred pounds!), but after a lot of eye-rolling and muttered curses, I was the proud possessor of the street guide.

Outside, a line of taxis was already waiting to ferry arriving passengers into the centre of town some four miles away, and we piled into the first in the line; Suze, Donna, and myself in the back and Dud next to the driver.

The short journey proved remarkable on a number of counts. We left the airport and were almost immediately into rural surroundings;

111

fields and forest, the occasional house. As the landscape remained consistently rustic, I began to think that the four mile estimate must have been on the short side, when we suddenly arrived at the town itself, the transition from trees to buildings occurring in no more than one hundred metres.

Another remarkable thing was the cost of the journey, which, by my rough mental calculation, came to more than thirty pounds. Of course, this could well be because we had been driven by a formula one pilot, judging by the speeds our man reached.

Luxembourg town itself brought its own level of surprise. Given my research the previous day, I had been expecting ultra-modern, steel, glass and marble constructions, maybe skyscrapers in the New York mode. Instead, the centre of the town proved to be anything but; the buildings no more than four or five storeys high, built of grey or brown stone with steeply pitched slate roofs and small, almost discreet, shop fronts.

I had eschewed the idea of staying at the two hundred pound per night *Royale*, and booked us into a more modest hotel, the *Molitor*, a couple of hundred metres from the bridge which marked the centre point of the town. It proved to be a pleasant, clean building on one of the town's main avenues, and, best of all (for me, at least), the staff were all able to converse in English. We were soon settled into our rooms on the third floor and I was finally able to go out on the room's balcony and light a cigarette – my first for nearly two and a half hours; another of my pet hates about flying, by the way.

"So, what do you think of it so far?" I asked Dud when he joined me there, drawing deeply on the Marlboro.

"Quaint is the word that springs to mind," he replied over his shoulder as he stared down onto the street below.

"Very apt. I'd rather expected something a little more modern."

"Donna said that there's loads of newer developments outside the town centre somewhere, but the local government have insisted on preserving the character of the town itself," Dud went on, "Apparently there were problems a few years back when the original Commission building was put up."

"Charming idea," I nodded, fervently wishing a few more planners felt the same way about my beloved City of London, "I can't wait to get exploring." A knock on our door indicated that I wasn't the only one.

"Fit?" Suze asked me when I opened it.

"As I'll ever be," I nodded.

We made our way down to street level. With a little help from Donna, I managed to work out our location on the street guide, and we decided that the first port of call should be the railway station, on the grounds that it was located in the wrong direction as far as our target search area went. I was surprised, maybe even disappointed, when we reached it a few minutes later. This area of town was more dilapidated, the buildings newer and less picturesque, although the station itself was clearly old. Inside the cavernous building, we were quickly directed to the booking office and even more quickly furnished with two tickets for the following Monday that would take the girls first to Brussels and then on the Eurostar to Waterloo station in London. Such efficiency in a British railway station is, as you are no doubt aware, unheard of, and I was already becoming enamoured of the place.

That task out of the way, we headed back towards the town centre, passing by our hotel and quickly arriving at the *pont Adolphe*. If the architecture was a surprise, then the view from that bridge can only be described as a complete shock. It spanned what Donna referred to as the *Grund*, a massive gorge that separated the two halves of the town centre, and it stood at least eighty metres above the floor of the valley. At some distant point in time, two rivers had tumbled ferociously through the area, carving this massive feature out of the surrounding rocks. Now there's just a tiny, concrete-sided stream far, far below us, probably incapable of carving through a single grain of sand.

The walls of the gorge are tree-lined, ancient fortifications dotted haphazardly among the firs, oaks, and cedars. I could make out a tiny chapel of some sort, and Donna explained that many of the buildings dated back to the thirteenth century, and that the gorge had been the town's main defence against the ever-present threat of invasion from the warring neighbours either side of the tiny Duchy. The view was both stunning and enchanting, and I couldn't think of a single natural feature to match it in any of the manifold cities I had visited before.

Donna, who had taken over as map-reader, told us that there were plenty of access points if we wanted to descend into the gorge, but that we should choose carefully, since a second gorge intersected this one less than a mile from where we stood, and it was all too possible to end up on the wrong side. If that happened, we would have to make two descents and, more dauntingly, two *ascents* to get back. Trusting to her judgement, we followed her to a second bridge a hundred metres away.

"This looks like the best bet," she nodded at a small, cobbled road which angled steeply down from one end of the bridge.

I was about to light a Marlboro but one look at the narrow street changed my mind, "Didn't you mention a lift?" I asked innocently.

"Yes, but it's on the other side, and quite a distance from here."

"Come on, Pa," Suze grinned, "It's about time you got some exercise." Rather charmingly, she took Donna's hand and began to descend.

"Oh, well," I sighed, "If I collapse on the way back up, at least there's three of you to carry me the rest of the way."

"No chance," Dud laughed, "It's a lovely warm evening. We'll just let you sleep down there. But don't worry," he added, "We'll bring you some food and stuff."

"Talk about finding out who your friends are," I complained.

Dud clapped me on the shoulder, and we began the long descent, soon catching up with the girls as gravity began to command our progress. Even with the steep gradient when we arrived at the bottom of the gorge, we were some hundred and fifty metres from our starting point at the bridge. If the view from the top had been spectacular, from this vantage point it was truly awesome. We spent more than an hour exploring the nooks and crannies, the tiny rooms carved into the rock walls, an ancient chapel, no more than ten metres long and four deep.

I normally prided myself on my sense of direction – whatever Suze might have to say on the subject – but I was thoroughly lost by the time Dud suggested that refreshments were called for. Donna consulted the guide and suggested that we head for the 'old-town'.

"Isn't that where we started out from?" I asked her.

She shook her head, smiling, "Nope. This is the really old town; some of it dates back four hundred years or so. According to this," she indicated the guide, "It's over in that direction."

I followed her pointing finger and saw a cluster of buildings on the far side of a small wooden bridge. I could just make out a tiny street angling away from river. "That doesn't look too steep," I remarked, happily.

"You can make it, Pa," Suze encouraged me, "Even at your advanced age."

Spurred on by my daughter's painful – and all too accurate observation – I took a few deep breaths and followed the two annoyingly fit youngsters. At first, the cobbled street wound through a few ancient buildings, its angle of ascent comfortable even for the near-geriatric that people seemed to think I was. However, that didn't last long.

"What about this bar?" I suggested, trying not to pant too hard.

"Dingy," Suze turned her nose up, "And no outdoor seating. I rather fancy one of those traditional European street café affairs."

"Me too," Dud agreed, "You know what they say: 'When in Rome' and all that."

"And think yourself lucky, Pa. If we *were* in Rome, there'd be seven hills to deal with."

Ten painful minutes later, we finally arrived at a place that the consensus view approved of, and I sank gratefully onto a chair at the nearest table. With slightly trembling hands, I plucked a Marlboro from its packet and fumbled around for my lighter.

"Pa!" Suze protested, "There's you panting away like some marathon runner, and the first thing you do is reach for a fag!"

"It's been medically proven that nicotine can soothe aches and pains," I guessed.

"He's hopeless," Suze sighed at Donna.

"He's breathless, you mean," Dud laughed.

A tall and pretty young waitress emerged from the café and approached our table.

"Over to you, Suze," I suggested, "Personally, I'd kill for a nice cold beer and I haven't a clue what beer is in French or German."

"As I said," my little princess remarked to the assembled company, "Hopeless. Beer is Biere or Bier. What does everyone else want?"

Before she had a chance to practice her language skills, the waitress spoke up, "You're English, right?" Her accent was pure London.

"Right," I nodded, "You too, by the sound of it."

"Yeah. Came over 'ere in ninety-nine and sorta never left. That 'appens a lot 'ere. What can I get you all?"

We gave her our orders and she disappeared inside the small building.

"Any idea of the size of the ex-pat population, Donna?" I asked.

"Massive," she said, "In terms of proportion of the overall population, anyway."

"Many Brits?" I went on, thoughtfully.

"Thousands."

"I think Sherlock's just had an idea," Dud grinned.

"That I have," I agreed. Just then, the waitress returned with our drinks, "Er, Miss?"

"I'm Donna," she informed me.

"Coincidence. So's she."

"It's worse than that," Donna, the waitress laughed, "So's the owner of this joint."

"And there's me thinking it was an unusual name," Donna, the girlfriend, sighed.

"Anyway, Donna, er, big Donna," I tried to avoid confusion, "Donna, that is little Donna, just mentioned that there's quite a few Brits over here."

"Too true," the waitress nodded, "Must be 'undreds and 'undreds. About 'alf of the bars and clubs over 'ere cater for British tastes. Want a few names so you know where to go?"

"That'd be nice, but actually I was wondering if there's some sort of ex-patriot club or some such?"

The waitress thought for a moment, "There's some sort of fing like that at the Commission. It's mainly fer older people like you," I swatted

Suze's thigh as she giggled beside me, "And there's a proper English pub a couple of miles outside of town where loads of Brits go; the *Red Lion*. Other than that, it's mainly just the bars and clubs." She produced a small booklet from her pocket and handed it to me, "I marked down the ones where it's mostly Brits wot 'ang out there."

I looked quickly through the booklet which turned out to detail the dozens upon dozens of nightspots that were on offer to the local populace, "They certainly seem to like their nightlife round here," I observed.

"They like their beer, an' all," the waitress agreed.

I took a sip of mine and was pleasantly surprised, "Very nice."

Dud, never a cautious one, drained half of his in one go, "Good stuff," he concurred.

We ended up staying there for another forty minutes – I, for one, wasn't anxious to resume our ascent – and discussed our plan of attack.

"I'm going to call the Commission in the morning and see if I can find out a bit more about this ex-patriot club," I told them.

"I guess I wouldn't mind taking on the responsibility of doing a tour of the bars and clubs," Dud grinned, "You up for that as well, Pete?"

"Count me out. Besides, I know what you're like in clubs; you'd probably get back to the hotel with a girl on each arm." I ignored his protestations of innocence, "Since you'll be out to all hours, perhaps we should organise some sort of rendezvous in the early afternoons. How does that sound to everyone?"

"Perfect for me," Dud said.

"Shall we say, the hotel at one o'clock?"

Dud had taken the booklet from me a few minutes earlier and he now opened it to a page he had marked, "How about here instead?" he showed me the page.

The *Black Bull* was described as a typically English bar, with a friendly and cosy atmosphere, frequented by the more discerning types. It was also located almost opposite our hotel. "Suits me," I nodded.

"Why is it," Suze sighed, "That whenever Pa and Dud work together, they're seldom out of a bar?"

"Alcohol frees up the thought processes," Dud explained.

"I seem to recall that trip to Norwich," Suze giggled, "You and Pa's thought processes were so freed up, you both fell into the river."

"We did not fall!" I protested.

"Absolutely," Dud agreed, "We were pushed."

"By each other," Suze rolled her eyes, "Oh, well, at least we don't have to worry about that here. The river's not big enough to fall into."

Invigorated by the local brew, I found the remainder of our hike less painful and we were back at the hotel in no time. Dud decided to rest up before his first expedition into the nightlife of the town, and the girls chose to carry out a bit more exploration. That left me alone and with nothing planned – which seemed like heaven.

18

The following morning I found myself eager to get started on the next stage of our investigation. I showered, dressed and went down to the breakfast room where I found the girls giggling together in the furthest corner of the room.

"Hi, little ladies. Sleep well?"

"Oh, yes," Suze giggled, "Well, eventually, anyway." What can I say? Hotels have that effect on me, as well.

I decided to steer clear of that particular subject, "Are you fit and ready to help out your poor, dear father, then?"

"Ready, willing and, more importantly, able," Suze agreed.

"Count me in," Donna concurred.

"But we've just finished breakfast," Suze went on, "So we'll be up in our room when you need us."

"Fair enough," I said, "I'll call the Commission first and then come and find you. Have fun."

"We will," Suze grinned.

'I bet they will,' I thought to myself as the two girls made their way out of the room.

After a light breakfast – the size of the portions served at the restaurant the previous night were practically American – I retreated to the room, stopping off at the reception desk on the way to obtain the telephone number of the Commission. After a number of false starts, I was finally put through to someone who could help me.

"I'm not quite the person you need to speak to," the guy told me after I'd explained the situation, "But I'm the next best thing. You really need to speak to Commodore Forbes, and I'm his driver. If you like, I can come over and pick you up? Where did you say you were staying?"

"That's awfully kind of you," I replied, "We're at the *Molitor*, do you know it?"

"Sure do. I'm Mike Nicholas, by the way. I can be there in about half an hour, if that suits you?"

"That's wonderful," I said, "Thanks again."

"No problem," the young guy laughed, "I'm just glad of something to do for a change. See you in thirty minutes."

It sounded to me that all those stories about Commission jobs being sinecures were right. I went next door to the girls' room and told them what we'd be doing that morning.

"Are you sure you really need us to come along?" Suze asked.

"Probably not, as it happens. Why? Would my little princess rather not trail around after daddy?"

"Definitely not if he puts on silly accents like that," she gave one of her theatrical gestures, "Oh! The shame of it." She swooned backwards onto the bed, every bit the silent film actress.

"What on earth have I done to deserve a daughter like this?"

"You just got lucky, Pa," she giggled.

"Yeah, right. But, anyway, you're probably right about me not needing your expert services this morning. So what say I meet you in the *Black Bull* as arranged?"

"Sounds good to me," Suze nodded.

"In the meantime we can do a bit of shopping," Donna suggested.

"I suppose you'll be needing some of this?" I opened my wallet.

"Judging by some of the shops we were looking in last night," Suze giggled, "We'll need all of it."

We compromised on three hundred Euro, and the girls had already scampered off towards the main shopping centre by the time Mike Nicholas arrived. He turned out to be every bit as young-looking as he had sounded on the telephone, and in person his manner was just as pleasant. I was quickly ushered into the car, a top of the range Jaguar in the only colour they should allow them to be produced – British Racing Green – and he pulled smoothly into the mid-morning traffic.

I was surprised to find Mike driving out of the main town centre and even more surprised at the district we arrived in. The Kirchberg Plateau, as Mike described it, was full of the most amazing buildings I had ever seen collected together. Each and every one was in a completely different style from its neighbours and the sheer extravagance of the ultra-modern structures spoke volumes for the wealth of the small Duchy.

I was staring, awe-struck, at a red-brick-and-glass building that seemed to be moulded into a small hillside when Mike announced with a flourish, "And on your left is where we're headed."

The small, blurry photograph in the guide could never have done justice to the sight that met my eyes. Nor could the term monstrosity be truly applied, although the Commission building was a monster structure. It stretched for as far as I could see, a four, five, sometimes six-storied structure of brown glass, flagpoles adorned with the member states' flags and the ubiquitous blue rectangle with the circle of yellow stars. Mike drove on for another two-hundred metres and then turned left. The building rambled on and on.

"I'm glad I don't have to work there," I said, "I'd never find my way around the place."

Mike laughed, "It's a real pain at times. All the staff are issued with maps, but there's still rumours about people wandering around lost for days. Especially the Italian contingent, for some strange reason."

Another left turn took us along the furthest side of the building, and inside I could make out figures moving around, "I never realised that the Commission did that much work," I observed.

"Don't worry, it doesn't. I'm pretty sure there are people in there that don't even have a job title."

Mike turned the car into the main entrance, its progress smooth and easy. I was reminded for a moment of Jenny's Aston Martin and made a mental note to get Dean to check on the vehicle's whereabouts. If she'd had it shipped over, or driven it over on a previous visit, it might make an easy target to look out for.

Mike parked just beside the main entrance, his boss's status made plain by the fact that his reserved spot was very close to the doors, and then led us inside where we were handed security passes by a uniformed guard. Mike used a telephone in the reception area to call the Commodore and then led me into a large room off to one side, where coffee awaited us.

"The Commodore is the boss of the British contingent here," Mike explained as he poured us both strong black coffee from the thoughtfully provided pot, "Nice enough bloke, but a bit... shall we say, old-fashioned."

"I know the type," I said, "I worked for an ex-military type three or four years back and I doubt whether the Commodore could be more old-fashioned than him. I think the Major fought in the Crimean War".

"This one was at Waterloo," Mike assured me.

"Did they have an air-force back then?"

"If you believe what the Commodore tells you," Mike replied, "It was a Spitfire squadron that turned the tables, not that Prussian guy."

I was still laughing when the doors opened and a tall, distinguished-looking grey-haired man bustled in.

"Welcome, welcome, welcome," he enthused, causing Mike to grimace.

"Hungover again, old boy?" the Commodore asked him cheerfully, and continued without waiting for the rather unnecessary reply, "Ah, youngsters today. Lucky buggers or what?" he directed this last question at me.

"We certainly are," I agreed, trying to make it clear that I still thought of myself as a youngster.

"And you must be our new friend from the old Smoke, yes? Spike Milligan or something isn't it?"

"Pete Cooke, actually," I couldn't help but smile.

121

"Ah, right, jolly good," the Commodore babbled on, "Wonderful, wonderful. I'm Commodore Forbes, by the way. Now, let's see what's what, shall we? I hear you're interested in meeting a few of our ex-pats at the club, is that right?"

"If it's possible. I'm trying to locate a couple of fugitives who have rather a lot of money that doesn't belong to them. I was hoping that some of the members might be persuaded to keep an eye out for them."

"Sounds intriguing. I'll just get you some details of the place." The Commodore set down the small attaché case he was carrying and fiddled with the catches for a moment or two. "Damn newfangled thing," he muttered, "Ah, right, that's got the bugger." The catches, together with the case's lid, snapped open and a stream of documents piled onto the floor. "Shit, damn and buggeration! It's always doing that." He bent to gather the documents together.

Mike and I exchanged amused looks before bending to assist the old man.

A couple of minutes later the documents had been returned, haphazardly, to the small case. After another couple of minutes rummaging, the Commodore grunted happily and plucked a small booklet from the morass, "Here we go! Everything you need to know about the ex-pats' club. Pity it's Thursday today, only that's the one day the club's not open. Could've taken you along, otherwise."

I took the proffered booklet and quickly scanned the contents. It contained details of the club's location and in tiny print, a list of the principal members. Many, I was glad to see, were bankers and investment specialists. Also, tucked inside it, was a letter of introduction which would enable me and a colleague to gain access.

"All in order, old boy?" the Commodore asked.

"It looks ideal," I nodded, "Thanks for your time and the introduction."

"Think nothing of it, old bean," the Commodore brushed my gratitude aside, "Any old how, must dash. Important snooker match lunchtime against the Krauts. Got to get some practice in, what? Can't let old Blighty down."

Before I could reply, the Commodore had grabbed his attaché case, closed it and strode out of the room with a final command to Mike to make sure he showed me where the club was when he took me back to town.

"Strange old bird, ain't he?" Mike smiled at me.

"And useful," I agreed.

"Well, if you're done here, I'll get you back to town."

"Sounds good to me."

I trailed out after Mike and we were soon back on the road, heading first away from the town so that he could show me where the clubhouse was located.

"If you like," he offered, "I could pick you up tomorrow lunchtime if you want to come along here?"

"That'd be great. But doesn't anyone object to you using the car for what pretty much amounts to private purposes?"

"Pete," he grinned at me in the rear-view mirror, "If I didn't use it for private purposes it'd never turn a wheel. The Commodore prefers to drive around in his Roller."

"Why on earth does he have another car and driver, then?" I asked, perplexed.

Mike laughed loudly, "At the Commission, it never pays to turn down anything."

I was definitely beginning to think that some of the more lurid press reports about European affairs were more accurate than I had originally imagined.

Mike dropped me off outside the hotel, and with two hours to kill before I met up with the rest of the gang, I decided to go for a quiet stroll.

Luxembourg felt a million miles removed from London, an air of *difference* hung about me; moreso even than when I'd been in Paris or New York. On all the main thoroughfares, people walked unhurriedly, no hustle or bustle about them at all. Traffic moved easily along the streets and the buses, of which there seemed to be thousands, were not at all crowded. The only thing that really bugged me was the proliferation of dog turds that made walking a somewhat hazardous process.

Perhaps they're all incontinent? I considered for a moment before changing my mind: 'Incontinental' seemed a much more appropriate word.

Without the guide book, I was quickly lost, and grateful to a passing Scotsman for pointing me back in the right direction when the time came. Perhaps my darling Suze was right about my sense of direction, after all.

The little darling was waiting outside the *Black Bull* with Donna when I arrived.

"Why didn't you go in?" I asked, "There's no restrictions over here."

Suze shrugged, "I didn't like to without your express permission."

"Will I always have to drag you halfway across Europe to get you to behave this well?" I grinned at her.

"Not nice, Pa! Just for that, I'm going to head back to the shops this afternoon."

We went into the small bar and sat on the broad window-ledge where a young barman served us with a beer and two Cokes. Dud had still not turned up by the time I ordered a second round.

"There wasn't so much as a snore from his room when we went back to change," Suze informed us.

"Knowing Dud, he's probably still out in some club," I nodded.

"Not true, partner," Dud announced, coming through the door, "Although I didn't actually make it back 'til six."

"So, how did it go?" I asked when they had drinks.

"Well, I started in that English pub the waitress mentioned yesterday, The *Red Lion*. And she was right; there must have been dozens of Brits in there – and get this: one of the guys knows all about ETA."

"Really?" I was astonished.

"Really. Unfortunately he was just about to leave, but he'll be back there on Sunday for lunch – apparently they do a full English roast – and I said we'd meet up with him, if that's okay with you?"

"I'll be there," I nodded happily. I had wondered whether this jaunt would turn out to be a complete waste of time, but already we were making steady progress.

"After that I went on to what? About thirteen different clubs?" Dud frowned, "I guess I lost count at twelve."

"And presumably had a drink in each one?"

"It's only polite," Dud grinned, "Anyway, I flashed the photos around at anyone who looked the banking type–"

"And probably to any young woman that looked vaguely available?"

"Not true. Well, pretty much not true. No-one actually recognised either of them, but I have got a couple of names of guys who work in the right departments with the local banks, and I've arranged to meet up with them tomorrow after work. So, all in all, not a bad start."

"It certainly isn't," I agreed happily, "What's the plan for later today?"

"Shopping," Suze and Donna said in unison.

"Clubbing," Dud nodded.

"I thought I'd maybe go back out to where I was this morning," I said, "There's loads of banks over that way and a few bars. If I hang out in one or two of them from about four, there's bound to be a few guys stopping off for a quick beer before they head for home."

"Sounds good to me," Dud nodded.

"Okay, that's all settled then," I said, "I'll meet you in here about three tomorrow, since I'll be at the ex-pats' club for lunch," I nodded at Dud, "And as far as you two go," I addressed the girls, "I guess the same applies. Do you need any more money?"

Suze giggled, "Always. But seriously, the only thing I've bought so far is this dress. Not that you've noticed it's new."

"Of course I had," I said airily, "I just didn't want to embarrass you by saying how beautiful you look in it." Not a bad excuse, don't you think?

"Since when have I ever been embarrassed when you say things like that?" Suze lifted her chin and tossed her hair back.

"True," I mock-sighed, "You can be a vain little mare at times."

She swatted my thigh lightly, "I am not vain."

"Narcissistic, then."

"But there again, so would you be if you looked as beautiful as me." You just can't win, can you?

I phoned Dean Samson and asked him to check the whereabouts of Jenny's Aston Martin and shortly afterwards, I left the others and spent a leisurely hour or so at the hotel watching BBC World News before heading off towards Kirchberg. I returned a couple of hours later, my efforts having proved fruitless, and decided that a nice dinner was called for. As well as the bars, clubs, banks, and, for some unfathomable reason, hairdressers that proliferated in the town, there was also a wonderfully wide selection of restaurants to choose from. After much internal debate, I chose a quiet back-street Italian place where I could eat outside, and where the food turned out to be absolutely delicious. I rounded off the evening by visiting a few up-market looking bars on the off chance of spotting either of the fugitives.

19

Friday dawned bright and clear. Well, presumably it had since it was sunny when I awoke at nine-thirty. By ten I decided that it was time for my hangover and I to get up and we took a leisurely late breakfast in our room before showering and dressing.

Mike arrived to pick me up at twelve, once again looking tired and hungover, and I was happily ensconced at the bar of the ex-pats' club by twenty past, Mike now acting as host and introducing me to various people he reckoned might be able to assist me. The first half dozen proved to be of no great help, although they all promised to keep their eyes open for my missing persons, but the seventh guy was like a gift from heaven.

He'd introduced himself as Graham Brooke, known to all and sundry, apparently, as GB, and he listened intently to my story. When I had finished, he nodded thoughtfully.

"I did say a little while ago that I'm an auditor, yes?"

I nodded, "Price-Waterhouse, wasn't it?"

He smiled, "That's what I said, but I'm afraid it's not actually true. You see, I'm an independent – one of those rare breeds these days. In fact, I'm not even really just an auditor," he motioned for us to move along the bar to where no-one would be able to overhear us. When he was happy that we were out of earshot, he continued his explanation, "Following all the fuss last year about bribery and corruption within the EU, an independent, international panel of audit and investigation was formed. I'm part of that panel, and, essentially, I work under cover, as it were; try to sniff out illegal goings on. From what you told me earlier, I believe that we might be able to help each other; I'm all too aware of what ETA gets up to – or, more accurately, what its true function is."

"You know ETA?" I asked, surprised.

"I was appointed by Westminster," he smiled, "It's not exactly difficult to obtain a little background information in that particular building."

I showed GB the photographs, "Recognise either of them?"

He laughed, "Rather. Stephenson has been a prime target of ours for some time."

"Why has nothing been done about him, then?"

"One individual's guilt is not nearly enough to put a stop to the various criminal activities that go on within the EU," he sighed, "Your Stephenson fellow is just a very small cog in a vast, corrupt machine. In fact, at one level, he's technically not guilty of anything; that he organises illegal payments we know, but it'd be damn hard to prove that *he* knows they're illegal. As for Winter, well, she's a little more problematic."

"Why so?"

"She, too, is known to us, but I'm afraid she's as elusive as the proverbial butterfly. We managed to have her followed on one occasion, but even so, we have no idea of who exactly she met, and what exactly might have been discussed. I rather think that she's a much bigger fish than Stephenson. What do you know about them?"

I told him everything I could remember which did not, apparently, give him much more information than he already had.

"What does intrigue me, though," he said, "Is that they seem to have finished with their little game."

"Surely there's two hundred million good reasons?"

127

"You would have thought so, wouldn't you? But it rarely happens that way. Once these people start to get into the realms of hundreds of millions, it just seems to spur them on. At a rough guess, there's maybe five hundred *billion* dollars' worth of black money floating around Europe and the UK."

I whistled softly, "So, how can you help me out?"

GB let out an ironic chuckle, "Believe it or not, by playing their own game. A little word and a promise in the right ears and I can get any number of bankers around here to look out for your two missing rogues."

"You'd do that for me?"

"It would be a pleasure. Of course, I can't cover every bank in this damn town, but a fair proportion. If we do manage to collar them, they might be open to a little name-dropping in return for certain favours on the part of the authorities back home."

"Sounds good to me," I shrugged, although to be honest, it sounded almost as criminal as what, apparently, was going on all around us.

We exchanged numbers and details, and I left him to his lunch, happy that progress was being made. At two-thirty, with no further successes, I decided to call it a day and had Mike take me back to town. I left him, promising to meet him at the *Red Lion* on Sunday, where I would treat him to lunch in return for his chauffeuring services.

The mood during my afternoon rendezvous with the other three was celebratory; not only was our European jaunt not a complete waste of time and effort, it was actually starting to show distinct promise. I made sure, also, to mention how lovely my little princess looked in another new dress, again, blue. I didn't think I'd give long odds on blue being Donna's favourite colour.

We were all laughing at Dud's recollections of his previous night's embarrassments when he had got carried away on the small dance floor of a club in the town centre when my mobile cheeped noisily.

"Yo, Pete," Dean Samson's rich, dark voice greeted me when I answered.

"Yo, yourself," I replied, stepping into the street where reception was better, "What's the news?"

128

"As far as I'm concerned," the big man chuckled, "Probably not good for business. But as far as *you're* concerned, it's probably as good as it gets."

"Okay, I'm all ears."

"First up is the car," he said, "A metallic green Aston Martin DB7 was collected from a secure garage under Winter's flat by a guy named Michael something or other at seven p.m. last night and driven South. June Davis, my contact at Customs in Dover spotted it being driven on to a cross channel ferry at eight-thirty, destination Ostend."

"Great work, Dean," I said happily, "That seems to prove that she's finished her business in London."

"It gets better, which is why I didn't call before. I've spent the morning persuading a West London estate agent to provide me with a little information."

"I won't ask for details of your methods, but why an estate agent?"

"Simple. Because a certain Jennifer Helen Winter left instructions with this guy to sell her flat. She apparently insisted that it should go on the market for well below the normal price as she wanted a quick sale. This morning, she got it."

"There's an 'and' here, isn't there?"

"There most certainly is," he continued, "I was able to… gain access to the details of the transaction. At eleven o'clock two-hundred thousand pounds were transferred from the account of a James Green into a Luxembourg bank account belonging to our Miss Winter."

"A named account?" I asked, my pulse quickening.

"Most certainly so," Dean laughed, "And, as you are no doubt well aware, a named account–"

"Always has an address attached!" I interrupted, one hand curled into a fist.

"So, grab a pen and get to it," he continued, before giving me the details.

I rang off after thanking him profusely for his efforts and returned to the bar to share the good news.

"I know just the man to help us out," Dud nodded when I'd related the new information, "Met the guy last night, and he works for that bank. Said he'd be only too happy to bend a few regulations to assist us. Hang on for a minute and I'll give him a call."

Unable to contain my mounting excitement, I followed Dud out onto the street as he contacted his man. Less than three minutes later he rang off and handed me a scrap of paper on which he'd scrawled the necessary information.

"This detective lark," he grinned, "Is a bloody sight easier than I thought."

"Maybe we're just brilliant," I laughed, staring down at Jennifer Winter's Luxembourg address. We went back inside to consult the street guide and share the news of our brilliance.

"It seems you're not so daft after all, Pa," Suze grinned, while Donna consulted the map.

"Where else do you think you get your intelligence from?"

"That address is down near the station," Donna informed us, "About a five-minute walk from here, I'd guess."

I looked across at Dud, "Fancy a stroll?"

He nodded slowly, "My very thoughts." He drained his glass and nodded towards the door, "After you, Sherlock."

"See you later girls," I beamed, "We shouldn't be long."

"We're coming with you," Suze spoke up for herself and Donna.

"I'm afraid not, ladies. Sometimes people don't take kindly to being located when they don't want to be, and I'm not about to put any of you at risk. Dud and I have done this sort of thing before, and we know what to expect. You two stay here, and we'll be back before you know it." Dud and I really *had* done this sort of thing before. What I didn't mention is that the last time we had, we'd both ended up at the nearest accident and emergency. However, I couldn't imagine that Jennifer Winter provided the same sort of threat as our last target, who had turned out to be a minor celebrity on the South London gangster circuit.

"But, Pa!" Suze began to protest.

"No arguments, princess. Really, we won't be long."

It took another five minutes of persuasion before Dud and I were finally able to leave the girls and we started off for the station, map in hand and spirits high.

Despite Suze's assertion that we'd be lost before we got to the corner of the street, we located the road in question within ten minutes and made our way along it. As I'd discovered before, the area around the station was more seedy than the rest of the town centre, and this road seemed to demonstrate my point. It was clearly part of the town's red light district, a mixture of tatty bars and strip joints; hardly the sort of place that I'd imagined the high-flying Jenny Winter to relocate to. Flat 2 at number 32, our destination, was located between a 'night-club' whose staff couldn't afford clothes judging by a large, photograph-covered board outside, and a shop selling all manner of rubber items.

"Well, this is it," Dud shrugged.

"Apparently so." I scanned the panel of buttons next to the wrought-iron door. The button for flat 2 was inexplicably the middle one of seven and I pressed it firmly. A few moments afterwards, a loud buzz indicated that the front door was open. Dud and I exchanged shrugs and walked into the gloomy interior.

A short flight of stairs took us up to an even dingier landing with a door on either side. Number 2 was on the right.

"Here goes," I grinned at my partner before knocking loudly.

I had adjusted my eyes in the expectation of seeing Jenny's, a couple of centimetres below my own, and so when the door opened, it at first appeared to be operated by remote control. It took me a moment or two in the poor light to realise that there was someone standing in the now-open doorway. Someone who could not have been more than five foot tall.

"Oh, er, Hi," I managed.

"Well, hello," the woman's voice almost purred, "For two of you, it'll be extra, but come on in, anyway." She stepped back into the room beyond.

I exchanged a seriously puzzled look with Dud and followed her. Inside, a window to our right provided more illumination which, in all honesty, I could have done without. For a start, it revealed details about the young woman.

She was possibly even shorter than I had at first imagined, and her slight frame, together with her short black hair, gave her the appearance of a young teenager. In stark, almost violent, contrast, was her clothing; or more accurately, the lack of it. She was wearing nothing more than a tiny, diaphanous robe which she now proceeded to untie and shrug off her narrow shoulders. She stood naked before us, her small pert breasts pointing almost accusingly in our direction, the innocence of her small body belied by her knowing, penetrating gaze.

"So, do you like what you see?" Her voice was as dark as the hallway behind us, the faintest trace of an accent hovering behind her words.

It was Dud who found his voice first, "I think there's been a little misunderstanding here. We're just looking for someone."

The girl-woman didn't seem in the least bit fazed, "Honey," she smiled, "You can look until the cows come home, but you ain't gonna find anyone as good as Marie." She ran her small hands over her breasts and down to her groin.

"No, you don't understand," I finally managed, "We're looking for a missing person, not, er, well, not someone like, er, you."

The little prostitute placed her hands on her hips and cocked her head to one side, "You mean you're not here for a fuck?"

"Right," Dud said quickly, "Just looking for someone."

"Why not have a fuck while you're here?" she asked, clearly an efficient businesswoman, "Fucks don't come any better than with Marie."

"No!" I insisted, "We really are just trying to find someone. Someone that's supposed to live at this address."

In retrospect, it was amusing to see the look on Dud's face as the little prostitute stepped up to him and cupped his genitals in one tiny hand. He gave a strangled squawk and stepped smartly backwards, a move I would have thought rather dangerous. "Really," he swallowed hard, "We're not here for anything other than trying to find her."

Shrugging, clearly recognising that she wasn't going to be doing business with either of us, the little woman turned and pulled on her robe, "You don't know what you're missing guys."

"What we're missing," I said, "Is a tall, blonde English woman. Name of Jennifer Winter. We were told that this was her address."

"Winter, you say?"

"Jennifer Winter. Have you seen her?"

"Not seen," Marie said, "But sure as shit heard of. I get loads of post for her these last six months, which is a bit odd 'cos I've been here nearly three years."

"She's never been here, then?"

"Not while I've been in, anyway."

Dud, clearly relaxing, joined in, "I don't suppose you've kept any of her letters?"

Marie crossed to a dark corner of the room and returned with a dozen or more envelopes, "Just these ones. I guess I'd better let you have them. This girl some sort of runaway?"

"Not exactly," I said, taking the letters, "More a fugitive from justice."

Marie's eyes narrowed, "You're not with Interpol or something, are you?"

"Not at all. We're... carrying out a sort of private investigation."

"Like private detectives?"

"Something like that," I nodded.

"Hey," she grinned, "I've never been dicked by a dick before. You sure you guys don't want to fuck me? I'll do you for a special discount?"

"No, really!" I insisted, "It's, er, a very kind offer, but we're, er, a little too busy."

"Ah, well," she shrugged, "It was worth a try. Maybe some other time?"

"Maybe," I couldn't help but grin.

"I really am one of the best," she continued her sales pitch, "I'm a raving nympho, you know? And what better job can a girl like that have, eh?"

"Makes sense," Dud said hurriedly, "But we've really got to get going."

We were out of the door and back to the street in seconds, the bright sunlight eye-piercingly bright after our few minutes in the gloomy apartment.

"Well that was entertaining," Dud sighed.

133

"Disappointing, more like," I grinned, "But at least we got something out of it."

"A very good view. Cute, wasn't she?"

"I was referring to these," I rolled my eyes and held up the letters.

"Let's have a look-see," Dud grinned.

The mail was of no help whatsoever; just a stream of letters from one of the local banks.

"Not exactly much use, are they?" Dud observed.

"Other than telling us that she's had a bank account here for more than two years, no. I guess we'd better get back and tell the girls what happened."

"You can tell the girls what happened," Dud laughed, "They'd never believe me if I told them."

"The only thing they wouldn't believe is that you didn't take up Marie's kind offer."

"You know, partner? Sometimes you can be really cruel."

When we got back, the girls seemed to find our news even more disappointing than we had, but with the important contacts already made that day, Dud and I remained pretty upbeat about things. He left at five to begin his evening stint with the contacts he'd made the previous night, and the girls and I headed back to the hotel to freshen up, before heading out for another quiet evening.

Saturday proved to be a success-free time with no new leads coming to light, and we abandoned our efforts in the early afternoon, determining that the rest of the day should be spent relaxing; an idea which appealed to everyone. Sunday lunchtime, though, was an altogether different matter.

Mike Nicholas picked up Dud and I at the hotel just after twelve and drove us out to the *Red Lion*, leaving Suze and Donna to their own devices. The pub really did look typically English – even down to the mock-Tudor beams and beer-slops on the bar counter – and, like most English pubs on a Sunday lunchtime, it was packed.

I was trying to work out the quickest route to the bar when a familiar voice called out to me.

"Spike! Over here, old boy!"

Commodore Forbes was standing at the furthest end of the bar counter, clearly the centre of attention for a small group of middle-aged men who surrounded his tall figure. Among them, I noticed Graham Brooke, the undercover 'auditor'. The three of us squeezed through the throng to join the group.

"Welcome, welcome, welcome," the Commodore enthused, before rapidly introducing us to the other nine people in his entourage. Other than GB, no names stuck, but I nodded to each of the men in turn. "Now where's me little girl?" the Commodore finished, gazing around him, "Nicola, dear?"

A vision of beauty appeared as if by magic at the far side of the group from where I was standing. Nicola Forbes was at least six feet tall but the thing that drew your attention immediately was not her height, but her eyes; the most dazzling shade of green I'd ever seen. With a full head of dark-auburn hair as a frame, they seemed to radiate emerald light from her fine-featured face.

"Ah, there you are, Nicola!" the Commodore went on, "Come and meet our new friend from the old Smoke; Spike, this is my daughter, Nicola."

I awkwardly reached across the group and quickly shook her well-manicured hand, "Actually, it's Pete. And this is my partner, Dud."

Dud, clearly as impressed as I was by this vision of loveliness, gave her a small wave.

"Pete and Dud?" Nicola raised one beautifully sculptured eyebrow.

I shrugged again, "It's to do with our names," I explained lamely.

"Perhaps," she smiled, "You could enlighten me at a later date? Only I really must leave now; Celestine's luncheon starts at one," she directed this last comment to her father.

"Righto, old girl," he beamed, the very picture of paternal pride, "Toodaloo, and all that. Have fun!"

Nicola sighed and gave the slightest shake of her dark tresses, "Surely," she muttered quietly, before making her stately way out of the throng.

"Wow," Dud whistled quietly.

"Wow, indeed," I agreed.

GB, who was standing on my right, let out a loud laugh, "She does rather have that effect on people. But," he modulated his voice to ensure that the proud father would not overhear, "Looks, I'm afraid, can be rather deceptive. A little bird or three have told me that she's an absolute cow most of the time."

"I'm into bovines," Dud grinned.

"Unfortunately," I explained to GB, "He means that literally to judge by one or two of his past conquests."

"I can see why people call you two Pete and Dud," GB grinned, "So what brings you to the Lion?"

"Dud, actually," I nodded at my partner, "He arranged to meet someone here today who might be able to help us. Any sign of him?"

Dud nodded to the young guy standing on GB's right, "Steve Standish."

Steve gave Dud a nod of acknowledgement, "Glad you could make it."

"It seems," GB grinned, "That you're both on the same wavelength. Steve works with me."

I quietly explained to Dud who GB was, and, after securing a round of drinks, the four of us moved away from the main group in order to gain some privacy. Quickly and efficiently, GB furnished Standish with the details of our investigation, Dud and I answering his occasional questions, and adding further details concerning the car and the bank account.

"Well," Standish said when we had finished, "This could mean one of two things; either your pigeons really have flown the coop and they've finished with their nefarious activities, or alternatively, the game, as far as they're concerned, is moving up a gear. If it's the latter, then we'd better throw everything into this. What do you say, GB?"

"Couldn't agree more. In fact, if you'd all excuse me for a minute or two, I think I'd better phone Duncan."

"Duncan Pressman is our 'man on the street', as it were," Standish explained when GB had left, "He's been here for years and seems to know everyone and everything. If Winter and Stephenson are here, then

I'd bet my life savings that Duncan could track them down within a week. Especially if a flash sports car is involved; he's a fanatic."

"Sounds great," I nodded, "But what did you mean earlier by the game moving up a gear?"

Standish looked levelly at Dud and I for a moment before nodding to himself, evidently deciding that we were worthy of his trust, "There's been a significant increase in activity over the last few weeks," he said quietly, "Certain, shall we say, 'known' faces have been appearing on the streets, and then just as quickly disappearing. We're fairly sure that their roles are as couriers for the much bigger fish. It could be that Winter and Stephenson are among their number."

"But surely, if they were merely couriers, they wouldn't have left the UK?"

Standish gave a snort, "Couriers are extremely well paid for a start; they'd likely end up with maybe twenty percent of whatever they were carrying, and I'm sure you'd agree that forty million dollars is not to be sneezed at. On the other hand, they may merely be relocating; after all, it must have been becoming apparent to them that the game was up in London; that the defences you'd prepared for the ETA systems had somewhat stymied them. They might also have been fearing that certain authorities were closing in."

"So you really believe they've come here to start again, or whatever?" I pressed him.

"Probably not. From what you've told me, the mistake they made with the draft means that they were forced to come here – or rather, that they *will* be forced to come here – I wouldn't imagine that they would feel any more secure here than in the UK; this is a very small country. Given that Winter, at least, has a good local knowledge judging by her bank account, I would imagine that they would stay away until the draft was valid."

"So you don't believe they're likely to be here right now?"

"Who knows?" Standish shrugged, "There is such a thing as a double-bluff, after all. You'd better let me have details of that bank account by the way. We won't block it – far too obvious a sign that we're onto them – but if it's with a bank that we have influence over I will get

137

someone to monitor it in case there's any activity. It's a long shot, but we've got to try to cover every eventuality."

"Steve," Dud said thoughtfully, "The only reason we've not been to the police or Interpol, or whatever, is that Forsythe specifically said that we shouldn't. What's to stop us now?"

He gave a loud laugh, "Corruption in Europe isn't so much a crime as a way of life. Everyone seems to think that it's just the bankers and politicians you can't trust. Personally, from what I've seen, I'd add police forces, accountants, auditors; Hell, I'm not even sure I can trust myself at times."

"So what's the next move for us, Dud and I, that is?"

"Just go about your normal business when you get back. Whatever you do, don't mention myself or GB to Forsythe – or anyone else, for that matter – we'll do what we can here and keep you informed. Perhaps it might be a good idea if one or both of you comes back for a few days nearer the time when the draft is to become valid?"

"Sounds fair," I nodded, "But are you sure there's nothing else we can do here in the meantime?"

He stared hard at me for a while and then nodded, "Maybe there is, given your background. Not all of the banks here are... co-operative; that's what I meant about having influence over some of them. But given your skills, maybe they don't need to be?"

I returned his stare, "What sort of jurisdiction would I be under if I were to... assist you?"

"Mine, directly. And I work directly for an organisation that is arguably higher in the grand scheme of things than our very own government. You would be under no risk whatsoever. You would also be on hand if our fugitives did show up, perhaps we might even be able to persuade them that you're not quite as straight as they think."

"And you believe that I'm straight?"

"Let's just say that, yes, I do. But that you'll not be working without very close scrutiny."

I laughed, "It does sound intriguing, and since our work at ETA seems pretty much finished, I guess I am available. What about you Dud?"

"I'll have some time free," he nodded.

I was thinking about my earlier pledge to myself to get out and about a bit more with work. And Luxembourg did seem rather pleasant. "Okay, then. We'll have to go back to London this coming week to finish off at ETA and to make it look as if we're at a dead end here. After that, I'll give you a call and see if we can arrange something."

"Good man," Standish grinned at me as GB returned, "GB? Looks like we might have a couple of new recruits."

Over a traditional English roast, we discussed a few more details before returning to the bar where Commodore Forbes was still holding forth.

"Ah! There you are, old things!" he was clearly becoming a little the worse for wear, "I thought you'd gone off after my lovely daughter."

"Absolutely not," I replied, alarmed. I needn't have been.

"They all do, you know," the Commodore babbled on, "Irresistible she is. Moths to a flame and all that, don't you know?"

We made our excuses as soon as was polite, and had the barman call for a taxi to take us back into town – Mike Nicholas having already left – and retired to the *Black Bull* in order to celebrate our luck. By the time the girls joined us at six, we were giggling like schoolkids.

"Oh, really, Pa!" Suze groaned, "Can't we leave you alone for two minutes?"

"Just for that," I grinned, "I'm not going to tell you some news that I'm sure you'd find really wonderful."

"Oh?"

"All right then," I chuckled, unable to contain my own pleasure, "How about I tell you that Dud and I will soon be doing some work over here? Two or three weeks' worth, starting the week after next?"

"You mean you'd be over here, and I'd be alone at home?"

"Quite so, my little princess. Although I don't think 'alone' is the right word." I grinned at Donna, who blushed.

Suze's face fell and she frowned at me.

"What's up, princess, I thought you'd be happy?"

"I am," she couldn't maintain her straight face any longer and giggled, "It's just that I was hoping you could start here tomorrow."

139

20

The following morning Dud and I accompanied the girls to the station – as much for the fresh air the exercise afforded as to make sure they got off safely; Dud and I were both finding the local brew a tad more potent than we'd first assumed it really was.

"Do you think they'll be okay?" I asked my partner as we waved at the departing carriages.

"Funny you should ask that," he grinned, "Only Suze asked me to keep an eye on you to make sure you'd be okay on the way back."

"If it wasn't for the fact that you were talking about my precious daughter," I sighed, "I'd probably not believe you."

We had a few hours to kill before our lunchtime flight and spent the time phoning round our new Luxembourg contacts and then checked out of the hotel, intent on whiling away an hour or so in the *Black Bull*. The luggage was left at the hotel reception for collection when we departed for the airport. It was as we were crossing the main avenue that Dud spotted, what to me, was a familiar vehicle.

"Look!" he pointed to his right.

It took me a moment or two to focus my gaze on the rapidly disappearing car, but there could be no doubt. How many dark green Aston Martin DB7s with British plates could there be in such a small country? "Christ! That's hers!"

Dud, showing a turn of pace that I never knew he possessed, took off down the crowded pavement at an Olympic-standard sprint. I immediately gathered what his intention was. The main avenue branched into two a couple of hundred metres from where we had crossed, and there was a set of traffic lights at the intersection. Although the traffic wasn't heavy by London standards, there were sufficient vehicles on the road to impede the Aston's progress; in all probability it would have to stop at that set of lights. I knew it was pointless for me to try to match Dud's pace, and so ambled after him at a gentle trot, discarding my Marlboro as I went.

I could see far enough ahead to observe the Aston's brake lights glow red in sympathy with the traffic light it was approaching, and turned my attention to Dud to gauge his progress; if the lights stayed red for another ten seconds, he should have been able to pull level with the vehicle. "Come on, guy!" I encouraged him, earning myself several strange looks from passing locals.

Just as Dud was about to draw alongside the Aston, the traffic lights flashed from red to green – there's no amber on many of the lights in the Duchy – and the sports car began to move forward. I was about to utter a load curse when its brake lights again flared red, the car stopping dead in its tracks. At first I thought that the driver had spotted Dud's frantic athletic efforts, but then made out the little old lady who was still struggling across the intersection. I turned my attention to Dud and saw him slow his pace, dropping back into the milling pedestrians, hoping not to be observed.

The driver of the Aston gave an impatient toot on the horn and then slowly eased around our geriatric heroine, before turning left and disappearing down the street, out of sight. Dud punched the air with both fists and began to make his way back to where I was standing. He was still panting heavily when he arrived.

"I take it your little celebratory gesture down there indicated triumph?"

"Oh, yes!" he gasped.

"Well done, Usain," I clapped him on one heaving shoulder, "So, who was behind the wheel?"

"You'll never guess in a thousand years," he managed a red-faced smile.

Dud, as I mentioned before, never likes to come straight to the point. "Not Jenny, then?"

He shook his head, and mopped his sweaty brow on his sleeve, "Wrong sex for a start."

"Stephenson?"

"Nope."

"Fess up, partner," I sighed.

"Mike," he said with a grin.

"Mike? What Mike?"

"Mike Nicholas. You know? That batty ex-RAF guy's driver?"

I stared in astonishment, "Are you sure?"

"I didn't sprint that far, *not* to be sure when I got a chance to see inside the car. It was the very man, himself."

For a moment nothing made sense, and then two things struck me at the same time. First, Dean Samson had said that the car had been collected from London at seven on the Thursday afternoon by a Michael something-or-other, which would leave plenty of time to drive it to Luxembourg overnight. Second, when Mike *Nicholas* had picked me up Friday lunchtime, he had looked tired and, I'd thought, hungover. Maybe though, he was just shattered after driving through the night...

I plucked the mobile from my pocket and speed-dialled Dean Samson's number.

"Dean Samson," his rich, dark tones greeted me.

"Yo, Dean. It's Pete."

"My man! How's it hanging in foreign parts? You and Watson making any progress?"

"Great and yes. And I think we may have just made a significant breakthrough – although I haven't the faintest idea what the significance might actually be. Remember you told me about a guy picking up the Aston Martin?"

"Of course. What about him?"

"You said his name was Michael. Any chance that you know the surname?"

"None at all, I'm afraid." You could hear Dean's apologetic shrug, "My man only got the first name because the guy he collected it from seemed to know the driver."

"That's interesting in its own right," I said thoughtfully, "How about a description of him?"

"Hang on, my man. That should be in the file; let me just go and get it for you."

I waited a few moments, listening to the background sounds of a filing cabinet being opened and paperwork being sorted. Dean came back on the line, "Okay, here it is. Mid-twenties, tall with dark, slightly curly shoulder length hair. Brown eyes and unshaven; that sort of designer stubble look that went out in the late eighties. Why, does this sound like anyone you know?"

"Indeed it does. You've just described a guy called Mike Nicholas. He's supposedly the driver for the head of the British contingent at the Commission over here." Dud was nodding thoughtfully as I spoke. "God knows what *he's* doing collecting Jenny's car; as far as I've been able to make out so far, no one at the Commission is in any way involved with this ETA thing. Maybe we're wrong about that though."

"Could be," Dean said.

"One other thing. You said that the guy the car was collected from seemed to know Mike Nicholas. Any chance of getting a little information from him? Like, for a start, how on earth does he know someone who works as a driver in Luxembourg?"

"Does sound mysterious," Dean laughed, "I'll check this guy out personally and get back to you this evening."

"Thanks, Dean. Speak to you then."

I broke the connection and turned to Dud, "Where the bloody hell does Mike Nicholas fit into all of this?"

"Buggered if I know, but I reckon we should pass on this little gem to GB and Standish. You never know, it could be that the batty Commodore's behind all this; just because he behaves like some eccentric throwback to the days of cavalry, trenches and Sopwith Camels, it doesn't mean to say that he's really like that."

"Or maybe it's just Nicholas himself. After all, he might well have met up with Jenny on one of her visits over here before."

"And without wishing to drag up any nastiness, she does seem to have a habit of, shall we say, ingratiating herself with menfolk that she sees as being useful to her," Dud said apologetically.

"True," I sighed, "Although that might mean that Mike was simply doing her a favour by collecting the car. He might not know anything about her criminal tendencies."

"Might not, but I think that's unlikely. How about we cogitate over a beer; all that exercise has given me a desperate thirst."

"Me too."

"What exercise have you done?"

"Thinking, of course. One of us has to be the brains of the outfit."

"All right, Sherlock, but you're paying."

I phoned Standish as we made our way to the *Black Bull*, and he seemed as surprised as I was when I told him of the driver's identity.

"Very strange," he said, "I think maybe I'll have someone have a closer look at Nicholas. And Forbes, too, come to that. I'll give you a call back in London if we find out anything of interest."

"Do you ever get the impression," Dud asked as we sipped at our first beers, "that we're digging ourselves deeper and deeper into a bottomless pit?"

I couldn't help but agree with him. There again, there was all that lovely money we were earning, with the prospect of lots more to come. Those little flashing dollar signs can be more seductive that a hypnotist's watch. Our journey back to England was spent mainly in contemplative silence. I, for one, was already looking forward to going back to Luxembourg.

Part 2

1

Dud and I parted at Heathrow after agreeing to meet up at Charing Cross on the Wednesday so that we could go along to ETA and discuss 'progress' with James Forsythe. I went straight home to await Suze's return, as usual, fretting over her safety. As usual, I needn't have bothered.

"Hi, Pa!" she called as she let herself in the door just after eight.

"Hi, princess. Good journey?"

"Fantastic!" She gave me a hug, "And thanks ever so for the weekend. It was out of this world."

"Donna gone home safely, I take it?"

She wrinkled her pretty nose, "Yeah. Apparently her mother's trying to work out whether Donna's already left home."

"She does seem to have become a bit of a fixture around here."

"You don't mind, do you?" Suze asked.

"Of course not. She's lovely company. As far as I'm concerned, she can move in if you like."

Suze surprised me by shaking her head, "No chance. Or not yet, anyway. It's a bit early to start thinking like that; we've only been… together a few weeks."

"A very sensible attitude. You *are* still getting on well?"

"Better than ever," she giggled, "It was all so strange at first, but I guess it's getting to seem normal. I think that's one of the reasons why the weekend was so lovely. You know? We were really able to relax? Thanks again, Pa."

"No need for thanks. Just as long as my little princess is happy." I was rewarded with another tight hug.

"Oh! By the way," Suze broke the embrace and fumbled in her shoulder bag, "I'd better return this." She handed me a bundle of banknotes.

"It was supposed to be there for you to spend," I grinned.

"And there's me thinking you were just playing the generous daddy to impress my friend."

"I'm always generous!"

"Not when I wanted that pony, you weren't."

"You only wanted a pony so that Sam could get closer to that stable hand," I pointed out, "You don't even like dumb animals."

"I like you."

"Sassy!"

"If I were a boy, that'd be 'sissy'; but surely you wouldn't want me any other way?"

"I guess not," I sighed. She was, as ever, quite right.

For what seemed like the first time in weeks, we spent a quiet evening at home alone together, and after Suze kissed my cheek and went up to her room, I was left wondering how many more times it would happen. My precious daughter seemed to have aged years in just a few short weeks, and yet I wasn't at all saddened by either that fact, or what it might mean for the future. Somehow, I think I'd come to realise that you never really let go; you just lengthen the leash a little at a time.

I spent most of Tuesday in my study, trying to figure out what was – or might be – going on in the tiny Duchy; although I might just as well have stayed in bed for all the progress I made. Jenny Winter and Paul Stephenson were clearly the principal villains of the piece; GB and Standish were, in all probability, on the side of right and justice. It was the wildcards that were puzzling.

Mike Nicholas could just have been doing Jenny a favour in return for goodness knows what – although I thought I could hazard a guess. If that were the case, then presumably there was no involvement on the part of the nutty air-ace; but if it wasn't... what then? There was also the question of what the bloody Aston Martin was doing in Luxembourg in the first place. If Jenny and Stephenson *were* in town, why draw attention to their presence with such a flamboyant vehicle. And if not, why have the car brought there?

To make matters worse, Dean Samson had phoned the previous evening and told me that Mike Nicholas was known to the former

146

guardian of Jenny's Aston Martin because they had once worked together at the Commission. The guardian, Thomas Davenport, had been Commodore Forbes driver before Mike Nicholas and now ran a car-parking and valeting service in the West End.

Then there was Forsythe: to all intents and purposes, an innocent bystander in all this – if you assumed that ETA wasn't guilty of anything. And how *could* they be when they were instructed by our very own government? Well, you see my point, don't you?

The extent and nature of Jenny and Stephenson's involvement also had me dumbfounded. According to Standish, they might merely be couriers; bit part players in some much bigger game. From my point of view – probably because I had no real grasp of how much corruption existed within the European community – I favoured the idea that they were straightforward criminals, defrauding a pseudo-bank of millions of dollars, and now intent on absconding with their ill-gotten gains. Nevertheless, I was beginning to make out the distinctive odour of a whole crate-load of crimson herrings.

I ask you. Wouldn't you have been confused in my position?

In an attempt to ease the stresses on my poor fuddled brain, I took Suze out for a quiet Indian meal that evening; favourite food for both of us. I was struck again by her sudden flowering into adulthood; in the blue summer dress she had bought the previous weekend, she could have passed for mid-twenties. With her new-found self-confidence, maybe even a decade or so older. I also noticed for the first time how many heads turned when she walked into a room. 'Prideful' doesn't even come close to describing how such things can make you feel.

That evening, everything was right with my world.

For once, it was Dud that arrived late the next day, and it didn't need a rocket scientist to work out what he had been up to.

"Lydia fit and well then?"

"Too bloody fit," he groaned, "Where's my coffee? I didn't have time to make one this morning before I left."

We spent a few minutes discussing what we were going to say to Forsythe and then wandered outside in search of a taxi, arriving at ETA's offices fifteen minutes later.

James Forsythe looked tired and haggard when we were shown into his office by Alice, Jenny's erstwhile secretary.

"Ah! Dear boys," his voice sounded as tired as he looked, "What news from the Grand Duchy?"

"Not a great deal, I'm afraid," I said, "But we've got people on the lookout and we've reason to believe that they might well have holed up there." I went on to explain about the Aston Martin, and how we'd made contact with some 'auditors'. I didn't mention Standish, GB or official investigations. "In addition," I concluded, "Dud and I will be going back there ourselves next week to keep an eye on things until the draft becomes valid."

"Oh, well," the big man sighed, "It's progress of a sort. It's rather good of you to keep such a personal involvement going, I must say. If you've got an invoice or whatever on you, I'll get Alice to sort out your fees."

"Er, fine," I nodded, suddenly realising that there was every possibility of Dud and I being paid by both ETA and Standish's organisation for our future presence in Luxembourg. Of course, I could hardly mention that to Forsythe. No, *really* I couldn't; it might let him get wind of the official investigation.

"In the meantime," Forsythe went on, "There's been no further developments here. I'm beginning to agree with your assertion that Jenny and Paul have finished with their activities with us. It's going to be a bugger to replace them though. Come to that, what with all the fuss the Westminster bods are making, we might not have to."

"Is it that bad?"

"Put it this way; our services have been suspended and we don't have any other source of business."

"Ouch. Well, rest assured, we're doing our utmost on your behalf." Sometimes in my line of work you can go days without uttering a single honest word.

"I'm sure you will, dear boys. Now, if you're free, what about a spot of lunch after Alice sorts you out?"

"Actually, I'm afraid we've got rather a lot to get organised," I said, "Maybe next time?"

"Oh, of course. How silly of me."

Forsythe looked almost as relieved as I felt – although I was used to playing less than straight with some clients, I've never enjoyed doing so, and in social situations, it's far too easy to let slip things which would be better left unsaid. We said our goodbyes and went in search of Alice and a nice large cheque.

In the first of the bars Dud and I visited on our way back to Charing Cross, I mentioned the prospect of being paid twice for our efforts.

"It seems a little bit unethical," I pointed out.

"Doesn't worry me," Dud shrugged, "I was born in Kent."

"Pardon?"

"In other words, I've never been an ethics-boy."

2

I spent most of the rest of the week organising our trip back to Luxembourg, a process made very much simpler when Standish called on the Wednesday.

"We've decided that you've been 'officially' seconded to the Commission," he said.

"Which means?"

"Well, since we've now reason to suspect that there might well be some involvement on the part of Commission employees within the British contingent, it seemed like a reasonable idea to base you there. I'm sure you can carry out your work from pretty much anywhere, can't you?"

"Absolutely," I agreed.

"Good. While you're actually there inside the organisation, as it were, you might also be able to keep an eye on what's going on around you. If you don't mind, that is?"

"Not at all." If nothing else, we might be able to glean a little information from Mike Nicholas.

"That's settled then. I'll have a word with Forbes and tell him that you're just using the Commission as cover so that no-one suspects your real motives – not that I'll tell him anything about your real 'real' motives. The old boy loves all that espionage claptrap; hasn't trusted the Germans ever since the Wall came down."

"He does strike me as the type," I laughed.

"Being seconded to the commission has the additional benefit of coming complete with accommodation," he went on, "So you'll not be needing to hole up in a hotel for the duration."

"Good news indeed. I've never been keen on long stays in a single room."

"Splendid. The initial brief will be for four to eight weeks, although, of course, we wouldn't expect you to spend more than a day or two there each week."

"That all?"

"My dear boy," he laughed, "If you work more than a dozen hours or so in any given week, you'd be sure to rouse suspicions; it'd be totally out of character for a Commission employee."

I was left once more feeling that the news media were being vindicated in my own mind for some of their more scandalous claims about the EU.

I relayed the information to a contented Dud, and we arranged to meet up that evening to work out flight schedules, a process, in the *Duke*, that for some reason took several hours.

"Oh. Not again!" Suze sighed when I giggled my way into the house just after ten.

"We were, er, celebrating," I said, following her into the kitchen.

"And now you're as celebrated as a newt. I'm getting really worried at the prospect of you and Dud spending several weeks in one of the major drinking capitals of Europe."

"We won't be there all the time," I said, "We're going to take it in turns to have a couple of days back over here during the stay."

"I'll stock up on Paracetamol then," she grinned, "When are you leaving, by the way?"

"Sunday afternoon. Why? Eager to get rid of your wonderful father?"

She crossed to where I was leaning on one of the counters and gave me a brief hug, recoiling slightly at the whisky fumes, "Not at all. After a few weeks, I might even start to miss you. Pity you couldn't leave it until Monday afternoon, though."

"Why so, my sweet little princess?"

"Well, if you're leaving on Sunday, you won't get to see Terri."

"Despite your best intentions, little one, I'm not really interested." A vision of the Commodore's daughter flashed into my mind – for some strange reason.

"Well you should be," Suze grinned, "I think she's taken a shine to you."

"Who wouldn't?"

"And you call me vain?"

"There's a small difference between vanity and self-honesty," I informed her.

"I've heard that whisky can have this effect on people. I'd better pour you a coffee."

The days leading up to the departure for Luxembourg seemed more like weeks, and I was surprised to find myself eager to get back to the job; fascinated by the intrigue and almost boyishly excited by what Dud and I might find out. With Suze seemingly settled, responsible for herself and constantly happy, I found it surprisingly easy to turn my attention away from her for a while and concentrate on my own life and career. Despite all of that, it was still strange when I finally climbed into the taxi on the Sunday lunchtime.

"Now, there's nothing I've forgotten, is there?" I asked Suze, "You've got access to the bank account, my mobile number, the–"

"Pa!" she groaned, leaning through the open window of the battered Sierra, "I'll be fine. Just make sure you behave yourself over there – and make sure you don't get into any problems with those guys, okay?"

Talk about role reversal. "I'll be okay. Remember, I've got Dud to back me up."

"Pa, that's precisely what *does* worry me," she giggled, "My sympathy goes out to your liver. Now, stop fretting about me and get gone; at this rate you're going to miss your flight."

And, with a final parting kiss, that was me on my way; missing Suze already, but nonetheless eager to get started in the tiny Grand Duchy.

3

The flight was a bumpy, turbulent affair, eased by the generous measures provided from the drinks trolley, and we landed at the tiny airport in good – and plentiful – spirits. Because of our exalted status on secondment to the Commission, we were met at the airport by a driver. I had been hoping that it might be Mike Nicholas himself, but was content anyway, when it turned out to be a pretty young woman who asked to be called 'Bridge'.

"Short for Bridget?" Dud asked.

"No," she grinned, "It's because I'm easy to cross." With her bright red hair, even brighter blue eyes, and a delicate Irish lilt in her voice, I wondered whether she might not be telling the truth. Stereotypes, are, as Suze had recently pointed out to me, based on fact at some level.

We were swiftly driven away from the airport and into town, Bridge keeping up a constant stream of chatter, pointing out places of interest that Dud and I might like to visit during our stay, and we sat back, relaxed and already experiencing a feeling of familiarity with our surroundings. Unfortunately, we were all too familiar with the district Bridge drove us to.

"Er, is this were our apartments are?" I queried.

Bridge took her eyes off the road for a moment to consult a clipboard laying on the front passenger street, "Seems so," she shrugged, "Not the prettiest part of town, that's for sure. Normally, the apartments over here are reserved from the Italians and Belgians. Now, let's see… number 44. There it is." She pulled up by the kerb and pointed to a building next door to what looked like a seedy bar on one side, and the ubiquitous strip club, this one *The Red Pussycat*, on the other.

Shrugging and grimacing, Dud and I clambered from the car and walked across to our new, temporary accommodation. Bridge followed us.

"Your rooms are numbers three and four, on the second story, according to this," she indicated the clipboard, "Seems a bit unusual, I must say. I'll go and get the keys and give you a hand with your bags."

"Perhaps we should have settled on a hotel after all," I said to Dud.

"If this place is anything as bad as it looks, I'm right with you on that score."

"There again," I shrugged, "It's really only somewhere to sleep."

We followed Bridge back to the car and retrieved our bags.

"Don't worry, guys," she smiled, "I'm sure we can sort something else out for you tomorrow; the Commodore's a bit funny about stuff like this. I'll take you to see him in the morning, if you like?"

"That'd be very kind of you," I nodded, trailing back to the front door of the building, "If you're sure it's not too much trouble?"

"Hardly. After all, I am your driver."

"*Our* driver?" Dud and I asked in unison.

"Didn't they tell you?" she said, fiddling the key into the lock, "People on secondment always get drivers."

"Wow," I whistled, "I'm beginning to feel like royalty."

"As long as you don't start treating me as one of your servants, I'm sure we'll get on fine," Bridge's grin broadened, "Now, let's see what's inside, shall we?"

We followed her into the dingy interior, and I was immediately reminded of the little prostitute's place we had visited the last time we were there. Four narrow flights of stairs took us up to a small landing on the second floor and in the gloom we could just make out a door on either side. We set our bags on the threadbare carpet and waited while Bridge found the right keys.

On the way up, Bridge had explained that the 'apartments' were actually 'apart-hotel' rooms – basically studio flats containing a bed, television, cupboards, cooking facilities and a separate bathroom; all of which would be serviced by the staff of the hotel that owned the property. Not quite as glamorous as we had both expected and hoped for, but it was, after all, only somewhere to sleep.

We went into number three first, and Bridge's description of the room was accurate insofar as it contained all the items she had listed. There was indeed a bed; a single bed covered in a couple of moth-eaten blankets with a 'mystery stain' motif, a television that was only slightly too large to wear on a watch strap and which was somewhat dwarfed by the telephone next to it, cupboards aplenty, some even with doors, cooking facilities consisting of two grease-encrusted electric hobs set in a rickety looking worktop, and a bathroom which lacked only a bath.

"Er, lovely," I said.

Bridge grinned, "Yeah, I guess it is a bit grim. I'll definitely be getting you to see the Commodore in the morning. Reckon it'll do for one night, though?"

"I guess so. I'm fairly sure we shouldn't catch anything too nasty in just one night." I crossed the room in three paces and hauled on the large rope that hung by the single window. An external shutter rolled noisily upward, doubling the level of illumination in the room to two candle-power. More light didn't help matters at all. "At least there's a view," I shook my head. The window looked out over a small courtyard, hemmed in on all sides by buildings similar to the one we were in, all of them looking just as shabby. Outside each window was a small balcony, and directly across from where I stood, a young woman wearing only a pair of greying knickers was busily hanging out what to me looked like a black rubber bedsheet.

"I'm really sorry about this, guys," Bridge wrinkled her nose.

"It's hardly your fault. And thanks for picking us up at the airport."

"Don't mention it," she said, "As I told you, it's my job. And talking of picking you up, how about I come back here at about nine tomorrow, or is that too early?"

"That'd be great," I replied. The sooner we could get to see the Commodore and sort out something accommodation-wise, the better.

Bridge gave Dud the keys to number four and then left us to 'not settle in'.

We were back outside on the street within five minutes, and off in search of a much-needed beer or five.

I left Dud in the *Black Bull* at ten and began to make my unsteady way back to the apartments, making a mental note to heed my lovely daughter's warning about Dud's drinking habits. My sense of direction seemed to be playing up, and it took me almost half an hour to find the apartment block. Double checking that I wasn't about to make an unexpected entrance into the *Pussycat*, I fumbled my way into the building and weaved my way up the ancient, narrow staircase. Opening the door to room 3 took considerably longer than it should have done, and I finally heaved an enormous sigh of relief as I stumbled over the threshold and closed the door behind me.

Just a place to sleep, I reminded himself, and only for one night at that. I heaved my unpacked bags off the bed where I had left them, yawned extravagantly and decided that food would have to wait until the morning. In deference to the dubious condition of the bed, I decided undressing was probably not a good idea and I climbed onto the bed fully-clothed. Sleep was my most immediate concern and two minutes later I was snoring gently.

Two *hours* later I woke with a start. At first, I thought there was an animal trapped in the room, one in the depths of deep pain. As my groggy head cleared, I realised that the animal was, in fact, on the other side of the wall by the bed. As it cleared further, I recognised that it was no animal – well not in the four-legged and furry sense, anyway. Evidently the *Pussycat* was open for business, and I was left in no doubt as to what the business entailed. Groaning loudly myself, but in rather a different fashion, I rolled over and buried my head under the pillow. *Just wait 'til the morning*, I told myself. The local brew was still coursing through me however, and within a few minutes I drifted off to sleep, dreaming of two-legged pussycats chasing me, a mouse, through the darkened streets of a strange town. In the morning I couldn't quite work out why I'd had a dream like that. There again, the gigantic hangover didn't let me work much out for an hour or two, anyway.

Dud, looking annoyingly – and surprisingly – fit, let himself into my room at eight thirty, smiling from ear to ear.

"Morning, partner," he greeted me, "All ready to get started?"

"I may never be ready again," I groaned, "I feel as if a small, incontinent rodent spent the entire night resting up in my mouth."

"You'll soon get used to the local brew."

"You honestly believe that I'll ever drink so much as another glassful?"

"I'd bet my share of our reward on it."

"I think Suze was right about you," I sighed.

Bridge arrived promptly at nine, her bright, cheery grin, almost too much for my delicate condition.

"So, you survived, then?" she asked me.

"Barely."

Twenty minutes later, we were shown into Commodore Forbes' office and provided with much-needed coffees. A few minutes after that, the man himself bustled into the room.

"Ah! You made it then," he greeted us, "All in order, old boys?"

Before either of us could reply, Bridge spoke up, "Looks like there's been a bit of a cock-up on the accommodation front, Commodore."

The Commodore looked aghast, "Where on earth did we billet the poor devils?"

"The apart-hotel down at the Gare."

"Oh, I say, young men, I'm most terribly sorry," the Commodore blustered, "We normally reserve that one for the Ities, don't you know?"

"The Commission can move us elsewhere, then?" I asked.

The Commodore was still full of apologies, "*Can!* My poor boys, this really must have been so dreadful for you. Of course we must move you elsewhere. We can't have our distinguished guests from the Mother of All Capitals shacked up next door to a knocking shop! Months of listening to East-European transsexuals practising their new-found fucking techniques! Shambles. Utter shambles." The old man was starting to take on a distinctly puce hue. "Bridge," he turned to the grinning driver, "Get the de-luxe apartment list and take our guests here around the five-star places. The least we can do for the poor blighters."

He turned back to Dud and I again, "I'm really so very sorry," he insisted despite our attempts to placate him, "Won't take more than a couple of days or so before you find ones you want. Let's say we'll meet up again on Wednesday, shall we? Say thirteen hundred hours at the ex-pats club, if that's okay? Bridge'll take you there."

"That's, er, very good of you," I replied, "And Wednesday will be fine."

"Least we can do," the Commodore waved away my gratitude, "Any problems at all just refer them to me," he handed me a grand-looking business card. "And, by the way, make sure you always call me Edwin. That way no one can doubt that you're an honoured guest, don't you know? Sort of a class-thing in the Commission."

"Er, okay, er, Edwin," I agreed.

"Well that's that all settled then," the Commodore said, rubbing his hands together, "Any old how, must dash. Bridge will show you where your office is, won't you m'dear?"

"Certainly, Commodore."

"One final thing, old boys," Forbes went on, "If you can't find anywhere quickly that takes your fancy on the accommodation front, have Bridge bring you over to my place. Plenty of room there, don't you know?"

Before either of us could reply, the Commodore had grabbed his attaché case and strode out of the room.

Bridge laughed, "That went well."

I nodded, "It certainly did. And thanks for bringing up the accommodation thing."

"No problem. As long as you use the right terminology, the old man will respond exactly how you want him to."

"Worth remembering," I nodded at Dud.

"Anyway," Bridge went on breezily, "It's always worth getting his dander up if you've got a hangover. Seems to blast it out of you somehow."

I was suddenly aware that Bridge was right. My hangover had completely disappeared. And so, come to that, had the headache over the accommodation. "He did say five-star, didn't he?"

"Too right he did," Bridge confirmed, "Hang on here for five minutes and I'll go and get the list. I guess you'd like to sort that out before you get settled in your office?"

"Oh, yes!"

"I think we might get to like it here," I suggested to Dud after Bridge had left the room.

He nodded his agreement, "Five-star apartments, two days' work a week, our very own – and very attractive – driver; what more could two young, single guys want?"

To my surprise, a mental image of the Commodore's stunning daughter flashed across my mind's eye, "Not a lot."

Neither Dud or I had much idea what to expect of 'five-star' quality apartments, but any ideas we may have harboured could not have come close to what we were shown. The 'day or two' estimate that the Commodore had given us when referring to how long he thought it'd take us to find somewhere suitable, turned out to be an hour or two. The second building we looked at, turned out to have twin penthouse suites overlooking the gorge in a quiet part of the main town centre. Each of the apartments was fully, stylishly and opulently furnished; two bedrooms with their own bathrooms, a vast kitchen, and a split-level living area with picture windows opening onto a secluded terrace.

Bridge didn't even manage to finish saying *'What do you reckon?'* before both Dud and I said, "We'll take them!"

By lunchtime, we had retrieved our bags from the tatty apart-hotel rooms, and were celebrating our good fortune with champagne that had been thoughtfully provided in the penthouse fridges.

"I could get used to this sort of luxury," Dud sighed happily.

"You're not the only one. Although I'd better not let Suze come and visit while we're here; she'll demand that I get a proper job at the Commission so that we could stay on or something."

"I must admit, the thought has crossed my mind," he grinned.

After our celebration, Bridge drove us to an out-of-town shopping complex where we stocked up on the basic necessities of life; beer, whisky, wine and instant meals, in that order, and we finally returned to the Commission building at four to check out where we'd be working.

Like the apartments, the office proved to be ultra-modern and chock-full of the latest technology. It was also a two-man office; meaning that we could carry on doing whatever we wished without fear of being overseen. It even came with a security lock on the door, so we could put our own equipment in there for the duration, rather than transporting it backwards and forwards.

Standish had left a message for us to contact him on the Wednesday morning, and we reasoned that until then, there wasn't anything else for us to do. I was already beginning to hope that Jenny and Stephenson didn't show up in two weeks' time when the draft became valid, and even if they did, maybe we could persuade Standish to keep us on for the full two months secondment… This was, as they say, the life.

4

"What do you reckon to our lovely little driver?" Dud asked me later that evening.

"Charming little thing. Don't tell me you've forgotten all about the lusty Lydia already?"

"No, no," he said airily, "Just wondering what you thought, that's all."

As I've mentioned before, Dud is nothing if not a lady-magnet. But the sort of magnet that doesn't seem to have the capacity to repel, "Well, as I said, charming. I suppose you're planning on getting to know her a little better, as you so often quaintly put it?"

"The thought might have crossed my mind," he shrugged, his insouciant air evaporating quickly, "I mean, it's not as if me and Lyd are… well, that close."

"You sounded that close in the back of the car the other week," I pointed out, grinning.

"Ah! But that's just physical."

"So you wouldn't want to get *physical* with the lovely Bridge, then?"

"Well, I'd never rule it out."

"There's a word for guys like you," I laughed.

"Handsome? Suave? Debonair?"

"Randy."

Dud began to ply his charms on our driver the very next day, disappearing with her on some trumped-up errand or other, and I was left alone to relax in peace. I decided that some ambulatory exercise might be a good idea, and I set off towards the old town to explore my new, temporary habitat. The simplest way to reach there other than by car, appeared to be across one of the bridges – I certainly wasn't going to tackle the gorge again in a hurry – and I ambled my way across the closest of the two, pausing frequently to take in the stunning scenery.

For a change, my sense of direction didn't fail me, and I was soon crossing the main shopping area in the centre of town, angling towards the cathedral, which I recalled was at the head of the old town. I was just passing a rather grand-looking boutique when a familiar figure emerged from it.

"Er, Hi," I said, "It's Nicola Forbes, isn't it?"

She paused in her stride and turned her elegant features towards me, her emerald eyes seeming even brighter than I had remembered them. Her expression was blank for a moment, and then she frowned, "It is," she said slowly, "I seem to recall your face from somewhere, but I'm afraid I can't quite place it."

"We met briefly at the *Red Lion* last Sunday week," I said, "Pete Cooke; I'll be working at the Commission for a couple of months."

Light dawned and her slightly frosty attitude warmed, "Oh, of course. Daddy mentioned something last night about some high-tech business people who had arrived. A bit of a problem with the accommodation, I hear?"

"There was," I laughed, "But that's all sorted out now. We've moved into the *Monet* Buildings."

One delicate eyebrow rose, "My, you must be important; they're normally reserved for high-ranking government officials. What exactly is it that you do?"

"I run a computer security company; we're seconded to the Commission to undertake a rather hush-hush investigation."

"Sounds fascinating," she rewarded me with a broad smile, "It's your own company, you say?"

"PC Security. My initials are rather handy in my line of work."

"How true. How are you settling in? It must all seem rather strange after London?"

"It's okay, but actually, I don't live in London; I've got a house a few miles outside. It's the best of both worlds in a way."

"Lucky you," she gave a resigned smile, "Since Daddy took this blessed job, I seldom get to go back. I really miss the bright lights at times."

"I can imagine," I sympathised.

She gave a shrug, an amazingly elegant gesture on her tall, lithe frame, "Perhaps you might allow me to show you one or two places that you might find interesting? There are some marvellous restaurants here."

"I'd be delighted." I took a deep breath, "Perhaps I could buy you dinner somewhere soon? Anywhere you like."

"That would be wonderful," she smiled. I nearly let out a whoop of pure delight. "The *Royale* is probably the best restaurant in town, although I'm afraid it's a tad expensive."

"That's not a problem," I assured her, eager to impress.

"Well, how about tonight, if you're at a loose end?"

I couldn't believe either my ears, or my luck, "Perfect!" I nodded, trying my best not to let her see how hard I had to swallow before I said it, "I'm, er, not sure our driver will be available though. Perhaps we could meet at the restaurant?"

"Fine by me. Shall we say, eight? Leave me to book a table; Daddy's name can have its uses."

"I'll be there." I'd probably be there at seven.

"Well, see you later then." She offered me a final radiant smile and strode elegantly away.

Now, obviously, I had only asked her out because there might be some Forbes family involvement in our investigation. Or at least, I remembered that little detail a few minutes later. The rest of my journey into the old town was made much easier by the fact that my feet were barely touching the pavement.

I suffered a slight sense of direction failure on the return journey, but eventually managed to find my way back by four o'clock. Dud arrived *sans* Bridge at the same time.

"Hi, partner," he grinned.

"Hi, yourself. How did it go?"

"Like a dream. She's not long split up with some guy and reckons it's about time she got herself out and about again. We're going out for a drink or two tomorrow night. Talking of which, fancy a beer this evening?"

"I'm afraid I'm already taken," I grinned, "I'm taking Nicola Forbes to the *Royale* for a spot of dinner."

"You're what!? Nicola Forbes as in the stunning, gorgeous, six-foot, I-could-be-a-supermodel-no-problem, daughter of a certain batty ex-RAF type?"

"The very same."

"You lucky bugger. How on earth did you manage to persuade her?"

"You're not the only one with charm around here," I said airily.

"So it seems," he, rather annoyingly, still looked shell-shocked, "I think something about this place seems pretty lucky for us both. Maybe we'll cap it all and pick up our million dollar reward."

"Now wouldn't that be nice?"

I spent the next three hours becoming increasingly nervous at the prospect of the evening ahead; gradually convincing myself that I would behave like a total idiot in front of the elegant, sophisticated and cultured Nicola. Dud, in an effort to boost my morale and calm my nerves, fed me a couple of large whiskies which seemed to help. I could almost light a cigarette without burning my nose by the time I was due to depart.

As I'd earlier predicted, I arrived far too early, and chose to walk around the block in order to waste some time. The restaurant was situated on the ground floor of the grandest hotel in town, and the building backed on to a small, secluded park. Determined not to arrive back at the eatery before five to eight, I took a seat on a bench and lit yet another Marlboro, beginning to fret seriously about what on earth we would talk about over dinner. After the tenth glance at my watch I decided it was time to go and ground out the half-smoked cigarette. A few deep breaths, a hastily crunched mint, a couple of stretches, and I was off.

The maitre d' greeted me in the restaurant's foyer as if I were one of his most respected and regular patrons, and I was quickly ushered through to a table overlooking the small park I'd just come from. I ordered a gin and tonic from an attentive waiter and glanced through the menu while I waited for both the drink and Nicola. There was a wide-ranging spread of fare on offer, and I could well believe Nicola's claim that this was regarded as the best restaurant in town; the prices alone should have guaranteed that.

At five past eight, I was beginning to fret, and was just checking my watch yet again, when I heard her voice from across the quiet room. I looked over at the foyer entrance, and there she was. I'm fairly certain that I stopped breathing.

It's difficult to find words to describe just how stunningly, jaw-slackeningly gorgeous she looked as she stepped into the room. Her dark auburn hair had been left to flow freely over her shoulders, perfectly framing her fine features. She was wearing a long, shimmering green dress, the smallest of straps passing behind her neck, the front low cut, and as she walked towards where I sat, it coruscated in the low lighting, wave upon wave rolling across her tall, slender figure. As she drew closer, I could see that it perfectly matched her emerald eyes as they, too, seemed to shimmer.

At the last moment, I remembered my manners and rose to greet this vision of delight.

"Nicola," I managed to smile, "You look wonderful."

"Why, thank you, Peter," she smiled back, perfectly straight white teeth framed by ruby-red lips.

She sat herself opposite me, affording me the tiniest glimpse of heaven as the top of the dress gaped when she leant forward, revealing an intoxicating nakedness beneath. I sat hurriedly and took a deep breath, still fretting about what subjects we could talk about; where, even to start. Nicola came to my rescue.

"So, Peter," I was favoured with another perfect smile, "You must tell me all about what you do; it sounds absolutely fascinating."

"It can be. But on the other hand, it can be dreadfully dull."

Despite finding it hard to concentrate on what I was saying at times, with Nicola's prompting I told her all about PC Security; how it was going from strength to strength; plans for the future, how I'd got started. The only subject I didn't talk about at length was the current investigation – just mentioning the two fugitives and nothing more.

I went on to talk about my precious Suze, earning myself unstinting praise for my selfless devotion to my daughter, and being told how proud I should be of her. From there we moved on to where I lived and how, despite poor Julie's untimely death, we were able to afford to live well thanks to the insurance and careful investment strategies.

I eventually managed to steer the conversation onto Nicola herself, learning that she was an only child, still unmarried at the age of twenty eight, how she had been educated at numerous private schools as her father traversed the globe in his career, and how, also, that she was desperate to leave the Grand Duchy; a combination of boredom and dislike of the ex-pat lifestyle fuelling her desire.

I was left with the impression that things at home were not particularly pleasant for Nicola. She twice mentioned that her father was an inveterate, and unsuccessful, gambler, and once that her mother took shelter under the influence of alcohol. The Forbes, she told me, were living beyond their means and it was as much this that prevented her return to the UK as the need to watch over her parents, who, she had decided, were not capable of running their own lives.

"I hope they appreciate how kind their daughter is being," I said.

She gave a soft laugh, "They seldom even notice I'm here. Daddy's always off to his precious club, or away at the casino and Mummy… well Mummy's always off somewhere in her own head."

Trying to move on to lighter matters, I diverted her attention by asking her whether she would like a dessert.

"I would *like* one, but I really shouldn't. I have to watch my figure as they say."

"It's well worth watching," I said before realising what I'd been about to say. Before I could apologise, Nicola laughed.

"Why, Peter! How very nice of you to say. It makes a refreshing change for someone to be so open over here. I promise you, a girl can get starved of compliments in this damned place."

Now that I'd begun, there didn't seem much point in stopping, and if Nicola had just been angling for a compliment or two, I thought she deserved them anyway, "I couldn't imagine for a minute that you wouldn't receive your fair share. You're a truly beautiful young lady, and charming with it."

"Very kind," she smiled, "But I rather think that it's you who's the charmer. You're like a breath of fresh air, as well as being wonderful company."

"It's my turn to thank you," I hoped and prayed that she couldn't see the blush that was rising on my cheeks, "Perhaps you'd like a post-prandial brandy or some such?"

"Well, I certainly don't want the evening to end so soon. But perhaps we could go elsewhere, if you don't mind? I find too long in a restaurant can stifle one's mood."

"I quite agree," I replied, "Perhaps you could suggest somewhere, though? I really don't have a clue as to where might be pleasant." I had thought for one giddying second that I should invite her back to the penthouse, but at the last moment decided that it might seem a little obvious. Having apparently made such a good start I didn't want to risk ruining everything by being too pushy.

"Well, there's a small wine bar just a few hundred metres down the street," she suggested, "It's always very quiet in there at this time of night."

"Fine by me," I nodded happily, pleased that Nicola had opted for somewhere quiet.

"If you'll excuse me for a moment, then?" She nodded in the direction of the ladies'" room.

"Of course." Gallant as ever, I rose and rounded the table to pull back her chair. Up close, I could make out her perfume, a heady but gentle fragrance that seemed totally in keeping with the lady herself. She thanked me and shimmered her way across the room, my eyes taking in every detail. When I turned my attention back to my surroundings in search of our waiter, I noticed that at least half a dozen men had been staring after Nicola. 'Smug' doesn't come close to the feeling I experienced right then.

By the time Nicola returned, I had paid the bill and we made our way into the foyer where I collected my jacket, and Nicola a tiny handbag and a small silk wrap which she draped over her shoulders. Outside, the night air was still balmy, and a gentle breeze had sprung up. Nicola led me slowly towards the wine bar and when we crossed the main street, she took my hand. Our fingers were still entwined when we reached our destination, and I was almost reluctant to let go, wanting to savour any contact, no matter how slight.

As in the restaurant, Nicola steered the conversation along, seemingly comfortable and at ease with herself and with me. She sipped cognac to my whisky, although for all I knew, I could have been drinking hemlock, such was my attention diverted by her. Nicola's voice had an almost mesmeric quality, the tones rich and deep, scaling down to an almost cat-like purr at times. And all the while, those beautiful emerald eyes held me entranced.

It was well past midnight before we knew it, the time flying past unnoticed as we talked and talked and talked.

"Sorry," I smiled when we realised what the time was, "I didn't mean to keep you out quite so late."

"Don't be silly. If I had my way, I'd not let the evening end at all. And, anyway, it's not me that has to go and work at that horrible place tomorrow."

I double-checked to make sure she really had said that she didn't want the evening to finish before I made any further comment, "It has been wonderful, hasn't it?" I tried to keep a note of hopefulness out of my voice.

"Absolute heaven."

My confidence at an all-time high, I posed the question that had been uppermost in my mind for some time, "If you'd like to, perhaps we can do it again? Or something different maybe?"

"I was rather hoping you'd ask," she smiled, "You've really cheered me up, you know?"

"I'm glad. Can I give you a call tomorrow, maybe? Or rather, today, given what time it is now?"

"Any time, Peter. I'll give you my mobile number."

With slightly tremulous fingers on my part we exchanged the details.

We left the bar and, emboldened, I took her right hand in my left. To my relief she grasped it firmly, and we walked back towards the restaurant where, she said, there would be a few taxis so that she could get home safely. Just before we reached the *Royale*, she slowed her pace and then stopped completely, turning to face me.

"Thank you again, Peter, for a wonderful evening," she said softly.

Just as when she had first walked into the restaurant, I could feel my heart freeze in my chest. "It should be me thanking you," I said, my throat drying up.

Her left hand found my right, and after the tiniest of hesitations, she leaned forward and gently kissed me. Slowly we moved closer, our hands slipping behind each other's backs, until finally our bodies were pressed tightly together, her firm breasts pushing at my chest. The embrace might have lasted ten seconds or ten minutes, but whatever the length of time, it certainly wasn't long enough. When we parted it, breathlessly, I felt a profound sense of loss.

"A wonderful way to end a wonderful evening," she smiled.

"I couldn't agree more."

"I'd... better get going."

The hesitation seemed to suggest that there was something she wasn't saying, but once again, I didn't want to push too hard, "I'll call you tomorrow," I promised instead.

"I'll have my phone in my hand," she gave a soft laugh.

We resumed our journey back to the restaurant, our steps even slower than before, both of us trying not to think about the parting of the ways that would soon follow, savouring each other's company. When we reached our destination we embraced once more.

"You won't forget to call?" Nicola smiled as we parted.

"Do you honestly think I could?"

I followed her over to the nearest taxi and held the door open for her as she climbed into the back. She did this as she seemed to do everything else; with a grace and elegance that were a pure joy to behold. Before I could close the door, she leaned towards me for a goodnight kiss, the top of her dress gaping once more in a manner which seriously threatened to send my blood pressure through the roof. I kissed her gently, savouring every second and already looking forward to the next time.

The driver coughed politely, and Nicola and I moved apart, smiling broadly, both once more a little breathless.

"Until tomorrow," she said.

"Until tomorrow."

I watched the taxi drive away with a mixture of pure elation and a crushing sense of loss.

5

"So, how'd it go?" Dud greeted me on the Wednesday morning.

"Like a dream." My smug smile, now some eight hours old, was still firmly in place.

"Details?"

"Great meal, wonderful conversation, a few drinks and a goodnight kiss, okay?"

"Sounds like a good start," he nodded, "Seeing her again?"

"You're worse than Suze! But, yes, I will be."

"Good for you, she's one gorgeous looking lady."

"You should have seen her last night."

Despite my supposed reluctance to go into details, I guess I must have bored Dud rigid on our way into the Commission. Even Bridge, who had picked us up at nine, seemed to find the subject tiresome after a while.

"So," she interjected as I was trying to describe the exact colour of Nicola's eyes, "Will you be needing me to ferry you around anywhere today?"

"We're lunching with the Commodore at one," Dud told her, clearly happy to change topics, "And we should be finished at the Commission around four, I'd guess."

"I'll be there," Bridge assured us.

When we arrived, she helped us ferry our equipment along to our office, and then handed us each a pager which meant that we could summon her whenever we wanted. I truly *was* beginning to feel like royalty.

The first task of the day was to call Standish and he answered the phone on the second ring.

"Standish," he announced.

"Hi. It's Pete Cooke, you left a message for me to call you."

"Indeed I did and thanks for doing so. Actually, I'd rather we met face to face so that I can fill you in on the details of what we need you to do. I'm not saying that the phone lines are bugged or anything – although, of course, I'd never rule that possibility out – but I think it would be simpler if I could show you a few things."

"Sounds sensible. When and where?"

"As far as 'when' goes, the sooner the better as far as I'm concerned. Are you free this morning?"

"Until we get the details from you, we're free all the time."

"Splendid," Standish went on, "I've taken up temporary lodgings in an office in the town centre; number 12 *rue des Bains*. Your driver will know where it is."

"I guess we can be along in about an hour," I said.

"Marvellous! See you shortly, then."

I rang off and told Dud the news.

"I'll page Bridge," he nodded.

Our driver arrived less than five minutes later. "I knew I shouldn't have given you guys pagers," she grinned.

"Sorry–" I began, but she quickly interrupted me.

"Don't apologise. It's great having something to do for a change."

"Mike Nicholas said that it could be pretty boring."

"Mike?" Bridge laughed, "Just recently he's been charging around like some blue-arsed fly."

"Oh? I thought he only drove for the Commodore?"

Bridge shrugged, "That's true, but apparently the old boy keeps sending him off on errands all over the place."

I looked across at Dud who was frowning thoughtfully, "Remind me to bring the subject up over lunch."

"I most certainly will," he nodded.

"Now," Bridge said, "Where do you need me to take you?" I showed her the address. "I know the place alright. Follow me then guys, you'll be there in fifteen minutes."

We were there in ten and Bridge told us that she would be parked around the corner when we were finished. In the meantime she was going to get herself a coffee. Still marvelling at the luxury of having our very own personal chauffeur, we made our way into the ancient building.

The modernity of the interior was at complete odds with the somewhat shabby external appearance, and we were quickly shown through to an almost space-age room by a cheerful receptionist. Standish joined us a couple of minutes later.

"So, down to business," he announced after a round of handshakes and welcomes. He opened a filing cabinet drawer and pulled out three thick dossiers, setting them on a broad desk. "In here are the names and numbers of all the banks in Luxembourg to which we have no direct access," he explained, pointing to the first file, "As I said to you before, what I'd like you to do is... gain entry into their systems so that we can

170

monitor activity." He moved the file to one side and opened the second, "This file contains the names and details of various persons who we suspect of being involved with illegal payments and so forth. Clearly these first two files need to be crossed linked according to what you manage to find out. Oddly to some, we do not keep computerised records because of the threat of... external access. With me so far?"

"Basically, you're asking us to find out whether anyone named in the second file has accounts with the banks in the first one, and, if so, check out any unusual activity within those accounts?" I summarised.

"Absolutely," Standish nodded, "Do you think that will take very long to set up? There's roughly twenty names and the same number of banks."

"Less than a day if we're on form. The monitoring devices that we'll be using look after themselves. We'll only need to check them occasionally."

"Splendid. And so on to the third one. This one," he pointed to the last file, "Contains all the information we've managed to gather about Winter and Stephenson. I was rather hoping that the additional background information might assist you in your investigations. There's been no new developments since you called me last time, and I take it you haven't heard anything more yourselves?"

"That may not be the case," I said, going on to tell him what Bridge had said to us earlier concerning Mike Nicholas.

"Very strange," Standish said when I'd finished, "I'll have Duncan Pressman check out things a little further."

"Your man on the street?"

"That's the boy. Okay, any questions?"

"Other than when should we contact you next, I don't think so. Anything spring to mind, Dud?"

He shook his head, "All seems fairly straightforward to me."

"That's good. As far as when I expect to hear from you, that's pretty much up to you guys. As long as you let me know when you've got the monitoring devices set up, and any information concerning our rogues gallery, here, I'll be happy to leave everything to you."

171

"Wonderful," I nodded, "We'll get straight on to it. I should think we'll have some basic information for you later this week."

"I look forward to it."

Two minutes later we were back out on the street, burdened down by the three thick files. "Sounds like a piece of cake," Dud grinned.

"That should be 'gateau' – we're in Europe now."

Back in our office, we went straight to work; Dud concentrating on gaining access to the systems, me setting up the monitoring and scanning software we would be using. By the time we left for lunch, we were halfway through the preliminary part of the task already.

When we arrived, the Commodore was in a mood best described as effervescent.

"Ah! My dear boys, so good to see you! Welcome, welcome!"

We shook the proffered hand and took seats next to him at the bar.

"Everything sorted out on the old accommodation front?"

"Perfectly, thanks," I replied.

"Splendid, splendid. What will you have to drink?"

Dud and I both ordered beers and the Commodore a large malt whisky. I didn't know about Dud, but I was fairly certain that I was going to need some fortification for the hour or so to come.

"So," the old gent went on when we all had drinks, "A little dickey-bird tells me that you and my daughter were spotted on the town last night?"

"Er, yes, we had a meal and a few drinks," I nodded, uncertain as to how the Commodore would react.

"Marvellous news. She's been moping around the place for weeks now; it was a real treat to see her smile for a change this morning, don't yer know?"

"That's good to hear," I said, truly delighted with the tidings.

"Just what she needs, I reckon," the Commodore went on happily, "A good seeing to always sorts the girlies out, what?"

It was all I could do not to spray a mouthful of beer across the bar. A few coughs later, I managed to find my voice, "Well, we're not... er, that close," I said, desperation in my tone, "I mean, we've only just met and all that."

172

"Oh, of course," the Commodore nodded, putting on a serious face, "But if I was you, I'd get a move on, what! She a stunning looker; half the chaps in Luxembourg have been sniffing around her."

Dud grinned at me, "Well, Luxembourg's only a little country."

I gave him a stern look, "Yes, well. I guess we'll just see how things go."

My further blushes were spared by the arrival of GB, who sauntered over to join us. After another round of greetings, welcomes and drinks, the subject was turned to work.

"Settled into your new office, lads?" GB asked.

"Yes, thanks," I nodded, "It's great; everything we need."

We went on to discuss the investigation and what we thought our chances were of apprehending Jenny and Stephenson, steering well clear of any mention of possible accomplices since one of them was present. When the Commodore excused himself for a couple of minutes to make a phone call, GB immediately brought up Mike Nicholas' name.

"Duncan Pressman has been asked to keep a very careful eye on what the old man's driver is getting up to," he said, "Standish reckons that his involvement is probably the chink in their armour that we're looking for."

"He's that convinced that Forbes is somehow involved?" I asked.

"And getting more so by the day. It seems the Commodore has been acting even stranger than usual up at the Commission recently. And of course, he's known to be rather heavily in debt at the moment."

"Nicola did say something about them living beyond their means. He's a bit of a gambler, by all accounts."

"A bit!" GB laughed, "Not only is that a gross understatement, it also doesn't bring home the point that he's completely hopeless to boot. Standish had a quiet word with the casino owner the other night, and he reckoned that the Commodore has never left the place in profit."

"It would certainly provide a motive for any involvement," I said.

"Our thoughts exactly," GB agreed, "Mind you, that's one useful thing about this place."

"What is?"

"Well, you see, gambling is illegal in this country. Unless you want to travel miles across the border, the casino's the only place where the old boy can go."

"Easy to keep tabs on him then?"

"And with the right words in the right ears, easy to find out how much he's losing."

"What sort of figures are we looking at?"

"Just recently, about a thousand a night – a thousand Sterling, that is."

"Christ!" I whistled softly, "Just at a casino?"

"Did somebody mention the casino?" Forbes asked, re-joining us.

"Er, yes," I replied quickly, "GB was just saying it's the only place for miles where you can have a flutter."

"It most certainly is," the Commodore nodded, "Perhaps I might be able to interest you in an evening or two down there?"

"Maybe." I'm not, nor ever have been a gambler, but I reasoned that it might be an idea to keep a close eye on the old man. You never knew, maybe after a few drinks and a few losses, he might just let something slip. Out of the corner of my eye, the nod that I saw GB give indicated that he was of the same opinion. "I'll probably have an evening free next week." I said.

"I'll sort something out then," the Commodore nodded happily, "In the meantime, you'll no doubt be busy with m'girl, what?"

"Well, I, er—"

GB came to my rescue, "Anyone know what the dish of the day is; I'm starving?"

The rest of the lunchtime passed without further embarrassment, although I was still pretty relieved when Bridge arrived to take us back to the Commission.

Back in our office, Dud decided that he needed to talk to Bridge for a few minutes and left me to my own devices. Uppermost in my mind most of the day had been an image of Nicola, and I reached for the phone the second the door closed behind my partner. She really must have been holding on to her phone as she had said she would be, answering on the second ring.

"Nicola Forbes," she announced.

"Hi, Nicola, it's Pete."

"Peter! How lovely!" Her voice was doing strange things to my knees.

"Well, I thought I'd better call to thank you for a wonderful evening, and see if we couldn't do something similar, maybe this evening?"

"It's me that should be thanking you," she said, "And as for this evening, I'm all yours. When would you like to meet up?"

I just *had* to sit down. "Any time at all." I was grinning from ear to ear, "I'll be finished here about four."

"Well, how about we meet up in the wine bar we went to last night, say eight?"

"That sounds perfect. Do you want to go on somewhere to eat, or anything?"

She laughed, "I had to endure another of Celestine's luncheons a couple of hours ago. I may never have to eat again, but if you want to—"

"No, that's fine," I said quickly, "I've just got back from your father's club, and I must say, their portions are rather generous."

"So they are. How was Daddy?"

"In high spirits."

"Oh, dear! Poor you," Nicola laughed, "I promise it doesn't run in the family."

"I'm glad to hear it."

"Well, until tonight, then."

"Can't wait."

I rang off, the stupid grin still firmly in place, and decided to call Suze; anything to stop me getting too overexcited about the prospect of the evening ahead.

"Suze's knocking shop," she answered gaily.

"Suze!"

"Hi, Pa!" she giggled, "Don't worry, I knew it was you."

I breathed a huge sigh of relief, "I do wish you wouldn't do things like that to your poor father."

"With two incomes these days, you're anything but poor. But how are you settling in?"

"Wonderfully. We've both got very, er, nice apartments and the office is well kitted-out."

"Meet any nice young ladies yet?"

"Er, well—"

"You have, haven't you?" she interrupted, "Talk about a fast worker. You sly old fox, you."

"I am neither sly nor old! And anyway, we only had a meal together."

"What's she like, then?" Suze asked eagerly.

"Gorgeous, witty and charming," I sighed, resigned to discussing my love-life – or what I hoped to be my love-life – with my precious princess.

"Just like me, then?"

"No! She's not nearly so nosy. But enough about me, what about you? Missing me like crazy?"

"Who did you say you were again?"

"Your extraordinarily long-suffering father!"

"Oh, right! Tall, good looking guy with no sense of humour. Yeah, I've been missing you."

"Likewise," I shook my head, an altogether different kind of grin on my face now, "You're okay though?"

"Of course I am," she said more seriously, "Donna came over yesterday, and she's going to be staying here for a few days."

"That's nice," I smiled at the receiver, "And I promise I won't call you too early in the mornings."

"No need. School starts back next week, so we're trying to condition ourselves for early starts."

"Practical as ever. Anyway, as long as you're okay – both of you, that is – then I'll leave you be. I love you, princess."

"More than life itself?"

"Much more."

"Then the feeling's mutual. Have fun with your new friend, and I'll speak to you soon."

She really is *so* delightful. Well, most of the time, anyway.

I was just hanging up when Dud returned, his own grin suggesting that he and Bridge were getting on well.

"Was that the lovely Nicola?" he asked.

"The lovely Suze. I spoke to Nicola just before, though. We're off out again tonight."

"Good man! So are Bridge and I. Apparently she knows some great clubs."

"Good man, yourself," I grinned, "But in the meantime, we'd better get on with the work. The sooner we get the basic set-up done, the sooner we can get going."

"True, partner. With a bit of luck we can start the searches and the scans tomorrow. Standish should have his info by the end of the week, as promised."

By the time Bridge came to collect us at four, we were pretty much finished, and content in the knowledge that we were well on schedule. She drove us back to the *Monet* building and left to prepare herself for her evening out with Dud, promising to return at seven to collect him.

6

To distract myself from thoughts of Nicola and the evening in store, I made myself a light snack and spent an hour luxuriating in the vast tub that occupied almost half of one of the bathrooms.

Dud knocked on my door just before seven and I let him in, leaving it open so we could hear Bridge when she arrived.

"Looking good, my man," he grinned at me.

I'd chosen black chinos and a jet-black shirt for my date – a look that has Suze running from the room, screaming – and was feeling far less nervous than I'd anticipated. Dud, on the other hand, was wearing his 'club-look', which basically consisted of leather trousers, a silk shirt and a lightweight cotton jacket with its sleeves rolled back. Despite being the same age as me, he could easily have passed for a decade younger and, whether you believe it or not, doesn't look at all sad dressed that way, "Not looking so bad, yourself."

Right on cue, the downstairs buzzer sounded, and Dud used my door release mechanism to let Bridge into the building. Unlike Dud and I, who always used the lift, Bridge came up the stairs, leaving me marvelling at her fitness. The transformation in her appearance was breath-taking.

Gone were the plain black trousers and white shirt that seemed to be a sort of uniform among the Commission's drivers, and in its place was a simple blue dress, its top low-cut, its skirt extremely short. Her curly red hair, normally tied back by day, had been let loose and tumbled over her shoulders, and, for the first time since we'd first seen her at the airport, she was wearing make-up; a little eye-shadow and mascara, and a high-gloss lipstick. The overall effect was, quite simply, stunning.

I could tell that Dud felt the same way by the position of his lower jaw – somewhere close to his waist.

Bridge gave an embarrassed laugh, blushing at our reactions, "I take it you approve?"

"Oh, yes!" Dud breathed.

"Who wouldn't?" I grinned, "You look lovely."

"Why thank you, kind Sir," she laughed, and to Dud, "Shall we?"

Taking her proffered hand, he nodded enthusiastically, "We most certainly shall."

They left quickly, and I'd have bet a lot of money on Lydia never once crossing Dud's mind the entire evening. I checked my watch and decided that a small whisky was in order – purely medicinal, of course – and after pouring a measure with slightly trembling hands, switched on the TV to see what was available in the way of channels. It turned out that there were more than eighty to choose from including, somewhat incongruously, I though, Channel 5 from the UK. More surprisingly there were three channels showing nothing but porn; not particularly soft porn at that. I didn't know whether to admire the openness of Europeans when it came to matters of sex or feel rather offended at having that sort of material beamed directly into living rooms all over the Continent. I've never been a great lover of pornography in general unless there was an element of humour involved; the humour that is inherent in the very act. This sort of material that I was seeing now simply bordered on pathetic with all the rapturous looks and meaningful groans. I smiled at my own ambivalence and checked my watch once more, finally deciding that if I took a very slow stroll, I wouldn't arrive too early.

Outside, another hot, sunny day had left the early evening air temperature once again balmy, and I was glad that I'd left early, enjoying the unseasonable warmth and the lush fragrances rising from the vegetation in the gorge. The wine bar, *Rico's*, was almost deserted when I arrived at ten to eight, and I settled myself at the bar where I could keep an eye on both the door and the ornate clock hanging above it.

At exactly one minute past the hour, Nicola arrived, and I found myself stunned once more by how beautiful she looked. That night she was wearing a dress not dissimilar to the one I'd seen Bridge wearing an hour earlier, low-cut, loose and summery, with a short skirt, showing off long shapely legs to the maximum effect. She crossed to where I was by now standing, delighting me further by greeting me with a warm kiss.

"Hi, Nicola!" I grinned, quickly taking in a couple of envious looks from two young men at a nearby table.

"Hello, Peter," she smiled back, "I've been looking forward to that moment all afternoon."

"You're not alone in that. What can I get you to drink?"

I'd not been quite so nervous about conversational gambits that evening, and I needn't have worried at all since Nicola once again led the way. We talked about similar subjects as the previous night; my work and family, her life in the Duchy, but this time in more detail, perhaps feeling comfortable enough to share a few of our deeper feelings.

After a couple of hours in *Rico's* we moved on to a small club, the atmosphere livelier, and watched a local band play a long set of soft-rock classics, happy to discover that we shared similar tastes in music. Nicola then took me to another wine bar, larger than *Rico's* but somehow even cosier. We stayed there until after midnight.

"I guess we'd better be making a move soon," Nicola sighed.

"I suppose you're right," I nodded, "But maybe–"

"Maybe a night-cap?" she said almost in unison.

179

Laughing, I nodded, "Sounds like a fine idea. Anywhere in mind?"

Nicola shrugged gracefully, "Let's have a stroll and see if we come across somewhere suitable?"

"Lead on."

I'd not been paying much attention to our surroundings or where we'd been, content to devote as much of my focus as I could on my companion, but once outside, I realised I knew the area we were in.

"I've just made out where we are," I laughed.

Nicola raised one of her eyebrows, "I would have thought you might," she smiled.

I looked around for a second or two and then nodded to my left, "The *Monet* building is are just around that corner, I think."

"You're probably right."

Heart beginning to race, I took a deep breath, "Since we're that close... maybe you might like to come back for a last drink there?"

"A lovely idea. Although I really shouldn't stay too long."

"Of course not!" I said, maybe a little too loudly, "Just a, er, that is, the one drink."

If she was aware of how suddenly uncomfortable I felt she didn't show it. Taking my hand, she said, "Let's see how good your sense of direction is then."

For a change, it turned out to be spot-on, and we arrived at the front door less than two minutes later. The key stuttered against the back-plate for a couple of seconds before I finally managed to insert it in the lock, and I realised that I suddenly felt two decades younger than I really was. We took the elevator to the top floor and stepped out onto the landing.

"The penthouse suites," Nicola said admiringly, "You *are* privileged."

"More privileged because you're here," I said, carefully inserting the keycard into my front door.

"Charmer," she laughed.

Once inside, I poured us both drinks and set them on the coffee table in front of one the living area's two large sofas. Nicola was standing at the picture windows, staring out across the town, and I crossed the room to join her, placing my right hand on the bare flesh of her shoulder. She turned to face me, her green eyes capturing mine in an instant. Without a word she pulled me tightly against her, our mouths meeting eagerly.

The embrace was passionate in the extreme, tongues probing, bodies press tightly together, hands roaming necks, backs and lower still. I let my right hand slip down to the hem of her dress, and then up and underneath the soft material. At first I thought she was wearing nothing at all under it, until my hand brushed across the tiny strip of material at her waist. If her breasts were firm and hard against my chest – and, believe me, they were – then my erection against her belly must have felt like rock.

After what seemed like the longest time, Nicola pulled back slightly, her face flushed, her breathing heavy. Those emerald green eyes were wide open, the pupils dilated, and I felt an instant of vertigo, as if I could drop straight into those two green pools, maybe never to surface. The slight parting of our bodies allowed me to raise my left hand to her bare shoulder, before sliding it slowly downwards, softly cupping her right breast through the flimsy material of her dress. As I softly caressed the firm mound, its nipple pressing hard into my eager palm, Nicola groaned loudly, a cross between the purr of a cat and the cry of a large bird.

"Oh, Peter!"

I let my hand wander back up to her shoulder, and slowly but slowly, eased the single small strap across to her arm, leaning in to kiss her once more as I did so. I repeated the process with my other hand before moving apart, letting the top of the dress side down to her waist. I let my eyes travel downwards to her now-naked breasts, perfectly proportioned, firm and pert. After my eyes, my hands; relishing every tiny square millimetre of contact, the softness, smoothness, the underlying firmness. I could feel Nicola's heartbeat against the inside of my right wrist and it felt as frantic as my own which was hammering so hard in my own chest, that I feared for the safety of my ribs.

At the first touch of bare flesh on bare flesh, Nicola's groans had increased in intensity, and as I let my lips follow the course so recently taken by my eyes and hands, they intensified still. Suddenly, she let out a more urgent sound, almost a yelp, and I straightened.

"Oh, Peter," she groaned, "I... I'm sorry." She must have seen my look of bafflement because she continued quickly, "I really shouldn't have let it come this far, this quickly. I... Please? Could we just sit and have that drink now?" She pulled the top of her dress back to her shoulders and I stepped quickly backwards.

"I'm sorry," I began to apologise, "I thought–"

She interrupted me by placing a hand on each of my cheeks, "Don't apologise," she instructed, "It's not you, I promise."

Still bemused, I let her lead me to the sofa, and sat quietly beside her while she seemed to be working out what to say. Finally, she began, "I... used to be a little... promiscuous, shall we say?" Her eyes were fixed firmly on the rug in front of her, "A few years ago, I made a promise to myself that I wouldn't allow myself to be like that again; that I wouldn't let a man get... that close, that fast. It's really nothing to do with you, Peter," she implored, finally looking at me, "You're... clearly someone very special, I just want to... be true to myself, I suppose you could say. I'm really terribly, terribly sorry. Can you ever forgive me?"

"There's nothing to forgive and nothing to apologise for. If there's one thing I've learned as I've grown older, it's that self-respect is a terribly undervalued thing these days. Don't apologise, because there's no need. If anything, this just makes me respect you all the more." That's what I told her and that's exactly what I meant. Aching balls or not.

"You're sure?"

"Nicola," I took her chin in one hand, staring directly into those wonderful, wondrous eyes, "You're a remarkable young lady, and I'm not about to do anything that might injure your self-pride or your self-respect."

"Thank you." She seemed satisfied with my veracity, "I... I'm glad you understand. I'll know... when the time feels right. In some ways it feels right now, but..."

"But, nothing," I smiled, "Everything should feel right for you. No buts at all."

She pulled me to her in a tight embrace, kissing me deeply. After a few moments, she pulled back and managed to smile, "You're a very understanding man, you know?"

"Thank my daughter for that. Until you've looked after a teenage daughter for a few years, you'll never really know the true meaning of understanding."

"Is she very much like you?"

I thought for a moment. "Physically, more like her mother, but I guess in some ways she does take after me."

"I'd really like to meet her."

"And I guarantee she'd love to meet you," I laughed, "She seems to take an inordinate interest in my personal affairs these days."

The tension that had sprang up between us a short while before, dissipated as quickly as it had arrived, and by the time Nicola left half an hour later, we were as relaxed as we'd ever been before.

I went to bed that night a very happy bunny. Make that, a very happy *frustrated* bunny; I'm only human, after all.

7

The next morning, feeling surprisingly refreshed despite the late night, I crossed the landing to Dud's apartment and knocked loudly, wondering whether he'd even made it back. I guess I shouldn't have been too surprised when Bridge opened the door, but it still took me a moment or two to remove the look of shock from my face.

"Oh, er, hi," I smiled.

"Hi, yourself," Bridge grinned, "And just so we don't have any confusion over the issue, yes, it is exactly what you think. Come on in."

I followed her into the room.

"Coffee?" she offered.

"Please."

"Dud's in the shower," she informed me, pouring us both a mug, "Don't get the wrong idea about me now, will you? I don't normally jump into bed with guys on a first date. Your partner's something a bit special though."

"He is that." I almost added that I was beginning to think that Bridge herself was, as well, but since all she was wearing – and, yes, you could tell – was one of Dud's plain white T-shirts, I thought that any compliments might give the wrong impression.

Bridge must have realised that she was somewhat underdressed – or noticed that I was studiously keeping my eyes raised to her face – because she blushed and looked down at the near-transparent T-shirt. "Oops! Guess I'd better get something a bit more decent on." She quickly set down her mug and scurried into the nearest bedroom.

I settled onto the sofa, sipping at the coffee, and wondered at Dud's innate ability to attract beautiful young women. Reflecting on my recent good fortune in that direction, I was beginning to think that maybe some of his magic was rubbing off on me.

Bridge emerged swaddled in one of Dud's dressing gowns, and I was sent down to the car to retrieve a bag from the boot which, she explained, contained a spare change of clothes for when she had long distances to drive. I returned to find Dud yawning loudly, a satisfied grin on his face. I handed the bag and the car keys to Bridge, and she went back to the bedroom.

"Lucky man," I smiled at the still-yawning Dud.

"Wonderful isn't she? What about yourself?"

"Pretty good, to be honest. Nicola came back for a while last night." Okay, it might have been a slightly misleading thing to say, but it wasn't an out-and-out lie, was it?

"Good for you," he grinned, "Perhaps it's something in the air over here?"

"Knowing you, it's more likely to be something in the beer."

The journey into the office was conducted in a mood not far removed from euphoria, the car containing what must have looked from outside, three identical broad grins, and nothing much else. That first Thursday promised to be the hardest day's work we would do while we were in Luxembourg, and one that had to be undertaken with the maximum levels of concentration and diligence. We told Bridge that we wouldn't be stopping for lunch and that we would be finished no earlier than five – our most optimistic estimate; we would page her when we'd finally completed our tasks.

This was work that Dud and I enjoyed, and the area in which we had the most expertise. I won't even try to pretend that we're the best in our field, but I wouldn't be being totally honest if I didn't say we weren't a damn sight better than most people. Breaking into corporate computer systems is not nearly as difficult as many people – including computer system managers – believe it to be; it's what you are able to do once you're in that separates the good security people – and hackers, come to that – from the mediocre.

The previous day, Dud had established gateways into the account systems of the nineteen banks that Standish had both targeted and furnished details of; he had effectively logged us on as ordinary users with supervisory capacities. While Dud had been busily setting up these links, I had been modifying our patented, copyrighted scanning software – in our jargon, a search engine which could be adapted to browse through any number of proprietary databases for pre-determined information; in this case, seeking out any bank accounts that might belong to the twenty-two named people in the second file Standish had given us. Although there are any number of software packages available in our particular market, the one Dud and I had devised on our own held two distinct advantages over those others: firstly, it was far more easily customisable, thereby reducing the time it took to set it up for any given task, and secondly, and certainly more importantly, there were no defences available against it since it was unknown to the world at large.

Perhaps I should add that there's a third advantage. There is, of course, *one* company that can establish adequate protection against PC Security's wonderful piece of software – who else but PC Security?

When we started out that morning, we were still unaware of the overall volume of data that would need to be scanned through, but we had estimated that there would be somewhere in the region of one million accounts of various types across all of the banks. By six that evening, we were somewhat surprised to find that the figure was close on three times that number. Nevertheless, out magical software had completed its first task – determining the account numbers of twenty-one of the twenty-two suspects. We recorded all of the information for Standish and then spent another hour resetting the software so that it would only monitor activity in the thirty-plus accounts that belonged to the named people, along with checking any new accounts being opened.

At eight, we sat back, the last connection established.

"Shit, that was hard work," Dud groaned.

"Think of the money," I suggested, "And besides, all we need to do now is keep an eye on the system from time to time."

"True. And I guess it's me who takes the first watch. I'll come in tomorrow morning and maybe pop back at close of business."

"Good man. I'll go and see Standish with what we've found out so far." I reached over to the laser printer and pulled a stack of sheets of paper from its tray. "There's some pretty weird stuff here," I frowned, scanning through the data.

"Such as?" Dud peered over my shoulder.

"For a start, the volumes involved. We're looking at millions and millions here; Dollars at that. *And* most of the activity seems to centre on just one of the banks."

"Looks like Standish really is on to something. Maybe that's why that particular bank haven't been co-operative with him?"

"I'd bet a lot of money on it," I laughed, "Perhaps you could download details of any other accounts they've got where activity is high volume?"

"My very thoughts, Sherlock," he grinned, scribbling a reminder to himself, "And talking of my thoughts–"

"Beers all round."

"I bet that didn't take too much deductive reasoning."

Dud paged Bridge while I called Nicola to tell her that I'd be free for lunch the next day if she was interested. I was still talking quietly to her when Bridge arrived to collect us.

"I just hope Daddy behaves himself," she was saying when the door opened.

We had arranged to meet at the ex-pats' club the next day, where she had promised to go for lunch with the Commodore, "I'm sure he will," I said. I signalled to Dud and Bridge that I was almost finished, ignoring Dud's lascivious grin, "I can be there a bit earlier if you like? Maybe we could have a quiet drink together before he arrives?"

"Now that *is* a good idea. Is twelve too early?"

"Five minutes from now wouldn't be too early, but I guess I can force myself to wait until then."

"I know what you mean. See you tomorrow then."

"You most certainly will," I promised before ringing off.

Although I'd much rather have had a cosy lunch alone with Nicola, the ex-pats' club would at least give me the opportunity to have a quiet word or two with her father, and there was also a chance that the elusive Mike Nicholas might make an appearance. Happy that the business of the day was finished, and that I'd be seeing Nicola in less than sixteen hours' time, I turned my attention back to the present and grinned at Bridge and Dud.

"Time for that beer, I reckon."

"I reckon you two deserve it," Bridge said, "I think you've probably set a new record at the Commission for time worked in a single day."

"From what I hear," Dud said, "We've probably set a record for an entire year."

"Come to think of it, you may be right," she nodded, "Anyway, where do you fancy?"

"You're the local expert," Dud shrugged.

"Just drop me off close to home, and I'll leave you two to go wherever you want," I told them.

"Oh, no you won't," Dud shook his head, "Okay with you Bridge?"

"Of course," she rolled her eyes, "Besides, it'll do my street cred no harm at all to be seen with a good-looking guy on each arm."

"One arm, anyway," Dud nodded.

"Well if you're sure?" I shrugged. To be honest, I wasn't in the mood for drinking alone.

"We are," Bridge insisted, "Now let's get going before you dehydrate. Have you eaten at all today?"

We'd had two monster salads delivered to the office at five and I pointed to the nearly empty plates, "Not that long ago."

"So we just need to concentrate on the other major food group," Dud added, "Alcohol."

Bridge drove us to a bar not far from our apartments and then parked the car up for the night while we greedily tucked into our first beers.

"All in all, a pretty successful day," Dud sighed happily, wearing a false moustache of white foam.

"Let's hope they continue that way."

I'd been slightly concerned that my presence would inhibit Bridge and Dud, playing Pete the Gooseberry all evening, but I needn't have bothered. We spent four exceedingly happy hours in the bar, laughing and chatting like three old friends, and when we left at one, I was feeling more contented than I had in years. We strolled slowly, and in my case a little unsteadily, back to the *Monet* building before taking the elevator to the top floor. Dud suggested I might like a night-cap and looked slightly horrified when I pretended that I might, before I bade the happy couple a warm goodnight and let myself into my own apartment, looking forward to nothing more than a good night's sleep. And sleep I did.

8

I was woken the next morning by a gentle tapping on my front door, and rose blearily, dragging on a dressing gown before opening the door. Bridge, looking alarmingly fresh and wide awake, was standing on the threshold, beaming from ear to ear.

"Morning, Pete. Thought you might like some breakfast." She handed me a warm paper bag which turned out to contain fresh croissants.

"Lovely idea," I yawned, "What's the time?"

"Nine-thirty. I've just got back from taking Dud to the Commission, and he said something about you going to see Standish this morning."

"That's right," I nodded, "Er, sorry, I should have invited you in already." I stepped back into the penthouse.

"Want me to put some coffee on while you shower or whatever?" Bridge asked, following me inside.

"You're an absolute angel." I headed for the bathroom.

After a long and much-needed shower, I dressed and joined Bridge on the terrace where coffee and croissants awaited. "This is the life," I said, settling onto a chair and sipping at the strong brew.

"The mutt's nuts," Bridge nodded.

I groaned, "Don't tell me he's got to you as well? Nothing," I went on when she gave me a bemused look, "Thanks for breakfast, by the way."

"You're more than welcome. Want me to phone Standish for you? See when he's free?"

"I won't have you accusing me of treating you like a slave," I grinned, "I'll do it myself when I've finished this."

"Suit yerself," Bridge grinned back, "But I really don't mind. You and Dud are really different from the normal type I get to drive around."

"We're abnormal, then?"

"I meant the usual type, not normal."

"Ah! We're just unusual then?"

"I can see why you and Dud get on so well," she sighed.

I called Standish after my leisurely breakfast and he suggested I come straight over to his office which suited me just fine; my thoughts were already turning towards my lunchtime with Nicola. Bridge drove me there, promising to return at eleven-thirty to take me to the club and I wandered into the reception area with a sprightly spring to my step. The same cheerful receptionist that had been there on our first visit took me straight through to the office where Standish would, she assured me, be joining me shortly. I was just taking the data from my briefcase when he arrived.

"Peter, dear boy!" he greeted me.

"Hi," I smiled, "As promised, we've got some news for you."

"So you said on the phone. I can't wait to see what you've come up with."

We went through the data together, me pointing out the most relevant information, Standish asking the occasional question. Twenty

189

minutes after we'd started, he sat back with a contented smile on his face.

"This is really splendid work," he said, "And so fast."

"We've had plenty of practice."

"Nevertheless, very well done! I'm almost positive this is going to be of enormous help to us. I know your real interest lies with Winter and Stephenson, and that their business might be at an end very soon, but I really must try to persuade you to stay on for a while longer; we could really use your services for some time yet."

I couldn't imagine Dud objecting. Nor Suze, come to that. And, of course, there was Nicola... "It's a pleasant change for us. I'm pretty sure I could persuade my partner to extend our trip."

"Splendid, splendid! Since everyone at the Commission already believes you're going to be there for two months, perhaps we could use that as a yardstick for your stay?"

"I don't see why not." I tried not to smile too broadly.

I went on to tell Standish that I would be going back to the UK that evening and returning on Sunday – I was taking the first trip back on the grounds that Dud had decided he'd rather stay in the Duchy for the duration – and that I'd contact Standish again on the Monday morning when we should have more information for him concerning activity in the suspect banks.

I left his office at twenty past eleven to find Bridge waiting for me in the reception area.

"Message from Dud," she informed me, "Apparently he's located two accounts where there's been exceptional volumes, but the details are a bit sketchy. He reckoned you might like to pop in this afternoon and check things out with him."

"He's right," I nodded, "Perhaps you could pick me up after lunch–"

"No need," she grinned, "All this detective work you're doing has got my interest up; I'm going to stay at the club over lunch and see if I can find out anything from Mike Nicholas. I saw him at the Commission this morning, and he said he'd be going there 'cos the Commodore needs him to drive him over."

"The old boy's not using his own car?"

"That's one of the things I want to find out," Bridge nodded, "It's the first time I can ever recall the Commodore actually using his Commission car."

"Are you sure you don't mind? I mean, I don't want you getting into any hot water, or anything?"

"Of course not! As I said, this is really fascinating."

"Oh, well, why not? Shall we?" I nodded towards the door.

"Sure thing, Sherlock."

We arrived at the club just as it was opening for the day, and went our separate ways; me to the bar to await Nicola's arrival, and Bridge to the games room at the rear of the premises where, she told me, Mike always hung out when he was there. At five to twelve the door opened, and the object of my desire strode into the room. I didn't even bother to check whether heads turned as she entered – if any male didn't stare at her, they'd have to be a raving homosexual. Nicola was wearing a short white skirt into which she had loosely tucked a green silk blouse. Her hair was once again flowing loose, cascading over her shoulders in perfect auburn waves. Without breaking her elegant stride, she crossed straight towards me and greeted me with a gentle, lingering kiss.

"That's better," she sighed as we parted.

"The best," I nodded, that silly grin back on my face.

"I know it's only been a day and a half, but I've really missed you."

"Likewise. I'm already dreading the weekend."

She smiled warmly at me, "I think it's wonderful that you want to make sure your daughter's coping okay, but I know I'm going to be longing for your return."

"Perhaps next time, you might be able to come with me?"

Her emerald eyes widened slightly, "You'd really take me with you?"

"Of course. In fact, knowing Suze, she'll probably *insist* that I take you with me."

"You must tell me when; I'll make absolutely certain that I'm available."

"Three weeks from today, returning on the Monday morning," I said, "If you're free, I'll book your tickets this afternoon."

Nicola fumbled in the small clutch-bag she was carrying and withdrew a small, old-fashioned diary. She riffled quickly through the pages and then nodded happily, "Nothing arranged at all. Can I borrow a pen so that I can write it in?"

"My pleasure," I beamed, handing her my favourite *Mont Blanc* – used only to write down the most important things.

We ordered drinks and retreated to a quiet table in the corner where our conversation would not be overheard.

"You've the most wonderful legs," I commented as she slid into her chair, the short skirt riding into the high blood-pressure zone.

"Thank you. And you've a wonderfully smooth tongue."

A mental image of where my tongue might prove to be at its smoothest had to be forcibly repressed, "I'm just being observant."

"As long as you like what you observe."

"I adore what I observe. You'll never know how proud I feel to be seen with someone as lovely as you."

"Why, Peter! You are in a complimentary mood today."

"I hope you don't mind," I smiled.

"*Au contraire*," she laughed softly, "It's one of the very few pleasures I seem to have these days, what with home-life and everything."

"Is it really that bad?"

"Probably worse," she sighed, "Daddy's having so many problems at the moment."

"Want to tell me about it? I don't mean to pry, but–"

"You're not prying. And it's very kind of you to offer, but I really shouldn't burden you with my difficulties."

"Sometimes it helps to share these things," I said, feeling the slightest twinge of guilt since I was rather hoping that she might be able to provide me with some background information for our investigation.

"Well, I'm sure he'll probably tell you about himself in a while, so I guess it won't do any harm to tell you. It's his car, you see; the precious bloody Roller. The old fool put it up as collateral at the casino, and now they've come and taken it away."

"His Rolls Royce?" I couldn't keep the incredulity out of my voice.

"The very same. God knows how much he's got himself into debt over this time."

"What on earth does your mother have to say about it?"

Nicola gave a derisive snort, "I really don't think Mummy's even aware of what's going on. She's been hitting the bottle pretty hard these last few weeks."

"You poor thing," I sympathised, taking one long delicate hand into my own.

"I'm used to it. But, really. That's enough about me. I'd much rather talk about you – and us, of course."

And so, for the next fifty, wonderful, entrancing minutes, that's exactly what we did, until, disappointingly, the Commodore arrived with Mike Nicholas in tow. We rose from our table and went over to join them at the bar.

"What a wonderful picture they make, don't you know?" the Commodore was saying to his driver as we arrived.

"Good to see you again," Mike nodded at me.

"Likewise."

"Anyway, must dash," he went on, "I've got an important snooker match to attend."

"Good luck," I smiled at his retreating back.

If the Commodore was upset about the apparent loss of his beloved old car, it certainly didn't show as he kept up a constant stream of banter over lunch, punctuated with bouts of innuendo aimed at Nicola and me. The man was, I realised, a master of the single *entendre*.

Although I was looking for clues into his apparently eccentric behaviour of late, it was to no avail. To be honest, I'd always found him pretty eccentric and he didn't seem any more so on this occasion. When he finally announced that he really *had* to return to the *'damned monstrosity'*, I found it hard to smother the huge sigh of relief that threatened to burst from my lungs. Forbes sent a steward in search of his driver and then said his goodbyes to his daughter and me.

"Wonderful to see you two so happy," his voice, fuelled by half a dozen large malt whiskies boomed across the dining room, "You really must invite young Peter home for supper, Nicola, m'girl. Mummy would love to meet him, I'm sure."

"Maybe," she shrugged, flashing me a quick lop-sided, apologetic smile.

"And don't forget, m'boy; next Wednesday evening at seven." I had promised to accompany him to the casino.

"I'll be there."

"And so will I," Nicola added, "I'm not having my own father running off with my fellow."

Mike Nicholas arrived looking rather miffed, "Bloody Bridge. She only went and beat me twice."

"Good for her," I grinned, "I must give you a game myself sometime."

"You play snooker?"

Dud and I had spent many a happy hour in the local snooker hall when we were younger, and with a best break of one hundred and twenty two, I considered myself a pretty good player, "I know which way round you hold the cue."

"You're on then," Mike nodded, "I'll give you a call next week and arrange something."

"Do that," I nodded. Whatever Bridge might have found out in the previous couple of hours, I still wanted to have a quiet chat with the Commodore's driver myself.

After another round of goodbyes, Mike led the Commodore outside, and Nicola and I let out the pent-up sighs of relief that we'd been holding back.

"Thank God that's over with," she said, "Sometimes I find it hard to believe that I really am his offspring."

"Likewise."

Bridge joined us, "Not interrupting, am I?"

"Not at all," I assured her. I checked my watch and gave a grunt of disappointment, "I guess I'd better get along and see what Dud's come up with. My plane leaves at half-five."

"I'll wait outside," Bridge grinned. Lovely girl.

194

"So, I guess this is it for a couple of days," Nicola gave me a sad smile.

"Guess so."

"Call me as soon as you're back," she insisted, "Or perhaps I could meet you at the airport?"

"That'd be wonderful. I should be getting in at four on Sunday."

"Then I'll be waiting," she promised.

We went through to the foyer to collect our jackets and embraced each other for a minute or two before sighing in unison.

"Until Sunday, then. Take care, Peter."

"I will, and I'll be thinking of you."

Before the mood made parting an impossibility, I gave Nicola a final, tender kiss and made hurriedly for the door, glancing back once as I opened it. We exchanged a brief wave and then I bolted for the sanctuary provided by the car.

At the office, Dud was in a remarkably cheerful mood when we arrived, and he eagerly went through the forty sheets of data he had downloaded that morning concerning two mystery accounts. Something about the figures involved seemed familiar, but it was Dud that had already spotted a connection.

"Okay, so the accounts don't have names, but I thought there was something about the pattern of transactions that rang a bell," he said, "Then it hit me."

"And so will I if you don't get to the point," I sighed.

"Simmer down, Sherlock. This is real good news." He pointed to one particular set of data, "These transactions – all major credits – occurred during the last six months, and all of them were originated in London or Geneva."

Light dawned. "They match the ETA losses, don't they?"

"Put it this way," Dud grinned triumphantly, "They are all for exactly half of the erroneous ETA transactions, and all occurred either one or two days after the money had gone missing from there, or, in two cases, a week afterwards. If you add the transactions together from the two accounts, we can – if you'll pardon the pun – account for ninety percent of what Forsythe believes to have gone missing."

"Or in other words, these accounts must belong to Jenny and Stephenson?"

"That'd be my guess," Dud grinned.

"Bloody good work, Watson!"

"It was your idea in the first place," he generously reminded me.

"Whatever. If you've got time, I reckon you should get down and see Standish with this news. And get a scan set up on these two accounts."

"The latter's already in place. And as for Standish, I'll phone him now."

Dud arranged to see our employer at six that evening in a bar close by his office. After completing the arrangements, it was Bridge's turn to provide us with more information.

"Mike Nicholas," she grinned, "Has a very loose tongue. Apparently, he's been tearing around all over the place on the Commodore's orders; picking up mysterious parcels and bringing them back to Forbes' place. And, on one occasion, he was told to fly to London and bring back–"

"A green Aston Martin!" Dud and I said in unison.

"Did he know who owned it?" I asked.

Bridge grinned, "No, but he does know where it was delivered to."

"Which is?"

"The long-term car park at the airport. The receipt was given to Forbes."

"Bloody hell," Dud whistled, "It looks as though Standish might well have been right about the old-boy's involvement. I'll let him know tonight; perhaps he can get someone to stand watch over the car."

"Good idea," I said, "I'm beginning to think that the reward money is as good as ours."

Bridge drove me back to the apartment to collect my bag, and we picked Dud up on the way back to the airport where the three of us had a celebratory drink before my flight was called. All in all, a most spectacularly successful day.

9

I arrived back at my house still overjoyed, my spirits not so much high, as in orbit. The house was deserted, but a large piece of paper had been taped across the living room doorway informing me that my precious angel had been taken out to dinner by Donna as a thank you for the hospitality. *A rather adult thing to do*, I nodded to myself, approvingly.

Like the well-trained househusband that I am, I emptied my washing into the machine in the utility room, added liquid and switched it on. The sum total of my chores for the weekend completed, I threw my case onto my bed and headed back out into the night in search of a beer. Dud had always described the *Duke* as a spider's web: once you were in, you tended to get stuck there for hours. That Friday night was no exception, and I arrived home to find the house in darkness, the girls – assuming they were both there – long retired for the night. As quietly as possible, I took myself off to my own bed and was fast asleep within a minute or two.

Despite the beers and the excitement of the previous day, I was awake at seven and rose almost eagerly, intent on seeing Suze and in great need of coffee and Paracetamol – what she referred to as the bachelor's breakfast. I pulled on a large, fluffy dressing gown and padded quietly downstairs. I was yawning widely as I pushed open the door to the living room, and it was only a sudden squeal that alerted me to Donna's presence.

She had been sitting in the middle of the room, totally naked, and she now scrambled to her feet and dived for her own robe which had been carefully folded on the sofa. "Oh, Christ! I'm sorry, Pete," she stammered an apology as she quickly pulled on the garment, "Suze said you'd be asleep for hours yet and this is the perfect room for my yoga–"

"It's okay!" I tried to soothe her, "Really. I'm sorry I didn't knock or something."

Donna turned to face me, blushing vermilion, "In your own home?" she managed a smile, "No, I really should have thought twice."

"Nonsense," I smiled, as much at her embarrassment as anything else, "Although maybe in future you should tape up a 'Do Not Disturb' sign, or something. If I see one, I'll go through to the kitchen the other way."

"I feel so stupid," she groaned.

"Well you shouldn't. Besides, neither Suze nor I are in any way prudish over a bit of naked flesh."

"A *bit*!" Donna's smile became more genuine, "Sorry again–"

"No more apologies," I laughed. I decided not to comment on her lovely figure, reckoning that she'd had enough embarrassment for one day. "I'll go through and rustle up some coffee and leave you in peace to finish your exercises."

"No need. I was just about finished anyway. I'll fix the coffee."

"That'd be nice." I figured that she'd probably get over her embarrassment faster if she had something to do, "Where's Suze, by the way?"

"She just popped out to get some bread," Donna explained over her shoulder, "She said she wouldn't be long."

I followed my daughter's girlfriend into the kitchen and sat myself at the table while she prepared the coffee machine, "Looking forward to going back to school?"

"Not as much as Suze, I guess, but, yeah, I think so. Everyone keeps saying it's a lot more relaxed for the A-level courses."

I was about to ask her what courses she was going to take when we were interrupted by Suze's return.

"Pa!" she greeted me, dropping the loaf on the worktop, "Lovely to see you!" She flopped onto my lap and hugged me tightly.

"It's lovely to see you as well, princess. Miss me?"

She leaned backwards and frowned at my face, "Aren't you a distant relation of mine, or something?"

"Not nearly distant enough at times," I grinned; my reward a giggle.

"I thought you'd still be in your pit for hours yet."

"You and Donna, both."

"Don't ask!" Donna groaned.

Suze looked first at me and then at Donna, who was once more blushing furiously, "Don't tell me you were in the middle of your exercises when he appeared?"

"Another thirty seconds and I would have been finished. I blame you for this!"

"Sorry," Suze giggled, "But you needn't worry. He might be a pain at times, but he's not the dirty old man type. Nudity is something we've always been pretty relaxed about, ain't it, Pa?"

"Absolutely," I said, "Really, Donna; don't fret about it, okay?"

"I guess," she shrugged, turning her attention back to the coffee.

After my bachelor's breakfast, I went upstairs to shower and dress, wondering what on earth I'd actually get up to for the day, and then went along to Suze's room to see if she and Donna had any plans. The pair of them were sitting on her bed surrounded by art books.

"Looks interesting," I commented.

Suze nodded, "I was just showing Donna some of your old books; the ones you and mum used to collect. Just trying to prove that you really weren't hung up about nudes and stuff."

The books had been collected over the first ten years I was married to Julie, mainly collections of photographic prints of nudes throughout the years, a subject that had fascinated the pair of us, "Why don't you show her the Decade Collection?" I suggested.

"Wow!" Suze giggled to Donna, "You *are* privileged. There's not many people that get to set foot in his famous study, let alone view his infamous collection."

She led Donna out of her room and down the landing to my office, with me trailing after them. Inside, there were twelve framed photographs on the walls, each depicting a nude form representing each of the decades from the eighteen-eighties through to the nineteen-nineties. The first pair had been bought for me as a birthday present by Julie about fifteen years earlier, and when we realised that they were from the first two of those decades, we had started to search for others, intent on building a collection which gave a feel for the photographic styles of the times.

Suze explained this to Donna as they progressed from the earliest to the latest. As she reached the nineteen-nineties photo, Donna paused and frowned. She cocked her head to one side and then turned to give Suze an appraising look.

Suze smiled, "Yeah, you guessed."

"Your mother?"

"Beautiful, wasn't she?" Suze's smile turned sad.

For nearly a year after Julie's sudden death, I'd kept that print in a drawer, unable to bear looking at it. It depicted her kneeling naked on a fur rug, her arms spread wide, and her head angled to her right and tilted slightly upwards. I had taken the shot myself after we hadn't been able to find anything that suited our tastes for the nineties, and it had become my favourite, and Julie's also.

"You really do take after her," Donna said, turning her attention back to the wall.

"I hope so," Suze said softly, "Thanks, D."

"She's right," I added, "Perhaps, now that you've, er, matured, so to speak, you might like to produce one of yourself for this decade? Maybe use the PC to come up with something really high-tech?"

"You really think I'd be good enough?" Suze raised an eyebrow.

"More than."

"Too true," Donna added.

Suze gave a shy smile, "Well, maybe we could at least give it a try. You'd help me, wouldn't you, D?"

"Love to."

"Maybe you could pose as well?" Suze suggested.

Donna visibly recoiled, "Hey, I get the picture about you two not being worried about naked flesh, but I don't think I could ever bring myself to pose for something like that! Besides, I'm not nearly as attractive as you."

"Nonsense!" Suze protested, "You've got a wonderful figure."

"She's right," I nodded.

Donna began to blush furiously once more, "Please? No more reminders of this morning?"

"Sorry," I said, trying to keep a straight face. My earlier impression that Donna was the one full of self-confidence and Suze, the shyer, more uncertain one, had begun to be replaced with the opposite view. "Anyway, I'll leave you two to decide who does what and when, but in the meantime, have you any plans for today? I thought you might like to join me for lunch at the *Duke*?"

"Sounds good to me," Suze nodded.

"Count me in," Donna agreed, clearly relieved to change subjects.

So, that's exactly what we did, and great fun it was, too.

The rest of the weekend flew past, the two girls surprising me by staying with me for virtually every minute of the day. As I prepared to leave on the Sunday, Suze came up to help me pack.

"When're you next coming back?" she asked.

"Missing me already?" I grinned.

"No, I just want to make sure that we know so that Donna can exercise without the worry of you peeping in at her."

"Suze!"

"Just joking," she grinned.

"Good. Anyway, it'll be three weeks this time. I'll be back on the Friday the same as this time."

"And you'll be bringing this Nicola with you?"

"I sincerely hope so."

"That's nice," Suze said, "At least you won't go sneaking around to cop an eyeful of my girlfriend if you've got one of your own in tow."

"Did you know," I sighed, "That in America, parents can now divorce their kids?"

Suze giggled, "You don't have the grounds, but even if you did, you wouldn't want to get shot of me, would you?"

I made out that the question needed consideration, earning myself a swat on the shoulder, "No, I guess not." The reward for the comment was a warm hug. "Are you sure you're going to be okay here without me?"

"I'll be fine. And, well, Donna'll be here most of the time."

"That's nice."

"You really don't mind about… me and her, do you?"

"Not at all. She's a very nice girl. Lovely figure as well," I added with a grin.

"Pervert!" she giggled, "But I guess you're right."

This was going to be the longest time I'd ever spent apart from Suze, and it really brought home the meaning of that old saw about 'parting being such sweet sorrow'. From the strength of the hug that Suze gave me when the taxi arrived to collect me, I imagine that she felt pretty much the same way. I think that some of that mutual missing-you-already feeling rubbed off on Donna as well, since she surprised me – and probably herself, too – by giving me a warm hug before I went out to the waiting car. I really was so happy for my precious princess.

10

During the journey, my thoughts turned gradually away from where I had just come from, and towards where I was headed – and who would be waiting there for me. By the time the plane finally taxied to a standstill at the tiny airport, a flock of eagle-sized butterflies had taken up residence in my stomach. Since I had nothing but hand-luggage with me this time, I was through passport control and the customs area within three minutes, and, taking a deep breath, I stepped into the arrivals' hall.

At first I couldn't see Nicola's tall, elegant frame but then a flash of auburn hair to my right caught my eye. I turned to see her moving quickly towards me, a vision of beauty in a short summer-dress. I dropped my bag and opened my arms, Nicola stepping swiftly into my embrace. We hugged each other wordlessly for more than a minute and it was in those seventy seconds or so, that I realised just how heavily I'd fallen for this wonderful woman. From the strength of her hold on me, I was even hopeful that she might have started feeling the same way about me.

When we parted, we both started to gabble away at once; the whole 'missed-you', 'wonderful-to-see-you-again' thing. After another hug, we parted again and then made our way out into bright, warm sunshine. Nicola's car, a modest BMW, was parked in the short-stay area, and she led me over to it, our hands entwined.

"Where would you like to go?" she asked as soon as we were inside.

"As long as it's with you, I really don't care," I sighed happily.

"Well, have you eaten, then?"

"Not since a late breakfast; I can't stand airline food."

"I know exactly what you mean," she said, starting the engine, "There's a quiet little place just outside of the town that's open on Sundays. We could go there, if you like?"

"I like," I nodded firmly.

The owner of the place seemed delighted to see Nicola, and he led us to a quiet table at the rear of the building which looked out towards the forest that surrounds that side of the town. I can barely remember what we ate that evening, or what it tasted like; such was my attention diverted towards the gorgeous woman sitting across from me. Afterwards, I recall us sipping drinks at the restaurant's tiny bar, before we finally left and headed back into town, more than three hours having just flown by.

"Maybe you'd like a night-cap at my place?" I suggested as we approached the town proper.

"I would. I love that terrace you've got up there. It must be such a joy to sit out there when it's warm like this. No-one overlooking you, the whole town spread out before you."

"It's glorious," I said, "And I'm sure it'll be even better with you by my side."

"Charmer."

Once upstairs, I opened the picture windows and went into the kitchen to pour drinks, my hands trembling a little. Back outside, Nicola was standing with her hands rested on the railing that surrounds the terrace, and I stood the drinks on the table before joining her.

"It's a wonderful view," she smiled.

"Not as wonderful as what I'm looking at," I smiled back.

"Thank you, Peter," she said, "Maybe it's something to do with being out here; way above everything. I feel almost... elemental; at one with the world about me. I could quite happily strip off and just luxuriate in the night."

"Why don't you?" I swallowed hard, "After all, as you said; there's no-one overlooking us here."

Even in the relative darkness, I could make out the flash in her green eyes. It took me a moment or two before I realised that she'd raised her hands to the top of her dress and was sliding the straps off her shoulders. "That's a marvellous idea, Peter," she breathed at me. The dress slid gently to the terrace floor and after a moment's hesitation, Nicola took a deep breath and then quickly tugged at the tiny G-string that was all that remained of her clothing. A second later, and she was standing gloriously, gorgeously naked before me. Her figure seemed even more beautiful than I had remembered it, every curve in perfect harmony with the rest, every line redolent of grace and elegance. I was finding it almost impossible to breathe.

She turned slowly away from me, facing out towards the distant lights, "This feels *so* good."

I stepped up beside her and brushed her long auburn tresses back over her shoulder from where they had been impeding my view of her naked breasts. As I did so, I could feel the fluttering of her heart, beating faster than even my own.

As slowly as she'd turned away, she turned back to face me. In complete silence, I gently pulled her towards me, our lips meeting with the tiniest clatter of teeth on teeth, already urgent, the sexual tension almost visible in the warm night air. I pulled her tighter against me, my hands on her firm bottom, our hips and lips grinding together. After what may have been one minute or ten, I broke the contact between our moist mouths and began to kiss her left shoulder. Ever so slowly, I worked my way lower taking each of her rigid nipples in turn into my mouth. As I progressed, I could feel Nicola's breathing quicken still further, the flatness of her firm belly acting like a drum. Finally, I dropped to my knees, my nose already pressed into the small patch of dark hair at her groin. She moved her left leg slightly away from the right, granting me access to the warm, moist centre of her, and the first touch of my tongue had her groaning loudly, her hands in my hair encouraging me.

I'd been aware since the first kiss that she might not want this to go too far, listening for anything in her voice that might suggest as much, feeling for any sudden tension in her body. I had begun to believe that she had decided the time was right when, as her gasping and panting were reaching the level I would normally associate with climax, she let out the same sort of desperate yelp as he had the previous week. I stopped my probing immediately, sitting back and staring up at her.

"Peter! I—" she began.

"It's okay."

"No, I really shouldn't I-I-lead you on like this," she was still panting heavily.

"Nonsense. We both know the rules and I respect you too much for there to be any problem between us."

"It's just that if you carry on… like that, I'll never be able to stop you… doing whatever else you want to me!" she was sounding frantic.

"I'll never do anything to you that you don't want me to," I tried to soothe her, rising slowly to my feet and pulling her tightly to me. A sudden dampening of my shirt where her head rested on my shoulder caused me to pull back, "Please! Don't cry, Nicola. It's really not an issue, here."

"I'm so sorry, Peter," she sniffed, "It's just I'm so… confused! One part of me – a really big part – wants you so much, but there's this little voice…"

"Listen to your little voice. It probably belongs to your self-respect, and it's the most important voice you've got."

She stared at me incredulously, her tears beginning to dry, "You're an amazing man, Peter," she shook her head, "I'm really so very sorry–"

"No more apologies," I interrupted, "I thought we'd agreed on that?"

It was her turn to draw me into a tight embrace. "Thank you, Peter," she whispered.

"How about that night-cap?"

Nicola nodded against my shoulder and then pulled back. She glanced down at her nakedness and gave a snort, "God! What on earth must you think of me?"

"I think you're truly beautiful."

She bent quickly to retrieve her clothing, stepping into her G-string and pulling it up her long legs. As she stepped into the summer-dress, I put a hand on her shoulder, "One thing?"

She straightened, the dress bunching at her waist, "What?"

"If you really don't mind?" I let the hand slip down until it was rested just above her left breast.

She drew in a deep, deep breath causing her breast to rise into my embrace, "Is that really enough for you?" she asked doubtfully.

"For now." After the gentlest of caresses, I dropped my hand to my side, leaned forward and kissed her softly on her warm lips.

"I won't make you wait forever you know?" she promised.

"I don't think I could," I smiled, "You're an incredibly beautiful woman. And not just physically."

"Thank you, again, Peter. For... everything."

"No need." I slipped the straps of the dress up her arms.

We retreated to the sofa in the living area for our night-cap and Nicola spoke more openly about her past; her earlier promiscuity. I guessed this was in some way to excuse her unwillingness now, but although I tried to tell her that she didn't have to go into details; that her past was *her* past, she seemed to need to unburden herself, somehow. I, of course, let her.

By the time she left, we were once more relaxed and happy in each other's company, although I can't say that my jeans felt that comfortable.

11

The Monday was scheduled to be my turn at the Commission building, and I rose at eight, showered and dressed, and then went over to Dud's apartment to see if he had any news for me.

"Morning, partner," he yawned when he opened the door, "Good weekend?"

"Lovely, thanks," I nodded following him into the kitchen, "Morning, Bridge."

"Hi," she smiled, "Coffee?"

"Perfect."

She poured a mug for me and another for Dud before putting them on the table. As she did so, she glanced down at herself, and then rolled her eyes. "Not again!" she sighed.

"Maybe a thicker T-shirt is called for?" I grinned at her hastily retreating form.

"Cute, ain't she?" Dud grinned.

"They don't come much cuter. Any news for me?"

"Not a dickey-bird," he said, sipping at his coffee, "Standish said he'd give you a call on your mobile around lunchtime. He was really interested in our discoveries, by the way."

"I can well believe it. It really does look like we're going to be able to collar the pair when that draft becomes valid this time next week."

"*If* they decide to cash it straight away."

"They're bound to know that we're on to them," I said, "I'd imagine they'd want to get things sorted out pretty quickly."

"Let's hope so, pal. Five million dollars each would sure go down well with me."

"You're not wrong about that."

Bridge re-joined us a few minutes later, and we all discussed the plans for that week. I was to be on duty, as it were, that day and again on the Friday, with Dud taking the rest of the week. Unless any of the men Standish was using came up with some news, it probably meant that we had less than four or five hours work between us; simple monitoring of the software we had already set up. I was more than happy about that and resolved to see if Nicola would maybe like to show me around the town and the surrounding countryside.

"Any plans?" I asked Dud.

He glanced over at Bridge, "One or two, maybe," he grinned, "We're going to do a bit of exploring when we've got some free time."

"Why don't I get a cab into the Commission today?" I suggested, "That way, you and Bridge can have the entire day to yourselves."

"But what if you need someone to drive you over to see Standish?" Bridge asked.

"Then I'll get another cab; it's no big deal."

"Well..." Bridge said uncertainly, "How about we compromise? If Dud and I are off exploring today, then I'll need to pass the Commission building anyway. How about I give you a lift in and you make your own way back?"

"Fine by me," I nodded.

They dropped me off outside the Commission at ten and I wandered inside in a chirpy mood, my good deed for the day taken care of. After checking the scanning devices and finding no new transaction to report on, I took the time to phone James Forsythe in London and tell him that we were appearing to be making progress. As far as he was concerned, the news was, judging by the tone of his voice, a much-needed boost, and I promised to keep him informed if there were any more developments.

After Forsythe, I checked in with Dean Samson to see if there had been any London sightings of our fugitives, which not surprisingly, there turned out not to have been, and then called Standish, on the grounds that I couldn't be bothered to wait for him to call me.

"Ah! Peter!" he greeted me, "Nothing new to report from this end, dear boy, but you'll be pleased to hear that the car's under surveillance, and we've also decided to keep someone posted to watch the two banks that you and your partner came up with last week."

"Sounds good to me," I said, "There's nothing new to report here, but Dud will let you know if anything's turned up tomorrow."

"Splendid, splendid. Well, I'll be in touch, dear boy."

I rang off and spent a moment or two savouring what was to come next, which was, of course, Nicola. As I reached out to dial her number, I experienced a few seconds of emotional déjà vu; recalling the feelings I'd had almost sixteen years before when I'd first begun to date Julie. Such was the strength of the similarity I pressed the wrong button twice before finally connecting to the right number.

I explained to her that other than for our trip to the casino on the Wednesday evening, and a brief check-in at the office later that day, I was free until Friday morning if she wanted me. In no uncertain terms, she did, and said she'd be over to the Commission in an hour to pick me up. I rang off and sat back in my chair, the Cheshire cat amongst the fat cats of Europe.

I was waiting in the reception area, trying not to look too eager, when her BMW pulled into the entrance, and in a further effort to appear nonchalant, I waited until she'd parked in the slot normally reserved for her father before sauntering out into the sunlight.

As I approached the car her door opened, and one oh-so long leg swung elegantly into view. She was wearing what appeared to be something akin to a sarong and as she climbed out of the car, a split in its skirt afforded me a sight of the entire length of her bare left leg. Swallowing as hard as I could, and praying that my voice didn't tremble too much, I stepped forward and offered her my hand to ease her progress. She smiled up at me and almost leapt into my eager embrace.

"Oh, Peter!" she laughed, "You don't know how happy you've made this girl."

From deep within her auburn tresses where my head was buried, I managed to find my voice, "That feeling is entirely mutual."

"You mean, you're a girl as well?"

"If I were, you'd have turned me gay."

She kissed me warmly and then stepped back, "So, you're all mine for three and a half whole days?"

"To do with as you wish."

Her emerald eyes flashed brightly in the sunlight, "Dangerous words. But seriously, what would you like to do? A bit of sight-seeing, maybe?"

A mental image of the sight of Nicola on the terrace the previous night flashed into my mind and I had to struggle hard to keep my voice neutral, "That'd be wonderful."

"Well, hop in, then," she said, "I've got one or two places in mind; I'm sure you'll love them."

"I'm positive I will." I scurried around to the passenger side.

We left the Commission building and headed north, away from the town centre, passing quickly through heavily forested areas, the occasional farm or smallholding the only signs of humanity for miles around. After half an hour, Nicola slowed the car and pulled onto a tiny track which I would have missed completely had I been driving. The heavily rutted lane wound through tall conifers for two or three hundred metres before ending at a tall, imposing gate.

"Another advantage of the Forbes name," Nicola smiled at me and climbed out of the car.

She went over to a small box mounted to one side of the barrier and inserted a plastic card into a slot. With a quiet electronic hum, the heavy gate began to swing inwards. She returned to the car and engaged gear, rolling us gently past the barrier, before stopping and climbing out once more. I watched over my shoulder as she returned to the gate and operated a mechanism which reversed the gate's swing, shutting us inside wherever we were.

When she returned, she started the car rolling gently forward once more, "This is private Commission property," she explained, "Although no-one much ever uses it. I doubt whether there'll be anyone else up here today."

"What's here exactly?"

"You'll see."

Less than a minute later, I did. The narrow track ended and we emerged into a broadly circular clearing, about four hundred metres in diameter, surrounded on all sides by enormous firs. Right in the centre and filling maybe two thirds of the area was a lake, its blue waters mirror flat, a tiny pier jutting out over it to our right. Behind the pier, almost buried within the forest was a small building which turned out to be a bar of sorts.

"This is amazing," I whistled, "I can't believe this place isn't teeming with people." There wasn't another car in sight and absolutely no sign of life.

"There's a bigger lake a bit closer to the town," Nicola explained, "They constructed an artificial beach there and have a proper clubhouse and stuff. Pretty much everyone goes there, but personally, I love *this* place; if nothing else for the solitude."

"I can see why. It's so peaceful." Other than for the quiet rumble of the BMW, there was only bird noise; even the gentle breeze seemed not to stir the branches of the trees surrounding us.

Nicola drove across to the small building and turned off the engine. "I brought some lunch with me. I thought maybe we could have a picnic; there's beer and wine and stuff in the bar there," she nodded at the building.

"What a wonderful idea."

We climbed out of the car and I stood for a moment, savouring the fragrances drifting from the forest, before helping Nicola with the hamper that she'd packed into the boot. We took it down to a spot close by the water's edge and then returned to the car to collect a large blanket and a drinks' cooler. Nicola used the same plastic card that had opened the gate to gain access to the bar and I followed her inside.

"Quaint," I said as I took in the rustic design of the place.

"Heaven sent, more like," she smiled, opening one of two massive fridges.

Inside was a vast selection of beers and wines, and we quickly selected a few bottles, placing them in the cooler.

"You don't have to pay, or anything?" I asked.

Nicola gave a soft laugh, "When you or your family works for the Commission you never pay for anything. It's probably scandalous when you think about it, but that's the way it goes."

"I thought all this 'gravy-train' stuff in the press was pure nonsense until I came here," I nodded, following her back out into the sunlight.

"Not a bit of it," Nicola said with a wry smile.

We settled onto the blanket and opened two of the beers. Once seated, the gentle breeze was lost, and the real heat of the day closed over us; sweat prickling at me within seconds.

"Phew! What a scorcher, as they'd say in the *Sun*," I loosened the collar of my shirt.

"That's another joy about the solitude here," Nicola grinned. She stood for a moment and untied a belt at her waist, quickly unwrapping the sarong-like garment and letting it fall to the ground. Wearing only the tiniest of G-strings, she sat back beside me. "I hope you don't mind?"

"Hardly," I managed unable to keep my eyes away from her perfect body.

"I just love the feel of the sun on my body," she sighed, angling her head backwards, her hair brushing the blanket behind her.

"It's one of the pleasures of living where I do," I nodded, unbuttoning my shirt, "No-one can see into our back garden and on really hot days, Suze and I pad about naked out there. We've got the pool as well which is an absolute godsend."

"It sounds wonderful. I hope the weather's nice when I'm over. Do you like to swim?"

"I love to," I said, pulling off the shirt.

Nicola rose to her feet in one graceful movement, "Shall we?" she nodded towards the lake.

"I... haven't got any trunks with me."

She laughed gaily, "Me neither, but that's another sensation I love; swimming naked in cool clear water." Without further ado, she quickly tugged her G-string down her legs, took two long strides and planed into the smooth water.

Hoping that the lake would have the same effect as a cold shower, I stepped out of my trousers and boxers and copied her actions. The water was considerably colder than I'd anticipated, and my initial gasp had me choking softly as I surfaced. I cast around for Nicola, and she appeared after a moment or two, some ten metres from where I'd come up.

"Wonderful, isn't it?" she laughed.

"It certainly is," I managed. The initial shock was beginning to wear off, and I duck-dived under the surface. The clarity of the water was amazing, and it allowed me to see that what I thought was a man-made structure was, in reality a natural phenomenon; the lake's bottom a rocky bowl. As I gazed around me, I caught sight of Nicola off to my right, angling towards me. In the water, as on the land above, her every movement was full of grace, and even the rapid scissoring motion of her legs seemed elegant. Just before she reached me, she angled her head back, her body straightening, affording me a clear and marvellous view of her form. Mimicking her action, I broke the surface less than a metre from her.

"Feel good?" she smiled, treading water.

"I'm in heaven."

With one sharp kick, Nicola closed the distance between us, our bodies colliding gently. After a moment or two of confusion, we managed to work out a rhythm that allowed us both to tread water without kicking the other person's shins, and then I took her into my arms, kissing her softly. Whatever hopes I'd had about the cold shower effect that the lake might possess were dashed as our bodies entwined.

"Sorry," I said, trying to ease apart slightly.

"Don't be silly," Nicola smiled, pulling me back to her, "I'd probably be disappointed if you didn't react like that..." she trailed off for a moment, her smile fading, "I hope you don't think this is a deliberate come-on or anything? I really do just love the feel of the water—"

"Of course not," I interrupted gently, wanting to avoid, at all costs, a repeat of her tears from the previous night, "I know the rules and believe me, if I could have any control over matters, I wouldn't let you feel how aroused I am."

The smile returned, "You're a lovely man, Peter. Maybe, when the time's right, we could come back here; make love right where we are now?"

"As if you couldn't tell, I'd absolutely love to."

Trying to reassure her as much as possible – under the circumstances – I kissed her gently, allowing one hand to briefly trace the contours of her body, and then floated backwards and away from her. With a final smile, I took a deep breath and rotated in the water, once more ducking under the surface. I turned and looked towards where Nicola was still treading water, hardly daring to believe how beautiful she was, how fortunate I was – or would soon be, at any rate.

We spent another fifteen minutes relaxing in the blissful waters, occasionally swimming close, occasionally kissing. Finally, one of us decided that it was time to return to dry land – I can't honestly remember who – and we climbed from the lake, returning to the blanket.

The heat of the day seemed somehow more intense after our cooling swim, and we lay back to let the sun dry our bodies; something it achieved within seconds.

"Do you mind if I... stay like this?" Nicola asked, nodding down at her nakedness, "I don't want you to think I'm a tease or anything, but, well, it just feels so good."

"Of course I don't mind," I laughed. Come on! What sort of right-minded, red-blooded guy would have? "As long as you don't mind me staring at you in awe from time to time."

"You're being charming again."

Perhaps it was the fact that her nakedness was not going to be covered quickly – not some brief, treasured glimpse – or maybe I was just getting used to her beauty. Either way I was finally able to, shall we say, relax, and I settled down happily beside her.

We stayed by the lakeside for the rest of the afternoon, undisturbed, unclothed and uninhibited with each other. The lunch Nicola had brought with her was perfect for our location; fresh bread, meats and cheeses, and we accompanied it with the wine we had taken from the bar. Afterwards we swam, drunk a couple of beers, chatted about inconsequential things, and dozed occasionally. The only time I felt that same urgent desire for her was when I woke from one of those dozes to find her leaning over me, staring into my eyes as they opened, her long hair falling either side of my head. When she saw that I'd wakened, she leaned closer still, kissing me deeply, her breasts brushing my chest as she did so. After a few moments, she sat back and seemed to laugh softly to herself. I wondered briefly whether she was struggling to maintain her own control, whether she was beginning to think that the time was right. I thought better of mentioning it.

The air began to cool around five, a sure sign that Summer was waning, and with a considerable amount of reluctance on both our parts, we slowly dressed. I realised as I pulled on my shirt, that I'd not had a cigarette in more than four hours and took this to be a very good omen. '*With Nicola around*,' I thought, '*perhaps I might even be able to quit altogether*.' Close to panic, I hastily lit a Marlboro.

An hour later, we packed up the things and made our way back to the car, depositing our litter carefully in the bins provided.

"What would you like to do this evening?" Nicola asked when we'd climbed into the car.

I eschewed the honest answer, as memories of her nakedness sprang immediately to mind, and instead tried to concentrate on the question. "I really don't mind. As long as it's with you."

I was rewarded with a bright smile, "Very kind. Perhaps a light supper somewhere?"

"Sounds lovely."

After a quick check on the scanning software back at the office, we dined at a small restaurant close by, yet another owner seemingly delighted to be allowed the privilege of provide fare for Nicola Forbes, and afterwards we made our way back to the town, stopping off *en route* for a drink.

"That was a lovely way to spend an afternoon," Nicola sighed as she sipped at a cognac, "What would you like us to do tomorrow?"

Despite my languor, I realised that I'd been presented with an ideal opportunity to prove how in control I was when it came to Nicola's body. Okay, and also that I'd been given an opportunity to see more of it. "As far as I'm concerned," I said as nonchalantly as possible, "I could do the same as we did today. It's sheer heaven out at the lake."

I think Nicola may have realised that I was trying to reassure her about my intentions because she gave a shake of her head, as if pleasantly surprised, and then smiled, "It was rather wonderful, wasn't it? Let's see how the weather is in the morning, though."

"Good idea."

"Shall I come to your place about ten, say?"

"I can't wait."

We went back to the penthouse around eleven and spent half an hour on the terrace and another on the sofa, sipping drinks, embracing passionately. By the time Nicola left, I was fairly certain that my genitals were close to exploding.

12

When I woke on the Tuesday, I was delighted to see brilliant sunlight pouring through my bedroom window, and I rose as eagerly as any child about to embark on an exciting day out. I was showered, dressed and sipping coffee by nine, when Dud knocked on the door.

"Looking fit," he nodded when I let him and Bridge in.

"Feeling it as well. How are you two doing?"

"Wonderfully," Dud grinned, slipping his arm around Bridge's shoulders. The look of affection that passed between them was enough to gladden the heart of the most miserable of men. "Any news from the office?"

"Nothing going on so far," I shrugged, "But there again, we don't really expect too much until next week, do we?"

"Let's hope not. I'm having far too much fun doing other things."

"I can well believe it," I grinned.

"Yes, anyway," Bridge said hurriedly, blushing, "We were just wondering if you needed my services at all today?"

"Not in the least. Nicola and I are off to do a little exploring and stuff."

"And stuff?" Dud asked innocently.

"And other things, I meant!" At least, I don't think it was a Freudian slip.

"Oh, well," he said, "Good luck and have fun."

"We will. You, too. Let me know if anything comes up."

"Pardon?"

"Dud!" I groaned, "You're getting to be like a young version of Benny Hill."

"Nah!" he shook his head, "He was always surrounded by loads of pretty women, and I only want this one."

I raised an eyebrow as he hugged Bridge; for Dud, that was an almost unbelievable statement. I guessed that Bridge didn't know how big a compliment it was. "Well, I can't say I blame you," I commented.

"We'd, er, better get going," Bridge said, her blush more pronounced.

"See you later, maybe," I nodded.

They left at a near trot and I decided that I could usefully fill some of the time until Nicola's arrival by going to a local newsagency and seeing if they had any English language papers. Computers were fine for immediate news reports, but sometimes good old-fashioned paper couldn't be beaten.

A tiny shop close by proved to have as broad a selection as any place in London, and I bought a *Times* and two packs of Marlboro, marvelling at how expensive the former item was and how cheap the last. Trying to keep my eagerness in check, I strolled back to the *Monet* building as slowly as I could, scanning the headlines as I went. As absorbed as I was, I didn't even notice the BMW at the kerb outside until the driver's door opened, and Nicola almost leapt from the vehicle.

"There you are!" she breathed a sigh of relief, "I thought you'd backed out on me."

I took her into a tight embrace, "Never. What time is it?"

"Just after half nine," she said, kissing my nose, "I couldn't wait any longer. What with the weather being so wonderful and everything."

"That's nice. I was just trying to fill in time by getting a paper."

"Well, you're here now," she smiled, "Are you ready to go?"

"I'll just need to pop upstairs and grab a bag. I thought I'd better take some trunks and stuff in case anyone else shows up today."

"Let's hope they don't," she said, smiling broadly, "But my bikini is already in the car."

On the way up in the lift, I wondered whether it had been in there the day before. Personally, I was glad that I'd not found out. I retrieved the bag from the bedroom and hurried back down to the street.

We arrived at the lakeside less than half an hour later, delighted to find the place completely deserted once more. After another visit to the small bar, we were quickly settled in the same spot as the previous day, sipping at coffee that had been brought along by Nicola in a space-age looking thermos flask. The morning air still retained a slight chill, and we waited for an hour or so before Nicola suggested that it might be warm enough for a swim. That day she was wearing the same short white skirt that I'd seen her in the previous week, and a plain white top, which hung loosely from her shoulders. She stood, and under my admiring, slack-jawed gaze, slowly undressed.

"Thank you," she laughed, "If the way someone looks at you can be called a compliment, then I've just received a very nice one."

"Sorry," I smiled sheepishly, slipping back into reality mode. As Nicola dived into the lake, I undressed as quickly as I could and followed her into the water, prepared this time for the shock of the cold.

That day, despite our occasional embraces, I found it easier to hide my excitement, more at ease in her gorgeous, naked presence. Around noon, we were dozing on the blanket when the sound of an approaching car engine roused us from our stupors.

"Damn!" Nicola sighed, "Looks like we've got company."

"Oh, well," my own sigh escaped me, "Perhaps whoever it is won't stay long." I reached for my boxers and hurriedly pulled them on, having left the bag with my trunks in it back in the car.

Nicola rose and recovered her skirt, pulling it on slowly despite the ever-louder engine noise. Just before the car came into view, she slid into the loose top and sat back beside me, putting her feet into the G-string and yanking it up her legs. I had already made it into my trousers, and pulled on my shirt, leaving it unbuttoned. The car, a Ford Focus, crested the slight rise at the entrance to the clearing and began descending towards where Nicola had parked.

"Damn again!" she muttered.

"You know who it is?"

"Rather," she pulled a face, "You're about to meet the dreaded Celestine."

"Isn't she the one you lunch with occasionally?"

"Am forced to have lunch with, you mean. Her father and Daddy go back a long way, and he pretty much insists that I socialise with her;

some sort of etiquette thing from the bloody colonial days." She was watching the car's progress with undisguised distaste.

"Is she that bad, then?"

"Bad isn't nearly close enough," Nicola sighed, "She's an absolute tart. In fact, she's one of the main reasons why I've become less promiscuous. If she's on her own, you'd better watch out for yourself."

"You've no worries on that score," I said, "I'm one of those old-fashioned one woman type of guys."

"You might very well be, but that won't stop our Celestine from climbing all over you."

The Focus stopped beside Nicola's BMW and the object of her antipathy emerged. Celestine proved to be a rather startling sight. She was a little shorter than Nicola and her hair ash-blonde, but she could easily have passed for Nicola's sister. Her movements as she climbed from the car were graceful and even her voice when she called over to us held resonances of Nicola's.

"Nikki, darling! What a lovely surprise."

"I bet Daddy told her where I was," Nicola said, *sotto voce*, "Celestine! How lovely to see you."

The young woman crossed quickly to where we were now standing, air-kissing Nicola and all the while giving me an appraising and apparently approving stare, "Darling, who is this delightful creature that you've been hiding from me?"

"Pete Cooke," I introduced myself, offering her my hand.

She took it in both of hers, her grip firm, "I'm so *very* pleased to meet you."

"What brings you out here?" Nicola asked, her voice struggling to maintain a pleasant tone.

"A sudden desire for a quick dip, darling," Celestine replied, finally letting go of my hand, "I do hope I'm not interrupting anything?"

"Of course not," I said firmly on our behalf, "Go right ahead."

"Marvellous!" Still smiling at me, Celestine reached down and in one swift movement pulled the T-shirt she was wearing over her head. Like Nicola, she wore nothing underneath, and, also like Nicola, her breasts were firm and proud. I did my damnedest not to look. And tried even harder when she quickly shrugged herself out of the remainder of her clothes. "Perhaps you two might like to join me?" she said, puffing out her chest.

"I think we're already all swum out," Nicola said, flashing me a warning look.

"Quite right," I agreed, feigning an aching back.

"Oh, I do hope I'm not embarrassing you?" Celestine stared down at her nakedness.

"Not at all," I assured her, my eyes focussed on hers.

She shrugged, a slightly puzzled look on her face, and then turned towards the lake, "Oh, well, if you change your mind, come on in." She dived elegantly under the surface.

"See what I mean?" Nicola sighed.

"I'm definitely beginning to. But really, you don't need to fret. And besides, you've got a much better figure."

"You shouldn't have been looking at hers," she grinned, "But thanks anyway."

Celestine stayed for another hour and spent the majority of it displaying herself for what she believed to be my pleasure, even going so far as to 'accidentally' fall against me on one occasion. When she finally gave up, dressed and climbed rather sullenly into the Ford, even I gave a huge sigh of relief.

"Okay," I nodded at Nicola, "I definitely believe you now."

We waited another fifteen minutes before stripping off once more, Nicola reckoning that Celestine might return to see what we were getting up to. Fortunately, that was the last we saw of her that day.

It turned out to be another afternoon of relaxation and joy and in many ways I was even more reluctant for it to end than I'd been the previous day. Before we finally dressed, Nicola and I took one last swim and she vowed once more that when the time was right, we'd return here to make love in the lake. After she told me, I dived to the bottom, arranging a number of rocks into a cross so that we'd know exactly where we'd been when the promise was made.

"Charming *and* romantic with it," Nicola smiled at me when I surfaced.

"And don't forget 'horny'."

We climbed out of the lake together and dried each other with towels that I'd brought along; the sun no longer sufficiently hot to dry us quickly enough in the rapidly cooling air. As she dried my front, I rubbed the towel over her shoulders and gasped as her hand brushed against what was rapidly becoming a full-blown erection. It was the closest moment we had that day to the terrible sexual tensions that we'd been suffering, and the look on Nicola's face as she apologised – unnecessarily, I thought – was tinged with sadness. I kissed her firmly and told her not to worry, not to apologise, and that seemed to ease things. By the time we were dressed and on our way she was back to being the relaxed, carefree young woman I was coming to adore.

We spent another evening of dining, drinking and embracing, rounding it off with what was becoming the habitual night-cap back at the penthouse. Around midnight, Nicola left with a promise to return the following morning, and I retreated to my bed where I dreamt of mermaids and sunshine. No, really!

13

Dud and Bridge paid their normal morning call on me the next day, although with nothing to report from the office, it hardly seemed necessary. I couldn't recall seeing Dud so happy in the company of a woman, and I was beginning to wonder whether he'd finally found someone he could be serious over.

Once more, I needed to fill my time before Nicola's arrival, and I decided to call Suze to see how things were on the home front.

"Suze Cooke," she yawned at me after answering on the eighth ring, "It's seven thirty, so this better be good."

"Oh, er, sorry princess. I forgot you were an hour behind us."

"Hi, Pa," she groaned, "So much for letting me get my beauty sleep."

"You don't need it. But sorry anyway."

"Any particular reason for dragging me from my warm cosy bed on the very last day of my summer holiday?"

"Um, actually, not really. I was just wondering how things were going there?"

"Apart from nuisance calls, wonderfully well," Suze's voice was lightening up, "How about at your end?"

"Marvellously. I've been seeing quite a lot of Nicola."

"Is that figuratively speaking?" she giggled.

"None of your business. Changing the subject; how's Donna?"

"Luckily for her, still in the nice warm cosy bed."

"I'm really sorry, Suze, but if you kept your mobile's battery charged I wouldn't have to use the landline—"

"Yes!" she giggled, "Three apologies in two minutes! You've just won me a fiver from Donna; we had a bet on how many times you'd say sorry if I made out you'd got me out of bed."

"You mean that you were up anyway?"

"For an hour at least. Getting into the swing of things before school starts."

"Devious mare," I sighed, smiling to myself.

"Well, you've always said I've got my mother's looks and your personality."

"I think maybe you're changing."

"For the better, of course. Anyway, I'd better be getting a move on, we've decided to spend our last day of freedom at the kart track."

"Have fun, then, angel," I smiled.

"We will. And have fun yourself. Tell Nicola I'm looking forward to seeing her."

"She's said the same about you, although for the life of me I can't think why."

"Sometimes," Suze sighed, "I can't imagine what women see in you. But I love you anyway, Pa." She made a kissing noise into the phone which I returned.

"Love you, too, princess. Take care."

I rang off happily, content that my precious little girl was doing alright and equally glad that she was happy. I checked my watch, only to find that Nicola wasn't due for another twenty minutes at least and cast around the spacious room for something to occupy my mind. My eyes came to rest on a large notebook and I crossed to the table and picked it up. The book contained my notes about the investigation and a summary of what we knew about each of the people involved. I figured that it wouldn't hurt to do a quick review of the information and began to scan through the pages, having a bit of difficulty deciphering my own spidery scrawl. If it wasn't for the security issue, I'd switch to computerising everything, and wondered whether PC Security should invest some time and money in coming up with a crack-proof tablet system. When I came to the page headed 'Stephenson, P.' something that had been nagging at the back of my mind came into focus.

It was fairly obvious that since I'd never met the guy, there wouldn't be nearly as much information on him as the other characters involved, and his entry took up less than half of the A4 page. What suddenly struck me was that one vital piece of information was missing; we'd been assuming that Jenny would be driving the Aston Martin out of Luxembourg when she and Stephenson left – after all, why else bring the damn thing over in the first place? But that's the trouble with making assumptions; you close your eyes to other possibilities. It was perfectly possible that Jenny and Stephenson would be leaving in his car – if, indeed, he had one – or maybe even a hired car. After all, what's an Aston Martin when you've got several hundred million dollars in your pocket? It was also not inconceivable that Jenny and Stephenson weren't having an affair; that it was just a cover to explain their sudden departures.

I slapped myself on the forehead and called Dud's mobile.

"Dud Moore at your service," he announced cheerfully.

"Hi, partner."

"Hi, Pete. What's up? Need some tips on bedroom technique?"

"Since I've mastered standing up in a hammock, I don't think that'll be necessary," I said, "I've just had a thought or two concerning the investigation."

"Two whole thoughts in a single day? Good going, Sherlock."

"Very funny," I sighed. I went on to tell him about my latest ponderings.

"You've got a point there," he said when I'd finished, "Leave it with me. I'll get in touch with Forsythe and Stephenson's missus; between them they're bound to know about any cars he's got, and I'll get Dean Samson onto it if we need anything checked out. I'll give you and Standish a call when I've got some info."

"Are you sure you don't mind? I thought you and Bridge might be going off somewhere when you're through at the office?"

"We will be, but not until this afternoon," he explained, "Cat's got a meeting of some sort this morning and won't be finished until about one."

"Cat?"

"Short for Caitlin; it's her real name."

"I thought it was Bridget?"

"Nope," Dud laughed, "She wasn't joking about being nicknamed Bridge because she's easy to cross. Let's just say that there's a few people around here who've been put firmly in their places when they've upset her."

"It looks to me like you're not one of them."

"Quite so, Sherlock. And I've no intention of ever *becoming* one of them."

"You're really taken with her, aren't you?"

"Put it this way, Pete," his voice grew serious, "I'm seriously wondering whether to stay on here when we're done. I mean, I can still work with you from over here; distance doesn't really matter in our game, right? Well, not with our normal stuff, anyway."

"Of course," I said, giving myself breathing space to eradicate the note of surprise from my voice, "She doesn't really strike me as your type, though. I guess I'm a bit taken aback."

Dud laughed, "Okay, so a short, slender redhead doesn't exactly match the typical Dud Moore companion profile. But there again, I've never fallen for any of my previous companions, have I? Cat's really amazing; witty, charming, intelligent – she's studying for an Open

University degree, by the way – and she's really cute, Sexy with it, as well."

"Good for you. This'll take a bit of getting used to, mind you."

"For me as well."

I rang off when the buzzer sounded by the front door, indicating that Nicola had arrived, and I crossed the room quickly and let her into the building. She took the lift up to my floor, and I waited eagerly for it to ascend, my pleasure for Dud being replaced by a purely self-centred feeling of contentment and excitement. When the lift door slid open, those feelings were joined by one of arousal.

Nicola was wearing another short skirt, this one blue, and a loose white T-shirt which hung off her left shoulder to almost halfway down her upper arm. She crossed the landing in four elegant strides and hugged me tightly.

"Hello, Peter," she whispered.

"Hi, yourself," I sighed, revelling in the feeling off her body pressed tightly to mine, eagerly breathing in her heady perfume.

We kissed for a moment or two and then parted, already a little breathless, and with silly grins fixed on our faces.

"What shall we do today?" she asked me.

I knew exactly what I felt like doing, but perversely knew that if I told her the truth, my chances of actually doing it would be considerably diminished, "Anything you feel like," I compromised.

She gave me a lop-sided smile and, not for the first time, I wondered whether she might be able to read my mind, "Well," she said at length, "Since we've got to meet up with Daddy this evening, why don't we have as much relaxation as possible beforehand?"

"Sounds like a good idea. What do you suggest?"

"How about I drive us up country? There's an area there which looks a bit like a scaled down model of Switzerland; there's loads of scenic walks we could take?"

"Lead on, Miss Forbes," I smiled.

Nicola's description of the region was spot-on, and we spent several hours wandering among the hills and forests, taking a short break for lunch at midday. The only interruption to the idyll was a brief call from

Dud informing me that Stephenson did – or used to – own a car, and that Dean Samson was busy trying to trace its whereabouts.

At around four, Nicola sighed and then smiled at me. "We'd better be heading back to the car."

"Must we?"

"Well, I for one need to get changed before we go out tonight," she laughed, "I can hardly bend over roulette tables wearing this, can I? She leaned forward, the loose T-shirt gaping open, her breasts clearly visible.

"I don't see why not," I swallowed hard, "I certainly wouldn't object." The already warm day seemed suddenly even hotter.

She laughed and straightened up, "Besides, I could do with a shower. I must be covered in dust and grime."

I tried to put an image of Nicola showering out of my mind before something inside me burst, "I guess you're right."

It was a good job that Nicola's sense of direction is better than mine, because I'm fairly certain I'd still be wandering around the hills to this day. She drove me back to the penthouse and promised to return at six-thirty to pick me up. I was already beginning to regret accepting the old boy's invitation but figured that it would at least show that I was concentrating on the investigation.

When I got up to the top floor, Dud came out of his front door, a bath towel wrapped around him.

"Hi, partner, how's it going?" I smiled at him.

"Wonderfully. Dean called about half an hour back and said that Stephenson owns a Pontiac Firebird – his wife reckons it's one of those midlife crisis jobs – but the best news is that it was collected from London on Monday afternoon by…?"

"Mike Nicholas?"

"The very same. Now, okay, I can go for the idea that he picked up Jenny's Aston as a favour for, say, services rendered, but Stephenson's penis extension, as well?"

"There's no chance of a coincidence here, is there?"

"Standish has already got his man out looking for the Firebird, and he's going to get another one to keep an eye on Nicholas."

"Good work," I said, "As it happens, I'll probably see Nicholas tonight at the casino – assuming the Commodore's still without other means of transport."

"Sounds like a plan. Cat and I are going to have a quiet evening in for a change; I've told her I'll rustle up a nice romantic dinner."

"Since when could you even boil an egg?"

"I said 'rustle up', not cook. I'm going to pop out to that Chinese place around the corner and order up half the menu."

"That sounds more like the partner I know," I grinned, "Well, have fun and don't break anything."

Bridge poked her head round the door, one bare shoulder indicating what sort of fun they might have in mind, "When you've quite finished talking shop," she grinned at Dud, "We've a little unfinished business of our own. Hi, Pete."

"Hi, er, Bridge? Or should I call you Cat? I think I prefer it somehow."

"You mean you think I'm catty?"

"Just full of feline grace."

"Charmer," she grinned, "Cat it is. Now, can I have my man, here, back?"

"He's all yours. You poor wee thing."

"How we girls have to suffer, eh?"

"Thanks, partner," Dud laughed, stepping back into his apartment, "And thanks, Cat. You'll pay for that, by the way." He made as if to drag her out from her hiding place around the door, and she squealed, dashing deeper into the room.

"See you tomorrow," I grinned at Dud.

"Or what's left of me, anyway."

14

I wasn't sure how formal a place the casino might be, and so after showering and grabbing a light snack, I dressed as smartly as my rather spartan wardrobe would allow; which, to be honest, wasn't particularly smart. It would, I decided, have to do.

Nicola arrived promptly as half-six, and I was relieved to see that she was dressed in a fairly casual manner; a bright green dress with a high neck and knee-length skirt. She seemed a little subdued.

"I take it you're not looking forward to this?" I asked.

"Not at all. The casino isn't much in any circumstances, but when your very own father is going to be there making a fool of himself it can be quite depressing."

"It probably won't be that bad. But if you don't really think you can stand it, why not just drop me off there and take yourself off someplace else."

She finally found a smile, "No chance. I'd much rather be in the grotty casino watching Daddy lose a fortune if you're there, than anywhere else in the world."

"Now who's being the charmer?"

We arrived at the casino – which turned out to be just as tatty as Nicola had indicated – to find her father already present, and more importantly for me in some ways, so was his driver.

"Peter!" the Commodore boomed, "Good man, come on in. Evening, Nicola, m'girl."

"Good evening, Commodore," I shook his proffered hand.

"That's 'Edwin', dear boy. Now let me get you both drinks and we can get started on the real business of the evening."

We followed him over to the bar where a weary-looking Mike Nicholas was staring moodily into a beer glass.

"Hi, Mike," I patted him on the shoulder.

He looked round slowly, "Oh, Hi, Pete."

"You're looking a bit tired," I commented.

"Tell me about it.". He dropped his voice so that the Commodore wouldn't overhear, "He's had me chasing all over the bloody place. God knows what's got into him lately."

"Whereabouts? Far?" I asked innocently.

"I've been to bloody London twice in the past three weeks or so. Picking up sodding cars and driving them all the sodding way back here.

The old boy reckoned they were urgently needed by a couple of his cronies but then all I did with them was park them up at the fucking airport!"

I had been hoping that Mike would lie about where he'd been – a sure sign of guilt – so this was disappointing news in a way, but at least I knew where the Pontiac was and made a mental note to tell Dud and Standish. Although Mike didn't appear to be hiding anything, it indicated that the Commodore was somehow involved with both Jenny and Stephenson. I determined that I would wait until he'd had a few and then gently grill the old boy. "Well, perhaps you'll have it a bit easier from now on," I suggested to Mike.

"I bloody hope so. I could have really done without this trip tonight. Knowing the old git, he won't leave here until two or three in the bloody morning. God, I'm knackered."

I was about to suggest to Nicola that we might be able to do Mike a favour and take the old boy home later, but when I turned to where she'd been standing, she had drifted off and was talking quietly and earnestly to her father. I decided against interrupting them just then. "Well, best of luck anyway."

"Thanks," Mike said, "Remind me to give you a call about that snooker game sometime soon."

"Will do."

I went over to Nicola and her father who were staring daggers at each other and coughed loudly so that they were aware of my approach.

The Commodore looked round and gave me a smile, "Are all daughters as bossy as mine?" he asked with a chuckle, "I hear you've a little lady of your own."

"They seem to be, and I do," I said.

"Sometimes I don't know what people see in her," he nodded vaguely in Nicola's direction, "Still, I guess she's a decent looking bit of totty, what?"

"Daddy!"

"She's a very beautiful young woman," I said neutrally, taking her hand and giving it a reassuring squeeze.

"Thank you, Peter," she said, "At least someone around here has decent manners."

The atmosphere, already cool to start with, was dropping into the Arctic zone; I swear I was able to see my breath condensing in front of me. "Well, anyway," I said breezily, "Perhaps you'd like to show me round?"

"Love to, old boy," the Commodore nodded, handing me a large whisky, "Follow on. You never know, you might bring me some luck."

Still holding Nicola's hand tightly in my own, I trailed after him. Before we'd gone five paces, Nicola let out a groan.

"Not bloody Celestine on top of everything!"

I looked round to see the object of Nicola's distaste closing rapidly on us, a very low-cut dress threatening to disgorge its contents at every stride.

"Nikki, darling! And the gorgeous Peter! How marvellous!" She air-kissed Nicola.

"Celestine. I didn't know you came here?" Nicola said levelly.

"Oh, now and again, darling," she swung her gaze onto my face, "A change is as good as a rest, and all that."

"Well, must be going, I'm afraid," Nicola went on, "Daddy's decided to show Peter around the place, and you know what he's like."

It was clear that Celestine couldn't take a hint. "Well, as it happens, I'm afraid my friend hasn't turned up yet so I guess I could join up with you for a while."

I could feel Nicola's grip tighten on my hand.

"Why don't I go off with the Commodore?" I suggested, "Leave you girls to chat. I'm sure you can catch up with me later, Nicola?"

"Good idea," she said, her look full of gratitude. Celestine on the other hand, looked decidedly crestfallen.

Before the blonde man-eater could object, I'd kissed Nicola and set off after the Commodore.

By the time Nicola joined us, almost an hour later, I was beginning to believe the stories about the old man's incompetence as a gambler. By my reckoning, he was already down three or four hundred pounds and showed no sign of reversing his fortunes. We had started at one of the

230

blackjack tables, moved briefly on to craps, and were by this time settled down and playing roulette. In order to keep the old boy company, I'd changed up some cash for chips and was betting modestly, pretty much breaking even. The Commodore, on the other hand, was gambling higher and higher amounts every time he lost – which was frequently. Another effect of his poor form was that he also increased the amount that he was drinking; despite Mike's assertion that he might well be here to the early hours, I couldn't see the old boy lasting the pace at that rate.

However, two hours later, he was still sitting there and didn't appear to be nearly as drunk as he should in all rights have been. Nicola excused herself to go to the ladies' room, and I took the opportunity to ask the Commodore one or two pertinent questions.

"Mike tells me he's been chasing all over the place recently," I said as casually as I could.

"What? Damn! Another bloody loser; I'm sure they're rigging the bloody tables. Mike, you mentioned?"

"Yes; chasing about?"

"Oh, that. Just helping out a couple of old friends," the Commodore nodded, "Although to be honest, m'boy, they're not really my friends at all. But you have to help one another out in the old ex-pat community."

"There's quite a few of you out here, aren't there?"

"Thousands, m'boy. But not many of the old school, these days. Mostly young computer chappies."

"So you tend to just mix with... the old school types, then?"

The Commodore turned his attention away from the table for a second or two, "I guess you could say that. Don't really give it much thought when you're doing it all the time. Prefer a little flutter meself, anyway."

"So your friend you helped out? Is he one of the old school?" I prayed that my prying wasn't as obvious as it felt, but I really couldn't just let this go.

The Commodore didn't seem to notice, "She, actually, but as it happens, yes."

There's no prizes for guessing what my next question was going to be, but before I could ask for the name, the old man suddenly rose from his seat.

"Got the bugger!" he crowed triumphantly, his loud voice turning heads all around the room.

I looked down at the wheel and saw the ball nestled in the twenty-one slot – the Commodore had just won somewhere in the region of six thousand pounds. Nicola rejoined us at precisely that moment.

"See, m'girl," he gave her a smug smile, "Told yer m'luck would change! Probably something to do with yer fellow, here." He patted me on the shoulder more forcibly than was comfortable.

"Well why don't you give up now, then?" Nicola almost pleaded.

"Nonsense, m'girl," her father settled back on his chair, "Never give up when you've started on a winning streak."

Despite Nicola's pleading, the old boy carried on playing for another two hours, eventually finishing the evening about level. He was also barely able to stand by that time, and it took both Mike and I to get him outside to the car. My chance of pursuing the identity of the 'she' that had instigated the assistance for Jenny and Stephenson gone. Or at least, gone for that night at any rate.

After Mike had driven off, I went back inside to find Nicola.

"I'm so sorry about that, Peter," she sighed.

"Don't be," I kissed her, "But I must say, I don't think I could quite stand another evening in here with him."

"Nor me. But at least that's over and done with. Would you like another drink here, or shall we go someplace less squalid?"

"I'm not sure I could handle another one," I said, beginning to feel the effects of the several whiskies I'd consumed during the evening.

"Well, I guess I'd better get you home then," Nicola smiled, "I want you all nice and fresh in the morning."

When we reached the *Monet* building, I decided that in my slightly squiffy state I probably wasn't able to fully trust my judgement or my self-control, and that it might be better if I didn't invite Nicola up to the penthouse. When I explained this to her, I was rewarded with the brightest smile she had given all evening, and I felt an enormous sense

232

of self-pride as I made my way unsteadily into the building after the longest and warmest of kisses.

15

The following morning, the Thursday, I felt remarkably fit given my recent assistance to the whisky exporters of Scotland, and I let Dud and Cat into the flat with a cheerful smile when they came knocking.

"Good night, was it?" Dud asked.

"Hell on wheels, but at least I managed to get a bit of info out of the old boy, and out of Mike. Stephenson's Pontiac is up at the airport."

"Reckon you'll be able to press him for the name, then?" Dud asked when I'd explained what I'd learned.

I shrugged, "That was probably my best chance last night, but I'll see what I can do tomorrow. He's bound to be at the ex-pats' club for lunch; I'll wangle an invitation from him somehow."

"Good idea, Sherlock. I'll give you a call later if I get any more news, and I'll let Standish know about the car."

The happy couple left me to finish my breakfast and, despite the first rain of our time in the Duchy, I was already looking forward to another fun-filled day.

When Nicola first arrived, she seemed even more subdued than she had the previous evening, but by the time we were lunching in a small Japanese restaurant in the old town, she'd regained her natural ebullience, and the afternoon was pure joy from start to finish. During the day and the pleasant evening that followed, I'd moderated my drink intake to ensure that I'd be perfectly *compos mentis* by the time it came for a night-cap.

"I sort of missed this last night," Nicola said as we sipped at our drinks on my sofa, "But thanks for being so considerate."

"No problem," I smiled.

"Peter..." she began before trailing off.

"What is it?"

"I... I know I just said I missed this last night, but, well, in some ways I'm beginning to dread these last drinks."

"Not so much the drinks as the closing of the door behind you, do you mean?"

Nicola gave me a strange smile, "That's exactly what I mean. From the second that door closes to the second I see you again, I don't seem to be able to think of anything else."

"I know the feeling."

"Look... I've got to go down to Metz early tomorrow and I won't be back until Saturday afternoon... Can I perhaps... stay here with you when I get back? For the night, I mean?"

My heart had begun to race, and I found it difficult to think straight, "Can you... Of course you can stay! I'd *love* you to stay."

Our goodnight kiss that night lasted for more than ten minutes, but somehow, knowing that there would be no need of a goodnight kiss when she returned the next time, it didn't seem nearly so difficult to finally escort her out to her BMW.

The following morning, Cat knocked on my door at nine and I let her in, a stupid grin on my face. Bless the little lady, she didn't mention it once. We arrived at the office half an hour later and she went off in search of fresh coffee while I checked through the scanners. Before she returned, I tried the Commodore's number to see if I could wangle the lunch invite that I so desperately wanted, only to be told that he wouldn't be in that morning.

"Damn!" I muttered after I hung up.

"Problem?" Cat asked, coming through the door.

"What? Oh. No. Well not as such."

"Want to share it, or is it a personal thing?"

I sighed deeply, "I was rather hoping that I could arrange to have lunch with the Commodore today. He nearly gave me some useful information the other night and I was thinking that I might get the rest of it out of him over a few post-prandial whiskies today."

"The name of this mystery woman that got him to send Mike over for the cars?"

"That's the one."

"Why don't we just turn up there at twelve and see if he shows?" Cat suggested.

"Good idea. I guess it can't hurt to try."

With the prospect of the missing draft becoming valid in just three days' time, I was conscious of the fact that we were running out of time. We knew who the villains of the piece were, but if there was someone else involved – and it was beginning to look more than likely – then all of our plans could be screwed-up. Right then and there, I'd have tried anything to get some more information.

Cat and I chatted idly while we waited for the appointed hour to arrive and she surprised me with her openness about herself and Dud.

"He's really great," she smiled, "I've not met many guys like him before. You know? Ones that you can talk to about pretty much anything, and ones that actually listen to what you say."

"He's certainly good at both talking and listening." I was wondering whether to mention that he was considering staying on, when Cat brought up the subject herself.

"He told me the other night that he might like to move over here. I guess I should really tell him to give it more consideration, but I can't seem to bring myself to do so. I just keep on encouraging him to do it. Selfish, I know, but there you go."

"I can't see why it's so selfish. I may be talking out of turn here, but, well, I've never seen Dud so... taken with a woman before. You've really got to him."

Cat raised an eyebrow, "You think so? I mean, I sort of guessed that he was keen on me – more than keen, really – but... half the time, I think it's just wishful thinking on my part."

"Not at all," I assured her, "And I can't say I blame him, either."

Cat laughed, blushing, "He said you were a charmer, but thanks anyway."

"I've always found it easy to talk to women, but I've never really considered myself the charming type. I prefer to think that I'm just being open and honest."

"You're a lot like Dud, you know?" Cat said.

"Me?!"

She nodded, "Nicola's a lucky girl."

As I've said before, I'm not comfortable with compliments, other than when they're directed at Suze; they tend to muddle my thought processes and I end up saying things which, if not downright stupid, then at least should probably not be said. This was a case in point, "Dud's luckier. You're pretty, intelligent and witty, and you've got a lovely little body."

I don't know which one of us blushed harder as I stammered an apology, "S-s-sorry, I didn't mean to be that, er, personal."

Cat laughed, "I guess I should be a bit more careful about what I'm wearing when I open the door of a morning."

The embarrassment soon passed, and we steered the conversation gently on to other topics; principally about what Dud and I hoped to achieve on the Monday – or whenever our villains chose to make a move.

"You both seem pretty convinced that they'll act as soon as possible," Cat said, half question and half statement.

I nodded, "It's the normal scenario with things like this. Especially so, since they've had four weeks to sweat and worry in."

"It sounds like a really interesting job you and Dud do."

"Not normally. Mostly it's just sitting in front of a computer screen for hours on end. Trying to track down fugitives doesn't happen that often; in fact, this is only the sixth or seventh time we've got involved with that side of things in the last ten years."

This was both true, and something that was worrying me; I really wasn't sure we were up to the task. Cat's confidence in us helped, though, and by the time we left for the club, I was in a fairly positive frame of mind.

We arrived there just as it was opening for business and wandered inside, settling ourselves at the bar. At twelve thirty, there was still no sign of the Commodore and I was becoming grateful for Cat's company as she related some amusing tales of what some of the Commission folk got up to in the town at night. I had just ordered a second round of drinks for us when the door opened, and Mike Nicholas strolled into the room. I was out of my seat in a second.

"Mike!" I called over, trying to peer around him to see where the Commodore was.

"Hi, Pete. Hi, Bridge." He made his way over to us, the door swinging shut behind him.

"Where's the old boy?" I asked, my manners deserting me in my eagerness.

Mike gestured to the barman before replying, "Fortunately, he's buggered off to Ostend for a long weekend with his missus. You really must thank Nicola for me when you see her; according to the miserable old sod it was her idea. Reckoned she couldn't trust the pair of them at home while she was away."

I groaned loudly. After seeing the old boy out on the town a couple of days previously, and from what Nicola had said about her mother, I could well believe that she wouldn't trust them to behave while she was gone. And of course, now that we'd arranged to spend the last part of the weekend together, she wouldn't be back home until Sunday night at the very earliest. In a way, I thought, this was my own fault. If the Commodore wasn't going to be back until Monday, and if our villains decided to act quickly, then we wouldn't have the information I thought we needed.

Cat, bless her, proved to be the only one of us thinking clearly.

"I presume you took them up there?" she asked Mike.

He nodded happily, "For once I was grateful for a long drive."

"So you know where they're staying?"

"Yup. The Grand. Why the inquisition?"

Nodding to myself, I said, "There's some information I need from the Commodore, and I need it pretty urgently."

"Before Monday," Cat added.

"Cat?" I went on, "Is there any chance you could drive me up there. I wouldn't ask, but this is really important?" I knew that if Forbes was involved himself somehow, then my turning up in Ostend and trying to prise information out of him was going to give the game away; that he'd then know we were on to him. But I also knew that if he wasn't involved, and if we didn't get the gen, then the chances of our recovering the missing draft were severely reduced.

"Why don't I go up there with Dud, instead?" she suggested, "We'd already planned to have a couple of nights away somewhere to rest up before the action starts."

I thought about this for a moment and then nodded, "Why not, indeed? Sort of killing two birds with one stone. Are you sure this is not ruining your plans?"

"Positive. I rather like Ostend. We'll be back on Sunday morning and we can phone you with any news while we're there."

"Well, if you're sure, then I guess it's a good idea," I agreed, "I'll phone Dud and fill him in with the news."

"I'll do it," she insisted, "I promised I'd give him a call around lunchtime, anyway."

"Fair enough. Thanks, Cat."

"No problem." She stood up and went off to find a decent signal for her mobile.

Happy that we might well get hold of the information we needed I began to relax.

"Since you're here," Mike said, "Why don't we have that game of snooker? If Bridge is going up to Ostend with your mate, then I can always give you a lift anywhere."

"Sounds good to me," I nodded.

We waited until Cat returned.

"Dud reckoned it was a brilliant idea," she told me, "But since it was mine, he probably would say that anyway. I'd like to get going as soon as possible, if that's okay with you?"

"It certainly is," I said, "Mike's offered to give me a lift if I need one. Why don't you take off now, if you're finished here?"

"Thanks," she nodded at both Mike and me, "I'll go get your lazy partner – he was still in bed when I called. We'll be in touch maybe this evening, and we'll be back early on Sunday."

"Good luck," I offered, "See you Sunday, sometime."

Cat left at a trot and Mike and I retired to the games room at the back of the building. Two hours later, I'd won three frames to Mike's one, and we decided that enough was enough.

"Where can I take you?" he asked as we sat back at the bar.

I checked my watch. "I need to pop back to the office for ten minutes," I told him, "And then I guess I'll call it a day unless anything's happened. If you could just drop me back in town, I'll be fine."

"Fair enough," he grinned, "Let's get to it. I've got a hot date tonight."

"Anyone I know?"

"Possibly. Celestine Fotheringham; she's a friend of Nicola's so you might have met her. In fact, wasn't she at the casino the other night?"

"I have, and she was, although I wouldn't have described her as a friend of Nicola's."

"Oh?" Mike asked, "That's news to me. I always thought they got on like a house on fire. Celestine's mother is always over at the Forbes; she and the Commodore have been friends from way back – something to do with time they spent in Singapore. If you ask me, they've had something going on for years; she only has to whistle and the old boy comes running."

I shrugged, "When we met Celestine out by the lake the other day and I got the distinct impression that her and Nicola's 'friendship' is more a well-disguised mutual dislike. The front they keep up seems more for the sake of their two families than anything else."

"Could be. What did you think of her, though?"

"Pretty cute," I laughed, remembering her stripping off at the lake, "Seems a bit on the wild side."

"Wild!?" he snorted, "Our Celestine is about as demure as you could get. I'll be lucky if I even get to kiss her this evening."

I was beginning to think that Mike's judgement of peoples' characters was way out of true. I decided not to pass any further comment. "Anyway, good luck. We'd better make a move."

We finished our drinks and made our way out into the car park where the Jaguar was one of only two vehicles left there.

"Not many in, today," I commented.

"Yeah," Mike nodded, "Very strange for a Friday. Maybe everyone's making the most of the end of Summer; having a weekend away while the sun's still shining."

"Could be," I said, climbing into the car.

There was still no activity from any of the scanned accounts when I checked them back at the Commission building, and I breathed a sigh of relief – I was looking forward to a quiet afternoon and evening, although a little worried about how I'd fill my time without Nicola around.

Mike dropped me outside the *Monet* building at four and I decided to shower and change before heading out to find something to eat. I had just let myself into the penthouse when my mobile rang.

"Pete Cooke," I announced.

"Peter, it's Nicola," came the angel's voice.

"Oh, hi!" I said delightedly, "How's things down in Metz?"

"Bloody awful without you. And I've just had the most horrible news."

"What's wrong?"

"I'm afraid I won't be able to get back until really late tomorrow, maybe past midnight."

I breathed a huge sigh of relief, "That's not so bad. I'll be waiting up for you even if it's three in the morning."

"You don't mind?"

"Of course not, I'm just looking forward to seeing you and, well, being with you."

"The feeling's mutual," Nicola laughed, clearly relieved, "I'm missing you like crazy."

"And I you," I said, "Take care down there, won't you?"

"As long as you promise to up there."

We chatted for another couple of minutes before ringing off, and then I took a leisurely shower, mentally calculating how many seconds there were to midnight the next day.

I dined early that evening, a monster fillet steak accompanied by a large green salad – food for lovers, I'd read somewhere – and then took a stroll round the town before settling myself in the small English bar that we'd visited when Dud and I'd first come to Luxembourg with the girls. Friday nights in the *Black Bull* seemed to be cause for celebration, and the small bar was already quite crowded when I arrived. By the time I left, some five hours later, it was packed solid and the cool night air came as something of a relief. However, it also served to make me realise just how much beer I'd consumed, and the journey back to the penthouse was not without one or two tangles with obstructions on the pavements; lamp posts, for instance.

Once inside, I stripped down to my boxers and sat out on the terrace with a soothing whisky, the coolness not bothering me in the slightest. I had just taken my first sip when my mobile started cheeping and I staggered back into the living area.

"Pete, it's Dud," he announced before I could say anything.

"Hi, partner. What's up?"

"A little bit of news for you."

"Which is?" I prompted with a resigned sigh.

"Does the name Forsythe ring any bells?"

"Loud ones," I nodded, feeling momentarily dizzy as I did so, "Is that the name of our mystery lady?"

"That's what the old duffer told me. Mind you, he was half pissed by the time I thought it safe to start grilling him."

"What are the chances that she's related to a certain James Forsythe?" I asked, my head starting to clear.

"That's the million-dollar question, methinks. And I mean that literally. I've just called Dean Samson – who was not, by the way, entirely delighted to be called this late – and asked him to run some checks. Can you call Standish tomorrow and get someone on to it from your end?"

"Consider it done," I promised, "Great work, partner."

"Let's just hope it leads us somewhere."

"Well, you and Cat have fun, and give me a call if Dean gets any news for us, will you?"

"He said he'd give both of us a call," Dud said, "You and Nicola have fun as well."

"Oh, we will."

I rung off and went back out to the terrace, trying to work out what this latest bit of news meant. The most likely scenario I could come up with was that all three directors of ETA were somehow involved; Forsythe staying back in London as some sort of diversionary tactic. I rather hoped that Dean would be able to tell me that the old boy, father of the dubious Samantha, had booked himself on an early flight to Luxembourg for the Monday morning. If that were the case, then I reckoned that capturing our fugitives would be a piece of cake. My only concern was that I didn't know exactly who was putting up the multi-million-dollar reward – if it was ETA themselves, then would they still pay up if all three of their senior executives were found to be guilty? I decided that it really didn't matter much at the moment, and that we could always pressure whoever controlled things from Westminster for some sort of recompense for our efforts.

Satisfied that I'd got everything figured out, I finished my whisky and tottered through to the bedroom for some much-needed sleep.

16

I was woken the next day by the insistent cheeping of my mobile, far earlier than I would have liked. Dean Samson's dulcet tones greeted me.

"Yo, Pete!"

"Yo, yourself," I yawned.

"News as requested," he announced, "But it ain't much use, I guess. James Forsythe has no known female relatives living in Luxembourg, nor, as far as I can make out has he ever had. I, er, had a word with one or two people, and I've got someone watching the old boy right now. The latest report I've got is that he and some blonde have booked themselves into the Savoy for the next five nights."

"Not Jenny Winter, by any chance?" I asked without much hope.

"No identity so far," Dean said, "And no good description. My guy only got the briefest glimpse of her when she appeared at a window. He's been briefed to find out as much as he can, though, and I'll let you know what he finds out as soon as he does."

"Good work, Dean, and thanks."

"No problem, Pete. Speak to you later."

After he hung up, I decided that since I was awake anyway, I'd call Standish to get him on the case. He didn't sound particularly pleased to hear from me at eight on a Saturday morning, but brightened up considerably when I explained what Dud had found out.

"Splendid work," he enthused, "I'll have one of my boys onto it straight away. If there's a female Forsythe anywhere in Luxembourg, we'll soon find her, and the name does ring a bell. I'll call you back later."

Happy in the knowledge that I'd done as much as I could for the time being, I climbed back into bed and managed to get another couple of hours' sleep. It would have been even longer but for the bloody mobile.

"Pete Cooke," I yawned.

"It's Standish. Good news. A certain Glenda Forsythe has been resident of the Grand Duchy since ninety-nine; exactly the same year that Forbes arrived. She's an old lady of independent means, as they say, and according to one source, she and the Commodore have, shall we say, a very close relationship."

"Not another one!" I couldn't imagine anyone fancying the old sot.

"Another one, old man?"

"His driver, Mike, was telling me yesterday about the Commodore and some other woman; Fotheringay, I think he said."

"Fotheringham, I'd guess. The old boy does have a bit of a reputation as a ladies' man. Bloody strange if you ask me."

"I quite agree," I laughed, "What are you going to do about this Forsythe woman?"

"Keep a very close eye on her. She doesn't have any known relatives over here, but that's not to say there aren't any. We're checking on that right now, and if anything turns up, I'll let you know."

He rang off and I called Dud to tell him the news.

"You do pick your times to call," he panted at me when he answered on the tenth ring.

I called back half an hour later.

"Having fun?" I asked.

"Yes, thanks. What's the news?"

I explained what Dean and Standish had told me and then left him to return to his 'fun', idly speculating on when Nicola would arrive. I tried for another hour's sleep but was by now too wide awake to do anything more than doze fitfully. I gave in and got up, taking a long shower and four Paracetamol.

After a light breakfast, I called Suze.

"Hi, Pa! How's things?" she greeted me.

"Hi, princess. They're going pretty good. How about your end?"

"There's certainly nothing wrong with my end, thank you very much," she giggled.

"I meant school and stuff," I sighed.

Suze's voice became more serious, "Pretty much okay."

"Only pretty much?"

"Well..."

"What's wrong, princess?"

She let out a sigh, "It's just... there's this new girl started, Dawn, and she's... really nice. At least, Donna thinks so anyway."

"Do I detect a touch of the green-eyed monster surfacing here?"

"I suppose so," she sighed again.

"Where's Donna now?"

"Here. Still in bed," I could almost picture Suze's shrug.

"Well, there you go then."

"I guess so," she said, "I'm probably just overreacting."

"I'm sure you are. But if I was you, I'd discuss this with Donna. I bet you haven't already, have you?"

"No," she said quietly, "I guess I'm too afraid of what she'll say."

"Don't be! It's far better to discuss these sort of feelings as soon as they surface; if you don't, things can sort of fester, and even though there's really nothing to worry about in the first place, it can spoil a relationship."

"Do you really think so?"

"I'm positive. Go do it now."

"I guess you're right. I'll... call you back afterwards, if you don't mind?"

"Of course I don't mind, princess!" I laughed softly, "I feel a bit guilty about not being there for you as it is."

"Don't be," she assured me, "Like we agreed; this is all part of the growing-up process. I'll call you back soon."

I really did feel guilty about not being there in my precious daughter's hour of need, but I was glad that I'd been able to give her some useful advice. When she still hadn't called back an hour later, I was beginning to worry about her.

I nearly dropped the phone when it finally began to cheep.

"Pa! You're an angel!" Suze exclaimed when I finally fumbled my finger onto the 'accept call' button.

"You've no worries about this Dawn, I take it?"

"None at all! Donna was thinking the same thing about me and Dawn would you believe?" The happiness in my daughter's voice made my heart soar, "We spent twenty minutes talking it over and then, well… sort of demonstrated what we feel for each other. That's why I didn't call back earlier. Donna sends her thanks as well, by the way."

"You're both more than welcome," I laughed.

We went on to talk a little about the investigation and a lot about Nicola, until the 'call waiting' warning cheeped at me. I rang off quickly, promising to call Suze on Monday, and took the next call.

"Peter, it's Standish. Excellent news, dear boy."

"I'm all ears."

"Glenda Forsythe does indeed have a relative in London; one James Forsythe, her nephew. I think your man over there might have missed something."

Dean Samson missing something was a very rare event, "I'll call him and let him know," I told Standish, "You'd better make sure your man keeps a very, very close eye on the old dear."

"No worries on that score," he assured me before ringing off.

I called Dean straight away.

"Yo, Pete. What's the news?"

"Forsythe *does* have a relative living here," I told him, "Her name's Glenda Forsythe and apparently, she's his aunt."

"Hang on a sec, let's see," I could hear him flipping through a notebook, "Got it. Glenda, aunt, seventy. Last known address in Mayfair, still in her name. No other addresses listed anywhere."

"She's been here since ninety-nine," I said, "Perhaps she's some sort of tax exile and just lists her London address with the authorities."

245

"More than a ninety percent probability, I'd say. And if she's cagey about stuff like that, then I could well see her involved in something dodgy like this shit that's going down now."

"My thoughts exactly."

I rang off and called Dud, praying that the phone's batteries would hold out a while longer. When I related the latest news to him, he sounded as if the case was closed.

"I'd bet my half of the reward that they're all in it together," he said, "And that they'll go for it on Monday. Can't wait, partner."

"Let Cat take your mind off it for a while," I suggested. I was hoping that Nicola could do the same for me; with Monday looming large before us, I was getting pretty nervous.

"I'll do just that," he laughed.

I told him that I'd see him the next day and rang off, surprised to find that it was nearly one o'clock, Nicola being due to arrive in less than twelve hours – if I was lucky. I wandered out into the street, stopping at the small newsagency to pick up the half a rain forest that comprised the Saturday edition of *The Times*, and went back to the *Black Bull* for a leisurely beer or three.

I left there at four and treated myself to another steak before returning to the penthouse. The beers and the meal conspired to make me feel drowsy, and I settled myself outside on the terrace, my eyes slowly closing in the afternoon sunlight.

It was dark when I woke, and I felt a little disorientated at first. I panicked when I realised that I could have slept for hours, missing Nicola's arrival but then breathed a huge sigh of relief when I managed to focus on my watch; it was exactly eight o'clock. I began to experience the first nervous flutterings in my chest as I thought of what would soon follow and I decided to calm my nerves with a generous whisky.

As midnight approached, my attention was focussed more on my watch than the TV which was burbling away quietly in the corner of the room and as the hands aligned themselves, I closed my eyes and muttered a prayer. My heart leapt into my throat as the door buzzer sounded.

17

I was on my feet in an instant, and over to the front door in less than a second. Taking a deep breath, I pressed the button that would allow Nicola into the building. The wait as the lift slowly ascended seemed interminable and I was almost hyperventilating by the time the doors finally opened.

Nicola was framed in the doorway for a moment or two, a small bag in one hand and a large smile on her face. "Hello, Peter," she said softly.

"Hello, yourself," I managed as she stepped into my embrace.

We stumbled back into the penthouse, still locked in each other's arms, the bag she was carrying dropped in progress. We parted at length and I stood back to admire her. Nicola was wearing the same dress as she'd been wearing on our first evening out; the emerald green number that shimmered with every movement she made, and I wondered whether it was a deliberate choice; somehow marking the event.

"Sorry it's so late," she said, "Any chance of a drink, though, I'm gasping?"

"No need to apologise. And as for the drink, what would you like?"

She gave an elegant shrug, "Beer maybe?"

"Coming right up."

I went through to the kitchen and rooted around for two clean glasses before going to the fridge and taking out two ice cold cans, pouring them with trembling hands. When I got back to the living area, Nicola had closed my front door and put her bag, now open, on the coffee table. I set down the glasses and joined her on the sofa, trying desperately not to let her see how nervous, eager and excited I was.

"Good trip?" I asked.

"Boring as hell. And I missed you like crazy."

"You haven't been far from my every waking thought either," I smiled.

Nicola picked up her glass and drained half of it in one long swallow, "God! That's better," she sighed, setting it back on the table. She half turned to face me, "I can't believe I made myself wait this long," she laughed, shaking her auburn locks, "Kiss me, Peter."

It was one of those instructions that you truly long for, and I moved forward, obeying her. At first my attentions were gentle, but the sexual tension in the air soon turned our clinch into a far more passionate affair, tongues darting into each other's mouths, hands urgently exploring each other's bodies. By the time we surfaced for air I was breathing heavily, my jeans already uncomfortable, and when Nicola raised her hands to her neck and untied the tiny strap of her dress, I was sure that my heart – among other things – was about to explode.

She rose from the sofa, that motion alone enough to send the dress sliding down her lithe form to the floor. After a tiny hesitation, she hooked her fingers through the top of her thong and sent it quickly after the dress. Naked, gloriously naked, she smiled at me and offered me her hand. I took it, standing to join her, pulling her close to me into another passionate embrace.

We seemed to glide into my bedroom – I certainly wasn't aware of making a move in that direction – still locked tightly together, and once we were through the doorway, she gently pushed we away from her. With trembling fingers, I undressed clumsily, flinging my discarded clothes in all directions as Nicola first sat, and then lay back on the bed.

"God! I want you so badly," she breathed, her firm breasts rising and falling rapidly as she began to pant hard.

"You've no idea how I've looked forward to this," I told her, moving swiftly onto the bed, beginning to kiss her shoulders and then her breasts. I worked my way down her graceful form to the sound of her moans of pleasure, relishing the very taste of her. I had left a box of condoms on the bedside table and heard her fumbling it open. I moved around as I kissed her thighs and gasped as I felt her mouth close over my erection. After a minute or two of her tender ministrations, she moved back, grasping me in her hand and then rolling a condom quickly onto me.

As soon as it was firmly in place I pulled back and stared down at her nakedness, barely able to contain myself.

"Now, Peter," she panted urgently.

I nodded, breathing hard, and swiftly slid on top of her. As I entered her, she let out a gasp that was almost animalistic, and her legs and arms grasped me tightly, pulling me deeply within her. Our first coupling was a wild, frenzied affair; a release of the pent-up sexual tension between us, lasting no more than four or five minutes, both of us climaxing within seconds of each other.

The sweat had barely dried on our bodies before we started again, this time slowly, savouring every sensation, relishing every touch and caress. If the first time had been a release, this one was a celebration; a rite of passage, of sorts. It lasted for what seemed like hours but was in all probability twenty minutes or so, and afterwards we held each other tightly, neither of us wanting to break this most intimate of contacts, neither saying much beyond whispered words of a pleasure shared.

After a while, Nicola gently pushed me onto my back and sat up, "Not only a wonderful man, but a wonderful lover," she smiled.

"All your doing," I returned the smile.

She stretched out an arm and plucked the half-empty condom box off of the bedside table, "Shall we?" she asked, her smile becoming lascivious.

"I don't see why not," I shrugged airily.

That third time was even better – as hard as that is to believe – Nicola riding me as I bucked beneath her beautiful body, my hands exploring every contour that was within my reach. My orgasm, when it finally happened, left me feeling drained and exhilarated at the same time; a truly wonderful sensation, and when Nicola slumped down on top of me, appearing close to exhaustion, I held her gently and kissed her softly, thanking her in as many ways as I could think of.

A few minutes later, she gave a soft laugh.

"What's funny?"

"Me," she replied, sitting up.

"Witty, maybe."

"No, I mean... Never mind," another soft laugh, "I guess it's just that I manage to surprise myself at times."

I raised an eyebrow, "How so?"

Nicola paused before answering, measuring her words carefully, "I suppose you could say that things never seem to turn out the way I expect. You're... more wonderful than I had any right to hope for." She leant forward and kissed me.

Incredible as it may seem, the tenderness of her words and her caress began to arouse me once more.

"Good God!" Nicola snorted laughter when she felt the stirring against her belly, "Am I that attractive to you?"

"What do you think?"

"I think I need a short recovery break," she smiled, "And all this frantic activity makes a girl very thirsty."

"I'll go get the beers."

Nicola shook her head, "Since I'm half up already, I'll go. Besides, I need to, er, use your bathroom."

I felt a distinct pang of loss as she finally broke the physical contact between us and left the room. I took the opportunity afforded by her absence to round up the discarded condoms and dispose of them – a fastidious habit of old – and then returned to the bed, lighting a much-needed cigarette. After all, what's the point of sex without the post-coital ciggie?

Nicola returned with our beer glasses and two fresh bottles, setting them on the bedside table before padding through to the bathroom. By the time she returned, I'd drained what was left of my first drink and was pouring a second.

"Thank you," I smiled.

"What for? The beer or the sex?"

"Come to think of it, if you'll pardon the expression, both."

She settled beside me and began stroking my hair, a strange look on her face.

"You look a little troubled?" I said.

Nicola shrugged, "Maybe a little. I guess I'm just confused."

"About what?"

Instead of replying, she shook her head and kissed me deeply. The kiss led to gentle caresses, the caresses to a hard embrace, and the embrace to another bout of energetic love making. When it was over, several centuries later, we both collapsed onto the pillows, too exhausted even to speak. But despite our mutual tiredness, neither of us wanted to sleep; to end that first full-blown passionate encounter, and the sun was rising as we entered into yet another bout of love making.

"I really never want this night to end," Nicola panted at me as I thrust deeply into her.

"I can always have back surgery."

"Don't hurt yourself on my account."

"It's as much for my benefit as yours," I assured her, my pace and my pulse quickening.

As Nicola began a particular pattern of grunts and groans which I was already recognising as a sign of her impending orgasm, I increased my pace further still, leaning back so that I could watch Nicola's expression as she came beneath me. We climaxed simultaneously and loudly before collapsing once more, sweating and gasping for air.

"God! You're good," Nicola managed.

"You're better," I assured her, kissing the tip of her nose.

She pulled me into a tight embrace and after a few moments, I felt a dampness on my shoulder. I leant backwards to find her crying gently.

"What's up?"

Nicola shook her head, "I'm just so happy, I guess."

"You couldn't be happier than me," I said, laying back beside her.

After a few minutes, Nicola insisted that she make us both coffee and I was happy to let her, seriously wondering whether my legs would stand up to a journey all the way to the kitchen and back. It was, after all, a very large apartment. I was smoking a Marlboro when she returned with two steaming mugs.

"Thanks," I smiled, taking a mug from her.

She gave another strange smile and sat beside me, surprising me by plucking the cigarette from between my fingers and drawing deeply on it.

"I didn't know you smoked?"

"I don't very often. I just felt like it right now; you don't mind, do you?"

"Of course not. Help yourself."

As we sat smoking and sipping coffee, I couldn't help but keep on touching and caressing Nicola, relishing her beautiful body. Despite being awake – on and off – for nearly twenty-four hours, I didn't think that I'd ever sleep again; I just didn't want to miss a single second of Nicola's presence. I finished the coffee and set the mug back on the table.

"You're beautiful," I murmured.

Nicola turned to face me, "You're too nice, Peter."

My eyes began to droop closed as she leaned forward and pulled me to her and my last waking thought was that I wanted to be with her for always. I tried to tell her that very thing, but my mouth seemed to have already dozed off. Reluctantly, I let the rest of me follow suit.

18

I'm not sure to this day whether it was a dream, but if it was, then it was the most realistic one that I've ever had: I'm fairly sure that I briefly woke some time later, to find Nicola riding me eagerly, thrusting herself hard against me, tears streaming down her face. I'm equally sure that she said, '*God help me, but I love you, Peter Cooke*". I don't remember much else, beyond truly waking in near pitch darkness and being offered a cup of water by Nicola which I drank thirstily before blacking out once more.

The next thing I recall is pain; an insistent pounding from inside my skull. As I gradually regained a little of my senses, I realised that together with the reverberations in my own head, there was an external source as well. With the utmost care, I opened my eyes, expecting bright morning sunshine, only to be greeted by the half-light of dawn or dusk. The thunderous pounding noise seemed to be growing ever stronger and I finally figured out that it was coming from another part of the apartment, probably the front door.

Grimacing, I struggled to sit up, my body wracked with pains in every joint, and then pushed the sheet off me, swinging my legs gingerly out of the bed. I took several deep breaths and then tried to stand, my legs immediately buckling beneath me, and I collapsed onto all fours by the side of the bed, my head reeling and my stomach nauseous. Hand over hand, I dragged myself into the living area, trying to call out to whoever was battering at my door that I was coming, but my throat was parched, the merest whisper the only sound I could make.

I made one last monumental effort to rise but I didn't have the energy and collapsed full length on the floor, gasping painfully for breath. Just as my head hit the carpet the front door crashed open and I was dimly aware of two figures falling into the room. The only one of my senses that seemed to be operating at anywhere near normal efficiency was hearing, but what I heard as I lay there made no sense at all.

"Jesus! Is he—" A female voice.

"He's breathing!" Male, familiar.

Soft hands rolled me onto my back, and I tried to open my eyes. I got the faint impression of red hair before I blacked out again.

The next time I came round there was a pillow under my head and I was covered in a sheet. Someone was holding my right hand. Although the pain was still immense, I managed to open my eyes properly and found Cat sitting beside me, concern radiating from her in enormous waves.

"Dud!" she said quickly and quietly, "He's coming round."

My partner's face swam into view as he leaned over me, "Don't worry, Pete," he said, "You're gonna be okay."

"What's..." my voice dried up.

"That would have been the million-dollar question, I'd bet," Dud said.

I changed tack as my senses began to unscramble. I pointed at my throat, "Dry."

Dud disappeared from my field of vision and returned quickly with a small cup of water. With Cat's help, they sat me upright and I swallowed greedily as one of them — Dud, I think — held the cup to my lips. When I had drained it, he went back to the kitchen and returned with a refill.

"What happened?" he asked me gently as I drank the second cupful.

"That's what I was going to ask you," I managed, my voice still croaky, "Where's Nicola?"

Dud and Cat looked at each other and nodded, "She was here, then?" he asked.

"Last night," I nodded, wincing as the movement sent another wave of pain crashing through my skull, "Or was it morning? What time is it?"

"Seven p.m. give or take."

"Then this morning," I handed the now-empty cup back to Dud, "What's happened to me?"

"Judging by the way you look and your eyes," Cat replied, "I'd say you've been drugged."

"What!?"

"Quite so, dear boy," I realised that Standish was in the room, "It seems Nicola needed you out of the way for a while."

"I don't understand."

"Pete," Cat said softly, "Do you realise what day it is?"

"Sunday, of course."

She shook her head, "It's Monday evening."

Realisation began to dawn, "You mean I've been out for what? Thirty-six hours?"

"If the last thing you recall is Sunday morning, then yes. Like Standish said, she wanted you out of the way. And not just you; Dud and I were arrested yesterday morning when we went to leave the hotel in Ostend. We were only released at two this afternoon, and only then because of my Irish nationality; they had, I guess, been told to hold us until tomorrow."

The full force of what I was being told hit me like a tidal wave. Despite the pain and nausea, I struggled to stand, but Cat held me firmly in place.

"No, Pete! Sit tight. God knows what she gave you but you're in no fit state to go anywhere yet."

"What about the draft? We need to check on the accounts."

"It's already been done," Dud sighed and I knew what he was about to say as surely as I knew I loved my precious daughter more than anyone else on the planet, "At nine o'clock this morning, the draft was deposited in one of the two mystery accounts. By ten-thirty, they had been drained – more than two hundred and fifty million dollars taken as gold bullion. The bank – after a lot of persuasion from Standish and his guys – finally fessed up an hour ago."

"Who took it then?"

"A young dark-haired woman and an older, grey-haired man," Dud said.

"Oh, God!"

Dud nodded, "Nicola and Commodore Edwin Forbes."

I stared at him dumbly, not really comprehending what I was hearing.

"That's why they wanted us out of the way. The guy watching the bank was on the lookout for a tall blonde and a middle-aged, dark-haired businessman so he didn't pay them any attention," he gave Standish a hard-stare, "Although you might have thought he'd be a bit suspicious given that the Forbes' family were supposed to be under our watchful gaze." Standish said nothing, staring down at the carpet. Dud continued, "Without us to monitor the scanners, there was no one capable of realising what was going on. To further complicate matters, a tall blonde woman climbed into the Aston Martin up at the airport at ten and drove off with another of Standish's guys hot on her heels. Two hours later she pulls off the road."

"So we've got Jenny Winter, at least?"

"Try Celestine Fotheringham."

"What!?"

Dud sighed deeply again, "According to her, Nicola asked her to pick up the car and take it to Ostend where it would be collected later. Being a good friend, she never even bothered to ask why."

"But she's not a good friend," I pointed out.

"From what everyone else says, that's not true. She and Nicola go back years and treat each other like sisters. Celestine also told Standish that Nicola had asked her to come on to you so that she – Nicola, that is – could be sure that you were the right sort of guy for her; if you didn't stray, then you were the faithful type that Nicola had been looking for. Celestine also reckoned that she'd never been so embarrassed as when she did what she did up at the lake, whatever that might mean. Her mother confirms everything."

"Oh, Christ! I've been duped all along, haven't I?" I shook my head, heedless of the pain this induced; perhaps even feeling that I deserved it. First Jenny and now Nicola.

"We all have," Dud nodded, "It seems that maybe the old boy isn't as daft as he makes out, and between them, they've led us a merry dance."

"But where do Jenny and Stephenson fit into all this?"

Standish finally decided to chip in, "My guess would be as couriers, probably on some sort of commission for their efforts. Even a very small percentage would be a rather attractive proposition."

"What about Forsythe, then?" I asked, "After all, he's got an aunt here."

"According to Dean, he's still shacked up at the Savoy with the blonde. Her name, by the way, is Alice Harper," Dud replied.

"His secretary, or rather, Jenny's?"

"The very same."

"So we now know who is behind it, but we don't have the faintest idea of where they've scarpered to," I groaned loudly again.

"Not quite true, but near enough," Dud gave a hard smile, "When Standish finally got around to having someone check on the Pontiac, it'd disappeared. Fortunately, the guy at the gate remembered a young woman with long dark hair and long legs presenting him with the receipt for the vehicle."

"Nicola?"

"Almost certainly."

"What about the Commodore, though? He's without a car at the moment."

"Wrong again. We spoke to Mike Nicholas while you were out cold and he said the Commodore had turned up this morning in his Roller; told him that he'd had a flutter in Ostend and won enough to get it back from the casino."

"And what do the casino say?"

"They never had the car in the first place," Dud shrugged, "It's pretty clear from that fact alone that it's most certainly the Forbes that we're after. The mother's nowhere to be found, either."

"They could be hundreds of miles away by now," I felt the crushing weight of defeat and foolishness bearing down on me.

"In all probability," Dud sighed, "But a silver-grey Rolls Royce and a scarlet Firebird aren't the most inconspicuous of vehicles – assuming they're still using them – we've issued notices to all port and airport authorities to report any sighting of them. I know it's a really long shot, but I've got Dean to get some of his guys down to Dover, Folkestone and any other damn place he can think of to keep an eye out."

"The trouble is, they could have easily already entered Britain if that's where they're headed," I frowned, "Does anyone have any ideas as to who they might know over there? Where they might be headed for?"

"Personally I couldn't see them going there in the first place," Standish shrugged, "But I've got my men out asking everyone they can think of."

"Which is also where you come into it," Dud said, "When there was no sign of you and you weren't answering your phone, Mr. Standish, here, suggested that you'd been in on it from the start and was away with Nicola and her folks," he gave the man a contemptuous glare, "Personally, I couldn't work out what had happened to you, but I knew it wasn't anything like that. The only thing I could come up with was that there'd been some sort of crisis back home, and you'd had to fly back to be with Suze. When I called her and she said she'd never been better and that she'd last spoken to you on Saturday, I began to get seriously worried–" he broke off and stared in horror at Cat and me, "Suze!" he exclaimed, "She'll be worried sick!"

In a flash, he produced his mobile and speed-dialled my home number, handing it to me. Suze must have been holding her phone, answering on the first ring, "Dud?"

"No, princess, it's me."

"Oh! Thank God!" Her sigh of relief was enormous, "Pa! Are you okay? What's been happening? I was going frantic here!" She covered the speaker with her hand and yelled "He's turned up!", presumably to Donna.

"I'm fine now," I assured her, "I've been, er, out of action for a while, that's all. In fact, I've been pretty bloody stupid."

It was a sign of how worried she must have been that she let such a golden opportunity slip by, "Are you hurt or anything?"

"Only my pride. I guess I got Nicola all wrong."

"She seemed okay half an hour ago," Suze said, "She told me she was really worried about you, though."

"Pardon? What do you mean 'half an hour ago'?"

"She said you'd asked her to drop off your briefcase on her way through. Why? Didn't you?"

I switched the phone to loudspeaker so that everyone else could hear, "I most certainly didn't. Suze, angel, it's Nicola that's behind everything. This morning they did a runner with all the money. Are you actually telling me she was there thirty minutes ago?"

"As large as life," Suze sounded stunned, "And twice as beautiful. What's going on?"

"I haven't the foggiest idea," I looked around at the others, their jaws hanging slackly, "The briefcase? Is it one of mine?"

"I guess so," Suze said, "Want me to go and fetch it?"

"Please," I muttered absently.

"I'll get on to Dean," Dud nodded at me, crossing to the apartment's telephone, "My guess is they're going to pick up Forsythe."

Standish strode out of the room, yelling back that he was going to get on to his own men.

Suze came back on the line, "Got it—"

"Wait! Be careful, princess. God knows what that woman might have done."

"I shouldn't worry," she said, "It feels empty; it's as light as a feather."

I heard the zipper being drawn slowly open, "Well?"

"Two small envelopes, nothing else," she informed me, "They've both got your name on the front. Do you want me to open them?"

"Yeah, please," I stared over at Dud who was talking rapidly into the phone.

"Jesus!" Suze whistled, and then went on excitedly, "The first one has what looks a bit like a cheque in it, made out for... Bloody hell!"

"What!?"

"It's for one million dollars!" her voice was filled with awe, "And it doesn't look like an ordinary cheque, either. It's gotta be a joke, right?"

I suddenly realised what it was, "A sort of joke in a way, I think. Does it have the words "I promise to pay the bearer" and suchlike on it?"

"Yeah," Suze said, "You mean this is real?"

"Absolutely. It's a bankers' draft. What you're holding there my precious princess, is effectively a one million dollar note."

There were a few moments of stunned silence before she cleared her throat, "Do you think that maybe I'd better put it in the safe?"

"Now that's a good idea," I swallowed hard. I wasn't sure of our legal position concerning the draft, but I could worry about that later, "What's in the other one, first?"

She tore it open and extracted the contents, "A letter." There was a pause while she scanned the first few lines, "Actually, it's rather personal," she coughed, "Are you sure you want me to read it out?"

Feeling that I probably deserved any embarrassment the letter might cause, I opted against switching off the loudspeaker, "Go on, angel."

"'Dearest Peter,'" she began, "'I'm finding this so difficult to write. I think some of my wretched father's bad luck must have rubbed off onto me, and I'm really so terribly, terribly sorry to have involved you in the way that I have. Sorry, also, for myself, believe it or not. I'd like to be able to tell you that I was only peripherally involved in this scam – or maybe that I was somehow coerced. But that's not true; it was my idea all along. I owe you at least this honesty. Jenny Winter and I were at school together for a while, and when she told me what she was doing and how she needed to get away from everything with some guy she was having an affair with, I got the idea.

"But I guess all that doesn't really matter anymore. I first set out to distract you and try to find out what you were doing to track down whoever was responsible. I certainly didn't count on falling for you. Just *when I finally find the right man, it's already too late; but I guess I should be feeling sorrier for you. I'm so sorry I led you on like that, Peter, even though I know you'll never be able to forgive me. I never had any intention of letting things develop as fast as they did – and as far as they did. It's just that I couldn't help myself. My father and I were originally going to wait for a couple more weeks at least, but I just couldn't trust myself. If I'd stayed with you for even another day, I don't think I could have walked away. I fell in love with you, Peter, and yesterday morning was more pleasure in a few hours than I've experienced in a lifetime – even though I was deep-down so sad about what was going to happen.*

"I pray to God that you're okay; that I didn't overdo things. I gave you Rohypnol and some sedatives, by the way; the so-called date-rape cocktail, and you should be awake by Tuesday morning. Unfortunately, that means that you probably don't have any recollection of what happened after the coffee yesterday, but I knew that it was a safe combination. I sat with you all day long, despite having no sleep, and I said sorry maybe a thousand times. I told you that I love you probably twice as often.

"Peter, I know it's far too much to ask, but, please, at least believe that it's true. You're a wonderful, wonderful man, and I'm sure I'll never get over you. Jenny had told me how marvellous you are, and how guilty she'd felt about the way she managed to get information out of you, and I guess I didn't really believe her. If you could see how hard I'm crying now, I'm sure you'd know the truth.

"Your partner and his girlfriend are being held in Ostend on a fake charge and will be released later today. Tell them I'm sorry to put them through that.

"Given the plans Daddy and I have for the future, I very much doubt that I'll ever see you again, and it's breaking my heart. I promise you this, Peter, if the scam had not already been in progress when I met you, then I would never have let it start. There again, if it weren't for the scam, I'd never have met you. I guess you could say that I now know what they mean by a vicious circle.

"I don't know what else I can say; how I could ever repay you for what you gave me. The draft in the other envelope seems inadequate, *but it's the very least I could do. And, although I promised her I wouldn't say anything, I could tell you that Jenny and Paul are living just off the main square in the centre of Geneva.'"* Suze read out an address, and then continued, *"'If betraying my oldest friend doesn't give you an idea of how I feel for you, then nothing will. I truly love you, Peter Cooke. I'll miss you forever. Nicola.'"*

There was the longest silence all round as Suze's voice drifted into silence.

Cat put an arm across my shoulders, "Poor you," she said softly.

"Foolish me," I shook my head.

"Hey, Pa?" Suze whispered, "If she felt that strongly about you, it's no wonder you didn't see what was happening."

"Maybe," I sighed, "But I don't feel that way right now. I'm not sure I'm up to travelling just yet, but I'll be home sometime tomorrow."

"You're not going to Geneva?" Suze asked.

"I'll go," Dud said from behind me, "Nicola's made a big mistake, Pete. She thought we'd both be out of things until tomorrow; she might well still be in the UK, and if she is, she won't get out. Dean Samson is organising everything with Customs and the police. Given that she was at your place less than an hour ago, I can't see her being able to wriggle loose."

"Dud's right, Pa!" Suze said excitedly.

"I reckon so," I agreed, "Dud? Can you or Cat get hold of a doctor; see if there's anything I can take to speed up recovery. I want to get back to the UK as soon as possible, but I don't want to risk flying feeling like this."

"I've got a better idea," Cat suggested, "Let me call Mike Nicholas. I'll get him to drive you over tonight; there isn't a plane until seven in the morning anyway."

"He'd do it, do you think?"

Cat laughed softly, "Does he call me Cat or Bridge?"

"I get your point. Did you catch all that, Suze?"

"Sure did. When do you think you'll be back; I'll wait up."

"It won't be for six hours at least. There's no need to stay awake."

"I'll never be able to sleep after all this excitement, and before you mention school, remember I'm in the A-level group this year and I'll not be missing anything much if I don't go in tomorrow."

For some strange reason I was really glad that Suze would be up when I arrived back. After all that had happened over the past few weeks, she seemed like the one true rock in my life, just then, "Okay, princess. If there's any change of plans I'll let you know. Love you."

"Love you, too, Pa. Have a safe journey and see you soon."

I rang off and handed Cat the phone. Two minutes later, she set it on the coffee table and gave me a triumphant grin, "Mike'll be here in twenty minutes."

"The doctor at the Commission reckons that a few gallons of water are as good as anything else, and some Paracetamol for the pain," Dud informed me, "I'll go and fill a few glasses."

"And I'll run a shower," Cat added, "You look like you need one."

Standish, who had just returned, gave a cough, "I, er, guess there's nothing much more I can do then?"

"Since this scam was nothing to do with your corruption investigation, I guess not," I shrugged.

"But you and your partner will stay on after you conclude your own matters?"

I looked across at Dud as he emerged from the kitchen with a tray full of glasses, "Dud?"

"I'd like to," he nodded, giving Cat a smile as he did so, "But there's no need for both of us to be here if you don't fancy it."

"I'll see how I feel in a day or two. And besides, until our own investigation is wrapped up, I don't really want to think about anything else."

I guzzled water along with four painkillers and then let Cat lead me unsteadily through to the master bathroom. On the mirror, in bold red lipstick were the words '*I love you, Peter*'. I turned to look at Cat and she gave me a sympathetic smile.

"I'm really sorry about everything," she said.

I nodded slowly, "Me too. But it's not over yet." The movement of my head brought on another bout of giddiness and had Cat not been there to support me, I'm sure I would have pitched headlong into the bath.

"Och! You poor thing," she sighed, holding me firmly, "I guess I'd better help you."

Despite my mild protests and one or two amused observations from Dud, she unwrapped the sheet I was wearing like a toga and guided me into the shower stall. A few very wet minutes later and I was feeling much better, even managing to towel most of myself dry. Cat, her clothes wringing wet, departed for Dud's apartment to change.

"Hey, partner?" Dud said as he led me carefully into the bedroom.

"What's up, Watson?"

He grinned, "You *are* feeling better. I've just had an idea – about that draft and Forsythe's offer of a reward."

"Which is?" I asked from the edge of the bed.

"If we do recover the missing millions, we should still be in line for the reward, right?"

"I guess so."

"Well, given the secrecy laws in Luxembourg – unnamed accounts and all that – why don't we cash the draft over here? No one will be any the wiser, and, let's face it, I reckon we deserve it after everything that's gone on."

"But what about the letter? If there's any prosecutions, it's bound to be wanted as evidence."

"Leave that to me and your precious princess," Dud grinned, "I hear she's a dab hand with that new computer of hers."

I realised what he meant, "Don't you think it's a little... illegal? Profiting from ill-gotten gains?"

"I'm not so sure that if it had gone to the intended target, that it was ethically correct in any case; just to line some already wealthy and corrupt politicians' pockets," Dud said slowly, "I'm sure that you and I could put it to much more worthwhile uses; Suze's future. Maybe, Cat's as well; let her study full time."

"I guess you may have a point," I nodded carefully, "Why don't we let Suze decide? After all, she's probably the only innocent one among the whole lot of us. But if she does think that it's not immoral, I'm not going to have her involved; I'll do whatever is needed to doctor the document myself."

"I'll go along with that."

He helped me to dress, assisted by a now-dried Cat, and we were ready and waiting when Mike appeared at my broken door.

"Looks like someone had some fun," he said.

"It's a long story," I sighed, "I'll tell you on the way."

"Good luck, partner," Dud patted my back.

"Good luck in Switzerland."

Cat gave me a tight hug and added her best wishes; Standish said nothing. With Mike and Dud's assistance, I descended to street level and into the Jaguar.

"Call me," Dud said.

"Likewise," I told him.

19

The journey back seemed interminable, made more so by a delay at Calais where we'd decided to get a ferry. Finally and thankfully, we arrived at my house at four a.m., and I climbed wearily from the car, feeling much steadier on my feet. Before I could even take a step towards the house, the front door opened, and Suze launched herself down the path. I braced myself against the side of the car and took her into a tight embrace when she reached me.

I let her almost drag me into the house and then introduced everyone to each other before settling onto the sofa to wait for phone calls. After my extended, drug-induced slumber I was still wide awake and although Mike protested that he wasn't in the least tired, he was soon snoring quietly in an armchair. Donna had retired soon after our arrival, and I was left with only Suze for company.

"Why don't you take yourself off to bed?" I said, "You're looking exhausted."

"I hope that's not the same as haggard?" she grinned.

"Not at all. You're a beautiful young lady."

"So was – is – Nicola," she raised an eyebrow.

"But you're beautiful on the inside as well."

"I hope so. But I think she's genuinely sorry for what she did."

"It sounded a little like that," I conceded, "But I think she's mainly feeling sorry for herself."

"Does that please you?"

"That's a very mature question. Also, a difficult one to answer," I pondered for a few moments, "I guess the answer really has to be yes. I think the last time I was taken in by somebody in that way was more than twenty years ago – not counting Jenny. Your mother would never have done anything like that."

The mood became even more serious, and Suze shuffled close to me so that I could hold her, "Am I really like her?" she asked quietly.

"Very much. In looks and in your personality. Haven't I told you often enough?"

She squeezed herself tightly against me, "I guess so, but I was wondering whether you thought I'd changed at all; you know? What with Donna and everything?"

"If you have, it's only for the better."

We went on to discuss Dud's suggestion concerning the draft and Suze came up with the perfect idea.

"Why don't you wait and see if anybody says anything about it? After all, you might not even catch them in the first place."

"Not just a pretty face."

"Beautiful face, you mean?"

"I do, indeed."

We were interrupted by the cheeping of my mobile.

"Pete Cooke," I said quickly as I answered.

"Yo, Pete!"

"What's the news?" I asked urgently.

"Your pigeons are due on the eight o'clock Air Canada flight from Heathrow to Vancouver; check-in is half an hour from now. Currently they're still at their hotel, but a large – or at least, heavy – freight package was collected twenty minutes ago. I've got a man at the airport right now getting it freed up from Customs."

"Brilliant work, Dean! What terminal?"

"Four. I've got three men on their way, and I'll be with them in about ten minutes."

"We'll be there in thirty," Mike, now awake, said from across the room.

"You get that, Dean?"

"Sure did. See you there!"

"Are you up to it?" Suze asked worriedly.

"I'm fine now." I rose stiffly.

"It's probably pointless to ask, but can I come along?"

"I'm afraid not, princess. You know my rules."

"Take care then, Pa," she nodded.

I followed Mike out to the car, Suze trailing after us, hugging herself against the chill morning air. "I call you as soon as I know anything," I promised her.

"You'd better."

"All set?" Mike asked from the driver's seat.

"Let's do it," I nodded, and with a last wave to Suze we were off.

"Christ!" I muttered five minutes later as the Jag thundered through the quiet streets, "Aren't you worried about getting stopped?"

Mike laughed heartily, "Hardly. I put diplomatic plates on before we left Luxembourg."

"Good thinking."

I'd never before made the journey between my house and Heathrow in twenty-five minutes, and seriously doubted that my poor Mini would even be capable regardless of police intervention. Mike squealed to a halt outside the main Departure entrance and, breathing a sigh of relief, I clambered from the vehicle. No sooner than I was upright, Dean Samson's giant black hand encircled my arm.

"Inside, quick," he ordered, "They're on their way."

"Mike, take off!" I called over my shoulder, "They're coming." The Jaguar disappeared in a cloud of burning rubber.

Dean hustled me inside and we dashed along to the main security gate where we were ushered through by two Customs officials. I was gasping for breath as we were led into a small interview room, and I collapsed gratefully into an institutional-plastic chair.

"Jesus!" I managed.

"Quit the weed, my man," Dean laughed. He wasn't even breathing heavily.

We waited in silence for four minutes and then the door opened. I rose and went to stand beside Dean, our backs to the wall next to the door.

"This won't take a minute, Miss Forbes," a young man said, entering the room.

Nicola, so recently the object of my every desire, walked in behind him, "What's going on?" she asked nervously.

"Hello, Nicola," I said.

She spun on her heel, her jaw hanging open, pure, unadulterated shock bursting from her. "Peter!?"

"I think you've made a slight error of judgement," I said, watching as she first grimaced and then slumped down into the chair I'd so recently vacated.

"Oh, shit!" she groaned.

Although the Customs officers were at first unwilling, I finally persuaded them to let me have five minutes alone with Nicola, Dean's looming presence seeming to tip the balance in my favour. When the door closed behind them, I sat opposite her.

"Why?" I asked.

"You know already," she sighed, resignation pouring from her in waves, "Just the money. I take it you read my letter since you're here?"

"Yes."

"Do you believe me?" There was a note of pleading in her voice.

"Pretty much."

"I have fallen in love with you, Peter. At least believe that." The look on her face could not have been put on by the best actress in the world.

"I guess I do. What are you going to do now?" I didn't want to dwell on her feelings for me.

"Confess all," she shrugged, "But I won't mention anything about the draft. Only you and I know about it anyway, not even Daddy does. As I said in the letter, it's never going to make up for what I did to you but, well, at least it might bring you a little happiness."

"Was Forsythe involved?" It was the one last mystery as far as I was concerned.

Nicola shook her head, "No. We didn't think we could trust him."

She was sobbing hard by the time the five minutes were up and it was almost a relief to leave her in the care of the Customs officers. I stepped outside, my legs feeling shaky.

"Yo, Pete," Dean called.

I went over to where he was standing and he nodded in the direction of another small room, "The old boy and his wife are in there."

"Thanks, Dean. By the way, if it's possible, keep your ears open for any mention of a million-dollar bankers' draft, could you? I'll tell you about it later." I went over to the door and knocked, letting myself in without waiting for a reply. Inside, the Commodore was sitting slump-shouldered, a tall elegant looking woman sitting next to him, her gaze fixed in the middle distance. They were alone and the old man looked up at me.

"Peter, old boy," he managed a tired smile, "I rather thought you'd be behind this; reckoned you was a bright one from the very first day. I suppose I should congratulate you."

"Thank you," I nodded, "Just a couple of questions. Was this really Nicola's idea?"

To his credit, the Commodore looked shame-faced, "She did it for us, really," he nodded to his wife, "I guess I drove her to it, what with all the gambling and things."

"What do you think will happen now?"

"M'girl told me that she'd own up to everything if we were ever apprehended, but I'll make it clear that I was involved," he sighed, "I just hope that it doesn't ruin her entire life. She's been crying pretty much non-stop since we left yesterday; I think she's regretting it all already."

"Me too," I nodded. I went back outside to where Dean was talking to an elderly man in a suit.

"But we've recovered the goods!" the stranger said.

"You mean there's a chance there'll be no prosecutions?" Dean demanded.

"We shall have to see. Right now, myself and Reginald need to take statements. I think I'll start with you two."

We followed him into another small room and emerged an hour later. I, at least, was beginning to feel tired, "I'd better call Suze and Dud," I said to Dean.

"Do that. I'll check with this Reginald guy and see what the Forbes have been saying."

Suze, apparently still awake, was overjoyed and rang off after I promised that I'd be home soon. Dud, if anything, was even more delighted, "Fantastic!" he yelled when I broke the news, "Remember to call Forsythe!"

Dud and Cat had just landed in Geneva and were on their way into the centre of the City and he promised to call back as soon as they tracked down Jenny and Stephenson. Dean had still not reappeared, so I had no way of knowing where James Forsythe might be. I decided to try the ETA offices and the man himself answered.

"Forsythe," he announced tiredly. I thought I knew why.

"James, it's Pete Cooke."

His voice brightened immediately, "Peter, dear boy! News?"

"Good news. We've recovered most of the money."

It took him a moment or two to grasp what I'd just told him, "You've...? Oh! I say! That's wonderful, wonderful news!"

I went on to tell him what had transpired, and he was almost crowing with delight by the time I promised to meet him the following day to sort out our reward and payment. The mention of the reward almost had me crowing, but I was just too damned tired to really enjoy things. Dean had reappeared while I'd been talking, and he clapped me on the back when I rung off.

"Good work, my man!"

"Good work, yourself," I smiled, "There'll be more than a hefty bonus in this for you. Talking of which, what have you found out."

269

The big black man chuckled heartily, "Lots. This Reginald guy let me read the Forbes girl's statement and she's pretty much confessed to everything. Didn't see any mention of any draft though."

"Let's check ourselves out of here and I'll tell you about it."

"Good man," he grinned, "I'll give you a lift home if you like?"

I realised that I'd forgotten about Mike Nicholas. "Let me just call the guy that brought me here, okay?"

Dean nodded and wandered over to see whether we were needed any further for the present. Mike answered on the second ring.

"How'd it go?"

"They're in custody and Nicola's confessed all," I said, "I'll fill you in on the details later. Look, I've got an offer of a lift home, so if you want to take off, feel free."

"If you're sure? I wouldn't mind heading back."

"I'm sure. I'll probably be over in Luxembourg in a few days. I'll catch you then."

He rang off and I walked over to Dean who was laughing loudly with two of the Customs guys. "Are we free to go?" I yawned, "Only I feel like one of the walking dead."

"We are. Need me to carry you?"

"I'll manage," I yawned again, "Or at least ways, I think I will."

On the drive back I told him everything I knew, and about Nicola's high-octane, dollar-rich method of apologising for her behaviour.

"Do what the lovely Suze suggested," he said, "But from what the Forbes girl confessed to in her statement, you won't have anything to worry about."

Just before we arrived home, my wretched telephone cheeped at me.

"Pete Cooke."

"We've got a full house," Dud announced, too loudly for my comfort.

"Jenny and Stephenson?"

"None other. They're not too happy with Nicola, I can tell you, since she was the only one who knew their location so must have been the one who shopped them; and from what they're saying they're going to cook up some sort of story about how she coerced them into helping her. But that's for later; right now, they're sitting in the car Cat hired and they'll be flying back to the UK this afternoon."

"Brilliant, Dud!" To Dean I said, "Any chance of meeting them on arrival?"

"Consider it done, my man."

I got the flight details from Dud and passed them on. With a promise to call him and Cat after I'd been to see Forsythe the next day, I rang off and settled back in my chair, already half-dozing. Maybe we were a modern-day Sherlock and Watson, after all.

EPILOGUE

The day after, I went along to see James Forsythe and was met at the ETA offices by two smartly dressed men as well as Forsythe himself. They turned out to be the 'bods from Westminster' that the old boy had mentioned, and spent much of the meeting praising the sterling efforts that Dud and I had put in. They also presented me with a cheque for ten million dollars made payable to PC Security.

"As it's a reward," the taller of the two informed me, "It is not subject to tax."

I left there whistling happily to myself, deposited the monster cheque in the nearest branch of my company's bank, and made the promised call to Dud from the comfort of a City pub.

At the weekend, I flew back to Luxembourg for a couple of days, a trip that was tinged with sadness, but considerably brightened by the news that Dud and Cat were to get engaged. After much soul-searching, they had decided to return to the UK so that Cat could study full time at a British university but had chosen to postpone the move until nearer Christmas.

Standish expressed extreme disappointment that I wouldn't be staying on to work for him but understood that I found too many bad memories associated with the tiny Duchy to countenance staying just then. He was happy enough that Dud would continue to monitor the rogue accounts.

In late October a most unusual trial took place. Nicola and her parents, together with Jenny Winter and Paul Stephenson, appeared before three High Court judges who, after four days of tortuous deliberations, found all but Nicola's mother guilty of a range of charges. However, they decided, it was not in the National interest for them to be formally prosecuted with all the attendant publicity that would generate. If all four were to agree to leave the country, they told them, then no further action would be taken. Sinecures would be arranged in any country of their choice with the exception of Luxembourg.

I had needed to be present, and when the judges explained their decision, Nicola turned to look at me, one delicate eyebrow raised. I gave her a sad smile and shook my head. I guessed she understood, and although she had begun to weep quietly, she turned back to indicate her acceptance of the judges' offer.

With any possibility of a formal trial gone, Dud and I deposited the draft Nicola had given me in an unnamed Luxembourg account. PC Security is now a seriously wealthy company. Suze and Donna came with me when I went out there with it, Dean Samson acting as bodyguard, and we all joined Dud and Cat as they celebrated their formal engagement; a party that lasted all night.

It's six months on, now, and both Dud and Cat, and Suze and Donna are still together; Donna is living with us on a full-time basis. Despite Suze's constant efforts, Terri and I haven't quite got around to dating, although we do have an occasional drink together. It's mostly down to me, I guess.

You see, Nicola's phoned me twice since the 'triahel'. The calls were from Nice, where she opted to go and work in our Embassy there, and each time, she has tearfully asked me to at least visit her. So far, I've refused, but I can't quite bring myself to rule out the possibility. Suze thinks I'm mad, but, there again, she always has. I tell her what I told you at the very start of my tale; *'Insanity is hereditary – you get it from your children'*.

The End

More Information

As I mentioned in the preface, this book would never have made it to the shelves were it not for the help and encouragement of a number of people – and the publication of many of my other stories.

Specialist publishers (and lovely people) **Regency Rainbow** can be found at:

> https://www.regencyrainbow.com/

Cover designer *par excellence* **Maria Spada** can be found at:

> https://www.mariaspada.com/

And then there's **me**, I guess. News, book links and my blog can be found at:

> http://www.johnmoneywrites.com/home.html

My final words though, must be:

> **Thank you** for reading **Hot in the City**, and I truly hope you enjoyed it!

26856663R00166

Printed in Great Britain
by Amazon